# JUST ONE SIP

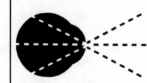

This Large Print Book carries the
Seal of Approval of N.A.V.H.

# JUST ONE SIP

# KATIE MACALISTER,
# JENNIFER ASHLEY
# AND MINDA WEBBER

**WHEELER PUBLISHING**
*An imprint of Thomson Gale, a part of The Thomson Corporation*

THOMSON

GALE

Detroit • New York • San Francisco • New Haven, Conn. • Waterville, Maine • London

# THOMSON

## GALE

*Just One Sip* Copyright © 2006 by Dorchester Publishing Co., Inc.
The publisher acknowledges the copyright holders of the individual works as follows:
Copyright © "Viva Las Vampires" 2006 by Jennifer Ashley.
Copyright © "Bring Out Your Dead" 2006 by Martie Arends.
Copyright © "Lucy and the Crypt Casanova" 2006 by Minda Webber.
Wheeler, an imprint of The Gale Group.
Thomson and Star Logo and Wheeler are trademarks and Gale is a registered trademark used herein under license.

**ALL RIGHTS RESERVED**
Wheeler Publishing Large Print Romance.
The text of this Large Print edition is unabridged.
Other aspects of the book may vary from the original edition.
Set in 16 pt. Plantin.

**LIBRARY OF CONGRESS CATALOGING-IN-PUBLICATION DATA**

Just one sip / by Katie MacAlister, Jennifer Ashley, Minda Webber.
    p. cm. — (Wheeler Publishing large print romance)
    ISBN-13: 978-1-59722-613-4 (hardcover : alk. paper)
    ISBN-10: 1-59722-613-0 (hardcover : alk. paper)
    1. Love stories, American. 2. Large type books. I. Ashley, Jennifer. Viva las vampires. II. MacAlister, Katie. Bring out your dead. III. Webber, Minda. Lucy and the crypt Casanova.
PS648.L6J87 2007
813.0850806—dc22                                                        2007022441

Published in 2007 by arrangement with Leisure Books,
a division of Dorchester Publishing Co., Inc.

Printed in the United States of America on permanent paper
10 9 8 7 6 5 4 3 2 1

# TABLE OF CONTENTS

■ ■ ■ ■

# Viva Las Vampires
## by Jennifer Ashley

■ ■ ■ ■

# CHAPTER ONE

"Her."

"Her what?" Water sloshed as Mario, all six feet six of him, stepped out of the sunken hot tub behind the sofa where Stefan stared at the flat-screen television on the wall.

Stefan half watched his friend's reflection in the monitor as Mario reached for a pristine Egyptian-cotton towel before collecting his half-consumed glass of wine and sauntering to Stefan's leather sofa. Stefan knew without looking that little pools of water marked Mario's footsteps across the marble and onto the cashmere carpet.

"I said, her what?" Mario parked himself on the end of the leather sofa and put his feet on the coffee table. Stefan's feet were already there in leather boots that disappeared beneath his jeans. Mario plopped his wineglass on the coffee table, slopping over a crimson drop.

Mario always drank red wine. He'd been

Italian for six hundred years, he said, and couldn't break the habit. Whether he meant drinking red wine or being Italian, Stefan never knew.

Stefan gestured with his remote. "Her."

*Her* was a late-twenty-something, tall woman with red hair scraped back in a sloppy ponytail and wide green eyes taking in every bit of Transylvania Castle's lobby. She wore a light cotton dress good for the baking temperatures of Las Vegas in July. Her limbs were bare, her feet in sandals. She carried a duffel bag over her shoulder as she walked through the casino, heading for the check-in desk.

Mario grinned in appreciation. "So you do have taste."

Stefan took a swallow of vodka, the liquid tracing a fiery trail to his stomach, and didn't answer.

The monitor showed feed that came through the security cameras trained on the lobby and casino forty-seven floors beneath them, piped to Stefan's penthouse at his request. He could assess his guests, watch for people who shouldn't be there, and generally make sure everyone staying at his hotel was having a good time.

This particular guest interested him very much. As she moved past the Coffin Bar and out of the frame, Stefan picked up the phone on the coffee table and spoke to his security team. "Give me camera three. Zoom in on the red-haired woman in the white dress."

The view changed to the clear lobby space in reception and the stream of people coming to check in, ready for their vampire fantasy weekend. The picture remained fixed a moment, and then the focus widened and blurred, the camera zooming to Stefan's woman.

It caught her just as she stepped up to the reception desk and smiled at the young man behind it. Stefan's blood warmed. Her crooked smile lit her eyes as she slung her duffel bag on the marble-topped counter and unzipped it. The way she spilled out pens, packets of tissue, books of matches, and various other jetsam was nothing short of adorable.

Stefan spoke into the phone. "Zoom closer."

The camera obeyed. Her round face and locks of flyaway red hair filled the screen, the light catching the gold flecks in her green eyes.

Mario laughed. "You twisted bastard."

"Have the desk clerk send you her name," Stefan told security.

"Yes, sir." Through the phone, Stefan heard him tapping computer keys. He saw the red-haired woman nod, then speak. Though there was no sound, he knew she was giving him her name.

"Meredith Black," the security man said in his ear.

"What room?"

A pause, more tapping of keys, another pause, and the security man's deep voice. "Ten twenty-two."

Mario's dark brows shot up. "Planning a midnight visit?"

Stefan spoke into the phone again. "Give her tickets to Vegas Vampires, vouchers for the restaurants and bars, and an invitation to meet me in my penthouse. I'll give her dinner."

"Yes, sir."

Stefan quietly set down the phone and returned his gaze to the screen. Mario stared at him, his long black hair dripping rivulets of water onto the leather sofa.

Then his coffee-colored eyes widened in understanding. "Oh," he said, voice subdued. "You mean it's *her.*"

In a thousand years of existence, Stefan had never been much for slang. He preferred precise speech to Mario's idioms that changed every decade. But Americans of this century had a phrase that he thought summed things up very well. He tossed back the rest of his vodka and slid the glass across the teakwood coffee table.

"Damn straight," he said.

The desk clerk had slicked-back black hair, a high-collared cape, and a mouthful of vampire teeth that made him talk with a lisp.

"Welcome to Tranthylvania Cathle, Mth. Black. You're in room . . ." He broke off, frowning at the terminal on the lower tier of the counter. "Room thhen thwenny-thoo." He slid an electronic key in a cardboard folder across the black marble. His cape moved and flowed as he plucked brochures and papers from various parts of his desk. "And vouthers for Have a Bite Rethrant, the Coffin Bar, and Fangth for the Memori-eth, our gift thop. Two free pathess to Veg-ath Vampirth, the all-male revue — eight and eleven every night and a matinee on Thunday, dark on Mondayth."

Meredith gazed at him in surprise. "What happened? Did I win a prize or something?"

"Complimenth of Mr. Erickson, owner of the hotel. He requeths that you dine with him tonight." He cast a doubtful look at her crumpled cotton dress that had lasted her

13

the drive to Las Vegas from Santa Fe. "A bellman will thow you the way after you retht from your trip and change."

Meredith raked the tickets toward her and started stuffing them into her already over-stuffed duffel bag. "Oh, he must have finally decided to give me an interview. I called at least twenty times. This whole hotel is going to be in the sequel to my first book." She dug into the bag, dislodging the vouchers she'd just shoved in along with crumpled napkins from roadside restaurants and a little cross on a chain, a joke gift from her mother because she was going to a vampire hotel.

At last she found what she searched for and hauled out a hefty hardback book. The black cover showed her name and the title in gothic-looking letters, "Meredith Black, *Vampires in Myth and Legend.*"

The next clerk over, a woman in bust-lifting black spandex, glanced at it in interest. "I read that. It was fascinating."

"Thank you." Meredith blushed, as she always did when given compliments on her book.

She stuffed everything back into the duffel bag, wrestled the zipper closed, then opened it again to dig out the key she'd accidentally shoved inside. Grinning ruefully, she slung the duffel over her shoulder and trotted away to find the elevators.

Transylvania Castle was laid out like a typical Las Vegas hotel — huge casino in the middle with restaurants and shops and elevators in the back. The layout forced guests to wander past rows and rows of slot machines, roulette and craps tables, blackjack and pai gow tables, and baccarat tables set behind carved Gothic arches for the high-dollar gamblers.

Huge cobwebs, dangling spiders, and glow-in-the-dark skeletons hung from a soaring black ceiling that pumped cold air and spooky music onto the tourists and dedicated gamblers. The occasional evil laughter gloated over the ring of slot machine bells and the steady *chunk-chunk, chunk-chunk* of falling coins.

Meredith glanced into the Coffin Bar on the edge of the main casino, where gamblers rested and smoked before venturing out to try their luck again. The lighting was murky, the bar itself was shaped like a coffin, and a cauldron of dry ice bubbled on one end of it. The tabletops looked like headstones, and the legs of the tables and chairs were shaped like chains. The bartender had forgone a Dracula costume for the black leather badboy look. Meredith peered at him with

15

interest as she sauntered by, and he gave her a wink and a smile.

This place could fill half her book. She was calling it *Vampires in Modern Popular Culture.* She planned to write about the fervor with which people had pursued anything vampire ever since Bram Stoker's *Dracula* hit the shelves a hundred or so years ago. The craze that never seemed to go away gave the world vampire hotels, vampire romances, vampire TV shows, vampire erotica, vampire nightclubs, vampire gangs, and vampire counseling. If there were as many true vampires as people who believed in them or wanted to be them, the world would be overrun.

Damn good thing none of it was real.

She at last found the elevators in a recessed hall in the rear of the hotel. The elevator doors were embossed to resemble iron gates, and dry ice flowed across the black marble floor. The throng of tourists waiting to ascend to their rooms wore everything from Bermuda shorts to traditional vampire garb to dominatrix Goth.

Meredith enjoyed the dark décor of her floor when the elevator spilled her out, the black walls and bloodred carpet, the open mouth with fangs painted around the peephole of her door. It was so cheesy she had to laugh, which she imagined was the point. She looked forward to meeting the man who'd thought all this up.

Stefan Erickson. The enigmatic owner of the hotel had made instant millions when it opened ten years ago, and the tourists showed no sign of abating. No one knew much about Mr. Erickson. According to his staff, he was rarely seen by his guests, nor did he grant interviews.

She'd looked him up when she began research for this book and repeatedly tried and failed to get in touch with him. She'd decided to come out to the hotel anyway and have a look around, and if he didn't like what she said about it, too bad. He'd had his chance.

Interesting how he'd suddenly reversed course and actually invited her for the interview as well as giving her all kinds of freebies. Was it so she'd praise his hotel and bring him more business? He'd discover that Meredith wasn't so easy to manipulate. *Defiant,* everyone called her, except her mother, who called her *stubborn.* Once Meredith had decided on a course, she didn't let anyone change her mind.

Inside her room, Meredith assessed herself in the Gothic-framed mirror and decided the clerk's hint about cleaning up was a good one. Her dress looked the worse for the long drive up and down mountains and across baking deserts, her nose was sunburned, and her throat was parched.

In the mini-refrigerator she found two bottles of blood — at least, they said "Blood, A Refreshing Drink." She opened one and sniffed cautiously, then took a sip. Cherry cream soda. She smiled and drank. The hotel really knew how to go for the yuks.

An hour later, she had showered and donned a yellow cotton dress hastily pressed with the room's iron, her hair still damp. A bellboy dressed in Dracula attire knocked on the door and told her to follow him.

He led her to the elevators at the end of the hall, and they rode back down to the lobby, two elderly ladies giggling when he showed them his fake fangs. Downstairs, he led Meredith through the casino to the other side of the hotel, past the theater for the Vegas Vampires, and stopped in front of an ordinary-looking door that he opened with a key card.

Beyond that was another cool hallway, this one tastefully decorated in marble and glass, holding an elevator with polished gold doors. Soft guitar music floated through the air to coat the silence. Not a vampire theme in sight.

The elevator opened with the bellboy's key card, and he gestured Meredith inside with his white-gloved hand. "This elevator only goes one place, the penthouse." He indicated the two buttons, one marked P, the other L. "Mr. Erickson will let you in when you get there. This is the only way down too."

"He must like his privacy."

The bellboy slanted her an ironic glance. "He must. He rarely comes down and lets very few people go up. Good luck."

He punched the button and withdrew his arm as the doors closed, leaving Meredith alone in a little gold box with a bench. Gently and smoothly, the elevator rose.

What would she find at the top? she wondered. An old man puttering around his penthouse trying to relive his glory days? A wannabe vampire convinced he had to drink blood to stay alive? Or a savvy businessman who knew people couldn't resist coming to stay at Dracula's castle?

The elevator let her out in a foyer decked out like an eighteenth-century anteroom. The high arched ceiling was embossed with gold-leafed curlicues, the floor was green and white marble, the curved-legged table probably a costly antique, the mirror over it huge and heavy. The double door she faced had curved panels picked out in gold and lavish door handles shaped like cherubs' wings. A round brass doorbell hung on the wall next to the door. She pushed it, expecting a foghorn sound like on *The Addams Family,* but she heard nothing.

Whoever was inside probably heard nothing either, because she stood for a full five minutes while nothing happened. She pushed the bell again and waited another five minutes.

A little annoyed, she turned around to take the elevator down again and discovered that there was no button to call it. A slot for an electronic card rested on the wall next to the elevator doors, a red light blinking quietly.

She made a noise of exasperation. Without a key card, she was stuck. No phone in the pretty anteroom either, so she couldn't call the front desk and tell them to let her the heck out of here.

"Oh, fine, Mr. Erickson, see what I write about your hotel," she muttered. She was hungry and tired, and Erickson leaving her cooling her heels in front of his door was nothing short of rude.

She rang the bell again, and then when she got no response, she tried the door handle. To her surprise, the door slid smoothly open.

Now she felt stupid. And more annoyed. If Mr. Erickson had wanted her to simply come in, the bellman should have told her.

She'd never been in a hotel penthouse and assumed they'd be pretty decadent, but what she found took her breath away. Beyond the front door, the foyer stretched at least a hundred feet in front of her, continuing the green marble and the high ceiling of the anteroom. Doors lined each side, and the end of the hall sported a huge mirror — not a wall full of glass, but an actual framed mirror that was at least one and a half stories high. In front of this mirror an ornate wrought-iron staircase wound upward to an opening in the ceiling.

Meredith padded slowly down this hall, her sandals whispering on the marble. Each ornate double door looked like the rest and gave her no clue what lay behind it. When she peered up the stairs, she could see nothing but darkness.

She opened the door at the foot of the stairs and stopped in astonishment. Behind it was a living room — at least, she supposed it was a living room but a hell of a lot more lavish than the cozy room with sofas and chairs she shared with her mother in Santa Fe. Two long glass walls, closed

21

against the heat, showed an outstanding view of the high mountains beyond Las Vegas — the beginnings of the Sierras. Sunshine lit the room but did not overheat it.

The floor was marble slashed with vibrantly colored deep-pile rugs. A sunken tub with whirlpool controls held a place of honor in the middle of the room, above which was suspended an ornate chandelier. In another area, lush leather sofas faced a flat-screen television mounted on the wall. A portion of the wall next to the television stood open to reveal every kind of electronic audio and video device known to man. A bar stood in another area of the room, small but well stocked with bottles and cut crystal glasses. The main drinks of choice seemed to be bloodred Italian wine and clear vodka.

But the room was empty. Beyond the glass wall on the shorter end of the room was a large outdoor area with a deck and full swimming pool. The deck had been landscaped with bougainvillea and orange trees to disguise the fact that it sat on the roof of a hotel. The wall around it was high for safety and aesthetics, but not so high that it blocked the view of the mountains to the west and the entire Strip stretching north.

The pool had what people in Santa Fe

called an "infinity edge," which meant that the far end didn't have a lip, but the water blended across an edge and spilled into a hidden basin below. When you sat on one end of the pool, it looked as though the water went on forever. Comfortable-looking chairs and lounges stood around the wooden deck, and a water system sprayed a cooling mist over it all to combat the hot summer sun.

Meredith approached the glass wall, wondering how a person exited to this Eden of a pool deck. She didn't have to wonder long because as she reached the glass it slid obligingly open for her.

She stepped out into cool paradise scented with orange blossoms. Her bathing suit was sitting downstairs in her bedroom, but the pool was so tempting that she wanted to strip off her dress and do a little skinny-dipping. After all, there was no one up here, and it would serve Mr. Erickson right for inviting her and then forgetting about her.

She would wade in it, anyway. Meredith slid off her sandals and stepped down onto the ledge that ran around the entire circumference of the pool. The water came to her knees, cool but not too cold. She felt like Goldilocks: it was just right.

She wandered around the ledge, sandals

in hand, holding her skirt out of the water. Whoever had created this place had done a marvelous job. This was how the rich lived, she thought, while the peons of the world eked out existences in apartments and houses they could barely pay for. *Oh well, if you have it, why not spend it?*

She looked back at the penthouse. The glass was not reflective, as she might expect in a hot climate, but she remembered how cool the living room had been. The glass was probably thick enough not to need reflectivity. She could see into the room next to the living room, which also opened onto the deck. It appeared to be a bedroom, also devoid of life.

She moved around the pool so she could stare inside. The bed was huge, the room as ornate and plush as the living room, but she saw nothing weird in there. No mirrors on the ceiling or heart-shaped beds or swings or stripper poles. As rich as he was, Erickson didn't go in for kink. At least, not obviously.

The water felt wonderful. She wouldn't put this in her book, but she'd tell her mom, who'd love it. "There I was, enjoying myself in a lavish penthouse pool on top of a Las Vegas hotel. All I needed was Raoul the pool man to come along and give me a hot-oil massage and chocolate-dipped strawberries and champagne."

The afternoon burned hot. It was about five o'clock, which around here meant baking time. The temperature had been a balmy 110 degrees when she'd arrived at the hotel, and the forecast she'd heard on the car radio said they expected to hit 117. Felt about that right now. In spite of the misting system, the sun seared right through her dress.

She was never sure if what she did next she did on purpose or accidentally on purpose. She slipped on the ledge and plunged down into the cold waters of the pool.

She surfaced, sputtering, spouting water and wet all over.

Meredith wiped the water from her eyes, slicked back her hair, and looked up to see Raoul the pool man standing on the edge.

Her gaze started at strong feet in flip-flops, firm, tight legs in bronzed skin, well-muscled thighs below shorts that hung low on his narrow hips. Up to a flat abdomen and hard torso in a tight white T-shirt, bronze-colored arms covered with wiry gold hair, and the hollow of his throat touched with perspiration.

Viking-gold hair, burnished with the sun,

skimmed across wide shoulders. He had a model's face — sharp cheekbones, square jaw, sensual, flat mouth, high brow. Yep, he had everything.

Dark sunglasses hid his eyes. Not just any sunglasses, some designer brand you had to custom order from a chichi boutique. So maybe Mr. Erickson paid Raoul the pool boy a good salary.

Those flat dark sunglasses trained on her from a long way up, about six and a half feet above the pool deck, and the slow smile that spread across his face confirmed that the dress plastered to her body hid absolutely nothing.

"Did you bring a towel?" he asked.

His low, rich voice heated the roasting air, his English a tiny bit accented.

Meredith blushed. "I fell in." She sank down in the water, clutching the edge of the pool, trying to conceal her hardened nipples.

His smile widened. "Next time take the dress off and enjoy yourself."

Next time? The pool was gloriously cool, the water licking her like a lover. She suddenly imagined herself stroking back and forth, water sliding into intimate places, while he lounged on the pool's bench and watched her. His hair would be dark with water, the sunglasses fixed on her, his bronzed flesh touched by the sun.

She gulped and beat away the heady vision.

"I have plenty of towels and robes in my bathroom," he was saying. "Through the bedroom. I will show you."

He started to turn around. Meredith's eyes widened, and she ducked below the lip of the pool. "Um, could you get me the towels first?"

The man turned back, smiling and drop-dead sexy.

"Very funny," she growled. "Are you Mr. Erickson? Or are you really Raoul the pool man?"

"I am Stefan Erickson. And you are in my pool, Ms. Black."

She flushed. "I didn't think anyone was home."

His smile could have melted butter on a cold sidewalk. "That is obvious, unless you make it a habit to walk into a perfect stranger's apartment and jump in his pool."

"I fell in. There's a difference." She gritted her teeth. "Stop laughing and get me a towel, and I promise I'll say nice things in the interview."

A crease appeared between his brows at the word *interview,* but he turned away and called into the apartment. "Mario, bring some towels and a robe. I've found a mermaid in my pool."

# CHAPTER TWO

Meredith gave a squeak of dismay and ducked under the water as a second man strolled out, his arms full of fluffy towels.

Good Lord, he was as buff as Erickson. He had the same tall body and delicious triangular proportion of shoulders to hips, but in coloring, he was Stefan Erickson's complete opposite. He had raven-black hair scraped back from sculpted cheekbones and square forehead, Italian swarthiness, and eyes the color of dark chocolate. His wide smile spoke of hot nights on the Italian Riviera and lovemaking by the blue Mediterranean. Meredith could easily imagine him whispering *"ti amo"* as his body covered some lucky woman's in the dark.

His English, though, was pure American. "A mermaid?" he said, leaning over to stare into the water. "I don't know, I don't see a tail."

Great. Two rich, hunky perverts and no

way out of the apartment without a key card.

"Just give me the towels. This is so embarrassing."

The dark man's grin widened. "I don't see anything to be embarrassed about."

"It isn't you who fell in the pool."

Erickson glanced at his friend. "Give her the towels."

Mario didn't look abashed. He plopped the towels on the end of a chaise and then he and Erickson stood aside. Waiting.

"Turn your backs," Meredith gasped.

Both men obediently turned around and studied the glass wall, which showed a nice, albeit faint, reflection of the pool area. "Close your eyes."

Mario did, but Meredith couldn't see Stefan's eyes behind the sunglasses. But she couldn't stay in the pool forever. The thin dress clung to her entire body, wrinkles suctioning to her skin. She kicked off her sandals and jerked at the wet zipper on her dress, but couldn't make the damn thing open.

"Could you . . ." Pant. ". . . help me?"

Both men turned around, still smiling. Face burning, Meredith stared over the wall to Las Vegas and the mountains while Stefan stepped behind her. His fingers brushed the nape of her neck as he found the zipper and easily drew it down her back. All the way down. She felt the whisper of his touch along each vertebra to the base of her spine.

"Thank you," she said, whirling around.

He stood there smiling at her like he waited for her to drop the wet dress. Under her glare, he chuckled and turned his back again.

One of the fluffy things in the pile was a long terry robe. Quickly Meredith peeled off the soaking dress and pulled the robe around her, tying it with shaking fingers before grabbing a towel to dry her hair.

"All right, you can look."

They were still grinning. She might be covered, but the way both men looked her over she felt stripped naked and spread out for their delights. That was nonsense — the thick robe covered her from neck to ankles, and she'd tied it tight — but still she felt as though every part of her was revealed to them for their pleasure.

They liked what they saw. Mario's wide grin and Stefan's slow smile made her burn all over. She was going to have to make this interview quick and get the hell out of here.

"You can stop laughing at me now," she said as she snatched up her wet clothes and sandals.

"But you are a delight," Stefan said. "I have not felt this light of heart in a long while. Come inside and have a drink."

To her astonishment, he slid his arm gently around her waist and led her inside.

Stefan's hunger flared high at the feel of her curved waist under his hand, but he'd learned to suppress hunger for so long that he could for a few more hours. Just a few more hours, and then . . .

And then, with any luck, this beautiful woman would set him free.

She was tall, her damp red hair just brushing his nose, and her limbs were long and sleek, in perfect proportion to her height. He remembered her from the hidden cameras in the lobby, her long-legged stride, her bright eyes taking in every bit of the tacky reception area, her red hair the color of fire. A luscious, sensual woman, and he hadn't been able to resist her.

Mario had cautioned him against getting his hopes up, but Mario was trying to be a friend. Stefan would gamble on her. After all, that's what Las Vegas was all about, the insane hope that long odds would pay off, and you'd walk away a millionaire.

What Meredith could give him was a damn sight more important than money.

She could not only give him life itself, but restore him to full power. If he did not soon regain his abilities as a vampire master, he would fade and die just like any other mortal, only in unbelievable pain. He'd seen a vampire master die before, and it had not been pretty.

He'd have to go slowly, introduce her to concepts she wouldn't believe at first, then teach her the duties he'd ask of her. By then she'd be willing and ready and wanting to fulfill every one of his wishes and desires.

Maybe. There was always a risk. And this was the last risk Stefan could afford to take.

Mario was talking in his usual cheerful way, flirting outrageously and behaving like an idiot. Women fell for it, and he claimed his payment easily.

Mario busily poured himself his usual glass of deep red wine. He asked what Meredith wanted, then competently mixed her a scotch and soda.

"Stefan?" Mario hovered behind the bar, his hands closing on a bottle of Stefan's favorite vodka. Stefan nodded once, and Mario poured him a shot, straight up, no ice, no mixer. He set Stefan's cut crystal shot glass on the bar with a thunk and pushed Meredith's highball of scotch and tinkling ice cubes at her.

"Salut," Mario said, raising his glass.

"Cheers," Meredith answered and took a sip. Her face smoothed into lines of pleasure as she tasted the smooth malt of the whiskey.

Stefan pictured that look of relaxed joy giving in to his touch as she lay spread beneath him. Her beautiful green eyes would be heavy with lovemaking, her breath sweet, her sounds of pleasure arousing.

Just thinking about her was arousing. Maybe *he* should jump in the pool and let the cold water calm him down. No, that brought thoughts of Meredith joining him, peeling off the robe he'd just watched her put over her lovely, lithe body . . .

Making no toast, he lifted his glass and downed his vodka in one swallow.

"I have to admit, this is the weirdest way I've ever started a research interview." Meredith set down her glass and crossed her legs on the leather-backed bar stool.

"Interview?" Mario said blankly.

"Yes. That's why I'm here." She glanced at Stefan. "I figured you stopped avoiding me once I actually showed up at your hotel."

"I don't grant interviews," Stefan said, not really listening.

Mario grinned behind Meredith. He was enjoying the hell out of this, damn him.

"What magazine do you write for?"

Meredith looked confused. "No magazine. I wrote a book, *Vampires in Myth and Legend.* I'm working on the sequel. I wanted to interview Mr. Erickson about owning this hotel — a mecca for wannabe vamps and people who love vampire lore. I think there's enough here for several chapters."

Mario swigged down his wine. "You want to write about us? Interview me. My name is Mario del Monico, and I'm a vampire."

Stefan saw Meredith start, her color rising. Very pretty color, beginning at her throat where it disappeared so interestingly into shadows he wanted to lick, rising up her long, kissable neck to flood her face. She thought Mario was making fun of her.

Then she relaxed and smiled. "Oh, you mean you're a Vegas Vampire. One of the dancers. I should have guessed."

"Have you seen the show?" Mario asked, his voice hopeful.

"Not yet, but I have a voucher." She shot Stefan a puzzled glance. "Which you had the desk clerk give me. Why? If you didn't know about the interview, why did you give me all those coupons and invite me up here?" She started to frown. "And why are you wearing your sunglasses inside?"

*Because you are not ready for me,* he

thought, but said out loud, "The light bothers my eyes. Come here, I want to show you something."

Curiously, Meredith hopped down from the stool, grabbing her glass of scotch on the way. She let Stefan rest his arm lightly on her shoulder as he drew her to the leather couch positioned in front of the flat-screen television.

She sat down on the leather and tucked her bare feet under her. Stefan sat beside her, sliding his feet out of the flip-flops and propping them on the coffee table. He lifted the phone from the table beside the sofa, rested it in his lap, and called his alert security team who waited for his every command. "This is Erickson. Play back the feed I was looking at earlier."

The security man said a smart "Yes, sir," and the screen in front of them flickered to life.

The picture showed the lobby of Transylvania Castle two hours ago, when he and Mario had watched Meredith walk in. A camera near the Coffin Bar swiveled and focused on a leggy woman in a rumpled cotton dress and wind-mussed hair carrying a duffel bag across the lobby to a check-in desk.

"That's me," Meredith said in surprise.

The feed tracked her from camera to camera, and then the lens above the reception desk zoomed down on her as she grinned and spilled things from her duffel bag.

"Freeze that," Stefan said into the phone.

"Yes, sir." The picture obediently stilled.

"So?" Meredith looked bewildered. "That's when I showed the clerk my book. You must have realized who I was."

"I had no bloody idea who you were," Stefan said. "I told my security to let you to have free run of this hotel and to bring you up to me."

Her red brows drew together, her glass of scotch hovering between lips and lap. "Why?"

"You truly do not know?"

"No."

Stefan slowly gestured at the screen. "That is why."

She looked back at the screen, which showed a beautiful young woman so full of life she sang with it. Stefan had wanted to see that life and feel it, touch it. Finding her in his pool, her dress outlining every delicious curve, had made his physical need soar into madness. She was perfect.

Her color rose again, a sensual flush that encompassed her entire body. Even her fingertips seemed to turn pink.

"Are you telling me you watch on your camera until you see a woman you like, and then you invite her up to your penthouse?" She slammed her glass to the table. "Oh my God, you *are* perverts."

"Hold on," Mario said, his smile dying. His voice took on the note of authority it must have had when he was an officer in the Venetian Army centuries ago. "Not every woman. Just you. He was looking for someone with very special qualities."

"What, big boobs?" Meredith sprang to her feet — her bare, sexy feet — and started to stride away. "Honestly, men like you make me sick. I am out of here, all right?" She caught up her wet dress and leather sandals. "I'll have your bellboy return the robe."

She stamped away, out into the marble hall, her feet slapping on the floor. Air stirred as she opened the front door, and then they heard it slam.

Stefan and Mario waited, Stefan studying the picture on the screen. He felt the weight of Mario's stare, but he had no intention of looking at him. Mario was worried about him and thought Stefan was crazy, and Mario was probably right. But Mario couldn't understand the drain on a master

38

who was losing power, the desperation that filled his body day and night. Not just anyone could destroy that desperation. It had to be the right woman, and he believed Meredith was she. He gambled with his life that he wasn't wrong.

The front door slammed open again, and they heard her bare feet tramping back down the hall. She stopped in the living room door, hands on her hips, her dress softly dripping water to the floor.

"Could one of you *please* let me into the elevator?"

Stefan rose. It was time. "Meredith," he said. "Come here."

For an astonishing moment, he thought she would disobey. They never disobeyed. But Meredith Black had a defiance in her, an unwillingness to submit that most women, even ones in this century, lacked.

Then, hands still on hips, she stomped across the room toward him and let out a heavy sigh. "What?"

"Look into my eyes."

"What for?"

Stefan slowly removed his glasses. Meredith's eyes widened as she took the full impact of his gaze, but other than that, her expression did not change. She was not going to crumple bonelessly to his feet and murmur, "Command me, Master."

Very strange. She was supposed to instantly submit. Few women could resist the eyes of a vampire master, and mortal women not at all. She should now be his to command, should be willing to do *anything* Stefan told her to, no matter how bizarre. She should do it and love it.

Meredith stayed on her feet, studying his eyes like she found him fascinating. Or maybe like she thought he was crazy. This was not a woman who would easily break, and the fact that she had the strength to defy him did funny things to his heart.

He heard Mario behind him, laughing under his breath. What the Italian vamp thought was so damn funny Stefan didn't know.

His eyes were golden. Meredith stood mesmerized by the dark gold the same tawny shade as a lion's eyes, framed with lashes as light as his hair. *Damn.* The man was gorgeous. He must have the women of Las Vegas falling all over him. No, not just Las Vegas, the entire world.

In fact, why didn't he? Why wasn't there a long-legged bimbo or three sunning themselves by his pool? They'd all look fantastic in bikinis and rise only to do something sexy like dive into the pool or saunter to the bar for another glass of sangria. Where were they?

*Oh no,* she thought in dismay, *maybe Stefan and Mario are an item.* That would just be too unfair.

But both men had been looking at her like they had hearty appetites and she was the main course at the lunch buffet. Like they hoped she hadn't tied the robe too tight and it might slip off. Like men who looked at a woman and thought, *attractive, sexy, maybe for me?*

Stefan's eyes pulled her thoughts back to him. Predator's eyes, mmm. She felt as though she was falling into them, and maybe he'd catch her in his big brawny arms and hold her safe against his tall, hard body. Wouldn't that be nice?

He made her weak in the knees too, and Meredith had never been weak in the knees over a man in her life. She had the sudden compulsion to kneel at his feet, maybe nibble his toes while she was down there. She resisted the compulsion, because she'd feel silly licking his ankles while Mario, who was already laughing at her, looked on.

And for some reason, Meredith pictured herself in a floating white gown, the kind women wore on bad Victorian-set horror movies, the ones who became slaves to the vampire masters. She must have been doing way too much vampire research.

"My," she said admiringly. "Why don't you dress up like a vampire? You'd look great in a black leather coat. You could walk around and inspire your guests. Oh, wait, your bellboy said you were something of a recluse."

"I am." His voice was rich and vibrant, as sexy as the rest of him. "But tonight you will dine with me."

"Yes, Mas — I mean, I will?" She drew on her resolve, wondering why she suddenly wanted to obey his every command. Obeying a man's every command was simply not like Meredith Black. "You could *ask* me, you know, and anyway, I had thought of taking in a show. Maybe the Vegas Vampires, maybe one of the Cirque shows, maybe the Blue Man Group."

"I will accompany you," Stefan said.

Mario, behind him, continued to grin. "He can get you the best seats."

"That's very nice of you. But I still want to interview you. You've obviously made a fortune off the vampire craze, and you too, Mr. del Monico." She found it almost impossible to switch her gaze from Stefan to Mario, but she did it. "The Vegas Vampires are known throughout the world because you claim to be real vampires."

"I hope good looks and charm have something to do with it," Mario said, pretending to be offended.

Meredith gave him a placating smile. "Having met you, I assure you it does."

Stefan slid his sunglasses back into place, sadly cutting off the glow of his beautiful eyes. "Now that you are mine, Meredith, you deserve to know the truth. Mario and I are vampires. Real ones, not like those who dress up downstairs for atmosphere. I do employ true vampires, vampires who are like me, but they remain incognito."

"Uh-huh." Meredith looked Stefan up and down, from the top of his golden head to his tanned toes bare on the cashmere rug.

"It is now safe to give you this knowledge because I have made you my blood slave, and you will be loyal to me."

"Blood slave. I see."

She'd written about blood slaves in her books, men and women enthralled to the vampire, like Renfield in Dracula movies, people who guarded when their masters slept in their coffins or fetched victims for them or, if women, provided sexual companionship and brought up the children of the blood.

Of course, if she had to be a blood slave, who better to be a blood slave for? She let her gaze linger on Stefan's throat, imagining licking the hollow there and what fun it would be. And she had just been accusing *him* of being a pervert.

"I have to choose the right one," Stefan was saying. "When I saw you on the camera in the lobby, I knew it was you. I hope you can save me, Meredith."

"Save you," she repeated.

Stefan chewed his lip, hands on hips. He couldn't know how utterly gorgeous he looked like that, his brow puckered in a frown, biceps stretching the sleeves of his T-shirt. "She does not believe."

"I see that," Mario answered. "She will."

Meredith burst out laughing. "Oh, come on, you two. Vampires? You have to be kidding me. First, I met you out there, in full sun. And you have a tan." She touched Stefan's forearm, then wished she hadn't, because she nearly melted at his feet again. His skin was smooth and satin warm, and she wanted to run her hands under his shirt to see if it felt the same there. "A vampire with a tan. Not to mention a reflection." She pointed to a large mirror at the end of the living room, which reflected her in a white terry robe towered over by the blond

44

Stefan and the dark Mario. "And you drink. Well, all right, vampires ate and drank on *Buffy,* but the writers deviated from classic literature to make the show more fun. *Buffy* gets a whole chapter in the new book."

Stefan said nothing. It was unnerving to have the flat black glasses fixed on her, so she reached up and plucked them off his face.

His eyes flared gold, almost glowing. "You will come to believe."

"You'd better hope so," Mario muttered.

"You don't have fangs, either," Meredith pointed out. "Honestly, I've studied every facet of vampire lore there is, and neither of you fits the bill. If you're going to pretend to be vampires, you should be more convincing." She scooped up her clothes again, wincing at their cold clamminess and hoping the dip hadn't ruined her room key. "I'll have to be going if you're taking me out to dinner. Fancy or casual?"

"Fancy. Most definitely fancy."

"Oh." Meredith deflated. "I don't have anything to wear. Business casual is about as fancy as I brought."

"I will tell the boutique to give you any dress you desire and send the bill to me."

"Free shopping? Well, if you insist, Mas— I mean Stefan."

45

Stefan took her hand, fingers warm on her palm, and lifted it to his lips. Trickles of heat twirled down her spine, and her usually steady heart took on a staccato beat.

"We will meet at eight," Stefan said. He pressed a key card into her hand as he released her.

"Eight. Right." She backed away and waggled her fingers at them, feeling very strange inside. "Ta-ta for now. You will see me again, resplendent."

She turned away from Stefan with reluctance and walked away across the marble floor. She felt their gazes on her all the way out into the hall, her mind a mishmash of what had just happened.

Somewhere deep inside her, a rational person was screaming that the Meredith Black she knew would never, ever let a man be her sugar daddy, buying her an expensive dress and paying for a fancy meal. She was a strong, independent woman who paid her own way.

Blood slaves, vampires. Stefan and Mario were cute but crazy. They had to be.

The rational Meredith got buried behind the somewhat buoyant Meredith who wondered what Stefan would like her best in — blue, green, rich chocolate brown? Humming, she slid on her sandals, then opened the elevator with her key card and stepped inside. As the quiet elevator took her swiftly downward, she realized Stefan had neatly made her forget all about interviewing him for her book, but that didn't seem as important anymore.

When he heard the elevator door slide shut, Stefan became bleak. He moodily sipped his vodka, lost in his thoughts.

"You still think she's the one?" Mario said behind him.

Stefan dragged his gaze from the door Meredith had just gone out. Mario watched him, black eyes holding knowledge with a hint of sympathy.

"Yes."

Mario shook his head and swigged back his wine. "Man," he said. "I wish you luck."

"I don't need luck."

Mario stared at him and then burst out laughing. "Yeah, you do. You poor slob." Still laughing, Mario picked up a towel Meredith had left, slung it over his shoulder, and walked out to the pool.

Meredith tucked the key card Stefan had given her into her pocket as the elevator took her swiftly and noiselessly downward. The fact that he'd just given her a key to, in effect, his entire penthouse pleased her a little. *Mom, you will never believe who just asked me out.*

She was still humming, paying little attention, as she stepped past the polished gold doors at the bottom.

By the time the doors slid shut behind her, she realized she was in the wrong place. She'd pushed the button for the lobby, not the basement, and besides, the elevator only had two buttons — one for the lobby, the other for Stefan's penthouse. So how did she get here?

She was definitely in a basement. Water and steam pipes, painted industrial white, gurgled overhead. She was in the belly of Transylvania Castle, in the real guts that ran the place. Interesting. Perhaps she could write a page or two on what the hotel looked like "backstage."

She took a few steps down the narrow hall and found more boring white walls, more pipes, cement floors. The entire basement must look like this — oh well, it was enough for a footnote.

She turned back to find the elevator and couldn't. Damn, she must have turned a corner and forgotten from which way she'd come. The boring monotony of the hall was easily confusing. Oh well, there would have to be some kind of elevator or stairway so the maintenance people could get up and down.

Unless they were real vampires and worked and slept down here and never saw the light of day. She giggled. She'd had way too much scotch upstairs in Stefan's penthouse. She'd almost started thinking it would be cool if Mario and Stefan really were vampires. It would do wonders for the book.

This was getting eerie. The pipes and cement floor went on and on, the same, the same, the same. At last she spotted someone up ahead, his black garb standing out among the monotony of white.

"Thank God." She hurried forward, her sandals loud on the bare floor. "Excuse me, could you tell me the way to the elevator?"

He moved faster than thought. One minute the man was looking away from her, the next, she was flat against the wall with his tall, cold body over her.

She looked up into an incredibly handsome face, perfectly formed, eyes the light blue of thick ice, and pure white hair that hung in a sleek wave over his leather-clad shoulders. Cold poured over her from his body, from his breath, from his fingertips that skimmed her cheek. Fear pounded deep inside her, the frantic fear of an animal that knows it's trapped.

She also knew that unlike Mario and Stefan, unlike the bartender in the Coffin Bar or the pseudo-Draculas of the clerk and the bellboy, this man was truly a vampire.

# CHAPTER THREE

Meredith didn't say, "What do you want?" because she knew what the vampire wanted. He wanted her.

Stefan's eyes were warm and golden, but this vampire's eyes were clear blue and so cold they burned. She was nothing to him, and she knew it.

He wrapped his hand around her neck, fingers powerful. She stood still, knowing she was going to die and could do nothing about it. She didn't bother to say, "Please," because she knew he didn't care.

His breath touched her neck, cold like he had nothing inside him. She stood with hands pressed against the wall, heart pumping, blood frozen. He threaded his fingers through her hair and pulled her head back while his other hand loosened the robe. She could only wait, fear leaking through her as he pressed his mouth to the hollow of her throat. His colorless hair brushed her skin like frozen silk, and she wondered dimly what it would feel like when he bit her.

He raised his head suddenly and looked into her eyes. They were nose to nose, his ice-blue eyes huge. She couldn't focus — but she would never, ever forget his face.

And then he was standing on the other side of the hall, arms folded, watching her. She had no memory of him releasing her and moving, but she now stood alone, five feet separating them.

Maybe he'd already sucked out her blood and made her a vampire, and she was just waking up. Her heart beating in her throat told her no.

"He's put his mark on you." His voice was rich, with all kinds of depth. "But it is only a delay."

She had no idea what he meant, and she didn't care. She only wanted to get out of there and back to the sane safety of the lobby with its slot machines and tourists in baggy shorts and silly vampire getups. She turned her back on him and ran.

This must be what hell is like, she thought, endless hallways of white and gray, everything the same, with a menace behind you. Where the hell was the elevator? It was freezing down here, the air-conditioning cranked to the max or something. The memory of the white-hot heat on the penthouse's deck and the soothing waters of the swimming pool were fading. There was nothing now but the cold dry air of this basement and all these damn pipes.

She nearly screamed with relief when the elevator appeared in front of her right where she'd left it, its mundane doors sliding quietly open when she slammed her finger to the button. She dove inside and jammed her finger on the Lobby button, jabbering, "Come on, come on, come on," as the doors gently closed.

She realized as she ascended, still clutching her bundle of wet dress, that there were only two buttons in the elevator, one for the lobby and the other for the penthouse. None for the basement. He'd brought her down there somehow, dragging her to him, using whatever vampire powers or magic he had to trap her.

The doors opened again. Meredith peered out fearfully and exhaled in relief when she saw and heard the warm rush of people in the lobby and the *clink, clink, clink* of coins falling from slot machines.

She joined the stream of humanity heading for the elevators to the guest rooms, really not out of place in her robe, because another group was returning from the pool in terry robes from their rooms. When she reached her door upstairs, she could barely shove her key into the slot, her hands were shaking so much. The pool water hadn't ruined the card, she saw with relief, as the door opened easily.

She secured all the privacy locks behind her, then stood in the middle of the room, shivering, trying to tell herself she was safe.

She didn't feel safe. Her skin burned where the vampire's cold fingers had touched her, and the look in his eyes had terrified her. He'd been strong enough to snap her life out right there, and there wouldn't have been a damn thing she could do about it.

The message light on her phone was blinking. She unclenched her body enough to go to the phone and check the voice mail. It might be her mother, wondering whether she'd made it to Las Vegas all right. Meredith had meant to call when she'd arrived, but the excitement of the invitation to meet Stefan Erickson had made her forget.

The first voice mail was the hotel telling her to make sure she checked out all its amenities, the world-famous gift shop, the coffee bar called Just One Sip, blah, blah, blah. She deleted it and went on to the next message.

The second message was blank. Silence filled her ears, blotting out the normal sounds of a hotel, like water in pipes and people tramping by outside the door. Her logical self told her that the blank message could simply be someone who'd hung up when they realized they'd dialed the wrong room, but Meredith knew it wasn't.

The white vampire had been on the other end of that line. The silence oozed his presence, quietly terrifying. He wanted her to know he knew where she was and that he could find her whenever he wanted.

She punched the Delete button over and over in panic and hung up the phone. She stood with her hands pressed to her face, shivering all over inside Stefan's warm robe, scared to death.

She'd never in her life believed vampires were real — they were stories made up by people intrigued because vampires were sexual beings as well as frightening ones. Vampires drank blood by taking it from the artery in the neck or in the groin, both erogenous zones. Hence, the popularity of vampires.

But she'd had no doubt that if the white vampire had put his sharp teeth into her neck, she'd even now be dead.

Meredith grabbed the phone and punched

the number for the front desk with frozen fingers. "Mr. Erickson, please," she said hoarsely. "Tell him it's Meredith Black."

The desk clerk's tone came back smartly. "Of courth, Mth. Black. Right away."

A split second later, Stefan's voice came over the line. "Meredith." The word radiated warmth, as though he'd been hovering by the phone, waiting for her call. "Meredith, love, it's all right."

And suddenly it *was* all right. The fear receded to a prickle at the back of her mind, easily buried and forgotten.

"He cannot hurt you," Stefan went on, his voice warm and soothing. "You belong to me now, and no one can take you away."

"How — how did you know what happened?"

"I sensed him. It's my hotel. But I've made him go away again."

Meredith exhaled in relief. "Thank God. Who was he?"

"Don't worry about that. Go buy your dress, love, and I'll take you out on the town."

"Yes, Stefan," she said, smiling. "Thank you."

"You're welcome." And he hung up.

Meredith stared at the receiver for a time, her body bathed in delight, before she gently replaced it in the cradle. Smiling and stretching, she threw off the robe, dressed in a new set of clothes, combed her still-damp hair and, humming a tune in her throat, went downstairs to immerse herself in the pleasures of shopping.

Meredith looked — what was the phrase? — awesome. She had chosen a sheath of dark blue velvet, short and sleeveless, a color that made her skin glow and her red hair shine. Her eyes, deep green and windows to her gentle soul, held specks of golden light.

She smiled at Stefan when he met her by the elevator and took her arm to lead her through the casino and to the car. Since he was rarely seen in public, he knew he was a point of interest and noted the people pointing him out to each other, murmuring. Tonight he was pleased to see that they looked not only at him in his relaxed designer tux, but at Meredith in her gorgeous velvet.

He paraded through the lobby because he wanted all eyes to see him with Meredith. He wanted everyone to realize she was his, wanted to send a warning to the other vampires to back off, don't touch.

The doormen scrambled to hold the huge glass doors open for them as Stefan led her, one hand on the small of her back, into the hot Las Vegas twilight. A limousine waited at the curb, an average everyday limousine, nothing vampire-themed about it. Long and white with smoked windows and a driver in front, it waited at the curb like an old-fashioned coach, complete with footman to open the door and usher Stefan and Meredith into its comforts.

Things hadn't really changed through the centuries, he reflected as they pulled away from the curb. If a man had money, he could take his lady out on the town in grand style, and the ladies liked to adorn themselves in the most sumptuous fabrics they could.

"Where are we going?" Meredith asked as the limo pulled smoothly away from the door and out the pseudo-Gothic gates to merge with the stacked-up traffic on the Strip.

"One of my favorite places."

Dusk had fallen, and the Strip began to blaze with light. Huge animated billboards advertised what could be found within the hotels, everything from major celebrities to lush female strippers to all-you-can-eat prime rib for $9.99.

Meredith stared out the window at the soaring hotels, the street as light as day, Las

Vegas just starting to come alive. The throng would grow to its peak after midnight, the die-hards lasting until the sun came up the next day. Some people came to Las Vegas and didn't sleep from the time they landed at McCarran Airport to the time they took off again.

Stefan had seen Las Vegas grow from just a few hotels owned by mobsters to a paradise of gambling and adult entertainment. Now it was a huge, thriving city surrounding theme hotels owned by large corporations. There wasn't anything anyone in Las Vegas wouldn't try. Stefan had enjoyed himself creating a playground for vamp enthusiasts. Vampires had moved from being scary and evil to the ultimate in cool.

Meredith didn't understand her role in all this, but she would. When she did, she might leave town and let him die, he didn't know, and he couldn't force her to stay. Mario advised him not to tell her, but Stefan did not think that was fair.

What Mario had said was, "Don't blow it by getting all angsty, undead, 'you are my chosen one' on her. Let her fall in love. It's supposed to be fun."

"I had forgotten what falling in love is like," Stefan had answered. "At least, until this afternoon."

In the limo, Stefan rested his arm across Meredith's shoulders, letting his fingertips glide over her satin skin. If the magic to restore him to full power stipulated that only *he* had to fall in love, the problem would be solved. He'd known the moment he looked at Meredith through the camera lens that she was the woman who would either save him or kill him.

The driver stopped in front of Ruglio's, an obscure restaurant off the Strip that only certain locals knew about. It catered to people like Stefan, a man behind the incredible success that was Las Vegas, and vampires.

"Mr. Erickson," the maitre d' greeted them, coming out to shake Stefan's hand. "Your usual table?"

Stefan nodded, and a silent and discreet waiter led them back. A few men and a woman acknowledged Stefan, greeting a colleague. The vampires averted their eyes from Meredith, letting Stefan know that they would never dream of trying to take the blood slave of a master.

These were warm vamps, living vamps, like himself and Mario. By Stefan's decree, the white vampires, the true undead like Armand, were not allowed. The white vamps wouldn't want to come anyway, but Stefan was never sure what Armand would get up to if he didn't enforce some rules.

To all intents and purposes, this was a normal restaurant, albeit with some of the best food in the country. The waiters moved in a choreographed dance, handing them napkins, filling glasses, and giving them menus without running into each other. They knew to give Meredith a menu that listed no prices. Stefan, in fact, had a running account here that a secretary settled up each month. Nothing so gauche as money changed hands at Ruglio's.

"It all looks so chichi," Meredith said. "Where I'm from, chichi is when my mom and I go for ice cream empanadas at our favorite Mexican place."

"Tell me about your life," Stefan said. He gestured to the sommelier who brought the best bottle of wine without being asked and poured the liquid into their glasses. "Every last detail."

"Not much to tell, really. Oh, this wine — it's fabulous. French?"

"Sonoma County. Tell me even if there's not much to tell."

Meredith shrugged her shoulders, wrapping her slender fingers around her wineglass. She should easily obey his commands, but the fact that she didn't was charming.

He sensed that if she told him anything about herself tonight, it would be because *she* chose. Her resistance to his mark fascinated him.

"I grew up in Texas in a little town, and then my mom and dad divorced, which was pretty scandalous even in this day and age. My mother is an artist — a good one — and we moved to Santa Fe to be closer to an art community. My mother shows her art in galleries, and we try to convince people to stop admiring her paintings and buy them for their walls at home." She made a face over her wineglass. "People think artists live on their love of art, but we still need to buy the macaroni and cheese. That's my job — take care of the accounts and buy the mac and cheese for dinner. I'm not very artistic myself."

"You wrote a book," Stefan said, watching her.

"A nonfiction book based on research. I write about other people's imaginations, not my own." She pointed a finger at him. "And I am not letting you forget about giving me that interview."

"That is not every last detail about your life."

She looked surprised. "Yes, it is. Unless you want to know every class I took in college and who I went to my high school prom with. He dumped me, by the way, for Wilhelmina Parker, who is now a sex therapist, in a bizarre twist of fate."

"I do want to know." He gave her his full vampire master stare. Until then, he'd either kept his eyes averted or damped down his power, but now he let her have it.

Her mouth relaxed into a smile. "Your eyes are glowing, did you know? You're sexy like that."

Definitely not the reaction he usually got. Blood slaves were supposed to either go into a trance and obey every word he uttered, or cringe and hide their eyes. Meredith only smiled and studied him with interest.

"Very sexy," she concluded. "I've never seen a man with golden eyes before, but they go with you." She reached out and touched a lock of hair that rested on his black-clad shoulder.

His nerves thrummed, every instinct aroused. He had the sudden urge to bend her over the chair and have at her. He could start slowly, nibbling and licking that long, pretty neck, lingering over the points of her pulse to tease himself. And then, when she was murmuring pleas and threading fingers through his hair, he could sink his teeth delicately into her and taste the sweet dark wine of her veins.

His whole body went stiff, including another part of him that wanted to feel her. Even better to have her naked in his bed, buried deep inside her before he drank of her. His blood warmed in anticipation — he had all night to convince her to give herself to him completely, and he looked forward to it.

She moved her fingertips to his neck, tracing it above the collar of his tux. "You don't have to pretend to be a vampire for me, Stefan." Her voice was soft. "You may have beguiling golden eyes, but you also have a pulse."

"I have a pulse because I am not dead. That doesn't mean I am not a vampire."

She smiled a little. "When I was doing research, I came across a story of teenagers who hung out on top of a mall and tried to live on blood. They used to sneak junk food when they thought no one was looking. People like to make believe — it's fun for them or gives them a sense of purpose in life."

"And that is what you think I am doing?"

She continued to stroke his skin, winding up his breath and his libido. "I think you're doing great PR for your hotel. Transylvania Castle, owned by a real vampire, rarely seen except to ride around in a limo and eat in a shadowy restaurant with exclusive clientele." Her eyes went dark, pupils widening. "A man of mystery — reporters make up stories about you, speculating on what and who you really are." She withdrew her hand and took a sip of wine. "I admit, it's brilliant. Your hotel is always full and gets wonderful ratings."

"Because I pretend to be a vampire?"

"Because no one knows anything about you. Who are you really, Stefan Erickson?"

Stefan traced the rim of his wineglass. "I am Stefan Erickson. Eric Bronson was my father. I was born in 1052 to the Wolf clan in what is now called Norway. When I was thirty years old, I was Turned by a vampire master who was the head of our clan. I was honored to be so chosen. I didn't realize that I'd also chosen a life of loneliness. I've befriended others of my kind, like Mario, and we've helped each other through the centuries. I've lived in England, France, Russia, and America throughout the years."

She cocked her head. "Trying to avoid villagers with pitchforks?"

"My power always kept villagers from wondering about me. And now, as you say, vampires are part of popular culture. A vampire no longer has to hide — people want to believe, or at least enjoy the make-believe."

"Like I do." She had dimples on the sides of her mouth. "I'm sorry, but your vampire pretense leaves much to be desired. You should at least try to look pale — like the vampire I saw in your basement."

Her smile died suddenly, and her eyes clouded with fear as her mind tried to break through the dampening effect Stefan had put on her when she'd called him, terrified. His voice had the power to comfort, even through the phone lines.

Her mind was fighting back, as it had from the moment he'd put his mark on her in the penthouse. Stefan countered it by leaning over to pour her more wine, a movement that let him edge closer to her in the booth. "You have nothing to fear as long as you are with me. And I am nothing like Armand."

"Who is he?"

She should not even remember her encounter with Armand, another vampire master, much less be curious about it. Her mind was certainly strong.

Stefan spoke into her ear, pitching his voice to be as warm and comforting as possible. "Armand Sebastien St. John. A cold vampire, a true undead. White vampires are

Turned after they are dead, usually after they die by violence. Armand was killed in battle sometime in the twelfth century and was Turned by the leader of his order, who wanted to raise an army of undead."

"Ick," Meredith said. "Well, he would have scared me into surrendering. But you aren't dead, so you're not like him?"

"I was Turned when I was still alive, and I made the choice," Stefan said. "No one else made it for me. I use blood to sustain my life, but I do not kill my victims — indeed, they must be willing to share their life essence with me. The cold vampires are killers."

Meredith listened with flattering interest. Stefan leaned closer and brushed his lips against hers. Mistake. His mouth tingled with the heady taste of her, and he needed her with an urgency that grew each passing moment.

She turned to meet his kiss. Their lips and tongues played, and he could taste the rich wine she'd just sipped. She was heady, like the wine, filling his mouth with sweetness. If he wanted, Stefan could freeze everyone in the restaurant to not see or hear for an hour or so, and he could take Meredith in this booth here and now.

An enticing thought, but how much nicer

simply to kiss her, moving lips on lips, building anticipation for what was to come. How much nicer to see her blush as he drew back, knowing she felt naughty for kissing a man she barely knew so blatantly in a restaurant.

She took a gulp of wine, red hair brushing rosy cheeks. "Why are you trying to seduce me? So I'll say good things in my book?"

"I care nothing about your book, Meredith. You are a beautiful woman." He drew her against him. Much better. Her warmth made him feel like he might stay alive a little longer, even if his power drained and he died in the end.

"You're very flattering." Her words were defiant, but he noticed she did not fight snuggling into his side. "You see me on a security cam, you invite me to your penthouse, you buy me clothes, you take me to dinner at restaurant that has *romance* stamped all over it, you ply me with fine wine, and you kiss me. You didn't have to go to so much trouble, you know. If you just wanted in my pants, all you had to do was get me drunk in your penthouse. You're gorgeous, and I nearly fainted when I saw you."

He drew his thumb along her jaw, tilting her chin to him. "You think all I wish is a physical encounter?"

Her brow puckered. "Isn't that what men like you do? You show off your money and power until a woman is ripping off her clothes for you, and then you take what you can and disappear." She flushed again as her words rang too loud in the quiet restaurant.

He said calmly, "Other men have done this to you, or tried? If so, they are boors and fools. I would not be so callous."

She made a face. "And now I've insulted you. I have foot-in-mouth disease, I know. I hope you don't walk out on me, because I have the feeling I couldn't afford this bottle of wine, let alone the dinner."

He tightened his arm around her. "I could not walk away from you, even if you had angered me. Viking warriors had better manners than that. Courtesy in a hall was a thing much prized, even with your blood enemy." He pressed a kiss to the warm line of her hair. "But I have a feeling that in this instance, the desire for a pure physical encounter lies with you."

She moved her shoulders, which let her breast brush nicely against his side. "What the hell?" she said. "You only live once."

"That is the point." He rested his forehead on her hair, breathing the beautiful scent of her. "You do not know me or anything of me other than what you have seen. I should not expect . . . I should expect nothing."

Meredith went silent for so long, the sounds of the other diners drifting to them, that Stefan opened his eyes. He found her staring at him, her lips parted. When their gazes met, she touched his face, smiling a little.

"Either you are the best sweet-talker who ever lived, Stefan Erickson," she said, "or the most wonderful man I've ever met." She touched a brief kiss to his lips, then moved apart from him as the waiters came to deliver the first course. "I sure hope I get all the rest of this night to find out."

# CHAPTER FOUR

If this was going to be a one-night stand, it would be the best one-night stand Meredith ever had. Not that she'd had many — both times had been blind dates with friends of friends, and Meredith hadn't planned them to be one-night stands. The men in question had never called or answered her subsequent e-mails. She'd learned how to take a hint.

At least Stefan was making it worth her while. They had a sumptuous meal at the restaurant, washed down with the bottle of exquisite red wine. Then the limo driver, whose name was Neal, drove them to an upscale club where Stefan led her out to the dance floor and took her around the room in an old-fashioned dance step. He pushed and propelled her so effortlessly, it was like he put the moves in her head and her feet obeyed.

He kissed her more than once while they

danced, his lips warm and hungry. Meredith saw where this was leading, but did she do anything to stop it? No. She rested her head on his shoulder and loved the feeling of his hand on her waist as he strolled with her around the dance floor.

Afterward, they drove back to the hotel, Neal quiet in the front while Stefan and Meredith sipped champagne and kissed in the back.

A dream vacation, that's what this was. The fact that she'd come to Las Vegas to gather material for her sequel was becoming a distant memory. The slogan was *What happens in Vegas, stays in Vegas,* so why not?

Meredith felt so safe with Stefan, like nothing bad could ever happen to her. His protection settled around her like a fuzzy sweater, the kind you hang on to long after it's worn out because it feels so good.

Yet he also thoroughly aroused her. Her eyes slid closed as the limousine wound through the traffic-clogged Strip, her body relaxing against his. A wicked fantasy made its way into her mind, and she seemed to see his naked body hovering over hers while he whispered, "Who do you belong to, Meredith?"

"You," she whispered back. She tried to

touch him, but her hands were tied to the bedposts with silk tethers. She wriggled in frustration, and he laughed, low and sultry.

He brushed his fingers over her bare breast, and she arched to his touch. "Mine," he said. "Never forget it."

"Yes, Mas —"

Her eyes opened as Neal stopped the car. The erotic vision had filled her head, so real that the limousine now seemed misty and insubstantial. Stefan was watching her, his eyes luminous gold in the dark, as though he knew her fantasy and liked it.

They didn't walk through the lobby this time. Neal pulled around to a private entrance in the back, and Stefan let them in with a key card. To her surprise, they did not adjourn directly to his penthouse. Stefan walked her down a long, plush corridor to another set of doors, behind which was a hell of a lot of noise.

She entered a world of black — black velvet curtains hanging from at least thirty feet above them and walls either covered with velvet drapes or painted a muted black. The floor was black too, and a black ramp about twelve feet wide ran upward to a bright emptiness.

Against this background people stood out in vivid hues. Men and women in oversized

T-shirts and shorts, the usual garb of the native Las Vegan, ran around with clipboards, headsets firmly planted against ear and mouth.

She realized they must be backstage in the Vegas Vampire Theater. The Vegas Vampires themselves mixed with the plainer techs, a dozen healthy, virile men in various stages of costume. They were specimens of physical male perfection — hard pectorals, broad shoulders, washboard abs, nipped waists, tight butts. They had hair every shade of brown, blond, and red and wore it long, short, tied back, or hanging in a waist-length wave. A Vampire with a mane of chestnut-brown hair and a leather vest winked at Meredith as he walked past.

A small group of Vampires gathered around a short woman with the body of a dancer. The men wore tight black pants, no shirts, and bow ties around their necks. They watched avidly as the woman thrust her arms out in front of her and her hips behind.

"Out and out and out," she said loudly. "Don't just flail about. It should be tight. It should be *sexy*."

The Vampires lined up and copied her movements.

Meredith knew she shouldn't stare. She

was with Stefan, and she should be as sophisticated and as oblivious as the women who ticked things off their clipboards, but she couldn't help it. All that muscle, all that oiled skin, and all those faces straight out of *GQ* did things to her healthy female hormones.

Several of the Vampires nodded or waved to Stefan, who gave them cool nods in return. Meredith wondered why Stefan had brought her here until she saw Mario heading their direction. Tonight he wore a tuxedo shirt and coat stretched across his broad chest, and black tuxedo pants. The pants didn't look quite right, and she realized after a minute that the seams were made of Velcro. Easier to tear off onstage, she guessed.

"Everything good?" Mario asked in his jovial voice.

"Armand made a visit," Stefan said. "Apparently to my basement."

Mario's dark eyes focused sharply, and he glanced at Meredith. "How did he get in?"

"I do not know, but I have reinforced the wards." He tugged Meredith's small velvet purse from her wrist and removed her cell phone from it. "I want you to program your number for her."

"Sure thing." Mario took the delicate phone and tapped the buttons, which beeped out a little tune. "If you need help, Meredith, and you can't find Stefan, you call me. For any reason, all right?"

"Sure." Meredith took back the phone, warm from his hands. *Warm vampires,* she mused. *Not cold like Armand.*

"Glad to help." Mario winked. "Hey, you staying for the show?"

Meredith glanced at Stefan to see what he had in mind, but he wasn't paying attention. He was looking over the sets going up on the stage, the hotelier interested in the quality of entertainment being provided for his guests.

"Stay for my act, anyway," Mario suggested. "It's the best one."

A passing blond Vampire gave him a scornful look. "In your dreams, Italian boy."

"Hey, the ladies love Italians," Mario told him. "Vikings are boring. Oh, sorry, Stefan."

"You do not offend me," Stefan said, almost absently. Mario shot him a look, but one of worry, which Meredith suspected had nothing to do with Stefan's Viking ancestry.

She could not help contrasting the two men. She liked Stefan better because Stefan was her mas — She liked Stefan better because he was incredible. Her heartbeat hadn't slowed from the intimacy she'd experienced with him all evening.

Mario was the same height as Stefan, but a little larger and more massive. He obviously lifted weights in addition to his dancing. Stefan had more raw muscle, like a leopard or panther. Mario would be a lion, big and stretched out in the sun, his harem around him, while Stefan prowled the jungle.

The vision of them as predators was vivid. It occurred to her that she should be afraid because she was Stefan's prey and he'd already caught her, but for some reason, she wasn't.

"Stay and watch, Meredith," Mario was saying. "You decide whose act is best."

"We'll stay a time," Stefan said, and that settled it.

She and Stefan watched the show from the wings. She listened to the theater fill, the chatter of excited women growing louder as showtime approached. An occasional whistle or whoop split the air. She imagined the audience, girls at bachelorette parties, ladies who'd left their husbands safely at home, local women on a girls' night out. She heard plenty of screams of "Mario! We love you!"

"He's very popular," she remarked.

"He knows how to please a crowd," Stefan said as he leaned down and nibbled her ear.

Stefan knew how to please Meredith. Anything he said made her happy. She wondered whether if he said, "Isn't it hot out today?" she'd start kissing him madly just from the joy of hearing his voice.

The stage got brighter. Glowing signs came on backstage warning all to be quiet as music started, softly at first, then swelled to fill the theater. The women beyond the black curtains let out a collective scream. The ripple of energy poured from the screaming women down the ramp and across the line of Vegas Vampires. They tensed, drank it in, and got ready to give it back in spades.

The first dancer turned and sprinted up the ramp to the stage. The screaming crescendoed, though Meredith hadn't thought it could. The Vampires dashed up the ramp one at a time, each to be greeted by another rocketing scream.

Stefan led Meredith partway up the ramp and off to the side where they could see without being seen. The audience's mass heat and sound nearly crushed her, the pulsing anticipation and excitement almost tangible.

Mario went onstage last. The screams for him were eardrum shattering. Meredith imagined plaster crumbling and girders groaning under the onslaught of noise. "Oh my God!" a woman's voice hurtled over the din. "Mario, I love you!"

Meredith saw Mario turn and blow a kiss toward the audience, which stoked their fever still higher.

The show was amazing. Meredith had thought a show called Vegas Vampires would be too silly for words, but the dancers played with the silliness and made the audience laugh with them. They took every element — the huge stage, the costumes, the raunchy tunes, the audience's excitement — and molded it into something sexy and playful and incredibly intimate. There must have been five thousand women in that theater, and the Vampires made every single one feel like *she* was the one for whom they danced.

They came off after that, and Mario stood with Stefan and Meredith, catching his breath. A gopher handed him a sports bottle and a towel, and he streamed water into his mouth and mopped his face. Meredith wanted to ask him all kinds of questions — like didn't all those screaming women unnerve him? — but it was too loud for conversation.

Stefan rested his cheek against her hair as they watched. For a moment, Meredith closed her eyes and enjoyed the feeling. Who needed dancing men when Stefan was her master?

Each Vegas Vampire went on and did his own act, while Mario watched with Meredith and Stefan, his dark eyes shining in the lights from the stage. Meredith ran her fingers along Stefan's strong arms. Occasionally, he'd lean down and kiss her neck, and Meredith closed her eyes and enjoyed.

Once, when she opened her eyes, she found Mario watching her with an intensity that made her think of predators again. Stefan ran his tongue along her neck, and her insides got hot. They stood like that, Stefan kissing her neck and Mario watching, until Mario's turn came to take the stage.

Two dark blue spots came on in back of the stage, and the women, obviously knowing what was coming, started to go insane. The blue light grew in intensity, then flared with the music to reveal Mario looking dark and dangerous in his black tuxedo.

A chair rested in the middle of the stage. Mario slid off his coat and slung it across the chair. He loosened his tie, like he was coming home from a dinner party, although Meredith suspected most men didn't remove their ties with a slow, sexy flourish.

He started to dance, his body rippling and graceful. As he undulated, each article of clothing started coming off smoothly and almost imperceptibly. He used the chair like a dancing partner, making it spin and leap as much as he did.

Every woman in the audience wanted to be that chair. Once he was naked but for a tiny thong across his hips, he stretched and danced around the chair, his movements taut and precise. When he turned to the audience and showed them his fangs — real ones? — she thought the women would have to be dragged out on stretchers. Mario looked over them all like a king with his adoring subjects, leaning into the cushion of sound like he loved it.

"So what do you think?" Stefan said into Meredith's ear.

"You still say he's a vampire?"

Stefan nodded once, like he was pleased she'd learned well. "He can protect you. That is why I put his number in your phone. If I am not around, and you need someone, you *call him.*"

She started at his urgent tone and tried to soften it with a smile. "Yes, master."

81

Mario ran down the ramp, grinning, his face and taut body covered in sweat. "Well? What did you think?"

"Uh," Meredith said, and gulped. "You were great. You're a wonderful dancer."

He looked slightly surprised. Then he leaned down and kissed her cheek. "Aw, you're sweet. I'm sorry Stefan got to you first."

"But I did," Stefan said, sounding amused.

Mario raised his bare hands. A tech girl, who pretended she didn't notice his naked, oiled body, was trying to hand him a robe. "Right. Enjoy your night, Meredith." He grabbed the robe, winked at the girl, and sauntered off, drawing the garment over his bare shoulders.

Stefan asked, "Ready?"

"Sure," Meredith answered, thinking she was.

He took her hand and led her out.

The penthouse was an oasis of calm after the outrageous din of the Vegas Vampire Theater, and Meredith breathed a sigh of relief. All was quiet inside the marble-floored rooms, but a bottle of wine stood open and breathing on the bar, the rest of the living room spotless. Stefan must have a staff who knew how to fade into the woodwork at just the right time.

Stefan poured wine and handed her a glass. "I want to show you something."

Meredith kept expecting their exodus to the bedroom, but Stefan did nothing so crass. Fingers on the small of her back, he led her out to the deck and the pool area.

The Las Vegas night was still hot, dry July heat seeping into her bones and relaxing her like a sauna. Stefan led her to the wall and gestured over. Below them the Strip stretched in a glittering stream of light from south to north. Lights of every color — blue, red, green, yellow, orange — lit the sky, the blackness above cut with laser displays from nearby hotels.

"It's beautiful," Meredith breathed. "I see why you live up here."

Stefan closed his arms around her waist. "Las Vegas is a city that hides evils behind its pageantry. It always has."

"You've lived here long?"

"Nearly one hundred years. I came to find solitude in the remote desert, but I became fascinated with this city as it grew."

She decided not to argue with him about this vampire business any longer. Meeting Armand had convinced her there were strange things afoot here, and she certainly felt Stefan's power, whatever it was. "If you wanted solitude, why did you stay here?"

"I take care of people."

His hands were warm on her abdomen, fanning fires already burning. He leaned down and pressed soft kisses to her ear, nibbling gently until she made a noise of pleasure.

Meredith turned around, wrapped her arms around his neck, and kissed him. She felt his body full length against her torso, hard muscle against her breasts and abdomen. His very real heart beat fast beneath his breastbone, his mouth fevered as it took hers.

They were going to make love. There was no coy question of *would they or wouldn't they?* She knew it with a certainty, and she had no qualms about it. She'd only met Stefan this afternoon, and already he'd outshone every man she'd ever known in her life.

She felt his fingers move to the top of her dress and begin to ease the zipper down. She laced her fingers through his hair, urgency filling her and making her wish his tuxedo was put together with Velcro like Mario's.

"This should come off, at least." She smiled up at him and tugged on one end of his bow tie.

Stefan slid one hand inside her dress to her bared back and with the other undid the bow tie and the top button of his shirt. The hollow of his throat came into view, tanned and enticing. Meredith leaned forward and licked it.

He made a noise in his throat, and her dress loosened, his hands parting the back and sliding it from her shoulders.

"No fair," she whispered. "I want you taking clothes off, too."

Stefan smiled into their next kiss, then shrugged off his coat and tossed it over the nearest chair, following it with vest and then shirt. Bare-torsoed, he went back to kissing her, while she traced her fingers over the muscles of his back and shoulders. She stroked his hard chest, pausing to touch his flat nipples, and skimmed her hands to the waistband of his pants.

He drew off the belt, then looped it around her backside and pulled her against him. "You are so damn beautiful," he informed her. "And all mine."

She licked his mouth. He tasted wonderful, like wine and maleness and Stefan. He caught her tongue with his and let her explore while he eased the gown down her arms, then unhooked her bra and dropped that, too.

It felt wonderful to be nearly naked with him, outside in the Las Vegas heat, open to the sky and yet so private in the nest that was his home. Their kisses went on while he got himself nearly naked, too, all hard muscle and smooth skin under her questing hands.

"I don't want to go into the bedroom," she whispered. "Let's stay here, under the stars."

His answering smile melted her bones. He slid his arm around her waist and led her to an armless, flat chaise sitting near the pool. The water, lighted, glared reflections on the window glass and across the deck, so it looked like they were in an underwater fantasy. As casually as though it were commonplace, Stefan stripped his briefs from his body and lay down flat on the chaise.

Meredith gawked. The most attractive man she'd ever met in her life was lying before her, stark naked, his cock straight and tall and inviting.

"Oh my."

He beckoned with his fingers. "Come to me, Meredith."

Meredith swallowed. Slightly more self-consciously, she slipped off her bikini briefs. There she was, standing nude under the starlight, the reflection from the pool dancing across her skin. It had been different when she had been in the water — at least then the water had covered her.

Bare and feeling both bold and vulnerable, she let him look at her, his eyes half closed. "Meredith, you take my breath away."

She put her finger to her lips. "In a good way or a bad way?"

He stretched out a hand to her again. "Come to me."

Who could resist a beautiful, naked man begging her to be with him? She moved toward him, not really believing she'd just stripped for him.

She took his hand, moving her touch to his wrist and all the way up his arm, wanting to feel him slowly, even though he was obviously rampant and ready to get on with it. His skin was hot and smooth, sleek over powerful muscles that moved as he quietly towed her toward him.

He didn't jerk her or slam her down to him, he let her take her time to get used to him. Which was good because he was big. Of course as hot and slick as things felt between her legs, he wouldn't have trouble sliding right in.

She sat on the edge of the chaise and continued her exploration of his body. His chest was firm under her fingers, his heart-beat strong and even. Vampires didn't have heartbeats. Didn't breathe, didn't tan, didn't eat tournedos of angus beef in wine sauce. She knew what vampires did — she'd spent two years researching every piece of vampire lore available.

They were supposed to ignite in the sun, sleep in coffins, keep a handful of the earth in which they'd been buried inside their shoes, not be able to cross running water. If Stefan had lived in Europe, then he'd crossed an entire ocean of running water. She thought of what he'd told her about being a warm vampire — having been Turned before he died and therefore im-mortal, not undead. He was turning all her research upside down.

He watched her with languid eyes as she teased his nipples, drawing the nubs into points with her fingertips. His chest rose under her touch, his lips parting.

She smiled at him. "Do you wish I'd get on with it?"

"Take your time. Better that you're will-ing than we rush it."

"Oh, I'm willing." She gently pinched his nipple. "I'm naked on the deck of your penthouse, bare for every passing helicopter or airplane to see."

"No one flies directly over Transylvania Castle."

"Have the FAA under your control too, do you?"

His brows drew together a little. "You are a most unusual woman, Meredith Black."

"Meaning I talk too much? There is one way to stop me."

Before she could think about what she was doing, she laid herself across his chest and kissed his lips.

He twined his fingers through her hair as they kissed, lifting it and letting it fall against her shoulders. He might be breaking every rule of vampire lore, but he sure knew how to kiss.

He moved his palm across her waist, sliding up her bare back to her nape, warm skin on warm skin. Beneath her she felt the muscles of his chest play as he busily touched her. Her breasts were pressed tight against him, the wiry curls on his chest warm and tickling.

She moved her hand lower, tracing the muscles of his abdomen, the flat indentation that was his navel. He moved his tongue in her mouth, tasting every corner of her. His own taste was like wine and spice, a heady combination.

He was aroused and getting hotter by the

minute, his skin under her fingertips roasting. His kisses grew insistent and intense. He slid his fingers between her thighs, stroking her heated folds until she thought she'd climax before she was ready.

"Stefan, wait. I haven't even —"

He cut off her words with a kiss that was brutal. "I can't wait. I need you."

So much for sweet talk. Liquid pooled on her inner thighs, which made him rub even harder.

Too fast, he was moving too fast. She wanted to touch him and learn his body, to arouse him with her fingers like he was arousing her. She wanted to explore his length and experience every inch of it before he slid it inside her.

And had one of them thought to bring condoms? Meredith hadn't been near a condom in more than a year, and she'd never dreamed her visit to Las Vegas would include sex. She wasn't a one-night-stand kind of girl, although now that she was experiencing one, it was kind of fun.

As though reading her mind, Stefan reached under the chaise and brought out a box of condoms, magnums of course. His cleaning staff really was prepared. How did they know they would choose this particular chaise? Unless this was the usual seduction couch.

Before she could say *Let me put it on you,* he unrolled it over his cock and dropped the box back to the deck.

"Stefan . . ."

"It must be now, hurry." His golden gaze held her. "Please."

The *please* was thrown in as an afterthought, a man remembering to be nice to the woman beforehand.

How could she explain that she wanted to savor this night, to draw it out as long as she could? She didn't want bang, bang, bang, good night. *If I'm going to be seduced and discarded, at least let me enjoy it.*

Her own body, on the other hand, was plenty happy to acquiesce to Stefan's urgency. Her heart beat swiftly, her body hot all over, blood thrumming through her veins. Her breasts lifted high and tight, warm and ready, and her opening flowed with honey. There wasn't one thing her body wanted more than for her to throw her leg over Stefan and join with him.

"Yes, Mast —" She clamped her lips closed. She'd never been remotely interested in bondage and domination, and now here she was wanting to call him "Master" and obey his every whim. She had no idea what had gotten into her.

She grasped the base of his cock where the condom didn't reach, liking the warm feel of his skin and the movement of his pulse. She slid her thigh across him and lowered herself until his tip pushed inside her.

It was incredible. Meredith tilted her head back and let her hair spill across her shoulders, the feel of the silken ends erotic. He sank hot fingers into her buttocks, pulling her slowly downward until every inch of him had entered her.

This man could tell her he was a vampire or whatever he wanted, as long as he kept on making her feel like *this.* He penetrated her deeply, her walls, long unused to anything inside them, aching as he stretched her. A good ache. She moaned and closed her eyes.

His hands moved on her back, a raw sound in his throat telling her he liked it just as much. She opened her eyes again and saw stars above the lights of the city, swirling in endless white across the sky.

"Meredith." His whisper held a note of desperation. "Help me. *Ride* me."

"Yes, Master," she said absently, then began to move her hips.

# CHAPTER FIVE

The sensation nearly killed Stefan then and there. He held her hips, loving the smooth feel of her skin, and watched her lips part in passion. Her red hair moved on her shoulders, the breeze stirring the ends across her cheek.

*Perfect, perfect, perfect.* He was so damn hungry, but he knew that if he just took her they'd both die. It would be a shame to see this beautiful woman stretched out bloodless on his floor for Mario to find. She was so full of life and fire, and she needed to stay that way. Better for him to die and get it over with than drag her into hell with him.

And die he would. He felt it coming. But what a way to go. He slid his hands along her thighs, prepared to love every second of this. Meredith was resisting his mark, and he wasn't sure how she did it. She had no power of her own — he knew that as he gently slid his thoughts into and out of her mind. She was who she seemed to be, an innocuous young woman from Santa Fe who wrote books and helped sell her mother's artwork.

Her slight defiance served as an aphrodisiac. She *almost* succumbed to him, but not quite.

She rocked her hips against his, and waves of incredible feeling roared through him. This was a woman and a joining he'd waited his long life for. He clenched down on the excitement rising like a black tide, wanting to hold on to his orgasm as long as he could. He'd always been able to draw it out, to control the situation, but with Meredith his body had other ideas.

*Take her, have her, take her again.*

*Why not?* If she did not choose to save him, at least he'd exit this plane of existence happy.

He drove upward, feeling her close on every inch of him. The pleasure was maddening, and he never wanted it to stop. As a Viking, he'd been a warrior and a hunter, and he'd learned the value not only of being strong and striking fast, but of patience. One struck only when the time was right.

The time was right — now. He was fading, and the signs that he'd learned to read in the wind and the weather and the stars

94

over the centuries told him she was the one who would save him. But while he could seduce her and coax her and make her his slave, the ultimate choice was hers. A blood slave obeyed every command but one. When a warm vampire said, *Let me drink,* a blood slave could refuse. That was their only power, the one check the universe had on vampires to keep them from taking over the world. Vampires had supernatural power, but in the end, they were as dependent on the slaves as the slaves were on them.

Most slaves willingly let their masters drink, though, being far gone in adoration for them. But Meredith resisted. He feared her resistance and at the same time, it intrigued him.

Her body certainly wanted his at the moment. She writhed on him, taking her pleasure, and he happily gave it to her.

"You are an incredible woman, Meredith Black."

Her answer was a moan as her climax took her over the edge. "Stefan," she gasped, and she rocked on him, hard, harder. *"Yes."*

He held her hips, pushing himself into her, meeting her thrust for thrust, while his own tension spiraled into the sky. The climax was like nothing he'd ever experienced. Darkness rushed at him at the same time he growled his delight and slammed into Meredith as hard as he could. "That's it, my love. Thank you."

He felt it coming, the end of the climax, the beginnings of darkness. *No, not now. I want to be with her a little longer.*

The darkness won. As her look softened into after-sex pleasure, cold took over his limbs. Under her stroking hands, he stopped moving and lay still, his heartbeat slowing until it thudded to a near halt.

Meredith rubbed his chest, liking the way his crisp gold curls wove around her long fingers. "Stefan? That was — amazing."

*Amazing* was an understatement. She'd never felt that way before, never felt such a connection with another person. She'd felt as though his climax had entwined with hers, her pleasure and his running side by side.

Stefan watched her with half-closed eyes, the gold glow in them fading. She stroked his smooth torso, loving the warm feel of him, feeling his pulse slow under her fingers.

"Stefan?"

He remained silent, his hands on her thighs, his fingers moving the slightest bit. Maybe he didn't like to talk afterward. Maybe he liked to sleep first and talk later.

He couldn't exactly go out for a beer and never see her again, because this was his apartment. He could throw her out, though. He'd seemed so gentlemanly earlier tonight, so tender with her, but she didn't really know him. Was he the kind of man who'd do the deed and then tell her to get out?

Apparently not. He continued to touch her thighs, his fingers featherlight. She lay across his body, reveling in his warmth. She wouldn't talk if he didn't want to. It was enough to bask in the afterglow. If all went well, they could do that again and again, until the roasting hot summer sun crawled upward to start another day.

He lay very still. Meredith raised her head to kiss his cheek and noticed that the stillness, except for the faint movement of his fingers, was absolute. He didn't even blink.

"Stefan?" she repeated. She touched his face, his lips. No movement, no response.

Alarmed, she sat up, pressing her hands to his chest. His heart still beat but very, very slowly, unnaturally so. She smoothed his hair from his brow and found it coated with icy sweat.

Her breath slammed into her, hot with the desert night. "Oh my God, I've given him a heart attack."

But how? Stefan was a virile male, in great

shape — but then, she didn't know anything about him. Maybe this was what vampires did after sex.

She slid from the chaise, scrabbling for the little velvet purse that went with her dress and had a cell phone inside it. Should she call 911 or hotel security? Call *someone.* Stefan could be dying.

Cold touched her, a chill in the air though the night was still roasting hot. Dry desert air that could peel the skin from her body was now overlaid with a coldness she'd experienced earlier today, when —

She turned. The white vampire was standing near the edge of the pool, his waist-length white hair stirring in the breeze. She could see his ice-blue eyes all the way across the deck.

The fact that she was stark naked hovering over a chaise on top of a hotel roof didn't bother her as much as what would happen when the white vampire reached her. The water reflected weirdly on him, making his face alternately white and bluish.

She never saw him move. One moment he stood near the sliding door to the apartment, the next he was in front of her, his icy eyes holding her gaze.

Her heart raced, but she held her ground,

though she was nauseated with fear. The vampire's gaze moved to her throat, where she knew her pulse pounded like a jackhammer. The more she tried to slow her breathing and her heart rate, the faster it went.

He reached a cold finger to her mouth. He moved his fingertips across her lips, which must be red and swollen from Stefan's kisses, tracing them slowly.

"Go inside, Meredith," the vampire said.

"No." The response came automatically.

*Do not obey.* She seemed to hear Stefan's voice inside her head, but a quick glance down showed he was still silent and immobile.

"Leave him to me," Armand said.

"No." Meredith yanked open her purse. The cell phone clattered to the deck, but that was not what she reached for. The cheap cross on a chain, the one her mother had given her, fell into her hands. She raised it into the vampire's face. "Leave me alone."

He regarded the plain gold cross with steady eyes before reaching up and firmly taking it away from her. He balanced the necklace on his palm while she watched, astonished. No screaming, no bursting into flames, nothing.

He raised his gaze to her baffled face. "I was a Knight Templar for many years, Meredith. The symbol of Christ holds no terror for me. I died with his badge on my chest."

"Oh."

He took her hand and dropped the cross back into it, closing her fingers. "Keep it for those who fear it." His grip was strong, and he was not about to let her go.

"I belong to Stefan," she tried.

"He wants you to think so. Fight him. Let his pull leave your mind and let him die."

"No." The voice behind her was weak. Meredith looked swiftly at Stefan to see him fighting to open his eyes. His body remained immobile, his eyes still half closed. "No." He tried to move, and collapsed, his arm trailing to the deck. "Damn."

The white vampire moved on him, blue eyes glowing. Meredith shrieked and flung herself on top of Stefan, holding out her hand as though she could stop a powerful undead being with her palms. "Leave him alone."

Armand stopped, his eyes as cold as ever. "He is using you, Meredith Black. He has made you his blood slave, and he wants sacrifice. He must drink of you or die."

His cold touched Meredith, and she shuddered. Her mind registered one thing — this man was a vampire, sure as shooting, and he believed Stefan was a vampire as well.

Armand noted her hesitation. "He has brought you here to feed from you, again and again, and you'll let him because you won't be able to resist." He threaded his cool fingers in Meredith's hair, his lips parted, and she saw the unmistakable white of fangs against his red mouth. "Let me Turn you now and make you my own, let me save you from him."

She stared at him in stark fear. "Wait, you mean you'll suck my blood and make me a vampire, and that saves me from *him?* What saves me from you?"

"You will be free. Not a blood slave. It is the only way."

"How about no way in hell? And I wish I would have phrased that differently."

He put his strong hand on her neck, moving aside her hair. "Come to me. I will make it the most exquisite event of your existence."

"Sounds like it will be all downhill from there."

He peeled back his lips, fangs sharp, his eyes flaring blue. As his mouth came down on her neck, she shoved him with all her strength and dropped to the deck. Her knees banged the hard concrete and she felt the sting of blood on them. She shoved her shoulder against Armand's leather-clad legs and scuttled out from under him.

She had a single moment's advantage, which she used to lunge for her cell phone. She grabbed it and rolled away, punching in the speed-dial number for Mario and praying she wasn't in a dead zone.

*Dead zone* — she really had to come up with new jargon.

Armand was on her the moment her finger lifted from the keypad. He threw the cell phone to the deck, where it spun and skittered into the glass. He jammed her head back, his hand on her shoulder, fangs ready.

"Mario!" she screamed, in case the phone had connected. "Mario!"

She heard Mario's voice faintly crackling in the faraway phone. "Meredith?"

"Help me!"

There was one second of silence, then a forceful Italian word. "Be right there."

He meant *right there.* As Armand's teeth connected with her neck, Mario's brawny hands yanked him from her and spun him around. Meredith collapsed to the deck, frantically feeling her throat for blood.

Armand easily threw off Mario's hold and the two faced each other, Mario breathing hard, the white vamp unmoving except for the wind stirring his hair.

"Get the hell out of here," Mario said,

voice menacing.

"You would help him? Or maybe you want to share in her blood. It's sweet." He flicked a drop from his lips and sucked it from his fingertip.

"I said, get the hell out."

Mario looked less like a dancer ready for a lady's pleasure and more like a thug you didn't want to meet in a dark alley. His dark eyes were steady, as cold as Armand's, his face hard.

Armand looked at him for a long time, no fear showing in him whatsoever. "Her blood will be on your hands," he said softly. "And you call yourself a man of honor."

Mario took a step forward, large fists curled. If Mario had looked at Meredith like that, she would have run far and run fast. Armand simply gave him a look of contempt. Then he whirled around, pale hair flying, leapt easily to the five-foot wall, spread his arms, and dove into empty space.

Meredith screamed, then clapped her hand over her mouth. She drew in several ragged breaths, her brain trying to comprehend what she had just seen. "He jumped — Wait, he's a vampire. He didn't turn into a bat, did he?"

She glanced above them in alarm, where a flying rat could even now be circling them.

Mario gave her an incredulous look, then burst out laughing. The cold, mean thug disappeared, and Mario the sexy dancer was back with her. "A bat? What kind of crap do you read?"

"I don't read it, I write it."

"Oh yeah, I forgot."

His dark eyes sparkled, and she realized his interested gaze was on her — all of her. She'd felt no embarrassment being naked in front of Armand — she'd been too terrified — but now she flushed as Mario's scrutiny went on and on. She drew up her knees and crossed her arms over her chest, her face hot.

"Hey, no need to hide yourself from me. I don't see anything bad here." He glanced at Stefan, who lay like a statue on the chaise, and his grin faded. "You had sex."

Meredith reached for her dress and lifted it on, trying to hide her body from Mario at the same time. "We're both stark naked beside the pool. Did you think we were fishing?"

"Don't get mad." Mario moved to Stefan and looked down at him. He brushed his hand over Stefan's face, gently lifting an eyelid. Stefan never stirred. "You couldn't resist her, could you? Idiot. It was too soon, and you knew it."

"Too soon for what?" Meredith struggled to zip her dress up in back. "Mario, too soon for what?"

Mario looked up at her, dark eyes unreadable. "He wanted to tell you, and I told him not to. Maybe I'm the idiot."

*"Mario."* Meredith glared at him. "What is wrong with Stefan? And what did Armand mean about you having my blood on your hands?" She touched her neck where Armand's teeth had scraped her. It had bled a few drops, but that was all.

"Armand is a vampire master, so he thinks he's always right. He has a big following, and his vamps do whatever he says. Kind of king of the cold vampires."

"The ones who are true undeads."

"Yep."

"Mario, could you please, please, please tell me what is going on? Is Stefan going to be okay, or did I slay him with sex?" She glanced at Stefan, who lay so still on the chaise, her heart hammering with worry. "Why did Armand want to turn me into a vampire to get me away from him?"

"Tell her." The whisper came from Stefan's throat.

Meredith dropped to her knees beside him, cradling his face. "Stefan. Are you all right? I'm so sorry." She kissed his forehead, not liking how cold his skin had grown.

"You didn't kill him with sex, Meredith," Mario interrupted. He grinned. "But if you want to try with me . . ."

"Tell her," Stefan repeated, barely moving his lips. "Jackass."

Mario chuckled. Meredith felt a little better that Mario wasn't freaking out and calling for an ambulance, but she saw nothing to laugh about.

Mario gently pressed Meredith aside and leaned to lift Stefan, as large as he was, over his shoulder. "Let's get this big guy to bed, and then you and me will have a talk."

Mario carried Stefan through the glass door that slid aside for him and into the bedroom. As Meredith had seen earlier, the bedroom was palatial but functional. The large bed did not look quite so large with Stefan sprawled across it — the man filled up a room.

Meredith helped Mario get him under the covers and arrange the pillows comfortably. Stefan tried to move now and again, but he seemed content to let Meredith position him in the bed and smooth the covers over him. She leaned down and touched a kiss to his lips. He moved them a little, trying to respond to the pressure, and then his eyes slid closed.

Mario waited for her in Stefan's ornate living room. He held up a glass and ice tongs. "Drink?"

"No." She'd drunk plenty of wine and knew if she had a cocktail on top of it she'd slide to the floor. She trusted Mario, sort of, but wasn't sure she trusted Armand not to put in a return appearance. A shiver ran through her, and she wondered if she'd ever feel safe sleeping alone again.

"I wish I'd stayed home," she began.

But she really didn't wish that. She wouldn't have met Stefan, and her night with him had been wonderful — up until he'd passed out and Armand had showed up, that is.

She accepted the bottled water Mario handed her. "Just tell me what's going on," she sighed as she popped the top.

Mario lounged on Stefan's leather sofa and propped his feet on the coffee table. He wore nonshow attire — jeans and tight black T-shirt, square-toed motorcycle boots, his black hair pulled into a ponytail.

"Stefan needs to feed," he said. "I didn't realize he was *this* weak, or I'd have re-inforced the wards around the hotel. Armand got in because Stefan is breaking down. He didn't tell me how far gone he was, damn it all."

"Stefan needs to feed — because he's a vampire?"

"That's right. Living vampires feed on the living. We need life to give us life. Understand? We make blood slaves who devote themselves to us, who are willing to sacrifice their own blood to keep us alive. But it's their choice." His dark gaze drifted to her neck, and Meredith resisted the urge to press her hand to it.

Mario's lips twitched. "Don't worry, sweetheart. Stefan's already marked you. I can't take you away from him, and if I try he'll kill me. Six hundred years of friendship don't matter when instinct will make him kill to protect his minion."

"Minion." Meredith made a wry face. "How flattering."

Mario's half smile became a grin. "It's just a term, not a description. Anyway, you're his, and I wouldn't violate the rules to try to steal you. Armand tried to take advantage of Stefan's weakened state to nab you for himself."

"Let me get this straight — Stefan needs blood, only the blood slave can give him blood, and I'm now the blood slave, but it's my choice whether to let him feed on me." She thought of Stefan lying so still and cold in the next room. "If he needs it so bad, why don't I just let him bite me?"

She grimaced as she said it, picturing Armand's sharp fangs and cold eyes. She fingered the shallow scratches on her neck.

"That's why." Mario took a speculative sip of wine. "You have to give yourself to him body and soul. You have to *want* him to bite you and not mind if something goes wrong and you die doing it. You make the ultimate sacrifice to keep him alive. If you go to him without giving all of yourself, he'll lose strength that much quicker. And he might not be able to stop himself drinking you dry and killing you too."

"Terrific." Meredith took a long swig of water, which she now wished was vodka. "So I can't just say *here, Stefan, have a sip.* I have to be willing to die for him if necessary."

"If you fall in love and become his true blood slave, you will. You won't want anything else."

"Gee, I thought when I met the right one it would be a little different. We'd pick out a house in the burbs and plant geraniums and get a cat."

Mario looked serious for once. "You can still do that. As long as you're there for him when he needs you."

Meredith traced the top of her water

bottle. "What about you? You seem healthy. Do you have a blood slave following you around, calling you master?"

Mario's grin widened and the hard look left his eyes. All he had to do was turn that smile on a woman and she'd be on her knees. He likely had no problem getting blood slaves.

"It's different for me. I'm not a vampire master." He took a casual sip of wine, his throat moving slowly, his eyes closing like he savored nectar. "My relationships with blood slaves can be a little more casual. They still have to be willing, but it doesn't have to be a life-or-death bond."

"How lucky for you."

"Not that I'm not looking for the right one. Just not ready to settle down yet. I'm only six hundred."

His smile was infectious. Meredith couldn't believe she was sitting here discussing blood slaves with a six-hundred-year-old who didn't look a day over thirty-two. Meanwhile, the man who wanted to make her his slave lay half comatose in the next room.

"Will he be all right? I mean, if I don't give him my blood right now, will he die?"

Mario shook his head. "I've seen him like this before. It comes on him suddenly sometimes. He'll recover and probably be pissed as hell." He gave Meredith an unreadable look. "It might help, though, if you stay with him tonight."

Meredith set down her water bottle. She gazed over the sumptuous apartment, from the flat-screen television to the lit pool gently moving beyond the glass doors. "I don't think I'd feel safe returning to my own room anyway."

"I strengthened the wards around the hotel. Armand won't be back."

Meredith remembered Armand's hungry mouth and the wild exhilaration in his eyes as he dragged Meredith's head back. She shivered, rubbing her arms.

"Well," she said, "I'll need my toothbrush."

# CHAPTER SIX

Stefan woke to Meredith's scent. He opened his eyes and found his nose buried in her hair, sweet red silk flowing over his skin.

He slid his arm around her waist, finding the thin, soft fabric of a T-shirt between him and her. She moved slightly, murmuring in her sleep. Stefan raised his head.

Light streamed in through the floor-to-ceiling windows, the Las Vegas sun already high. The windows were so insulated that the sun barely warmed the cool air in the bedroom. Meredith lay against him, covered by a thigh-length T-shirt, her bare legs tangled in his fine Italian cotton sheets.

He ran fingers lightly up under her T-shirt, finding her hip bare, no underwear to mar it. His heart beat faster, strength returning. He inched the shirt up as he kissed her face, willing her awake.

"Stefan," she murmured, not opening her eyes. Her lips curved to a little smile.

She was not quite awake. With his thoughts, Stefan grayed out the windows so that the fierce sunlight dimmed into cool shadow. He kissed her hair while he slid his fingers between her parted thighs, warming her. Her honey was already flowing, her body wanting him even in her sleep.

He pressed his erection into her slowly, savoring her all the way. She made a noise between a whimper and a moan, then wriggled her hips, settling back against him.

Half cradling her, Stefan made love to her in a quiet softness contrasting the wild frenzy of last night. Out on the deck, he hadn't been able to have her fast enough. He'd known he should go slow, but he hadn't been able to. He needed her, he wanted her.

Now that his body had calmed and rested, he could enjoy slow moments with her, breathing her scent, feeling her body around him. Lovely woman. He wanted her to belong to him, body and soul, he craved it, and not just to keep him alive.

"*Stefan.*" Her eyes were open now, aware of him and what he was doing.

"Good morning, love."

Her laugh turned to a throaty moan. "A girl should wake up like this every day."

He pressed her backside against him as he

slid deeper into her. She scrabbled for the sheets as though needing to hold on to something, and her face twisted into an expression of pure pleasure. "This is the best trip to Las Vegas I've ever had."

And the best time of Stefan's life. He kissed the sensitive skin at her temple, loving the heat of her body. She'd been made for him. He couldn't remember anything after his coming last night on the chaise, a feeling like his body had been ripped in two. She must have gotten him into the bed before curling up beside him. He was sorry he'd passed out, but he'd make it up to her today.

Their frenzy built, his orgasm rising up to drown him. He splayed his hand over her breasts, feeling her tight nubs against his palms as she strained against him. Her eyes closed in her climax, her breathy female noises washing excitement over him and making him come almost at the same time.

They collapsed back into the pillows, breathing hard, Meredith laughing.

When he withdrew, she rolled over on the sheets and touched his face. "I guess you're all right."

"Mmm. I think so."

"I was worried about you."

There was true worry in her eyes. Stefan

often took women to bed, not necessarily to feed, but to sate himself. Most were turned on by his flat-screen television and the restaurants he took them to and simply being seen with Stefan Erickson, powerful man-about-town.

Meredith's expression told him she didn't care a flying damn about his gadgets, his limo, and his money. He could build a one-room adobe hut for her in the desert, and she'd still look at him like she cared. Maybe she'd insist the one-room hut had air-conditioning, a bathroom, and a patio, but the point was she didn't equate him with his money. It was all bullshit anyway, just nine hundred years of patience and knowing how money worked.

"I apologize for inconveniencing you," he said. *But thank you for caring.*

"Not your fault." She smiled, her lips swollen from his kisses. "I was afraid I'd killed you, but Mario says no."

"Mario?"

"Yes, he put you to bed."

Stefan stifled a groan as he imagined Mario's laughter. Stefan wasn't surprised he'd passed out after having sex with Meredith. He'd needed her so much that he'd sacrificed his strength to be with her.

He traced her cheek. "At least you stayed."

"I wanted to. I wanted to make sure you were all right."

Her hands moved across his shoulders, and he turned his head and kissed one of them. Her waist curved enticingly under her breasts, her navel a shadowed dent. He leaned down and licked it.

"Now I know you're feeling better." She laughed.

He made love to her again, starting slowly and building to the near frenzied pitch of the night before. He knelt on the bed and lifted her feet to his shoulders, entering her while she writhed on the pillows.

"Love you," he said as he came. His voice was hoarse and rasping. "Love you."

"Tell me more about this blood slave business," Meredith said as they wound down together, limbs tangled with sheets. "Would I have to wear one of those white nightgowns? I don't have long floating black hair, though I suppose I could dye it."

He chuckled, running his hand through the silken wave of red on his pillow. "I love your hair just as it is. And wear what you want. I was thinking of a black leather bustier." He cupped her breasts in his hands in approximation.

She half glared at him. "You would." Her

look softened instantly, showing she knew he was teasing. Well, he was mostly teasing. Thinking of Meredith in nothing but a black leather bustier was heating things up again.

She went on. "Mario told me that if I don't become your blood slave and be willing to give up my life to you, you'll die."

Stefan's hand hesitated on her skin. "Did he? What else did he say?"

"That he hadn't wanted me to know, but you thought it was only fair. Of course, you were in a coma at the time and couldn't really explain." The worry flared again in her eyes. "What happened to you?"

"If I get too weak, my body shuts down until I regain my strength."

She pushed at his chest. "See, I *knew* I almost killed you with sex. You should have warned me."

"I hadn't meant for it to happen last night. Besides, I wanted to be with you."

He kissed her fingers, the growing warmth in his groin becoming a full-blown erection. "I want to be with you now."

"I can see that — or feel that anyway. It's dark in here."

"I like it dark."

"Of course you do, you're a vampire."

"You believe me now?"

Meredith smiled into his kiss. "Let's just

say I saw things last night that convinced me. You sure you won't fall into a coma again?"

"I feel stronger than ever." Stefan stopped her words with another kiss, parted her thighs with his hand, and began to make love to her again.

He knew she hadn't made the decision to give herself to him, and he had the feeling that her ultimate answer would be *no.* But for now, he would enjoy her — enjoy this — to savor when he was alone again.

He could find another blood slave — Mario would find one for him — and convince her to give him blood, but it would be a stopgap. Only Meredith could restore him to full vampire master strength, and he knew it. Without her, he would weaken and eventually die. All vampire masters did when they got too ancient, unless they found a pure love that would restore them. Armand would face this soon himself.

Meredith was the one for Stefan, no other. He'd take that knowledge with him into true death.

Several hours and a shower later — one that involved soaping each other down — Meredith faced Stefan over the table in an alcove enclosed on three sides by glass. A waiter in white had appeared and laid the table, then presented a meal on white porcelain plates with wine in cut-crystal goblets.

"Don't you ever just eat off paper plates in front of the television?" she asked as she slid into her seat. The waiter discreetly shook out a linen napkin and placed it in her lap.

Stefan sent her a smile that warmed her bones. He'd resumed the sunglasses, and she remembered that he told her the light sometimes bothered him. Ha — one proof that he was a traditional vampire. But she hungered to see his eyes. Waking to find him watching her with his tawny gaze had been most pleasurable, not to mention what they had done after that.

The round circles of opaque black unnerved her. Otherwise he seemed relaxed, gesturing quietly to the waiter who set plates of lobster salad in front of them and withdrew.

It was the best lobster salad Meredith had ever eaten, and she didn't even like lobster. She toyed with the lettuce, savoring the cool flavor of the salad and bite of the sauce.

"Sometimes Mario and I watch football and drink beer," he said. "Is that better?"

"Yes, but you probably have four hundred different channels, a hundred of them unavailable to most people, and I'll bet your beer is served at the perfect temperature in an ice bucket. Must be a hard life, being rich."

"I have acquired money over the centuries. I learned how to turn little into much with nothing but patience."

"Are you patiently waiting for the blood slave who will save you?"

Stefan laid his fork down as though no longer interested in food. He lifted his wineglass. "Yes."

She twirled designs through her sauce. "So you're asking me to devote my entire life to you, let you feed on me when you need to, and basically be your minion?"

"The rewards would be spectacular."

His voice was warm, with only the hint of a waver. Meredith watched his face, trying to read his expression, but with the damn sunglasses it was hard to tell what it was.

"I have a life already, Stefan. Compared to yours it might seem boring, but it's mine."

"Tell me more about it." As he had last night, he sounded hungry to hear what she had to say.

She shrugged. "There isn't any more. I sell my mother's paintings — liaison with the galleries and buyers, keep the books.

Research and write about what strikes my fancy, like vampires. My mother and I share a house but we spend whole days without seeing each other. She stays in her studio and I do my thing. We like our space."

Stefan looked out of the long window, across the deck and the glittering pool to the stark mountains beyond. "You wouldn't want to leave that."

"I don't know."

"And there is no one in your life, no man to marry you?"

"Damn, you're nosy. No, there are no men beating down my doors. I was asked once, but I turned him down because I found out he was a complete asshole." She swallowed on her words, remembering the hurt she'd felt when one of her friends had gently explained that the idiot had a girlfriend in Albuquerque and figured he'd continue seeing her even after he and Meredith married.

Stefan's sunglasses trained on her. "Thank you for telling me."

"It was years ago. I'm over him. I've dated, but nothing . . ."

Her life had evolved into a safe routine, interrupted occasionally by her friends trying to fix her up. Sometimes the relationship lasted a few months, usually he found someone more interesting to be with or she decided to end it before she strangled him, or they just never called back.

"What I want to give you is nothing like that." Stefan's words were flat.

Meredith laid down her fork. "It's a hell of a lot to ask, you know. You're sexy as hell, and I still want to put you in my book, but I barely know you — although what girl wouldn't be swept off her feet by a big spender who looks like you, I don't know."

"I do not want you to be swept off your feet. The choice must be yours, and you must decide what is best for you."

She glanced through the glass at the pool. It was so beautiful out there, despite the roasting sun, with flowers kept lush by the hidden misters. "Armand wanted to make me a vampire to keep me away from you." For some reason she was no longer afraid of Armand. With Stefan awake and back to full power, the miasma of fear had faded. "Wasn't that charming of him?"

She felt the weight of Stefan's stare. His face had gone granite hard, his body still, the sunglasses trained on her like shining voids. "Armand was here?"

"Yes, don't you remember? Last night, as soon as you pretty much passed out, he materialized and said he'd save me from you. I tried to tell him to go to hell, but I was too terrified. I was able to get Mario on the cell phone, which is why he was here to put you to bed."

The sunglasses didn't move. Meredith sensed a change, something malevolent entering the conversation, the room, the planet.

"It wasn't your fault, Stefan," she said quickly. "You were lying there nearly unconscious. You couldn't have done anything."

She closed her mouth. The last thing men liked was to be placated, especially when it was about a territory violation. Men were like that — obstinate, territorial, testosterone-laden. Vampires probably even more so.

A sudden wave of power rocketed from him, sending furniture, objects d'art, and the glasses at the bar crashing into the windows. A piece of marble tile came up and slammed into the thick glass.

"Shit," Meredith whispered.

Stefan threw his napkin on the table and left his seat. With strong hands he turned Meredith's head to expose her neck to the sunlight. She moved her hand self-consciously to the scratches Armand had left.

"He didn't bite me, not really," she babbled. "I managed to get away from him before he could."

His stillness was more frightening than the fact that he'd just destroyed his living room without lifting a finger. He turned abruptly away and crossed the room, his booted feet crunching on porcelain shards of once-priceless statuary.

In alarm, Meredith rose. "Where are you going?"

Stefan reached into a closet tucked near the door and pulled out a leather jacket. "To take retribution."

Meredith took two steps toward him, wondering how on earth she would stop him and even if she should. Stefan removed his sunglasses. His eyes glowed golden and harsh, the light in them forbidding and powerful.

Then he turned away, and vanished.

Mario answered her cell-phone summons almost as fast as he had the previous night. He listened to her incoherent explanation of why she called before grabbing her by the hand and dragging her down the elevator and through the casino, yelling at the valet parkers to go get his car *now.*

In minutes, Meredith was scrambling into a black vintage Corvette and bracing herself while Mario screamed out onto the Strip

and then around a corner to a road less traf-
ficked.

She dragged in a breath as they hauled ass
down the street at least double the legal
limit. "Why do you have to drive?" she
gasped. "Why don't you just disappear like
Armand and Stefan?"

"Because I'm not a master." Mario's face
was grim as he wove through slower cars
and ran a red light. Meredith clapped her
hands over her eyes, but miraculously no
other cars touched them. "I can slide
through spaces within the building but no
farther. I just hope to God Stefan and Armand stayed in the Ice Palace. If they
transported to the middle of the desert or
Paris, there's not a damn thing I can do."

"What is the Ice Palace?"

"Armand's hotel."

She'd never heard of it. The researcher in
her filed it away as another thing for her
book, but most of her brain was taken up
with worry. "I know Stefan is angry, but Armand didn't bite me. I got away."

Mario shook his head, black hair sliding
over his leather coat. "The point is Armand
tried. The two of them have a gentleman's
agreement not to poach on each other's territory. Armand doesn't touch what's Stefan's, he doesn't touch what's Armand's.

They're two vampire masters, and they divided this town between them. If Stefan dies, Armand and his vamps will feed and kill as much as they like."

Meredith swallowed. "No one will come to Las Vegas anymore, then."

"Armand is subtle and very, very powerful. They will come."

Meredith thought about that while the grungy street full of warehouses zoomed by. "If Stefan is a vampire master, isn't he strong enough to take care of himself? I mean, he destroyed his living room without even blinking. Why are you so worried?"

"Because Stefan is unpredictable. He's weaker, he's pissed about it, and hell, he could flatten this entire town to get his vengeance if he wanted, even not at full strength. I live in this town — I want to stay here."

"That's not the only reason you're worried."

"No. Armand's just as powerful as Stefan, and Stefan's the one who's been having draining spells. You zapped his strength — Armand moved in."

"Wait a minute, you told me last night I hadn't hurt him." Her face got hot as she remembered just how she'd hurt him.

"You didn't." Mario floored it around a

complicated curve back to an intersection that crossed the Strip. He was forced to wait from sheer press of traffic, but once across the Strip he careened into an alleyway beside another tall hotel. "You showing up at all has weakened him. It's like his body knows you're the one and is shutting down to wait for you."

"Oh, hey, no pressure," Meredith said. "If I don't become his minion, he dies, and I feel terrible. I become his minion, and I'm his slave-girl for life."

Mario swung into a garage, slamming his car through the wooden gate, tires squealing on the slick pavement. "If it was up to me, I'd chain you to his bed and tell him to go for it. I owe him my life, and I'm running out of ideas to keep him alive. But he needs you to have the choice, so I won't do it, sweetheart." He slammed on his brakes, and Meredith braced herself against the dash.

A dozen white-haired vampires poured into the garage to surround the car. Most wore leather, some had chains wrapped around their arms, all had eyes even more bloodless and soulless than Armand's.

"And now I'm in the middle of a vampire gang war," Meredith said. She yelped as the door opened and a white-haired vamp dragged her out. "Watch it, this is a new shirt."

"Leave her," Mario snapped. He glared at the white vamp and amazingly, the white vampire backed off.

The group didn't depart. They surrounded Meredith and Mario, looking mean. Chains leapt to hands, and Meredith knew these men could kill her faster than she could even think about running.

They were a little more wary with Mario but not much. Mario held up his hands. "I only came to get Stefan out. I'll take him home so he won't bother your little party anymore."

One of the white-haired vampires whose close-cropped hair reminded her of Spike from *Buffy the Vampire Slayer* spoke. "Yeah, he's there with the master. Armand figured you'd come for him. You send her in, the master will let him go."

Mario didn't move, but Meredith felt his power touch her like heat from a radiator. "She's not going anywhere without me. And we're not leaving without Stefan, so get used to it."

Spike's gaze went remote as though he were listening to an inner voice. Then he snapped out of it. "I have orders. I'm to bring you both."

"Like I said," Mario growled.

Spike grinned, a malevolent glitter in his eyes. "He didn't say anything about letting you go again." He licked his red lips and gazed speculatively at Meredith.

There wasn't much they could do but allow the white vamps to herd them toward an elevator. Six of them, including the Spike vampire, crowded into it and the doors shut before they zoomed downward.

The elevator opened into a cavernous room deep in the bowels of the hotel. It was decorated lavishly, like Stefan's apartment — but where Stefan's place was light and glass, Armand's emphasized black and shadows.

"Why do people stay in this hotel?" she murmured. "The Ice Palace — sounds cold to me."

Spike grinned. "For the atmosphere. Vampires, and it's haunted. They love it."

Meredith agreed that some people probably wouldn't be able to resist. This was Las Vegas — no doubt the staff had been trained to provide an experience that was scary but not too scary. The scary people were the ones behind the glitz and glamour of the hotels. In early days it was mobsters, now it was CEOs and vampires.

Double doors at the end of the black room

opened by themselves, and Meredith and Mario were ushered into an office. At least, it was nominally an office. There was a desk with a computer, but the rest was decorated in early medieval. Stools and benches covered in opulent brocade throws stood in every corner, tapestries covered the walls, and a heavy sword hung in a glass case beside the tattered remains of a blue sur-coat with a red cross emblazoned on it.

Meredith gazed at it in wonder. *I was a Knight Templar,* Armand had said. *I died with his badge on my chest.*

One entire wall of the room was glass, and behind it lay a view of the city — a real view, but of course there couldn't be windows this deep underground.

"Cameras feed him real-time images," Mario told her.

"Where is Stefan?" she demanded, glaring at Spike. His cold blue eyes unnerved her almost as much as Armand's did, but she lifted her chin and tried not to let him know that.

Spike jerked his thumb at another set of doors, which opened at the moment to let in Stefan and Armand.

Meredith sagged with relief to see Stefan unhurt, but the look in his eyes bothered her. So did the look in Armand's. The man was almost glowing in triumph.

"Mario," Stefan said, training a glare on his friend. "Take Meredith out of here. He'll let you go freely. I've agreed to pack up and leave Las Vegas."

# CHAPTER SEVEN

"You've got to be kidding me," Mario shouted.

The white vamps moved closer to him, recognizing danger when they saw it. Meredith stayed close to the Italian vampire's side, though an urgency to rush to Stefan nearly overpowered her. But she'd have to fight her way through six white vamps plus Armand to do it, so she stayed put.

"If you leave, the rest of us have to go with you," Mario continued, angry. "Without a master, we'd be toast. I have a career here. Think about your friends, Stefan — the ones who need to make a living."

"I've stayed too long already," Stefan said. He sounded drained of emotion. "And you don't need to stay in Las Vegas. You own a city in Italy."

"That's not the point."

"I am fading, Mario. There's nothing anyone can do. Armand has agreed to let us leave so I can die in peace."

"And you believed him?" Mario snorted.

Meredith slid past the enclosing vamps and made herself walk up to Armand. She looked him in the face, Stefan's presence helping damp down the fear. "How do we know you'll let him leave? You could just kill all of us right now and be rid of us."

"Thanks, Meredith," Mario said. "Don't give him ideas."

Armand met her gaze with unflinching coolness. She could see the ancientness of him, eyes that had looked upon countless centuries, countless lives, and countless deaths. "I gave him my word," he said.

"He does have that kind of honor," Stefan answered. "So do I. If I agree to his terms, I'll abide by them."

"I see both of you have already made up your minds about me," Meredith said, her own anger flaring. "What if I decide to stay? What if I decide to let Stefan feed off me and restore him to his full strength? I haven't made up my mind yet."

"I have made it up for you." Stefan's voice was quiet. "I'm no longer asking you to stay with me, Meredith. Go home and live your life."

"Wait a minute." She transferred her glare to Stefan. "Just like that? I'm not good

133

enough for you anymore?"

"Meredith." Stefan put his hands on her shoulders and drew her aside. "Armand is right about one thing. I'm weakening and have lost perspective. I am using all my power to coerce you to stay, to trick you into believing you love me. I used to believe myself an honorable man, but what I am doing is not honorable. Armand has made me understand that."

"Meaning —"

"Meaning that if I take my mark off you, you'll see me for what I really am."

Meredith stepped back. "All right. Fine. Take your mark off me now. I remember being pretty impressed by you *before* you made me your slave. Let's see how I really feel."

"I can't here and now. You need protection from Armand's vampires. If you're unmarked, there's nothing to stop them from taking you."

"Oh." It unnerved her to suddenly realize she was the only human in the room. Mario and Stefan might seem like ordinary men, but they'd proved to her beyond doubt that they weren't. And Armand still terrified her, even if she couldn't help thinking he'd be a fascinating person to put in her book. Who around these days could explain what it was like to be a knight on the Crusades?

"I will protect her," Armand said.

"No," Meredith and Stefan and Mario all said at the same time.

Armand smiled slightly. "You would always be safe with me, Meredith."

"Maybe, but like I said before, would I be safe *from* you?"

Armand's smile widened. "Take her and go, Stefan. You will be unmolested."

Stefan slid his warm hand through Meredith's. "Let us depart. I will have my staff pack you a meal for the road."

There wasn't much use in arguing with him right then. Meredith wasn't the kind of woman who liked having her fate decided by a bunch of men, especially vampires, but she realized it was more important to walk away slowly now, yell at Stefan later.

Stefan began to lead Meredith out of the office. Mario fell into step with them, as did the other vampires. Spike looked disappointed he couldn't bash heads and snack on Meredith, but he obeyed his master and kept his hands to himself.

"Did you drive her here?" Stefan asked Mario.

"Yeah, I brought the 'Vette." He glared at the white-haired vampires. "Which had better not have a scratch on it."

"It will not," Armand said behind them.

Meredith looked back. The former knight stood in the middle of the room, his long white hair hanging still and long to his waist, his ice-blue eyes holding surety of his power.

Meredith raised her hand in acknowledgment of what he'd done, and Armand nodded quietly in response. Spike, on the other hand, looked positively disgusted. With barely concealed anger, he shoved them into the elevator and sent it rocketing up to the garage, leaving Meredith's stomach behind. She wondered just how far underground they'd been and decided, as her ears popped, that she didn't really want to know.

The Corvette was intact, black paint gleaming, right where they'd left it. Mario got in and started the engine, watching the vampires in suspicion, but nothing dire happened.

Stefan opened the passenger door and assisted Meredith into the seat. Meredith clung to his hand. "Aren't you coming with us?"

Stefan shook his head. "I'll see you there." He glanced across her at Mario. "Get her back to the Castle. Safely."

"Hey, I know how to drive," Mario growled.

Stefan straightened up and shut the door before Meredith had a chance to protest. Mario gunned the engine and stomped on the gas, sending them hurtling around a row of cars and out toward the sunshine.

Meredith looked back at the circle of vamps through the Corvette's tiny back window, but Stefan had vanished.

Stefan waited as promised on the deck of his penthouse, outside his living room, which had been restored to rights. His superefficient staff must be used to his wild surges of power.

He waited in the sun, bronzed hands resting on the top of the wall as he gazed over Las Vegas and the craggy mountains that lined the horizon. The desert wind stirred his wheat-blond hair and the sun reflected off the sunglasses he'd resumed. His back made an almost perfect triangle between shoulders and hips, pure muscle atop long, strong legs.

Meredith's heart broke as she watched him through the glass. Why couldn't they be two ordinary people meeting under the Las Vegas sun and getting to know each other slowly? No vampires and slaves, no rival vamps or masters. Just Meredith and Stefan falling in love.

She knew she couldn't have that, because he wasn't going to let her.

As soon as she walked out onto the deck, he turned his head, his hair sliding over his shoulders.

"Come here, Meredith. Please." Again he used *please* as an afterthought, softening the command.

She could resist, but her body had already said *yes, Master,* and propelled her forward. Stefan slowly drew off his sunglasses and folded them in his hand. Meredith caught one flash of power from his eyes, and then she got lost in studying the beauty of them. Tawny like a lion's, she'd thought at first, with flecks of green in them, framed by long lashes.

"I love your eyes," she said.

Stefan leaned forward and pressed a kiss to her forehead. "Go home," he said softly.

"I thought you were going to take the mark off me."

"I just did."

"Oh." She stepped back, waiting to feel completely different. She did, and she didn't. She no longer wanted to throw herself on the ground and hug his legs, but she still wanted to kiss those lips that knew how to drive her crazy.

What woman wouldn't? He didn't have to

go around putting women under his power to make them want to kiss him. He just had to pass them in the hall.

And then she felt a great chasm in her heart, a void that was going to hurt like hell when the numbness wore off. She tried to look into Stefan's eyes again, but he'd resumed the sunglasses. Mere mortals probably couldn't handle the gaze of a vampire master, and to him, she was a mere mortal.

With tears stinging her eyes, she asked, "Can we start over?"

Slowly he shook his head. "What I need is not what you need. Go back to Santa Fe and write your books and sell your mother's paintings. You will sell enough that she can open her own gallery."

She sniffled. "You can predict the future, can you?"

"I can make the future. It will happen." He trained the sunglasses on her, his mouth turning down at the corners. "Go, Meredith. Your luggage is already in your car. The bellboy will take you out."

"I came here to write a book, Stefan. You can throw me out of your hotel, but what I do for my career is up to me."

"I do not want you in Las Vegas when Armand takes over. Get in your car, drive out of this town, drive out of this state, and don't come back. If you are still here when the balance of power shifts, you will belong to Armand."

"That was your agreement?"

He nodded once. "That was the agreement."

"So glad I was consulted."

His face went grim. "I love you, and I want you safe above all things. Either you drive out yourself, or I tie you up and have someone drive you out. Those are your only choices."

She stopped. "You love me?"

"Yes. That is why I am letting you go."

"I wouldn't say you were letting me go as much as tossing me out of your life. You could give me the chance to decide how I feel without your mark on me."

"No." Stefan didn't move, but she felt his power touch her. "I can't be near you without wanting to make you submit. If I take you over, it will kill both of us. So please go while I still have the strength to control myself."

Meredith's feet wouldn't move. Stefan half turned away from her, looking out at the city and the desert again, a city where so many people arrived with hopes of winning it big and limped away days later, back to reality.

It seemed anticlimactic to say thanks or good-bye or even *I love you too,* so she turned around and walked back into the penthouse, across the marble floor of the living room, then down the echoing hallway to the double doors at the end.

The same bellboy who'd brought her upstairs waited for her by the elevator. He noiselessly slid the key card into the slot to open the doors and ushered her inside. The elevator took them straight to the lobby, no funny side trips to the basement, and the bellboy led her out through the crowd to the front entrance. No checking out — Mr. Erickson had already taken care of that, the bellboy informed her.

Her car waited for her in the circular drive, her old Toyota looking rather frumpy next to the Lexuses and Mercedeses and Cadillacs that waited, purring, for their owners. Her duffel bag rested across her backseat and a hamper with the promised meal waited for her on the passenger side.

The bellboy held the door for her and shut it firmly after she got herself inside. Stefan was making sure she left.

She nodded good-bye to the bellboy and drove past the valet parkers in their Dracula capes, down the drive, and through the arch constructed to look like a Gothic gate. She blended in with the traffic on the Strip, increasing now as the afternoon waned to evening, then pulled onto the freeway to head south.

It was rush hour in the real world, commuters leaving their corporate offices in the hotels and downtown for their homes in the burbs of Henderson and Boulder City. Meredith blended in with them, inching along the freeway while her eyes threatened to overflow at every curve.

The sun sank behind the high mountains in the west as the city fell behind her. Even in summer, the desert darkened fast. Navigating the hairpin turns around the Hoover Dam at night blinded by tears didn't appeal to her, so she took the turnoff that went down a bluff and straight across the desert floor toward Laughlin and Arizona. She'd drive to Flagstaff, an easy two or three hours, and spend the night there, far from casinos and lights and gorgeous vampires.

Why had she gone to Las Vegas in the first place? To research her next book, of course. Not to have her ideas about vampires and life and love twisted around all over the place.

The road was pitch-black, cut only by the headlights of passing cars. There was the tiny town of Searchlight out here and not much else. In the privacy of darkness with only red taillights far ahead for company, Meredith gave in to her tears.

How did she feel about Stefan? She had no idea and the jumble of the past day and night confused the hell out of her. He made love like the most romantic hero, teasing and pleasing and demanding and rough. He'd wanted her and needed her, and sex had been like nothing she'd ever experienced.

She couldn't separate what he made her feel from what she really felt. He'd shocked her and twisted her up and then tossed her out before she could figure out what was going on inside her.

"Stupid men," she growled at the windshield, and then sobs took her.

She pulled all the way off the road and stopped the car, knowing she couldn't drive under the storm of weeping. She banged the steering wheel and let out all her tears. No one could hear her, no one passing cared why she'd stopped. It was just her and the car and the desert night and her ripped-out heart.

As the sobs died away to dry-heaving, she rummaged in the picnic hamper for whatever had been stocked to drink and found chilled water, flavored gourmet iced tea, and a thermos of coffee. She chugged some of the water and wiped her stinging eyes.

"I finally find the right one and he turns out to be a dying vampire with issues." She drank some more water, nearly choking on it. "Damn it, damn it, damn it."

She toyed with the idea of calling her mother for comfort, then discarded it. What would she say? *Hi, Mom, I met a guy, but it didn't work out. In the end, he wouldn't bite me.*

Maybe she could lie low in Flagstaff a few days before she had to face her mother. She could always claim she was checking out galleries in which to exhibit her mom's art.

She opened the door and stepped out of the car. Hot desert wind, only slightly cooler than daytime temperatures, buffeted her hair and dried the tears on her face. She gulped the air like she did the water, liking the clear, sage-scented breaths of it.

A motorcycle slowed and pulled in behind her. Meredith sighed, wondering what to say. *Sorry, Officer, I just needed a good cry.*

The man who approached her wasn't a policeman. He wore black leather and no helmet, and she recognized the cropped white hair of Armand's vampire minion who looked like Spike. Fear hit her and she grabbed the door handle, thanking God she'd left the engine running.

Before she could even open the door, he was on her. His tall body pressed her against the car, leather chafing her exposed skin, his lips pulled back in a snarl. His eyes glowed light blue in the dark and his fangs glittered.

She struggled. Screamed for help, praying someone out in the desert would hear. Her cell phone was out of reach in her car, and she wasn't sure it would work out in the boondocks anyway. And would Mario respond or leave her to die?

Because she was going to die, that was all there was to that.

"Stefan," she screamed.

The vampire slammed her head against the car. The world reeled, and she tasted blood in her mouth. He tore open her blouse, knife in hand, exposing her breasts.

"I love leftovers," he hissed. Then he raked his talons across her eyes, blinding her. She felt his knife all over her body, ripping her open, his teeth tearing her throat. He was not going to bite her to savor her or Turn her, he wanted one thing and one thing only. Her blood. Her life.

*Stefan!* her mind continued to cry while pain arced through her, followed by a numbness that made her so dizzy she started to vomit.

And then a bright light flared, brighter than anything she'd ever seen in her life, blinding her even through the blood in her eyes. The vampire who was busy killing her shuddered and screamed, his keening loud in her ears, and then the world vanished.

When she woke, she expected a hospital — a white room, machines beeping, tubes snaking into and out of her body. But the bed felt luxuriously soft, the sheets ultrafine, not hospital utility. She couldn't focus her half-closed eyes to tell what color the room was, and she heard no beeping, only low masculine voices.

An all-male nursing staff. That might not be so bad.

She tried to move, to open her eyes, to ask a question. Pain roared through her and all she could do was groan.

"Meredith."

Stefan's voice, cut with worry. His hand warm on hers. Meredith closed her eyes and began to weep with relief.

Another touch, this one cool, skin like satin. "I do not know if it will work. She is almost gone."

"We have to try. I will try, anyway. Whatever it takes."

She felt Stefan slide his hand under her neck and raise her body. It hurt, dear God, it hurt. Was he going to bite her? She remembered the Spike vamp's foul breath on her face, his teeth in her skin, the knife blade cold sharp. She whimpered.

"It's all right, love. I have you now."

She tried to say, "Stefan," but it came out a gurgle.

Someone banged into the room, out of breath. "Is she all right?" Mario's voice asked. "I was driving like a maniac. I thought he'd kill her."

"He nearly did." The cool voice belonged to Armand, the Spike vamp's master. She tried to squirm away from him.

"I thought you said she had free passage," Mario growled, the very thing Meredith would have asked if she could talk.

"He broke away from me," Armand said. "He is dead now."

"He almost took Meredith with him." Mario went silent as though looking her over. "Damn."

Stefan's tone was flat. "She will die if we don't help her. I am glad you're here. We need someone to watch, to keep it from going too far."

"What are you going to do?" Mario

sounded very worried.

"The blood of a master can save her," Armand said.

"Yeah, and put Stefan in a coma again, from which he might not recover." Mario leaned over the bed — Meredith felt his warmth and smelled leather and sweat. "That's what you wanted, wasn't it, Armand? For him to weaken himself all the way trying to save her? Maybe you'll kill him while he lies helpless?"

"No," Armand said, the word harsh.

"She will drink from both of us," Stefan said. "A little from each."

"You'll still be weaker than he is," Mario pointed out. "Which I bet he's counting on."

"I would give her all of it to save her life," Stefan returned.

"Shit."

"Just stand by and make sure she doesn't drink too much. We want to heal her, not Turn her."

"Right," Mario snarled. "You maybe don't, but what about him?"

Armand's cool voice cut through Mario's blustering. "I gave my word."

"He's serious, Mario. I trust him." Stefan hesitated, a catch entering his voice. "I have to."

"All right, but she drinks from *him* first,"

Mario stated.

"Agreed," Armand answered.

Meredith felt herself lifted — in Stefan's arms, she knew every inch of him intimately. It was wonderful to snuggle against his shoulder, to breathe his scent and feel his warmth envelop her.

"Drink from him, Meredith," he whispered. "It's the only way."

She heard a soft grunt of pain from Armand and smelled the bite of blood. She tried to turn away. "Don't want to be vampire," she mumbled.

"You won't be, sweetheart. His blood will make you better. You need to get well."

Or she'd die. She knew that. The Spike vampire had torn her apart, she felt that in every aching limb and stinging slash of skin.

Stefan lifted her again, and Armand slid a leather-coat-clad arm behind her back. Stefan's hand rested in her hair while he guided her mouth to Armand's neck.

Blood filled her mouth, hot and tangy like fiery spice. She gagged and tried to spit it out, but Stefan's hand and Armand's arm held her fast. "Drink," Stefan whispered.

Gasping and nearly choking, Meredith swallowed. Fire burned its way to her stomach and flowed out to her fingertips. She felt the slightest, tiniest bit better —

enough to realize how truly bad things had been.

She drew in another mouthful, the spicy taste not as harsh this time. Armand made a soft noise in his throat, and his fingers moved in her hair. Meredith opened her eyes to see his leather-clad back, his tail of white hair slide across it as he tilted his head. His blood filled her mouth and she swallowed, another burning sensation scouring her body.

She took a few more gulps, feeling less nauseated after each. Finally she drew a breath that didn't hurt and gave a little sigh of relief.

"Enough," Stefan said.

Just a little more. She would never dream of doing this to a normal human being, but the blood of a vampire master wasn't bad. Tangy. *Let me have more. Just one sip.*

"Enough." Stefan pulled her away.

Meredith still felt weak and dizzy, but a hell of a lot better than she had. She sagged against Stefan, enjoying breathing without too much pain. Armand stretched his long legs out on the bed and rested his head on the headboard. His eyes were half closed, his lips parted as though he were in the ecstasy of an orgasm. A gash of red stained his neck.

"Mario," Stefan rumbled under Meredith's ear.

A blade glinted as Mario handed a knife to Stefan. Meredith flinched, not liking knives anymore, and looked up to find Mario's expression grim and angry.

Stefan made a small cut in his own skin and guided Meredith to his neck as the blood began to flow. She caught it between her lips, understanding now why vampires loved what they did. The hot taste of blood, of Stefan's life force, was almost like the excitement of sex.

Stefan tasted different from Armand. Stefan's taste was darker, more mellow, and yet it had a bite, like brandy aged in old wood. She licked him and slid her arms around his strong waist, loving him for making this sacrifice for her.

Mario was right, he was seriously trusting Armand not to attack him while he was weakened. Armand might be languid with afterglow at the moment, but Meredith could sense the white vampire's power. He could flatten them all in the blink of an eye. And if Armand was that powerful, what must Stefan be like when he was at peak strength?

As healing flowed through her, Meredith decided she wanted to know. She would find

151

out what Stefan was like as a vampire master. She would make him let her.

Stefan's strength filled her and made her shudder in reaction. She drew back, licking his heady taste from her lips, her heart pounding but not in pain or fever. She'd never felt this good in her life.

"Oh God," she said, dragging in a breath. "I think I'm going to come."

Armand made a small noise as though he were, too. Mario grinned down at her. "I guess that means you're better."

Stefan said nothing. His own breathing ragged, he gathered her close and held her hard, pressing soft kisses to her hair.

# CHAPTER EIGHT

Meredith looked cocky. That was the only word for it. Stefan watched her strut around the deck in her bathing suit — even a one-piece showed off her curvaceous and beautiful body to perfection. She was laughing with Mario about something. He lounged in a chaise, his skin exposed to the heat, sunglasses protecting his eyes. He looked smug too.

Stefan rose from the bed where he'd been resting since the night before and strolled to the window to watch them. Mario had insisted on staying, not trusting Armand to keep his word to stay away while Stefan lay sleeping.

Armand would not descend upon them, and Stefan knew it. Armand wanted Stefan out of the way, to tip the balance of power in this town to his side, but he'd play by the rules. It was unusual for two masters to exist side by side, but they'd managed it —

Armand and Stefan, cold and warm — keeping the balance in a town that could so easily erupt into chaos. Armand had taken responsibility for his vampire's betrayal and had not held Stefan to his promise to leave. Armand's sense of honor far outweighed his desire for power and revenge.

"I'm doing it for Meredith," Armand had said in his ice-cool voice. "Not you."

Stefan had nodded, understanding. They'd have a truce if not complete trust.

As Stefan watched, Meredith dove into the pool, swam a few laps, then stepped out, slicking her water-dark hair back with one hand. Stefan had not lost one bit of yearning for her. If anything, their connection through her tasting his blood had made it worse.

*Her choice. It must be her choice.*

The bestial part of Stefan wanted to throw Mario out, toss Meredith on the ground, and have at her. Would she laugh and twine her arms around his neck? Or scream in terror and try to flee?

Right now she looked healthy and vibrant and yes, cocky. He didn't want to take that away from her.

He touched the control to slide open the glass door, and strolled out onto the deck. Mario glanced up, his expression cautious, but Meredith ran to Stefan and enfolded him in a wet hug.

"Stefan! It is so good to see you. Are you better?"

"I am now."

He kissed her smiling mouth, remembering what it had felt like to have her drink him — erotic and exciting. The hardest thing he'd ever done was to tell her to go yesterday, and he wasn't certain he could do it again.

She drew back a little, her eyes cool green in the strong sunlight. "I'm better too. What happened to Spike?"

"Who?"

"Armand's vampire who looked like Spike. The one who attacked me."

Her words faltered, and he felt the fear in her. Stefan touched her forehead, absorbing the fear and returning calm.

"Armand killed him," he said. "Armand can sense what his vampires do, and he knew you were being attacked. We found you just in time."

The vampire had nearly finished her off. Armand's power over his vampires was so great that he'd made the rogue vamp burst into flames with a thought. Meredith had lain against her car, bleeding profusely from gashes all over her body, her throat half torn out, barely alive.

Now, except for a few pink lines where the deeper cuts had been, she looked healthy and whole. And cocky.

"I'm glad you did," she whispered. She rose on tiptoe and kissed him again, stirring hungers that he'd kept buried inside him while she rested. He put his hand under her wet hair and lifted her to him. He could kiss her forever.

He heard Mario noisily get to his feet. "Looks like I should leave you two alone."

His grin was knowing. Mario was convinced that now Meredith would stay and give herself to Stefan, and everything would be all right. Stefan knew that Meredith bathed in the afterglow from feeding from two vampire masters, which meant she might come to her senses and run any minute.

Mario gave Meredith a wave and sauntered out. He was as cocky as she was.

"So what were you two talking about?" Stefan asked as he led Meredith to the chaise Mario vacated. He lifted the terry robe that lay in a snowy heap and pulled it around Meredith's wet body.

"You." She grinned. "Mario was telling me stories about you."

"Hmm. Why don't I want to know about that?"

"Oh, it was all good. He told me how you rescued him way back in the early fifteenth century and how powerful you are. I think he wants me to be impressed with you."

Stefan stroked her sleek hair. Water droplets beaded on her lashes. "And are you?"

"Somewhat."

"Somewhat?" He felt a little offended. "Only somewhat?"

"Well, you are pretty arrogant. *I am a vampire master, everyone must obey.* And as soon as you put your touch on me, I wanted to fall at your feet and kiss your toes. You have to be proud of yourself to expect a woman to do that."

"I don't think I specified you had to kiss my toes." He pursed his lips. "But if you *want* to . . ."

"And this *yes, Master* thing has to go."

He felt a grin breaking through his despair. She stood with her hands on her hips, a glint in her eyes that said if she became his blood slave, it would be on her terms and nothing else.

"You can call me Stefan," he said.

"In fact, the whole *slave* part of it has to go to. I want my own career and to come and go as I please. I don't want to ask your permission every time I want to leave your side."

"Fine." The grin was growing. "In fact, if you wanted to open a gallery here for your mother's paintings, I can do it. Big spenders come to Vegas."

She stopped. "You'd do that?"

"Why not?"

She pressed an excited kiss to his lips. "You're a sweetheart. Now, let's see, where was I? Oh yes — the wardrobe. Diaphanous white gowns aren't really me, and neither are leather bustiers. Something sexy but tasteful, I think — I'll have to go shopping and see what I can find. And shoes. Manolos, definitely. A whole closetful — no, I think I'll need a whole room. You know how women are about shoes."

The wicked twinkle in her eyes made him burst out laughing. He hadn't laughed, not like this, in centuries. "What are you saying, Meredith?"

She slid her arms around his neck. "That I want to stay with you. As a blood slave, girlfriend, wife, whatever you have in mind. And I *will* make you bite my neck, if that's what it takes to bring you to full strength —"

Stefan stopped her words with a kiss. "Be sure, Meredith," he said in a low voice.

"Please. Be sure."

A smile blossomed on her lips. "I think that's the first time you've said *please* like you really mean it."

He did really mean it. He pressed his forehead to hers, his hard fingers framing her face. "I do mean it, Meredith. *Please.*"

"Well," she said, her breath coming faster. "If you put it that way . . ."

Ten minutes later, Meredith found herself stark naked on Stefan's bed with his incredible body on top of hers. Her bathing suit lay in a wet puddle on the floor where Stefan had swiftly peeled it from her, probably ruining the priceless carpet.

Stefan didn't look like he cared. He'd stripped off his clothes and now lay spread on her, one hand stroking her hair.

"Look into my eyes," he said.

Meredith suppressed a laugh and readily stared into tawny eyes that could melt her heart. His irises began to glow, golden light that flared as bright as the Las Vegas sun. His power hit her full force, sending her dropping into a dark abyss, down, down, down.

But the abyss held no fear because she knew Stefan would catch her. She was safe in his arms and always would be.

"Are you ready?" he whispered.

"Yes." Meredith arched her body against his, wrapping her arms snugly around him. "Yes, yes, yes."

With a strong hand, he parted her thighs and slid inside her, stiff and definitely ready for her. She lifted her hips, loving the way he opened and filled her, as though her body had been waiting for him all her life.

He closed his eyes, his mouth twisting as the erotic excitement filled them both. He nuzzled her, kissing her lips, then drew his tongue from the corner of her mouth to the pulse point at her throat.

"Please," she babbled, wildness washing over her. "Please, please, please."

"I thought you liked me to say that," he murmured.

"Stefan," she gasped. "Shut up and bite me."

He laughed, his chest rumbling against her. He licked her neck, tongue hot and wet, and then she felt a brief, sharp pain. His mouth closed over her flesh, and he suckled.

Meredith screamed. She bucked up into him, feeling his cock inside her and his mouth buried in her neck. Her climax hit her full force, excitement jolting through her. She swore that the apartment disappeared and they were floating in the blackness of space, surrounded by stars, or maybe she had half passed out from her wild climax. She was never sure, but she knew she'd never had an orgasm like this before.

Whatever she screamed and babbled, she didn't know, but her throat was raw with it. Her muscles ached from slamming herself into him, but she couldn't stop. Stefan fed on her and made love to her without mercy, and she hung on and loved every second of it.

He lifted his head. His eyes were bright like stars, his power flaring even as her frenzy wound down. He growled low in his throat, a sound of triumph — and then the sex they had after that blew everything away.

"I love you, Stefan," Meredith said. Or maybe she screamed it loud enough for the entire hotel to hear, she couldn't tell. "Love you."

Stefan didn't answer, being too busy giving her mindless, pounding, brutal, wonderful sex.

When they were gasping and shaking and trying to catch their breaths — and on the floor for some reason, with Meredith's bathing suit ice-cold on her shoulder — Stefan smoothed her hair, his eyes gentle now.

"I love you," he said. "Thank you."

■ ■ ■ ■

"Does this mean you're restored to full power?" Meredith asked.

She sat on the chaise lounge by the pool, enjoying the heat of the night. The sun had long since set and Stefan's well-paid staff had laid out a supper for them on the deck. Above the laser light shows, stars showed thick in the desert sky.

Stefan and Meredith had devoured the supper, hungry after their long afternoon of sex, probably not appreciating the fine flavors Stefan's personal chef had chosen for them. They'd been too hungry to notice.

"Yes," Stefan said.

He looked so smug, sipping his wine while he lounged in his bathing suit on a chair, smiling like a man who'd finally gotten what he wanted. His eyes still glowed with the warm golden light they'd taken on in the bedroom.

He hadn't resumed the sunglasses all afternoon, and now he bathed his world in his own light. When he blinked, it was like watching a shutter on a lighthouse. She wondered if he would always be like that or just when he had good sex. She wouldn't mind experimenting to find out.

"How can you be sure?" Meredith asked. "That you're at full power, I mean?"

He smiled, a man in full control. "I am sure. How do you feel?"

"Me?" She took stock. "Great. Wonderful. Better than ever, in fact. Fabulous, fantastic. Want any more adjectives?"

"That is how I feel. As strong as I've ever been." His expression softened. "You not only saved my life, but restored my powers. Maybe gave me even more."

She dangled her wineglass from her fingers. "Enough to kick Armand's ass?"

"Easily." He took a sip of wine. "But I'll leave him alone. The power in this town needs to be balanced, and we do a good job of it. Besides, he helped save your life, so I have a mushy feeling about him here." He pressed his fist to his heart.

"That's true, he could have let me die. He didn't stand to gain anything by saving me."

"He likes you."

Meredith blinked. She thought of the tall, cold vampire with black leather clothes and long white hair, the vampire not afraid of God and his symbols. She imagined what he must have been like as a knight, his strong body encased in mail, his surcoat with its cross, the huge sword in his upraised hand. He'd probably scared the crap out of his enemies.

"He likes me?" she asked. "Hmm, how does that make me feel?"

"He admires courage, and you have it in abundance."

Meredith sipped her wine, remembering how she'd twice tried to threaten Armand and how he'd regarded her as though he were a tiger being screamed at by a mouse. "Some would call it foolhardiness."

"You stood up to him to protect me," he said. "You amazed him. And me."

"You made me your blood slave. I thought it was my job to protect you."

Stefan laughed. He set aside his wineglass and got to his feet, the look in his glowing eyes making her shiver in anticipation. His body was beautiful, tall and hard with muscle, his golden hair scraped back from a sculpted face, and those eyes . . .

"A vampire cannot compel a blood slave to protect him. He protects the blood slave."

"Really?" She stood up as well. "So when I wanted to charge after you to Armand's to rescue you, that was just me wanting to do it?"

"Mario's panic might have had something to do with it."

"Mario's a good friend."

"He is." Stefan slid his hands to her hips

and drew her against his warm body. "I do not wish to talk about Mario right now, or Armand."

Meredith kissed his warm chest. "Fine by me. We can talk about them later. Maybe invite Mario out to dinner. Or breakfast."

"I want to show you that I've returned to full strength, and then some. You seem to need convincing."

Meredith smiled, excitement racing down her spine. "I don't know, you seemed very convincing in the bedroom. We should be more careful, though, about breaking things. Your poor staff has to clean up after you."

Stefan laughed. She loved the sound of his laugh, low and rumbling and warm. He wrapped his arms around her and did a slow spin with her, a dance step that they'd done at the club when he'd wined and dined her.

After a moment Meredith realized they were twirling together *above* the deck, rising into the balmy desert night. The stars spread out above them, and below them the glittering lights of the city created starlight of their own.

She knew that if she let go of him, she'd fall, but also that he held her safely and would never let her fall.

"Where do you want to go, love?" he asked, breath warm on her skin.

"Anywhere you go." Meredith snuggled her head on his shoulder, feeling protected and loved and deliriously happy, and incidentally enjoying the view. "Master."

Stefan's smile grew feral, the glow in his eyes threatening to light up the sky. He kissed her hard on the mouth.

"As Mario would say," he intoned, stroking her hair, "you got it, babe."

■ ■ ■ ■

# Bring Out
# Your Dead
## by
# Katie MacAlister

■ ■ ■ ■

# CHAPTER ONE

"Braiiinssss."

"Yes, I know."

"Braaaaaainnnsss!"

"Ysabelle?" The front door thumped shut with an audible grunt from Noelle, one of my two flatmates. "One of these days we're going to get Mr. Sinclair to fix that door . . . Ysabelle?"

"*Elle est* right here *avec le* sitting *chambre du femmes*," Sally, my other flatmate, called out as she drifted through the room. Sally had issues.

"Braaaains!"

"*Vous parlez* a mouthful." Sally beamed at my client as she wafted past him, through the wall, and into the room beyond.

"Oh." The door to the sitting room opened and Noelle stuck her head in, a worried frown puckering her brow. "Did you know there's a small herd of zombies in the hall?"

I sighed, giving my client what I hoped

was a reassuringly cheerful smile. "Yes, I know, and please, Noelle — zombie is so politically incorrect. The preferred term is revenant, or functionally deceased."

"Well, there's a group of *fuctionally deceased* in the hall playing strip poker, and if Mr. Sinclair sees them, he's going to have a fit. You know how he is about using the flat for business."

"Ahem! Brains!" Tim, a new revenant in need of counseling, glared at me.

"I apologize for the interruption," I said in a calm, reassuring voice as I waved Noelle away. She rolled her eyes and closed the door, leaving me with my client. "You were telling me about the taunting you experienced recently?"

"Yes, brains. Or rather, *braiiiiiiiins.* Spoken in a slurred, repugnant voice that was accompanied by a fine spray of spittle. That's all they said, over and over again, as if I were supposed to stagger toward them with a fork and knife, and start hacking away at their heads. I am more than a little offended by the stereotype portrayed in modern films, and which people such as those at the bus stop wholeheartedly embrace. Isn't there something we can do about it? Must we endure such things without speaking up? Is there no way to educate the public about the true nature of revenants?"

"We're working very hard to do that, but as you know, public acceptance is a hard-fought battle, and frankly, I don't see an end in sight any time in the near future."

"*Qu'est que le* hell?" Sally, who had drifted back into the room on Noelle's heels, paused to look out the window.

"Sally, language, please!"

"*Pardonnez.* But holy *merde! Voici est* a whole boatload *du* zombies *en l'rue. J'allez* to get *le* cricket bat in case *ils* try breaking *dans le* flat."

"There, you see?" Tim pointed at Sally. She gave us a cheerful smile and flitted past to the next room. "Your . . . whatever she is. That's just the sort of negative stereotypical reaction I object to!"

"Sally is my spirit guide," I answered. "I apologize for her, as well. Some time ago she decided she wanted to be French, so she changed her name to Fleur and began speaking in that atrocious Franglais. We're hoping it's a phase that will pass. *Soon.*"

Tim's eyes, which reminded me of a particularly obnoxious form of boiled sweet, bugged out at me in the manner of an elderly pug. "Spirit guide? *You* have a spirit guide? I thought you worked for the Society for the Protection of Revenants."

"I do, but counseling is only a part-time position," I explained. "I also occasionally tutor English and history, and sometimes I act as a medium for persons wishing to contact the deceased. I'd probably have more of the latter work if I had a spirit guide who wasn't quite so . . . well, you saw Sally. But my personal problems are neither here nor there. We were discussing your successful reentry into a meaningful and productive life filled with satisfaction."

"It's neither successful, productive, nor meaningful thus far," he said in a rather petulent tone. "Surely there must be something we can do about the prejudice I've been forced to face?"

I gave a helpless shrug. "What would you suggest?"

"Well . . . I'm a pacifist, so I won't go the route of violence, despite what the public seems to believe of us. Perhaps a picket, or a boycott of nonrevenant companies, or oh! I know! An Internet letter–writing campaign! That worked wonders with the Save the Hedgehog folk! You should suggest that to the Society."

I opened my mouth to explain that the SPR had spent decades working to educate the public as to the true nature of their members with little success to date, but I bit back the inevitable lecture. It would do no good. Tim was newly reborn, as were many in this time of upheaval. He'd learn with time how to hide his present state. My job was not to teach him to pass as mortal — it was to get him past the first hurdles of rebirth. "I'll be sure to pass along your suggestions, but you know, something like that really needs someone with excellent organizational skills to head it up. Perhaps you'd like to start a grassroots campaign yourself? Your resume says you were very active with a human rights organization."

"Hmmm. That's an idea," Tim said with a thoughtful pause. "I suppose I could do something along those lines. Perhaps if we started small, say, a sit-in consisting of new revenants like myself to show the public that we aren't the mindless, brain-eating zombies popular movies paint us as."

"Excellent idea," I said, relieved that he was channeling his energies into something worthwhile. Most new revenants spent several months at a loss as to how to restart their lives.

"Somewhere popular, obviously. Leicester Square?"

I frowned. "There are a great many restaurants there . . ."

"Is that bad?" He looked puzzled for a

moment, then nodded. "Ah, I see what you mean. You believe the proximity of fast food and other restaurants will be a temptation for us to leave the vegetarian lifestyle behind."

"It's been shown that revenants function much better in society if they severely limit their intake of animal flesh," I said gently. "It seems those who turn feral tend to indulge in feeding orgies at local fast-food restaurants. That's why the Society insists all members adhere to a strictly vegetarian diet. Most members have no problem, but for new people, it can be difficult to avoid the lure of a quarter-pounder with cheese. We recommend you avoid temptation for the first two months."

"Surely a hamburger now and again couldn't hurt?"

"You wouldn't think so, would you? But we've found that animal flesh is like a drug to revenants — it leaves them addicted, needing greater and greater quantities to satisfy the craving. Thus, the no-flesh diet."

For a moment, a red light lit the depths of his eyes, but it faded quickly. "Er . . . yes, point taken," he said solemnly. "Perhaps we can do the sit-in somewhere less likely to lead to a fall. A park? Hyde Park?"

"That sounds perfect."

"Yes. I will do that. Thank you, Ysabelle — that was an excellent suggestion. You will help with the sit-in, naturally?"

I smiled. "I'll do my best. If you have any problems, feel free to contact me."

"Very well." With a brisk nod, Tim gathered the orientation and welcome packets I'd given him. "I'd like to get started on it right away, but I suppose I should look up my wife and see what she's done to the house in the six months since I died. Knowing her, she's run amok with gingham or some other hideous scheme."

"Your family was notified last week about your resurrection, so they should be ready to greet you," I said, getting up to show him out. "If you have any questions or problems, please don't hesitate to call. My number is on the card."

He nodded and said good-bye.

I waved him out, then hurried to Noelle's door, knocking before opening it. "How did the infestation go?"

She looked up from her laptop. "Hmm? Oh, it went well, although there were a few more coblyn than I expected. But given Salvaticus, understandable. Speaking of that, how are you holding up? I know this can't be an easy time for you."

I sighed and rubbed my neck for a moment. "I'm tired, but I think my head is still above water. This is so different from anything I've experienced as a counselor, I'm a bit overwhelmed."

"It's bound to be. How many zombies do you normally have to deal with?"

I rubbed the back of my neck again, and wished for a couple of aspirins. "Usually fewer than five a year are raised by intervention."

"Intervention? You make it sound like revenants are drugs users."

I smiled. "Intervention in this case means someone petitions a being with the power to raise the dead. It's not an easy process. Because Salvaticus is traditionally the time of rebirth, the Society says we can expect more than three hundred new revenants over the next few days. Thank goodness this only happens every five hundred years. All the counselors are working around the clock to cope with the influx. Speaking of which, if my clients are playing poker in the hall, I'd best see to them before the neighbors start to complain about naked revenants. Sally?" I poked my head out into the flat's hall.

"*Oui? Vous* called?"

"Can you show in the next person? And please — watch your language. Some of these people have been dead for over a hundred years, and they're bound to be scandalized by any cursing."

My erstwhile spirit guide snorted and rolled her eyes as she drifted toward the front door. "*Années du* hundred *est rien. Moi, je* will be *cent soixante-douze* next March."

"And you don't look a day over one hundred and fifty," I said. "Please give the client the welcome packet, and tell him or her I'll be right there. I need to talk to Noelle first."

"It will have to be quick," Noelle said, glancing at the clock and saving her file. "I'm on duty tonight in the Tower of London's portal. It's been spewing out huge numbers of imps the last few nights, and the Tower's regular Guardian is too overwhelmed to cope with all the crossovers."

I frowned. "Salvaticus is the time of rebirth for revenants. Why would that make the imps come into our world?"

"Lots of reasons," Noelle said, snatching up her bag of tools and a small purse. "It's the week before Vexamen, the time of upheaval in Abaddon when demon lords struggle with one another for surpremacy. Those battles generate an excess amount of dark power, so the imps and other beings use that to access portals that would normally be beyond their abilities. And speaking of that, I wanted to remind you to be especially careful when you go out."

"Me?" I watched as she crossed over to her bedroom window and drew a protection ward on it, then followed when she marched out and repeated the process on all the windows in the flat. "What are you doing? I thought you warded the flat every weekend."

"Those are normal household protection wards. These are different — these will keep any being of dark powers out. They don't last as long as the others. I'm drawing them because you're at risk right now."

She turned to face me as Sally showed a middle-aged woman into the sitting room. I told the woman I'd be with her in a minute.

"What are you talking about?" I asked Noelle in a low voice. "Why am *I* at risk? It's not like I'm a sex bunny or anything like that."

"You're sex bunny enough to capture five husbands," Noelle said with a laugh.

I thinned my lips. "They weren't captured. They were all very nice men, considerate and thoughtful, if a bit . . . well, that's not a discussion for today."

"That's not the danger I was talking about, but you know full well you're attractive enough. *You're* not cursed with red hair and freckles."

I smiled. Noelle's hair and fair skin were the bane of her existence. "Oh, you're not going to tell me that men don't like red hair, because I know that's not true. You have lots of boyfriends."

"Perhaps, but there was only one who really mattered." She stopped next to a desk, her face drawn.

I put an arm around her. I had been in the country visiting a relative when she had met, been madly attracted to, and ultimately rejected by a mysterious man about whom she was oddly reticent to speak. "I'm sorry, Belle — I don't mean to be a wet blanket about this, but it . . . well, it still hurts."

"Men are scum," I said sympathetically. "Most, that is. Certainly the one who dumped you is."

"He didn't dump me so much as reject what I had to offer him," she said with a sad little sigh. "I just don't know how he could do that. It doesn't seem possible — it was against all the rules — but he did."

I murmured platitudes, feeling her pain. "I know it's hard now. It's only been, what, seven months? But in time, you'll realize that this man was not meant for you."

"That's just the problem — he *was* meant

for me," she said, turning away. "He was . . . oh, what does it matter? He refused me, and that was the end of it."

"Then more fool him. You are charming, attractive, smart, and a wonderful person. And for the record, I quite like your red hair and freckles."

She laughed and gave me a hug. "And I like your dark hair and gray eyes, but that's beside the point. We're quite a pair, aren't we?"

"I still don't see what any of this has to do with Salvaticus."

"Then you're being unusually obtuse. You must know that your double soul presents an extreme temptation to any servants of demon lords who are about."

My smile faded. I'd never been too comfortable with my unusual status.

"Anyone with my handicap will be a target," I said, crossing my arms and looking out the window at the rainy London morning. A thin drizzle spotted the window and made the street gleam damply, casting a gloom over the day that had me shivering slightly.

"Oh, for heaven's sake, you aren't handicapped. You're unique! There aren't that many of you around, are there?" she asked, her head tipped to the side as she continued to study me, evidently cheered out of her own glums by my moodiness.

I shifted restlessly, uncomfortable with such close scrutiny.

"That wasn't a condemnation, you know," she said softly, then *tsk*ed when the sitting room clock chimed. "Bloody hell, I'm late. Just watch yourself. Stay in and don't go out for the next few days just to be sure."

She was off to the front door, snatching up her coat and umbrella en route.

"I can't stay in — I have to go tutor a new child this afternoon who was sent down from his school."

"Cancel."

"I can't! I need the money. I'm tired of borrowing from you just to pay for groceries and things."

She paused at the door to make a face. "Why you continue to spend every spare minute of your time with that Society when they don't pay you —"

"You know why I volunteer with them. They need me. It's not their fault they don't have the budget to pay their counselors. I was lucky to get this tutoring job, so I'm not going to cancel and risk losing the only source of income I have."

She touched a blue and green tapestry that hung on the hall wall. "You could always sell some hangings."

I wrapped my arms around my waist, a little prick of pain burning deep within me. "I've sold my loom. I've sold all my wools and other equipment. I've sold everything I could, but that piece is the only thing I have left of myself. I can't sell it, I just can't."

Noelle smiled. "I'm not asking you to, Belle. I know how much this means to you. Don't worry about money — we'll get by somehow. I can always take on some extra work if need be. Just stay here and take care of your zombies."

"Revenants," I said automatically as she slipped out the door, her red curls bobbing madly.

Worry held me in its ever-present grip, tightening across my chest until every breath was an effort to take. Noelle might be willing to do my share as well as hers, but that was a situation I couldn't tolerate. Despite her warning about being a target of the dark powers, I had to go to the tutoring job. A girl's pride could only take so many blows.

"*Vous est* coming?" Sally asked, poking her head through the door. I rubbed the goose bumps on my arms that remained as Noelle's words echoed in my head. "*Qu'est-ce qu'il y a?* You look *tres* worried."

"Nothing's wrong, and yes, I'm coming. I'm not worried, it's just . . ." I rubbed my arms again, trying to disburse the somber feeling that had been left in the wake of Noelle's warning. "It's nothing. Just someone walking over my grave."

Sally pursed her lips but said nothing as I entered the sitting room. Considering the obvious, I counted that as a minor miracle.

# CHAPTER TWO

"Yip, yip!"

"Oh God, not more . . ." Followed by a dozen or so tiny yellow imps, I burst out of the tube station and ran like a maniac down the street, tossing apologies over my shoulder as I occasionally bumped into people on their way home. It was early evening, and the sodden sky did nothing to lighten the way as I raced down streets, cut through alleys, leaping over fences and rubbish bins in the manner of a hyperactive Olympic hurdler. "Pardon me. So sorry. My apologies, sir."

"*Belle! Vous êtes* banging my head *dans la* bottle of water!"

"I'm a little busy at the moment, Sally," I muttered through gritted teeth. Mindful of my spirit guide's head, I spun around the corner as carefully as possible, but ended up skidding on the wet pavement and slamming into a large figure that loomed up out of nowhere.

"Oooph," the man grunted as I collided with him, falling backward. Inside my purse, Sally yelled out copious curses in mangled French.

My arms flailed as I attempted to regain my balance, but it did no good. We fell in a tangled heap of arms and legs, my nose bumping his cheekbone, his warm lips pressed against mine. For a moment I lay stunned — both by the blow and the fact that I was inadvertantly kissing a total stranger.

I opened my mouth to apologize, but his arms tightened around me. His lips moved, sending little zings of excitement down my body. For a moment, I could taste blood, but the second his tongue swirled across my lip, teasing me, *tasting* me, all thoughts flew out of my head.

He must have been eating a spicy sweet or chewing clove gum or something, because his mouth tasted of a heavenly ambrosia I couldn't begin to put into words. A distant part of my brain was shocked that I was lying on a stranger in the middle of a London street, surrounded by passersby as I kissed him with everything I was worth. But at that moment all I wanted was to enjoy the spicy sweetness his mouth offered.

His body stiffened. I had a momentary glimpse of gray-blue eyes flashing surprise beneath the black rim of a fedora before they narrowed and he spoke. "Beloved!"

The sound of his voice brought me back to reality. My cheeks flamed with embarassment as I squirmed out of his hold. I got to my feet and gathered my backpack from where it had fallen. "I'm so very sorry, sir. There's no excuse for my actions other than the ground was wet, and I'm being chased —"

"*Tabernak! Peut-être vous* would like to murder *moi?*"

The man leaped up with a grace I lacked, looking toward the voice issuing from my backpack.

"Sorry. It's a little confusing, isn't it? That's actually my spirit —" I started to explain, still red-cheeked at my uninhibited display. But at that moment, the imps found me.

"Yip, yip, yip," clamored the murderous little monsters (imps seldom have good on their minds) as they poured around the corner in a yellow wave of menace.

"Bloody hell!" I scanned the street quickly, searching for the best escape route, but before I could make a decision, the man shoved me toward the entrance to a narrow

186

unlit alley.

"Down there. Quickly!" he ordered, turning to block the alley with his body. I hesitated a moment, unwilling to place my Good Samaritan in potential danger, worried that he could be harmed. "Run, you foolish woman. I won't be harmed."

I didn't wait for him to tell me twice. I ran, my arms outstretched in a blind attempt to avoid trash bins and boxes of refuse that hid in the darkness.

"*Belle! J'ai entendu le* voice *du* man. Who was it?"

"Sally, I really don't have time — ow! Damn it, this is ridiculous."

The tiny alley ran behind a row of connected buildings, allowing little light to intrude from the shops and streetlights. Judging by the smell of rodent droppings and urine, I gathered the alley was not the safe haven I had hoped it would be. I swore again as my shin connected with something hard and pointy, then turned back to see how my champion was doing, prepared to go to his rescue if he was being overwhelmed. All I could see was his silhouette in the entrance of the alley, bobbing and weaving as he beat off the imp attackers.

"*Vous avez arrêté?* Why?"

"Because the man may be in trouble."

*"Run!"* he yelled, spinning around toward me. "Turn left at the end of the alley."

His voice was strong and confident, not at all like that of someone who was about to be overwhelmed by imps.

"Do as he says," advised the muffled voice. "*Il retentit tres* Sexy Pants."

"I am doing it," I snapped, sprinting down the last half of the alley with only minor injuries to my abused shins. I burst out into the lights of the busy street, turned blindly, and raced straight into a demon.

Pain exploded through my head and shoulder. Sally shrieked, her high-pitched screams piercing the fog in my brain and the stench of demon smoke. Woozy, I realized the demon had instinctively thrown me off him, no doubt believing I was an attacker. The pain, along with the sharp, coppery taste of blood helped clear my head. It focused its attention on me.

"Demon! Demon! Demon!" Sally screamed from inside the backpack.

"You smell of revenants," the demon said, sniffing the air. Its eyes narrowed on me as I got painfully to my feet.

"I mean you no harm," I said slowly, showing my palms so the demon would know I was unarmed.

"Get away, Belle! Demon! *Zût alors!* It will

have you!"

My gesture of good faith did little good. The demon snarled one word at me, a word that made my blood curdle. *"Tattu!"*

I leaped backward as it lunged at me. If only I hadn't taken the tube. The imps never would have found me, and I'd never have run into the delectably kissable man outside the alley, and he'd never have sent me careening (intentionally, or accidentally?) straight into the arms of one of the few beings who could do me damage.

I whirled around, about to sprint away in a desperate attempt to escape the demon, but at that moment the man I'd been kissing burst from the alley, flinging himself between the demon and me.

I didn't wait around to see whose side he was on — I ran. Judging by the demonic curses and screams that followed me, the man must have been an ally. When I stopped three blocks away in a small square, one hand on my side to ease a stitch as I gasped for air, there were no demon or imps in pursuit. No mysterious man in a dark hat with glittery blue eyes, either.

*"Qu'est que* going on? *Porquoi* have you stopped?"

For a moment, I was disappointed that the stranger — back in the savior role —

hadn't followed me, but I quickly regathered my wits.

"Economy be damned," I said grimly, limping to the nearest taxi rank. "The streets aren't safe for someone like me."

"*Vous* said it, sister."

"Tell me you're the tutor."

"I'm the tutor."

"Oh, thank God." The woman who opened the glossy black door of the three-story town house yanked me inside without any ceremony. She looked to be in her mid-twenties, and bore a frazzled, wild glint in her eyes. "Ew! What is that?" She asked, eying the paper bag I carried.

"I'm so sorry. It was an imp who got a little too personal with my leg. You know how they are — they'll mount anything that moves."

"Imps," the woman said, her eyes round with horror.

"*Il était seulement* one imp." I gave the backpack a little shake to remind Sally that I didn't want her speaking until I'd had the chance to check out my new employers. Not everyone is thrilled to see a tutor who has a spirit guide following her everywhere.

The woman's eyes widened even more at the words emerging from my backpack.

190

"Ignore that," I said.

"Yes, I think I'd better," she answered, her face tight. She said nothing more about either my unsavory package or my talking backpack, simply pulling me inside and slamming the door behind me. She frowned a moment, opened the door again, and dashed out to where the taxi driver was attempting to merge back into traffic.

"Save me from having to order one," she said breathlessly as she returned. She stopped in front of me, running an agitated hand through her hair. "What's taken you so long? I thought you'd never come."

I glanced at my watch. If she didn't appreciate hearing about the imp who had been hiding in the taxi, I doubted she'd care to hear of the demon I'd run into earlier. "I take it you're Mrs. Tomas? I apologize for being late, but it is only five minutes past my appointment time —"

"It doesn't matter, you're here now," the woman said, grabbing a raincoat from a nearby chair. I looked around the small entrance and noted the dark paneling on the walls, marble tile, and sparse but elegant furnishings. I had been told by the private tutoring agency I worked through that the child I was being assigned had been sent down from an exclusive boarding school.

Coupled with what I could see of the house, I assumed the family must be pretty financially comfortable. "I don't know where he is right now, and frankly, I don't care. He's probably dismembering a cat or planning some evil crime against nature or plotting to overthrow the government. I don't know and I don't care! He's your problem now. I've had all I can take!"

"Erm . . ." *He,* I took it, referred to my pupil. What a very odd response this woman had toward her own son. She grabbed two large bags and her purse before turning to face me again. "You're Damian's mother?"

"Goddess, no!" The woman actually shuddered as she spoke.

"Ah. Then you must be the nanny. I was told there would be a new nanny. I'm Ysabelle Raleigh."

*"Was."*

"Pardon?"

"I *was* the nanny. They hired me yesterday, but I hereby quit. I don't care how many bonuses they pay me to stay with him while they're gone, it's not worth living with that little monster."

A loud crash sounded from the floor above, startling me into an exclamation of surprise, but the agitated woman in front of me didn't even blink an eye. "Tell them they

192

can send my wages to me. They have the address."

"I'm sorry," I said, completely lost. "I don't seem to follow you. You're the nanny but you're quitting?"

"Yes. You're here now. I didn't leave him until you came — you can tell them that. But he's your problem now!"

*"Ce qui est celui?"*

We both ignored my backpack. "My problem? I hardly see —"

"That's part of it, don't you understand?" She grabbed my arm in a tight grip, her eyes wild. Outside, the taxi driver tapped on the horn. "Everything looks all right, but it's not. Not any of it. And if you can't see that before it's too late, then all will be lost."

Before I could ask for clarification, the nanny grabbed her bags and hauled them out to the taxi driver. "Don't go anywhere, I'll be right back," she told him.

I waited until she returned for the last of her things. "I'm sorry, there seems to be some confusion. I'm not here for the nanny job. I'm just here to tutor —" I dug out the employment card. "Damian Tomas, male child, age ten."

The woman paused dramatically in the doorway. "If you take my advice, you'll clear out right now. The monster can take care of himself."

"Monster?" asked a muffled voice. "*Qui est le* monster?"

I desperately clung to shreds of hope that it was all a big misunderstanding, but sneaky little tendrils of dread kept tugging at me. "What about his parents?"

"Got away while they could. Smart people." She grabbed a cloth bag and a cardboard box, sending a glance of loathing at the ceiling before pinning me back with a look that had the hairs on the back of my neck standing on end. "Be afraid, tutor. Be very afraid. Guard your soul."

My mouth opened in surprise, but before I could form a coherent sentence, she shoved her things at the taxi driver and got into the black car, slamming the door behind her.

"The hell!" Sally said.

I watched the nanny leave, slowly turning to look at the stairs behind me. "I don't know about you, but I'm a bit worried."

"*Une* bit is all?"

"Well . . . all right, more than a bit. What could be so wrong with a child that he drove away his nanny in less than a day?"

"*Merde!*" Sally swore. "*Il est temps pour vous* to get away! *Cette* minute! But first take me *hors de* backpack."

"I'm not taking you out until I know it's all right —"

A rhythmic pounding started upstairs, interrupting both my sentence and my thoughts.

*"Allez, allez!"* Sally urged, the backpack beginning to twitch.

I squared my shoulders. "You know there's not a lot that can scare me." Brave words considering the feeling of dread that permeated my bones, leaving me with the unwavering suspicion that I had just gotten myself into a situation way over my head. I marched to the bottom of the stairs. "Hello? Is someone there? My name is Ysabelle. I'm the tutor."

The pounding stopped. A hushed, expectant feeling settled over the house.

*"Ce n'est pas* normal."

"Hush." I took a deep breath. "There's nothing to fear from a small child, not even one who frightens nannies."

Sally snorted. I set down the backpack and started up the stairs. Before I got halfway, a head poked around the corner and looked down at me.

"Hello. I'm Ysabelle. You must be Damian." I released a breath I hadn't realized I was holding. I don't know what I had been expecting, but the boy in front of me looked

195

perfectly normal. Dark blue eyes watched me from beneath two thick slashes of eyebrows. He held a hammer in one hand, a small can in another. "It's a pleasure to meet you. Are you working on some home-repair project?"

As I rounded the landing and walked up the last few stairs, Damian frowned. "Where's Abby?"

"Is that your nanny?"

"I'm too old to have a nanny," he said, scorn dripping from his words. He had a slight accent that sounded vaguely Germanic to my ears. "She was here to watch the house while my dad and Nell are away."

"Nell being your . . . stepmother?" I guessed.

He nodded, turning to stride down the dark upper hall. I followed, looking around for signs that the boy had been engaged in nefarious acts, but there was nothing I could see. From what I could glimpse through the partly opened doors, the upper floor contained only bedrooms. None of them held dismembered cats, evidence of crimes, or mechanisms to overthrow the government. Abby the ex-nanny must have been of a high-strung personality not at all suited to the care of a child.

"She smells."

"Pardon?" I stopped in the doorway to the room Damian entered. I judged by the clothing strewn on the floor, the TV on but blessedly silent, and the number of electronic toys and game machines that this was his room. Two windows looked down on the square outside, but Damian had nailed a couple of dirty planks across one window, shutting out all light. He hefted a flat piece of board, grunting a little before glancing over his shoulder at me. "Nell. She smells. Are you going to stand there or help me?"

Autocratic little . . . I stopped before I could even think the word, and reminded myself that I had promised the tutoring agency I was good with children. "Perhaps you'd like to tell me why you're boarding up your windows?"

"Because —" He plucked a nail from the can he'd set on a small desk and wrestled the board into place. At another arrogant glance, I obligingly held up one corner of the board so he could nail it into place across the window. "Sebastian is coming."

"He is? Does he always come in through the windows?" I relaxed. Why didn't the agency tell me the boy was special-needs? No doubt the nanny had been unable or unwilling to deal with a child who had a different way of looking at life, but that was nothing new to me.

Damian shot me another look filled with scorn. "He can't use the door. Nell warded it. And the windows on the lower floor, but she didn't do the upper ones."

"I see. Who exactly is Sebastian?"

"He's my dad's enemy. He tried to kill Nell and Papa. Now he's coming for me."

"He's coming for you?" I added paranoia to my list of qualities most evident about Damian.

"Yes."

"How do you know that?"

"He said so." Damian stood back and admired the wood he'd nailed across his windows for a moment. He nodded, then gathered his tools and headed for the next room.

For someone riddled with paranoia, he seemed oddly unconcerned. I couldn't help wondering whether this was an attention-getting device, but that wasn't my major concern at the moment.

"Is there anyone else here?" I asked as he proceeded to nail a board across another window. "A . . . a housekeeper? Or sitter? Anyone?"

"Just Abby, but she's left. I'm glad. She didn't believe Sebastian was coming. She said I was . . ." He paused a moment to recall the word. ". . . delusional."

"Hmm. Well, here's the problem — I'm a tutor, not a nanny. I have my own home to go to, and other work I must do, so I can't stay here to take care of you."

"I can take care of myself," Damian said matter-of-factly. He nailed up another board.

"I'm sure you can. Regardless, I believe it would be best if I spoke with your parents." I sat on the edge of the bed, next to a cordless phone. "Do you have their number?"

"My mum is on a cruise. You can't talk to her unless she calls. My dad and Nell are in Heidelberg. But there's no phone because they're building a new house."

It took some doing, but after fifteen or so minutes, Damian was persuaded to hand over a slip of paper with his father's mobile phone number on it. Two minutes after that, I found myself talking to a pleasant American woman who identified herself as Damian's stepmother.

"I'm sorry, but I just can't stay," I said after explaining what happened. "I have many other clients, and although Damian seems like a delightful child" — Damian huffed and puffed past me hauling a handful of cobwebby two-by-fours from the basement, shooting indignant looks at my lack of helpfulness — "I simply cannot put it all aside to take on a nanny position."

"I wouldn't ask you to do so permanently," said the woman named Nell, a distinct note of pleading in her voice. "But we would be so very grateful if you could stay with Damian overnight. Just overnight. I will call the agency right away, but I know for a fact they won't be able to send someone out until tomorrow morning, and we can't possibly get away until after that. I realize this is a great deal to ask you, but if you could see your way clear to just staying with Damian until morning, we would be happy to pay you a bonus on top of your regular fee."

I bit my lip, swayed against my will by the word *bonus.* "I hate to appear mercenary, but I'm a bit tight right now financially, so it really does matter when I ask how much this bonus would be."

Nell was silent for a moment. "How does a hundred pounds sound?"

It sounded like heaven, but I had enough presence of mind not to blurt that out. Evidently Nell took my momentary silence as disapproval, because she quickly added, "I'll make it two hundred if you can stay until the new nanny arrives."

My hesitation wasn't due to greed. I

quickly ran over a mental list of everything that I needed to do in the next twenty-four hours. "I will agree if you don't mind my clients coming here to see me."

"Your clients?"

"I'm a counselor," I answered.

"Oh. Occupational? Emotional?"

"Sort of a cross between the two. I counsel people who've undergone a major change in their life and need a little help to get going again. I have three appointments tonight, and a handful more in the morning."

"Ah, I see. Well, so long as no one unbalanced or dangerous is brought to the house, I don't see any objection. Thank you so much for doing this, Ysabelle. Adrian will be relieved to know his son is in such capable hands."

The son in question chose that moment to stalk by me with a fistful of kitchen knives.

"Erm . . . yes."

After a few basic instructions on where things were located in the house, and promises that a new nanny would be on the doorstep bright and early, Nell hung up. "Anything else you need, Damian will help you. He's very precocious," she said before she disconnected.

*Precocious* was one word for it. I promised

to call if there were any problems, after which I set the phone in its cradle and watched with interest as Damian bustled around the room arranging knives, electrical tape, and more wood.

"Your backpack is talking."

"Hmm? Oh. Erm . . ." My wits, somewhat shaken with the events of the last half hour, attempted to pull together an explanation of why a spirit was in my backpack. "Damian, have you ever wondered what happens to people after they pass on?"

He shrugged. "Not really."

"Ah. Sometimes people who pass on unexpectedly are a bit . . . well, confused is as good a word as any. Many of them don't realize that they're dead. Some do, but they might remain behind in spirit form for other reasons — there's something important that needs to be done, amends to be made, revenge, that sort of thing. What remains of those people after their bodies fade are often called ghosts or spirits —"

"Sally speaks horrible French."

I did a quick mental double-take, upping my estimation of Damian a smidgen. "Ah. You chatted with her?"

"She asked me to let her out." His eyes narrowed for a minute before he dismissed me and turned back to his work. "I figured you had her trapped in there on purpose, so I didn't."

"Thank you, but she's not actually trapped . . . One second, I'll let her out and see if I can explain a bit."

It took a few minutes to smooth Sally's ruffled feathers, but at last she settled down enough to listen to me while I told her of our change of plans.

"What about *votre* clients *du* zombies that are *programmé ce soir?*"

I shot a glance at Damian, but he didn't seem to be listening, instead preferring to pound planks over the window. "I'll just have to see them here instead. There are only three more tonight, aren't there?"

She nodded.

"Excellent. I'll just deal with them and send them on their way. That should be the end of it."

Sally had a few choice things to say about the change of plans, but I pointed out to her that we needed money to live. By the time I was finished with her, Damian had used the electrical tape to attach a couple of knives to each window. Sally took one look at the knives and headed for safer ground. "*Je* go leave *une petite* note on our door for *les* zombie appointments."

"Revenant appointments." I waited until

Sally left for our flat before saying to the industrious boy in front of me, "Um . . . Damian . . ."

"Just in case," he said, not waiting for me to finish my question.

A few minutes of close scrutiny of his handiwork made it clear that Damian was not a stupid child. He handled the knives carefully, respectful of their ability to cause injury. I debated making him take the potentially lethal booby traps down, but decided that so long as he was not harmed — and did not harm anyone else — the rest was an issue for his parents or his nanny.

"I see. As fascinating as that is, I'm here to give you lessons, and even though your stepmother has asked me to spend the night here just to make sure all is well, I think we should proceed with the original plan and take a few lessons in English and history."

"I'm busy right now," Damian answered, not even looking at me as he went into a room made dark by more boarded-up windows. He selected two skinning knives and arranged them on each side of the window. "Why do you have a spirit guide?"

"She . . . er . . . was a bit of a gift. And just so you know, attempting to distract me isn't going to work. There are many other things I would like to be doing at this moment as well, but tutoring is what I'm being paid to do, and do it I will."

"Protecting us from Sebastian is more important than lessons," he said with a black-browed scowl in my direction. "My dad would want me to save your life over learning some stupid dates and writing compositions."

"I don't even know this Sebastian person," I pointed out. "Why do you think he would pose a risk to *me?*"

The look the boy gave me was rife with irritation. "You've got a double soul."

I swear, my mouth hung open for a moment at his statement. "I . . . I don't know what you're talking about. People don't have two souls," I said slowly, a chill running down my arms. How on earth could a mere child see my handicap? "Everyone is granted one soul only when they are born."

Damian shrugged and said nothing.

"What does Sebastian have to do with souls?" I couldn't keep myself from asking. "Is he a demon?"

"No. He's a Dark One." He looked up and grinned, two pointed canines clearly visible despite the gloom. "Like my dad and me."

I took a couple of steps back, a hand at my heart. I'd heard of Dark Ones — vampires, tainted by the dark powers, parasites who preyed on the lives of mortals — but I'd never seen one in person.

"I think . . . I don't know . . . I think I need a little air," I said, stumbling backward as my words jumbled together. Blindly, I made my escape, clutching the banister as I ran downstairs, aware now what Abby had found so wrong with Damian.

I wanted to run away, to go home and hide, to forget I'd ever been here, but as I stood with my hand on the front doorknob just about to bolt, my conscience took that moment to kick in and remind me that although Damian might be a vampire — *vampire!* — he was also a child. I couldn't just leave a ten-year-old alone.

"I'm hungry." Damian's voice drifted downstairs. "Do you have any blood?"

A flight instinct I didn't know I possessed kicked in. I yanked the door open, a survival instinct overriding my better sense into running. But a dark shape looming in the doorway had me shrieking instead, stepping backward in horror as a familiar man — tall, built rather solidly, and covered in blood — staggered through the door.

"You, woman, give me the ring!" he demanded in an authoritative voice that was immediately contradicted when his eyes rolled up and he collapsed at my feet.

I stared down at the man in shock, a thousand questions racing through my mind. What on earth was the kissable Good Samaritan from the alley doing here? Had he followed me? Was he a stalker rather than a lifesaver? How could anyone who kissed the way he did have harm on his mind? And what on earth was he babbling about? "What ring? Who are you? What did you have to do with those demons? God's mercy, you're bleeding! Are you all right? Should I call the paramedics?"

"Oooh," Damian's voice said from where he stood on the stairs, looking down at the scene before him. "You let Sebastian in. That isn't good. Now he'll try to kill us."

# CHAPTER THREE

"Who are you?" The voice was as rough and low as I remembered. "You are not the charmer. You cannot be. What are you doing in this house?"

Sebastian was bound to a chair, held by a thin nylon laundry line Damian had found in the basement. Before I could answer, Sally, only just returned from a quick trip to my flat, gasped and floated over until she was directly in front of him. "*Elle est* very charming! *Vous êtes tres* rude!"

"He said charmer, not charming," I said slowly, racking my brain to dig out information on charmers. Fleeting thoughts skittered away as I was swamped with the memory of Sebastian's mouth on mine.

"So?" Sally contined to stand with her hands on her hips, glaring at Sebastian. He glared right back at her.

"A charmer is someone who can unmake curses," he said, turning his gaze to me. I felt it as if it were a physical touch.

"That's right — they lift curses and wards and things. You are quite correct; I am not a charmer. My name is Ysabelle Raleigh. I am tutoring Damian. I take it you are Sebastian?"

"Yes. Where is Adrian?" His brows pulled together as he looked down at himself, noticing that his arms had been tied behind him. When he looked back up to me, his gray-blue eyes were flashing with indigation and just a smidgen of disbelief. "You think to hold me prisoner?"

Sally's form shimmered indignantly. "*Oui, vous êtes dérangé* man! And there you'll stay *jusqu'à ce que vous expliquiez* why you're attacking *pauvre* Belle!"

Sebastian's eyes narrowed at her for a moment. "You are aware, are you not, that you are not speaking actual French?"

"*Le* gasp!" Sally said, following word by deed and gasping in a thoroughly shocked manner. "*Je suis* too!"

"No, you are not. You are mangling a perfectly nice language —"

"*Zût alors!*" she interrupted, shaking an ethereal fist in his face. "*Je frapperai vous* on the nose —"

"All right, that's enough, you two." I gave my spirit guide a very stern look. She bristled, her eyes flashing. "Sally, please leave us alone."

"Like *enfer* I will! You are not safe —"

I shooed her toward the door. "Don't be silly. He's bound quite tightly, and if I need any help, I'll yell for you."

*"Mais* —" She shot both of us a shared indignant look as I shoved her through the door.

"I'm sorry about that," I said, giving Sebastian a wide berth as I returned to the desk I'd been leaning against. "She's a bit ecentric."

One of his eyebrows rose. "An understatement, but one I am willing to let go in order to deal with more important issues."

"Yes . . . your injuries seem to be healing. I take it you received them fighting the demon? Why did you do it?" I asked, desperate to distract myself from the strange attraction.

Damian and I had half dragged, half carried the unconscious Sebastian into the library, a room filled with comfortable leather chairs and several bookcases, all dominated by a large rosewood desk. As my aching arms attested to, he was a big man — imposing, but not fat — with hair the color of rich honey, his eyes a stormy grayish blue. Despite his arrogance, my fingers itched to run along the stubborn line of his jaw, to feel his touseled hair, to gently brush the width of those broad shoulders, tracing the solid planes of his chest down to that flat belly, and still farther below to where tight jeans accented masculine attributes. My lips positively burned with sensual delight at the thought of kissing him again.

"I disabled the demon . . . after a bit of a fight. What were you thinking, running straight into it?"

"I was running down the alley because you told me to."

He had the audacity to look annoyed. "I told you to turn left. You would have been safe if you'd done so."

"Moot point," I said with a smile. "I am . . . erm . . . sorry about running into you. And the . . . er . . . kissing. I'm not normally so forward."

He frowned. "That also is a moot point. Where is Adrian and the charmer? Why have you tied me to this chair?"

"Mr. and Mrs. Tomas are in Germany at the moment. As for the bonds — I'm sorry, but I felt it prudent given the nature of your arrival and Damian's avowal that you've come to destroy him."

"I have," Sebastian said simply, pulling uselessly at the ropes. Because of my weaving experience, I could tie a quality knot. "Germany. I should have known. Very well, we will go to Germany once you give me the ring. You will release me now and bring it to me."

I rested my hip against the edge of the desk, considering the man before me. "We? We will go to Germany? We as in you and who, exactly?"

"You try my patience, Beloved. You know full well I am referring to you. Now cease these games and release me. I have limited time to destroy Adrian, and we must Join as soon as possible."

"Hold on," I said, raising a hand to stop him. "Back up a moment — you expect me to go to Germany with you?"

"Of course. You will go wherever I go."

"Are you insane?" I couldn't help it, I goggled at him for a moment. "I don't know you! Wait — is this because I kissed you back?"

The look in his eyes was almost insulting. "Why do you pretend ignorance? I am a patient man, but you are pushing my limits. Release me!"

"Not on your life. This is about that kiss, isn't it? You think you're going to take me away to Germany just because I kissed you? Once? God's blood, what do you do with the women you sleep with — marry them?"

"I will marry you, yes. Now cease with this useless conversation and release me."

I shook my head. "I'm going to call in some professional help. Honestly, I think you must have bumped your head on the pavement when we fell. You're not making any sense —"

He swore in French, and his muscles bunched for a moment before the rope exploded around him. One second he was sitting, the next he was before me, his hands hard on my hips as he yanked me up against him. "We do not have time for these games. Your presence complicates matters some- what, but we will overcome the obstacles you present. The first task at hand is to complete the Joining. Remove your cloth- ing."

"What?" I shrieked, trying desperately not to melt against him.

"We must make love to complete the Join- ing. We will do that first, then retrieve the ring."

His body was hard against me, hard and aggressive and overwhelming to my senses, but it was an oddly exciting feeling, not at all the frightening one I'd expected. He was a vampire, I desperately reminded myself. A cold, heartless parasite who preyed on humans.

*We prefer the term Dark One, actually,* he said. With a start I realized he was speaking directly into my head. *And I assure you I am anything but cold and heartless. Right at this moment, I am very, very hot.*

My eyes widened as his head dipped toward mine, freezing as his gaze narrowed for a second on me. I had the sensation that he was seeing deep into my soul, baring all my secrets. I knew then that he'd noticed my handicap, and I turned slightly to avoid his piercing gaze. I felt like a succulent bit of prey watched by a dangerous predator — a feeling I did not enjoy, no matter how many tingles of excitement rippled down my body.

His voice, which had been deep and forceful, softened. "You do not know what I am talking about, do you?"

"No, I don't. All I know is that you mean Damian and me harm —"

"Beloved, I could never hurt you," he said, his thumb sweeping along my lower lip, teasing me until I turned back to look into those all-seeing eyes.

"You are a vampire. Hurt is what you do best, isn't it?" For some reason, I felt it necessary to remind my errant body that this man was not for me.

"I am as you see me. And you are —"

"I am quite well aware of my handicap, thank you," I interrupted, looking down, trying to control my breathing. Being pressed up against him was proving to be an overwhelming experience, one my body wanted to explore more fully.

"Handicap?" His heavy dark honey brows pulled together. "You consider having a double soul a handicap?"

"We are not here to discuss me," I said sternly, trying my best to ignore the bizarre attraction. It had been too long since I had been married, that's all. My hormones were simply kicking in and focusing on the nearest male body they could find.

"On the contrary, at this moment I can think of nothing more I wish to discuss." His gaze flickered over to the clock on the mantel. He sighed. "But I do not have time to indulge myself. Very well, since you are not aware of what has transpired in the last hour, I will give you a summary. You are a *tattu,* bearer of a double soul, and my Beloved, the one woman who can redeem my soul and save me from millenia of anguished existence. I knew that the moment we exchanged blood."

"Exchanged blood?" I asked, my head

whirling. "When did we exchange blood? I kissed you, that's all! And, for the record, you started it by licking my lip!"

"Your lip was cut when you landed on me. I bit my tongue when I was knocked backward. We exchanged blood when we kissed. And now we must complete the other seven steps of Joining for you to be safe from the demon that will be pounding on the door at any moment. Once that is completed, I will be able to protect you. Until that time, you are vulnerable."

I touched my lip. It was sensitive, still tingling from Sebastian's kiss, and in one spot, slightly tender from our collision. I shook my head again, unable to digest it all. "Even assuming that I am your soul-saving person, why do you think that demon will be coming to Adrian's house?"

"He will follow your scent just as I did," he answered matter-of-factly.

I wanted to bristle at the idea that I smelled so strongly people could track me all over London, but the heated look in his eyes generated an answering heat that pooled deep within me, and left no doubt in my mind that whatever it was I smelled like, he did not find it offensive.

"You are *tattu,* a great prize for the demon's master. Do you believe it will not do everything it can to find you and take you to Abaddon?"

I shivered, leaning into him for a moment. I had just met this man, this vampire, but already I felt safe with him. It was as if an empty part of me was suddenly filled with life. "I . . . I don't know what to believe. This is all going too fast for me."

"I am sorry," he said, his eyes filled with regret. "I would do this differently if I could, but, Beloved, we have no time. We must Join now so I can protect you. It is my duty. I do not wish to frighten you, or force you into something you are not ready for, but you must believe me. We have no time for wooing."

His lips brushed mine, gently teasing the edges of my mouth until I sighed and started kissing him back. The world had gone mad, everything I knew was being turned on its head, but damn if I didn't care.

"We have completed several of the steps," he murmured into my mouth, his tongue flicking against my lips. I moaned and sucked his bottom lip, shamelessly pressing myself against him. "But we must exchange fluids once again for the Joining to be complete."

"I'm not going to make love to you," I whispered just before I deepened the kiss, tasting his mouth, twining my tongue around his.

"You must," he groaned, pulling my hips tight against his. I had no doubt that he was as aroused as I was, but even though I was giving in to this unexplained attraction, I wasn't stupid.

I pulled my mouth from his. "I have been married five times, Sebastian. I'm no stranger to either men or lovemaking. But I do not indulge in casual sex, no matter how . . . metaphysical the relationship is. There seems to be something between us that I wouldn't mind exploring further, but I am not sleeping with you."

*Your souls are at risk,* he said, nibbling my lower lip. My knees buckled, leaving me swooning in his arms, my head spinning with the scent and taste and feel of him against me.

*Do you think they have never been so in the past?* I slid my hands under his shirt and let my fingers dance across his back. I wanted to touch him, all of him, but I knew one of us had to keep some control, and clearly Sebastian was not going to be that person. I confined myself to stroking the planes of his back as he kissed me, allowing him to explore my mouth.

*This is Salvaticus,* he reminded me, his

tongue dancing against mine. *For a week, all will be chaos, but even when Salvaticus is over and Vexamen upon us, the demon will not forget you. You will be in danger from here to the end of your days if you do not Join with me.*

"I can take care of myself," I mumbled against his mouth as we came up for air. "I always have."

"That was before you were marked by a demon. No, Beloved, the only answer is for us to Join. *Now.*" Hot kisses burned my neck as he found a spot that sent shivers of absolute pleasure down my back.

"Can you explain . . . oh, dear God, yes, right there . . . can you explain just how this Joining is going to save my souls? As far as I can tell, it's just some sort of emotional commitment. I don't see how that will help protect me from a demon or its lord."

Unbidden, my hands skimmed around to his sides, sculpting the long, sweeping lines of his torso. He nipped my neck when I found a pert nipple that was all but begging for attention. "A Beloved is the mortal woman who redeems a Dark One's soul. In return, he is bound to her, and protects her at all costs."

"You don't have a soul?" I pulled back enough to peer into his eyes. They glittered hot with desire, but I didn't see anything in them to indicate he was soulless. There was no sick feeling of dread emanating from him, as was common in a creature of the dark. The only feelings I got from him were desire, need, want, and an overwhelming sadness that pulled at my heart. "You don't look like a demon."

"I am not a demon. Dark Ones are cursed to remain soulless until their Beloveds regain it for them, but we are not demonic."

His eyes, dark navy-gray, regarded me as I tried to sort through what he'd told me. "You seriously believe I can regain your soul for you?"

"I know you can. It follows the Joining."

A little burst of pain zinged through me at the realization that I was means to an end for him. I was certain that the whole business with him protecting me from a demon was simply a little sugar-coating over the more important issue of his soul. Regardless of all that, I was shaking my head even before he finished the sentence. "I can't be your Beloved."

"You are."

"No." I pushed back on his chest. To my surprise, he released me. My breath came hard and rough, my heart beating wildly as I tried to regain composure. "I'm sorry, Sebastian. I realize that I look like a *get your soul back free* card, but there's a big point you are missing."

He watched me for a moment. "That is not an issue. You are my Beloved. I feel it. I tasted it in your blood. I know it in my heart."

I said nothing for a few minutes while I tried to sort through my tangled thoughts. If what he said was true, then I had very little time to make a decision that would change the path of my life. I hated feeling pressured into doing anything, and here I was being asked to commit myself body and soul to a man — a *vampire* — I'd just met. Could I do it? Did I even want to try? He said my handicap made no matter in the issue of Belovedness, but did he truly know that? What if we tried and it failed? What if he were just using me, manipulating me into giving him what he wanted without regards to the future? Did I really have any alternatives? Salvaticus would be over soon . . . but somehow, I knew that he spoke the truth. The demon had seen me for what I was, and it would move heaven and earth to return to its master with me as a prize. The man before me held the key to my salvation, just as I did for him.

Sebastian said nothing as I wrestled with

my thoughts, simply holding me in a loose embrace, his eyes flashing bluish gray lights that mesmerized me.

"Very well, I will Join with you," I said finally. He needed a soul, and I could redeem it for him. I would do it his way because the alternative was unthinkable.

I didn't want to die. Not again.

# CHAPTER FOUR

"What . . . er . . . do we have to say something?" I asked, more than a little nervous now that I'd agreed to bind myself to the man whose mere physical presence filled me with a strange excited happiness. "Is there something I need to swear to? Or is it like a ceremony?"

"There are seven steps to Joining," he said solemnly. "The first two are marking and protection from afar."

"The demon and the mind-talking," I said, recalling his soft voice in my head urging me down the alley. I hadn't thought anything of it at the time, but I recognized it now for what it was.

"Yes. The third and fourth steps involve the first exchange of bodily fluids, and entrusting the Beloved with the truth."

"That would be the kiss and . . . well, I guess telling me who you are."

He nodded. "The fifth step is the second

exchange."

"I assume that" — I waved a hand to indicate the necking session in which we'd just indulged — "qualifies?"

"It does. The sixth step is for the Beloved to overcome the darkness within the Dark One."

"Oh." I thought for a few seconds, frowning as I ran over our conversation. "I'm afraid I don't quite see where we've done that."

"That's because you haven't promised yet to assist me in bringing down the Betrayer."

"Who?"

"Adrian the Betrayer. The man who sold me to Asmodeus."

I gawked at him for a second or two. "He *sold* you to a demon lord?"

"Yes." Sebastian's eyes grew as pale as a foggy dawn. "That is why I seek revenge against him and his family. I swore my vengeance as Asmodeus drained my blood away. Nothing but death will satisfy such a betrayal."

The urge to take him in my arms and comfort him, to lighten the darkness visible in his eyes, was almost overwhelming, but before I could act upon it, the door opened.

"Sally told me to make sure Sebastian doesn't try to do something bad to you,"

Damian said, marching into the room with a pugnacious set to his jaw.

Sebastian's entire body tensed. I put a warning hand on his arm. "Damian, we're having a bit of an adult conversation. Sebastian isn't going to do anything bad, so you can go back and tell Sally —"

"She also said to tell you that there's a demon outside the house demanding to see you. And a bunch of imps. She said she's called Noelle already, too."

I closed my eyes for a moment and wished for the sane, normal life I had when I woke up that morning.

"There are also five zombies outside with big signs, saying they need to talk to you about being kicked out of Hyde Park."

All right, maybe my life wasn't so normal. Still, it had been better earlier in the day.

. . .

"To delay any longer is folly," Sebastian said, turning to me. "The demon is here. He will fight to gain control over you. We must Join now."

Damian wrinkled up his nose at us. "Ew. Joining. That means you're going to kiss her. That's gross."

I sighed at the boy. "Would you please tell Sally that we'll be right out, and tell Tim and his fellow sit-in revenants that I will be happy to talk to them as soon as I can. When did Sally say Noelle will be here?"

"She said she caught her on the tube, and it would only take a couple of minutes. Who's Noelle?" he asked as I gave him a gentle push toward the door.

"Our roommate who is also a Guardian."

Sebastian jerked, as if he was startled by something. I shot him a curious glance, but his face was blank.

"Oh. That's good?"

"Yes, very good. If there is a demon to control, Noelle is the best person to have around. Go on now. We'll be right out."

Sebastian ground his teeth as he watched the boy slowly walk to the door, his body tense and poised to strike. "We must leave now, Beloved. We must Join and leave this house."

I touched his cheek, wondering how he could live through such atrocities and still show so much control. "How did you survive?"

His eyes flickered toward me. "Christian, more of a blood brother than a friend, helped me track down the Betrayer." Sebastian's expression darkened until his beautiful face was a vision of stark vengeance. The sight of it chilled me with frozen dread. I had seen such a look once before . . . and now to see it on the face of the man to whom I had just promised to bind myself was unbearable. "He later turned on me, throwing in his lot with the Betrayer."

"Papa isn't a betrayer," Damian said abruptly, standing at the door. His scowl was almost as fierce as Sebastian's. "He had to do what he did. Nell said he's a brave man because he let everyone think he was bad so he could save people."

"The charmer is deluded," Sebastian snapped, turning back to me. "Christian claimed the Betrayer was saving others by sacrificing me, but I know it was not so. Christian forswore me to distract me from my plan."

"Uncle Christian would never do that," Damian muttered, glowering at us both. "He knows Papa wouldn't do anything bad like you say he would."

"No? The Betrayer skewered me to the wall with a knife in the neck, nearly severing my head. But perhaps you do not call a near decaptitation 'bad.' " Sebastian took a step toward Damian, pulling down the neckline of his black sweater to expose a faint, ragged white line. I tightened my grip on his arm and gently touched the scar.

"No," I said simply.

Sebastian misunderstood me. "I will not

ask you to participate in the actual killing of the Betrayer — that act is one I must do myself. But you understand now why I must seek justice for the crimes committed against me. We have delayed too long; we must leave now. We will go to Paris first —"

"No," I repeated, rubbing my arms against the chill that seemed to leech out from within me. "I understand what you've gone through. But I will not help you if you insist on this path of revenge."

Disbelief filled his eyes. "You will not —"

"No," I said again, lifting my chin so he could better see my determination. "If you wish for me to Join with you, you must first swear to me that you will release your oath of vengeance against Adrian and his family. I will not lift one finger to help you otherwise."

He swore softly to himself. "Why would you deny me what is mine? Do you not think I have every right to exact revenge for the betrayal?"

"I think you have a right to be hurt, yes. Angry, absolutely. Changed by your experience — without a doubt. But I have seen firsthand what revenge against another can do, and I will have no part in it. So make your choice, Sebastian — either you have a soul and a Beloved, or you can have revenge against someone who is probably just as much a victim as you were."

"Papa was cursed by Asmodeus," Damian chipped in. "He didn't have a choice. He had to do what Asmodeus told him to do because his papa gave him away."

Sebastian growled something rude in French. I gave Damian a narrow-eyed look of warning and made a shooing gesture. With head held high, he nodded, and reluctantly left the room.

I knew the second the door closed Sebastian would start in on me about my demand that he give up his plans of vengeance, but I haven't survived as long as I have without learning how to deal with men.

"I think you're incredibly brave," I told him as he turned toward me, clearly about to lecture me.

"Ysabelle —" He stopped, frowning. "You do?"

I smiled to myself. Nothing distracts a man like a bit of flattery, especially when it's sincere. "Yes, as a matter of fact, I do. You had to be incredibly brave to survive being in the control of a demon lord and an attack that could have severed your head. I also think you're intelligent, charming, and . . . well . . . sexy as hell, to be honest."

He stood in front of me, his toes touching

mine. I held his piercing gaze, happy to let him see in my eyes that I meant exactly what I said.

That puzzled him. His frown deepened. "Then why did you just threaten to leave me unless I did what you wanted?"

"I told you why — I've seen the effect of the sort of vengeance that you plan, and frankly —"

"Belle!" Sally swept through the door, her hands on her hips. *"Le* demon *est à la porte!* And *il vous* wants *parler!"*

"Yes, I know. Damian told me."

"Ysabelle?" A man's voice sounded muffled on the other side of the door. "Tim McMann here. I'm sorry to bother you here, but you did say to come to you with problems. Might I have a word about the sit-in? We seem to have a spot of trouble with one of the participants."

"What sort of trouble?" I asked, momentarily distracted from the grave decision Sebastian was demanding of me.

"It seems William here inadvertantly ate two squirrels and a small ferret en route. He's fully willing to participate in the sit-in, but the others were wondering if that's quite proper since we are espousing the nonflesh lifestyle."

"They were very small squirrels," another

man said with obvious distress, clearly the William in question. "Tasty, but not much meat on them. I'm still hungry, in fact. Anyone want to pop into the McDonald's for a quick bite?"

I sighed and hung my head for the count of five, wishing once again that I could rewind the day and start it all over.

"Ysabelle?" Tim shouted.

"I'll be right there. Don't let him eat any more meat."

"I can stop any time I want," William yelled through the door. "I'm just a bit peckish right now. Here, Jack, you doing anything with that arm?"

A squawk followed, presumably from the man named Jack. I rubbed my forehead and wondered how hard it would be to fall into a little coma.

"Ysabelle? We really could use your help out here. William just bit Estabon and Jamal when they pulled him off Jack. I believe he's frothing at the mouth. Surely there's something we can do to save him?"

"Brainnsssss," came the reply from the now thoroughly meat-poisoned William. I sighed again. I hated to lose a client to meat.

"Pull yourself together, man!" Tim bellowed. A sharp thwacking noise followed, as if the sit-in members were beating William on the head with their signs. "That's the very stereotype we're protesting against! Remember what we're standing for! Ysabelle!"

"Tie him up if you need to, but don't get within range of his teeth. Sally will show you where there's rope," I answered, turning back to face Sebastian.

The look of disbelief on his face was priceless. Sally rolled her eyes.

"Is Noelle on her way?" I asked her.

"*Oui.* She's coming *ici bientôt,* just a tube stop away. But —"

"Beloved, we must go now," Sebastian said. He grabbed my hand and pulled me toward a door at the opposite end of the room. "We do not have time to delay any longer."

"Just a moment, Sebastian. I'm not moving until we get a few things straightened out."

"Belle! *Le* demon!" Sally shouted, her hands gesticulating wildly.

"Yes, I know, but this should only take a couple of minutes. Until Sebastian and I have an understanding —"

A huge crash rocked the house.

"*Là, vous* see?" Sally's voice was complacent as both Sebastian and I ran for the door. "*Le* demon has blown up the house!

*J'* hope that *vous êtes* happy."

"Bloody hell . . ." I beat Sebastian to the doorway, but he grabbed my arm and pulled me behind him as he raced out into the hallway. The sharp, stinging smell of explosive powder filled the air, making my eyes stream and clogging my throat. I coughed, peering through weeping eyes at the destruction. The remains of the front door hung drunkenly open, attached only by one bent and damaged hinge. The small couch and end table that sat at the far end were covered in bits of wood and plaster, and part of something I hesitantly identified as a revenant. Tim and the others emerged from under the remains of a large potted palm that had exploded.

"Brainssssssss," came the eerie wail from the bits of revenant on the destroyed couch.

Sally picked up an unattached leg and floated her way across the debris to where the still animated upper half of William sat. "Is this yours?"

"Oooh. That looks lovely. If you could set it just here next to me . . ."

Sally was about to give the revenant his leg, but heeded the look in my eye and retreated to a corner with it instead.

Damian, crouched at the top of the stairs, peered over the rail at me, his dark hair powdered gray, but he appeared otherwise unhurt.

"Are you all right?" I asked him.

He nodded, then pointed to the gaping hole that was now the doorway. Sebastian and I turned to look.

*"Tattu!"*

The demon I'd surprised earlier stood in the doorway, its eyes glowing with hate.

"Oh, crap," Sally said, brandishing the leg as if it was a weapon. "It's *ici*."

Sebastian moved to block the demon's view of me. I stared at the back of his neck for a second, amused but touched by his protective attitude. I'd barely met the man, and already he was acting like . . . well, like a doting husband. I couldn't help wondering . . .

"*Tattu!* Come with me and I will not harm the Dark Ones."

"Who is this now?" Tim asked, giving the demon a haughty look. "Is he holding us hostage? Are we in a hostage situation? Will he adhere to the proper rules governing treatment of hostages? Shall we designate one of us as a negotiator?"

I sighed and moved to Sebastian's side to confront the demon. Sebastian stood absolutely still, his eyes the color of bleached granite, his muscles tense. I slid my hand into his, not sure whether it was to restrain him from hasty actions or to comfort myself. His fingers tightened around mine, sending a little wave of warmth up my arm.

"This woman is my Beloved," Sebastian told the demon, his body language screaming that he was not about to take anything from anyone. "You will leave now."

"Beloved?" The demon's gaze turned to me. My skin crawled as it examined me, leaving me feeling tainted and foul.

A wave of imps washed up and over the demon's feet, collecting in a pool on the hallway floor before him. They yip-yipped aggressively, hopping up and down and shaking their little fists at us until Sebastian cast a glance at them. One look from him had them scampering back to the safety of the doorway.

"Imps," said William's remains. "I could go for a nice imp fry right about now."

*You're a handy guy to have around,* I told Sebastian.

*In more ways than you can imagine,* he answered, and for one brilliant moment, my head was flooded with the most erotic images, thoughts and desires and urges that all involved me. My knees almost buckled at the things Sebastian wanted to do to me. The images were gone in a second, leaving me to wish we were alone so I could investigate futher some of the arousing thoughts he'd had. A snarl from the demon returned my attention to the moment at hand.

"The *tattu* is not your Beloved," the demon sneered at Sebastian. "You have not Joined. She belongs to my master. I will take her now, and there is nothing you can do to stop me."

"Can I have my leg back, please?"

*Beloved, we must Join now. It is the only way I can protect you.*

"*Vous et ce qui* army?" Sally floated over to stand in front of me, her arms crossed over her chest (she'd given William's leg to Tim). My heart warmed at her brave — but completely useless — attempt to protect me.

*Ysabelle, we do not have a choice. We must Join before the demon attacks. Without help, I can disable it only for a short time. It will no doubt return with minions and other demons.* Sebastian's voice was rich with regret that he was forcing a decision on me, but there was a faint echo of satisfaction that had me wondering again.

The demon walked right through Sally and stopped a few feet in front of Sebastian. It smiled. The lights in the chandelier near the stairs exploded, tiny bits of glass raining down on the floor behind us.

"Here now! Broken glass can be very dangerous!" Tim protested, taking a firm grip on William's leg as he started forward. He immediately beat a retreat when the demon turned its eyes on him. "Er . . . sorry for interrupting. Continue."

"Do not delude yourselves," the demon said. "You cannot stop me. I will have the *tattu*. Will you be destroyed as well, Dark One?"

Sebastian snarled something that was anatomically impossible (even for a demon), his muscles bunched as he was about to strike. A movement behind the demon, a dark shape faintly visible in the streetlight, caught my attention. Sebastian must have seen it as well, for his fingers loosened their painful grip on mine.

*Ysabelle, this does not change anything. The demon will return, with reinforcements. We must Join!*

"Just the foot would do. Surely you could spare me one little foot?" William pleaded with Tim.

I heaved yet another sigh, knowing in my heart that what Sebastian said was true. Now that the demon had found me, there was no way it was going to let me go. I knew even without asking that anywhere I went, it would find me, just as it found me in the middle of London.

"A couple of toes? Just tide me over?"

I had no choice. I could either save myself and Sebastian, or I could damn us both by trying to avoid the inevitable. Sebastian's thumb stroked over my hand for two heartbeats while I wrestled with my thoughts.

*What about Adrian and Damian?*

Pain lashed through him, mingling with his anger and regret and need for justice. I held my breath, knowing if he made a choice I could not condone, we were both doomed. *I will do as you demand,* he said at last, the agreement costing him much. *I will forfeit my right to revenge myself on them if you will Join with me.*

Relief filled me. *I am not going to make love to you. Especially not right here in front of everyone!* I thought at him indignantly.

*That is the preferred method, but not the only one. Another exchange of body fluids would do.*

*Body fluids?*

*Blood. I wish things were different, Beloved.*

*I know.* I smiled at him as the demon whirled around, finding itself face-to-face with a short, red-haired Guardian barely visible through the doorway.

"What —" The demon was cut off in midquestion.

238

*Now, Beloved.*

"Belle?" Sally asked, her brow puckered as Sebastian pulled me into an embrace. "What are you — *mon Dieu!* Not that!"

A disgusted "Ew!" drifted down the stairs as Sebastian's mouth descended upon mine, his lips starting a desire inside me that I doubted would ever be extinguished.

"Here, you, little boy. Fetch me that thigh I see peeking out from under the chair."

"You're gross," Damian told the remains of William.

Despite the confusion of everyone surrounding us, the demon who was now hanging upside down in the doorway screaming curses, the revenants, the imps, and Noelle dimly visible outside as she began banishing the demon, I kissed Sebastian back with every tangled, confused emotion I had, and prayed I was making the right choice.

His mouth trailed heat as he kissed a path to the base of my neck. *I wish this were different, Ysabelle. But it is right we do it.*

I said nothing as his teeth pierced my flesh, my body quivering with both the sensation of him taking life from me, and the images he was sharing with me, feelings of arousal and need, of a bone-deep satisfaction, and surprisingly, a strong sense of rightness that resonated within me. My body went up in flames as his mouth moved on my neck while he drank deeply, my breasts aching and straining against him, my hips rubbing in a suggestive manner, heat deep within my core flaring outward in a rush of ecstacy. Every inch of my flesh was sensitized to the point where I thought I would climax right then and there.

The demon screamed, causing the windows near the door to shatter. Sebastian pulled his mouth from my neck, his eyes almost ebony as he looked down at me. Without a word he kissed me again, his tongue painting the inside of my mouth with a familiar, sweet, spicy taste.

*Drink, Beloved.*

He'd nipped his tongue. As I suckled it, drunk on the heady sensation of taking from him what he'd taken from me, I merged with him, almost crying out at the dark emptiness where his soul should have been.

I filled him with as much light as I could give, dimly aware of Noelle as she yelled the words of banishment above the clamor of the revenants and imps. Sally sputtered around us helplessly, trying to gain my attention, but that was focused solely on the man I held in my arms, the man to whom I had just bound myself body and soul.

"Well, that's done." Noelle's perky voice

drifted across the hallway to us as she dusted off her hands and entered the house. "Nasty fellow. We're going to have some trouble there, Belle, now that he's seen you. Hello, Tim, nice to see you again. Did one of you explode? I found a knee out on the walkway. We'll have to . . . oh my God. Sebastian?"

I pulled away from Sebastian. His eyes were clouded as he turned to face my room-mate.

"Good evening, Noelle. You look well."

"You know each other?" I asked, looking from her to the man who still held me close to his side.

"I should say so," Noelle said, giving me an unreadable look. "I'm his Beloved."

# CHAPTER FIVE

"You *lied* to me!"

"I do not lie."

"You told me I was your Beloved!" It's difficult to put indignation, betrayal, hurt feelings, and a healthy dollop of menace into a whisper, but I gave it my best shot.

I'd quickly discovered that Sebastian's eyes were a barometer to his mood. Dark midnight gray indicated sexual arousal. The lighter his eyes turned, the less happy he was. Right now they were a pale bluish granite. "You *are* my Beloved."

"Don't you dare lighten your eyes at me," I warned. "You have no right to be angry here. I'm the victim. I'm the one you used."

Noelle, who had been standing in the middle of the hall, moved over to join our whispered conversation. The revenants were busily blockading the gaping hole where the door used to be, while Sally had been sent to double-check that all the windows on the ground floor had been warded against possible imp or demon infiltration. Damian sat on the stairs, his chin in his hands, watching everything with bright, interested eyes. The remains of William were propped up against the wall next to him, alternating between offering the revenants advice on how to use the couch to block the doorway, and pleading for just a bit of flesh to appease his hunger.

"I'm not quite sure I understand this," Noelle said slowly as she looked from me to Sebastian. "He told you that you were his Beloved?"

"Yes," I said, glaring at the man in question. He crossed his arms and tightened his jaw, as if he were going to stand there until doomsday before he spoke another word. "I believed him. I Joined with him — oh, I can't believe I fell for that old 'You're my Beloved, save my soul' line! What a fool I've been."

To my surprise, Noelle exploded in anger . . . at me. "How could you do this to me, Belle? How could you betray me like that? I thought you were a friend! I never thought you would stab me in the back!"

"Wait a second," I answered, holding up a pacifying hand. "How could I do what? I had no idea that you were anyone's Beloved, let alone his!"

She gaped at me in disbelief. "I cannot believe you can deny that just this morning I was baring my broken heart to you."

It took a second for me to put the pieces together. I blamed my sorry mental state on Sebastian. "The man who dumped you was Sebastian?"

"Of course it was!"

I turned my attention to him. "You *dated* my roommate?"

His jaw tightened. "I refuse to be drawn into this argument. You are my Beloved. We are Joined. You belong to me now, and nothing and no one can sunder that."

"She is not your Beloved, I am," Noelle said, socking Sebastian on the arm. I knew just how she felt. "You admitted as much the last time we went out."

"You have two Beloveds?" I asked. "Is such a thing possible?"

"I have only one. You are she," he answered, with a particularly obstinate set to his jaw.

"You can say that as much as you like — it won't change the facts," Noelle whispered fiercely. "I know the truth."

Sebastian had evidently had enough. He grabbed me by the wrist and started pulling me toward the door. "It is a waste of time to stand here and argue. We must leave this house immediately. I must move Ysabelle to a safe area before I contact the demon who is no doubt rallying an army to take her."

My heart felt like a lead weight, thumping painfully in my chest. My mind was numb with disbelief and confusion. I'd felt the emotions inside Sebastian — he truly believed we belonged together. But how could that be if Noelle was his Beloved? And how could I stay with him when I knew how heartbroken she was over his refusal? "I'm sorry, Sebastian, but I'm not going anywhere with you until we get this sorted out."

"There's nothing to sort out!" he bellowed, causing everyone in the hall to stop what they were doing. "You are my Beloved! You hold the key to my salvation. We are Joined! Previous relationships are not relevant here!"

"*Qu'est-ce fiche* he say?" Sally stopped in the center of the hall. "Noelle is his Beloved, *aussi?*"

"Please, Sally, not now," I said absently, trying to make sense of the confusion.

"Evidently the Dark One used to date the Guardian," William's remains said with a sickening cheerfulness. "This is as good as a telly show, eh, lad? Wish I had a little something to eat while we watch. Do you

. . . eh . . . need all ten of those fingers?"

Damian scooted down to a different stair.

*"La la,"* Sally said, looking at Sebastian. "*Il doit être* Mr. Sexy Pants to have *deux* Beloveds."

"Prove it," Noelle said to Sebastian, ignoring everyone else as she confronted him. She straightened her jacket and gave him a quelling look.

"Prove what?" I asked, torn by the conviction that Sebastian spoke the truth.

"If she's your Beloved," she said, "and you Joined, then where's your soul?"

I looked at him, remembering the dark, tormented emptiness inside him. *You didn't get your soul back?*

He hesitated a few moments before answering. *It may take some time before I have it.*

I closed my eyes against the pain that swamped me at the unspoken acknowledgement. *She's your real Beloved, isn't she?*

*No. She is a Beloved, but not mine. In all senses of the word but one, you are my Beloved. Can you not feel how we complete each other? You bring me light, Ysabelle. You stir feelings in me I never imagined existed. I want to protect you, to keep you safe. I wish to spend the remainder of my life discovering all there is to know about you. I have known you less than an hour, but already you have become vital to me. Only a Beloved could bind me to her in such a way. You complete me. We are one now, and nothing Noelle or anyone else says can change that.*

I stood with my arms wrapped around myself, sorrow stinging behind my eyelids. Sebastian didn't try to touch me, just stood watching me, his mind open to mine, willing me to merge with him to read the truth for myself. I allowed my mind to fuse with his, rocked by the powerful emotions he held in check. He didn't lie — he was thoroughly convinced that we were meant to be together, that my very presence brought him immeasurable pleasure.

How on earth could I resist a man who so completely believed the sun rose and set on my word?

How could I betray the one friend who had stood by my side for so many years?

"What you're saying is that she's your Beloved in name, but I'm your Beloved in fact? Is such a thing possible?"

"Yes." With infinite gentleness, his thumb brushed away a tiny little tear that had crept from my eye. *Forgive me, Belle. I would have saved you this pain if I could.*

"So touching," Tim said quietly to another of the revenants. "Just like a chick flick."

"That it is," the revenant named Jack agreed. "Romantic."

"Romantic, my arse. I'm sitting here starving to death, and all you can do is yammer on about this drivel? Someone give me a bite to eat!" William's remains demanded.

Damian stood, picked up William's discarded leg, and walloped the half-a-revenant over the head with it.

*You don't believe me?* Sebastian asked.

*Yes, I believe you.* I couldn't disbelieve him — the regret he felt was so strong I didn't need to merge with him to feel it.

"Noelle?" Her stormy green eyes turned to me. "I have known you your entire life. Your mother gave you into my care when you became a Guardian, but I think we've become more than just roommates — you are my friend, and I love you. I would never hurt you. I know you and Sebastian had a less than amicable parting, but what I want to know now — what I *need* to know is what your feelings are for him. Are you . . . are you in love with him?"

"Well, it doesn't matter now what I feel, does it? You've gone and Joined with him. There's nothing left for me," she snapped, the words hurting me almost as much as the anger in her eyes.

"Noelle —"

"*Zut. Elle est tres* pissed," Sally said in a clearly audible undertone.

"Very," Tim said, nodding.

"I'm leaving now," Noelle said with icy dignity, gathering her bag of tools. She marched to the door, ruthlessly pulling down the barricade the revenants were building from bits of the door and part of the couch. "I am bound by the laws governing the Guardian's Guild to answer any summons you may make for help with a demon, but I would advise you to think twice before you call. I fear I would be quite, quite delayed in answering."

"Noelle, please, we can talk about this —"

She ignored my outstretched hand and marched out of the house, her back rigid.

I dropped my hand, pained by her actions but aware that I had hurt her deeply.

"She will understand in time," Sebastian told me, his fingers whispering across my cheek. "Do not feel guilty, Belle. You are innocent of any wrongdoing."

"*Où* the imps *sont allées?*" Sally asked, peering out into the darkness as the revenants rebuilt their barricade.

"They probably went back to Abaddon." With reluctance, I took a step back from Sebastian. I needed time to think things out, and I couldn't do that with him touching me, stirring feelings that had lain dormant for so long.

"That should hold it," Tim said as the men moved the last bit of hall furniture across the doorway. "We should be safe from those little yellow devils now."

"I could eat them, you know," the remains of William answered. "I'd be happy to do it. That would solve a big part of the problem, wouldn't it? I could probably put away a couple dozen braces of imps with no difficulty."

Sally frowned, looking up and down the street before coming back into the hall. "*Non. Les* imps don't just disappear, *hein?* They *doivent être* banished properly by *le* Guardian. *Ils ont disparu* somewhere else."

I frowned at her words, glancing through the part of the doorway visible around edges of the barricades. "They don't go off on their own? Then where did they go?"

A muffled crashing noise drifted up from beneath the floor. We all looked down.

"You checked the windows?" I asked Sally. "They were all warded?"

"Well . . . *oui*. So far as I know. *Je ne* quite sure what a ward looks like. . . ."

Sebastian swore.

"What's down in the basement?" I looked at Damian.

"It matters not. Beloved, we must leave now." Sebastian grabbed my hand and tried to haul me toward the door.

"Nothing is down there," Damian answered, shrugging. "A few broken crates, the furnace, a wine rack with no wine in it, and one of those big old-fashioned radios that Papa says everyone used to listen to."

Sebastian's gaze met mine. "Furnace?" I asked him.

"Pilot light," he answered, and without another word, snatched the back of Damian's shirt with one hand and my arm with another, kicking aside the barricade before shoving us both through the doorway. "Run!" he ordered.

I grabbed Damian and ran down the steps to the street below, heartened to see the revenants and Sally spilling out of the house after us. Sebastian brought up the rear.

"Here, what about me?" wailed a voice from within the house.

"Oooh, we've left Will," Jack the revenant said, but the rest of his sentence was drowned out by a loud explosion. Sebastian hurled himself at me, knocking both Damian and me to the ground, covering us when a fireball exploded from the house, consuming everything in its path.

# CHAPTER SIX

"Damn the imps," Tim muttered, as behind us Sebastian's door closed. Ah, sanctuary.

I collapsed into the nearest chair, heedless of the soot that no doubt came off my charred clothing. "Amen to that."

"Mmrfm wbrbl mnplm." Damian, on his way to investigate the video-game equipment in the entertainment center also housing a flat-screen television, paused long enough to pull a faintly smoking object out of a plastic carrier bag. He set the remains of William's remains — now just a blackened head — on the coffee table, propping it up next to a bowl of seashells.

"Ta, lad," William's head said politely. "I'm a bit peckish . . . anyone not using all their fingers or toes?"

"Did we have to bring *that?*" Sebastian asked, glaring at William's head. William grinned back and blew a kiss.

"Tim felt it would be wrong to leave a

sentient body . . . er . . . part of a body behind," I explained wearily. "I suppose I can see his point. Once a revenant, always a revenant, until the entire body is destroyed."

"That's right, and I've still got me old noggin," William said, nodding. Unfortunately, the act sent the head rolling across the table until it was lying upside down.

Damian shoved it aside to perch on the coffee table, a game controller in his hand.

"Ooh, Xbox 360 car racing!" William said. "Give us a turn, will you? I love this one."

Sebastian's look become more pointed as Damian set a controller before William's head and positioned it so it could be manipulated by the revenant's mouth.

"I admit it's stretching the precepts set down by the Society a bit far, but his head is still sentient."

"Vroom!" William said. Sebastian pursed his lips.

"Okay, just barely, but it still seemed wrong to leave him behind just because the imps blew up the rest of his body."

"I'm done. Next!" Jack said as he emerged from the suite's guest bathroom. Although we'd all survived Damian's house exploding, we were all a bit singed about the edges and covered in soot and dirt.

"Ysabelle?" Tim asked.

I waved an exhausted hand. "I'll wait. You all go ahead."

"You may clean up in my bathroom while I have a word with you," Sebastian said, hauling me to my feet again. "The bedroom is through here."

"Dibs on *le* couch," said Sally as Tim kindly let her out of another carrier bag. "Oooh! *Très bon* hotel room, Sebastian! *Je l'aime*. Is there service *du* food *en la* room? *Je suis* starved."

"I have a few things I'd like to say to you, as well, but I'm not going into your bedroom," I told Sebastian, sitting back down.

He stood in front of me, his hands on his hips. *Why not?*

*Because you'll just try to seduce me, and quite frankly, I'm not sure I could resist.*

The rotter had the nerve to smile. It lit his eyes, sending little tremors of excitement through me. *We are Joined. We will be together until the end of our days. Your body belongs to me, and mine to you. There is nothing wrong with me seducing you now.*

"I'm sure that's what you think, but I still have a billion or so issues to work through over this whole Beloved thing," I said blandly, and refused to let him pull me out of the chair again.

"*Est ce le* bedroom? Oooh! Huge bed!"

Sally drifted into the bedroom.

"Anything you have to say you can say to me here," I told Sebastian as he continued to glare and send me thoughts that just about steamed my blood. "There's nothing you can't say in front of my friends."

"That's right," Tim said, emerging from the bathroom with a damp shirt but a clean face. "I feel we owe a lot to Ysabelle. Clearly you two are having some sort of relationship crisis, and we all want you to know that we're here to help you work it out."

The other revenants nodded. Sebastian said rude things in French under his breath.

"That's very sweet of you. I greatly appreciate the support, although I'm a bit concerned about your safety." I glanced at Sebastian. "How long do you think we have before the demon tracks me down again?"

Before I could brace myself, he grabbed my wrists and pulled me into his arms. *You are the single most irritatingly stubborn woman I have ever met.*

I kissed the tip of his nose. "Oddly enough, I was just about to say the same about you. How long do we have, do you think?"

He sighed, his hands stroking gently down my back. My body — against my better intentions — melted against him. "I would say an hour or less, depending on the resources the demon is able to utilize. If it searches for you on its own, longer. If it rallies an army, perhaps twenty minutes at best. I must find it before it does either."

"Find it? Why find it? It's going to be here soon enough," I pointed out.

"I must destroy it before it can find you again," he answered, striding to a desk upon which sat a black attaché case. He rifled through it and extracted a small burgundy notebook. I couldn't help watching him move, admiring the lines of his impressive body, the strength and controlled power that he seemed to bear so easily. His every movement was filled with an almost feline grace that warned of a ruthless, potent being behind the sophisticated exterior.

"How do you destroy a demon?" Tim asked, holding out a chair for Sally. She beamed at him.

I raised an eyebrow at Sebastian, waiting for his answer. He didn't look at me. "A Guardian can destroy demons."

Tim glanced at me. "That's the only way?"

"Not the only way, no. Talismans created for that purpose can also be used, but unfortunately, the one I was trying to locate has no doubt been destroyed in the fire that claimed the Betrayer's house."

"A talisman?"

The color in Sebastian's eyes faded. "Yes. A ring of power, actually. It was thin, rimmed with gold, made of horn."

"Oh, you're talking about that ring you mentioned when you staggered into the house. I don't know where it is."

"It was in the possession of the Betrayer. In the right hands, it was capable of the destruction of the demon lord and his minions." His hands tightened on the notebook. "But now it is destroyed."

"It's broken, but not destroyed," a voice piped up over the muted sound of electronic cars racing down virtual country roads.

We all turned to look at Damian.

"You've seen the ring?" I asked him.

He shrugged, his eyes still on the TV. Beside him, William's head grunted as it manipulated the controller with his mouth. "Yes. It broke when Nell saved Papa. He gave me the pieces, saying it was a souvenir."

The last hour and a half spent talking to fire officials made it clear that there was not going to be anything salvageable from the house. "Damian, I'm sorry — I thought you heard when the fire captain said that the fire destroyed everything in the house. Not even a magical ring could survive it."

"The ring isn't in the house," he said, his

shoulders twitching as he manipulated his virtual car through a hairpin turn.

Sebastian all but pounced on the boy, grabbing him by both arms. "Where is the ring now, boy?"

"You're hurting me," Damian said, frowning.

Sebastian loosened his grip. We all watched breathlessly as Damian reached into his pocket and pulled out an assortment of grubby items. He picked carefully through bits of string, a couple of shiny rocks, a key, hard sweets, and assorted fluff to pluck out three items. He handed them to me. Everyone but Damian and William's head crowded around me to see the three thin bits of curved metal that lay across my palm. They looked more like a broken hoop earring than a ring. I touched one of the pieces. "This is a ring of power?"

Sebastian slumped down onto the love seat, his eyes closed for a moment. "It *was.*"

"Hmm." The pieces of the ring lay cool on my hand. I touched them, pushing them into a rough circle, looking closely at the edges of the breaks. "This isn't gold. It's carmot."

"Carmot? What's that?" Jack the revenant asked, peering at the ring so closely his nose almost touched my hand.

"Have you ever heard of a man named Edward Kelley?" I asked Sebastian.

He frowned for a moment. "No."

"Really? Erm . . . how old are you?"

"Two hundred and seventeen," he said, looking nonplussed for a moment.

"Ah. That would explain it. Edward Kelley was a bit before your time — he was an alchemist during the reign of Elizabeth the First."

Sebastian's eyes narrowed on my hand. "That ring was reputed to have been created in the mid-sixteenth century."

I nodded. "Edward Kelley claimed to have found the tomb of a bishop in Wales that contained not only the basis for his tinctures, which would transmute base metals into gold, but also of a manuscript that explained the secrets of the manufacture of the tinctures. He was a fraud, of course, since the tinctures were not as he claimed, but he did contribute one true finding to science — carmot, the basis for which philosophers' stones were made, and, when treated properly, a yellow metal a thousand times more rare than mere gold. This ring was made of horn and carmot, not gold."

"Why do I suspect there is more to this than a rare substance?" Sebastian asked, his gaze steady on me.

I smiled, my fingers closing over the broken bits of ring. "Because you're a smart man. One of the reasons carmot was used for items of great importance like this ring is because of its restorative property."

"Restorative in what manner?"

My smile deepened as I whispered three words: *magis plana conligatio.*

Before I could open my hand, Sebastian was on his feet, his expression startled. I stood as well, turning over my hand as I opened my fingers. The pieces burned a bright reddish gold for a moment before subsiding into a more mundane horn ring edged in a gold-colored metal.

"You remade it," Sebastian said, touching the ring with the tip of his finger, as if he were worried it would break again. "But . . . how?"

"Anyone who knows about carmot knows how to restore it to its manufactured form," I said, and pressed the ring into his hand. My fingers touched the pulse of his wrist. "I am giving this to you now because I know you will not use it unwisely."

His gaze flickered to Damian, now thoroughly engrossed in the video game. "I made a vow to you, Beloved. I am a man of my word."

I touched his cheek, the anguish inside

him so great it leeched into me. *I know you are. I could not have bound myself to you if you were anything but an honorable man. I'm just sorry that I couldn't give you back your soul.*

*Do not worry, Beloved. I can exist without a soul — so long as I have you.*

I didn't know what to say to that. Sebastian seemed to have no difficulty sharing his thoughts and feelings with me, blithely accepting his emotions rather than questioning how such a strong relationship could develop almost instantly. I couldn't deny that some pretty strong emotions were building within me on what seemed to be a minute-by-minute basis, but I was not yet ready to either confront or accept them. There were other issues to deal with first.

"That's amazing," Tim said, peeking over Sebastian's shoulder to see the ring. "You just pressed it together?"

"*Elle est la fille de* alchemist," Sally said, sashaying forward to look at the ring.

I frowned at her.

"You are? I didn't know they still had such things," Tim said.

"They don't. If the loo is free, I'll go clean up."

"Who exactly was Edward Kelley?" Se-

bastian asked, following me into the bathroom.

The revenants had left me a clean towel. I
scrubbed my face and neck, wishing I had a
change of clothes. "He was a liar and a thief,
a man whose ears were cut off early in his
career as a laywer because of fraud. He later
turned his talent for prevarication to al-
chemy."

"But it wasn't all false, was it?" Sebastian
fingered the ring. "This carmot seems
legitimate enough."

"It is. Carmot is the one thing in Kelley's
life that was real, only he didn't understand
that until the end of his life."

"What happened to him?"

I rinsed out the now-soiled towel. "The
common belief is that he died during an attempt to break out of a Bohemian prison."

"The common belief? What's the truth?"

"Mind if I use your brush? Thanks." I tow-
eled my hair quickly to get any soot out of
it, then applied Sebastian's brush to the
unruly mess, studying myself in the mirror.
What could Sebastian see in my face? My
eyes? Did he see the truth, or had some inner sense prompted him to press the subject? "He lost a leg during the prison break
attempt, but he survived. He lived in seclu-
sion for several years more, a broken man

who could never recapture the fleeting fame he acquired in his earlier years."

"I assume he had a family?" Sebastian's eyes were watchful. Damn him, he knew.

"That would be a reasonable assumption." I set down the brush and turned to face him. "He had two children by a Gypsy woman: a son and a daughter. One was captured and burned at the stake for his sins. The other escaped and was not heard of or seen again."

"Fascinating," he said, but I could tell what was coming next, and I dreaded it. Offense was my only option.

"If your next question is going to be, 'Was his daughter named Ysabelle?' I will walk out of the room."

Three seconds passed. "Was his daughter named —"

I left the room. "Damian, I'm going to have to go out with Sebastian for a bit. You're perfectly safe here, but Sally will stay with you —"

"Oy!" Sally said at the same time Sebastian, emerging from the bathroom, announced that I would not be accompanying him.

"Why not?"

He slipped on his coat and tucked the ring into the pocket. *You do not seriously believe*

*I would allow you to come within range of this demon's powers?*

*I thought the whole point of us Joining was to keep me safe from the demon.*

*It was. And you are safer now that your souls are bound to me, but if the demon destroys me, you will be unprotected again.*

I rolled my eyes. "Then you should stay here, and I'll use the ring to destroy it."

"That would be the height of foolishness."

I started to bristle at the implication, but common sense kicked in and reminded me that while I was many things, powerful enough to destroy a demon was not on the list.

"You will stay here with the others where you are safe. I will destroy this demon, and return to you as soon as I am able." He moved to the desk and flipped open an address book. "Then we'll alert the Guardian that Asmodeus will shortly be making an appearance."

"Asmodeus?" I asked, startled. "Isn't that the one who held you prisoner —"

"Yes," Sebastian said with a smile. At the sight of it, a burning memory coursed through me. "The demon belonged to Asmodeus. I have no doubt that by now, the demon has told its master of the existence of a *tattu* in London. By destroying the

264

demon, I will draw Asmodeus himself out."

I said nothing, rubbing my arms against the sudden chill that gripped me. Sebastian was almost through the door when he paused and looked back at me.

*Beloved? You are distressed. You burn with fever.*

*It's not a fever, and yes, I'm distressed. I understand why you wish to destroy Asmodeus, but I don't like the way thoughts of revenge consume you.*

His eyes glittered, pale. I felt his curiousity, but all he asked was, *Why?*

The air left my lungs, making it diffcult for me to breathe. I rubbed my arms, reminding myself where I was, that there was no threat to me in this hotel room. Despite that, my flesh crawled. Black dots appeared before my eyes. I couldn't breathe, I couldn't think. I was trapped, immobile, a prisoner of my own mind. Panic mingled with dread, flooding me with its inky, blistering presence, consuming every bit of me until nothing was left but a charred shell.

# CHAPTER SEVEN

Sebastian reached me before I hit the floor, shouldering aside the revenants and Sally as they asked questions about what was happening.

"I will see to her," Sebastian said to Sally as she ignored the closed door and followed us into his bedroom.

"She is my charge," Sally started to say, but Sebastian cut her off, waving her out of the room.

"She is mine now. I will let no harm befall her."

To my great surprise, Sally just looked at him for a few seconds, nodded, then left without even glancing toward me. I felt oddly bereft . . . for the space of time it took for Sebastian to lay me on the bed.

"Why did you not tell me, Beloved?" he asked, his fingers gently brushing a strand of hair back from my cheek.

I turned my face so I wouldn't have to see

the pity in his eyes. He didn't like that, gently but irresolutely forcing me to meet his gaze.

"It was not your brother who was burned at the stake for his father's sins, was it?"

"No," I said, choking on the word, desperately pushing back the memories.

Sebastian slid behind me, cradling me against his chest. I fought the temptation for a moment, but he offered too much of a sanctuary to resist.

"I have not asked you how you became a *tattu* because I felt you would tell me when you trusted me," he said. I turned in his arms, holding him tight as I buried my head in his neck. Tears, hot and thick, squeezed out of my tightly shut eyes. Desperate to escape my own torturous mind, I merged with him, falling into the blackness that filled him. "Do you wish now to tell me how that came about?"

Images flashed through my mind — a gray-haired man bent over a flame, muttering obscure alchemical spells as he poured one liquid into another; another gray-haired man, flinching as the first swore eternal vengeance for his betrayal; the flash and pomp of Elizabeth's court; the snow and sleet of endless icy winters in Prague; the smell of smoke as it curled up around me, stealing from me not only my breath, but my very life.

"Your father threatened another?" Sebastian's voice was soft and caressing, his presence calming the panic within me. I didn't want to answer his questions, didn't want to think back on that part of my life, but I knew I would have to sometime soon if I wanted him to understand me.

"Edward Kelley befriended a scholar named John Dee early in his life. Dee helped him with much of the alchemical work he later used to parlay favors and money from various monarchs and patrons. But Dee realized that Kelley was little more than a con artist and broke off relations with him. Kelley had some success with carmot, but never fully understood its properties, and soon Dee's fame eclipsed his. He swore vengeance, claiming Dee stole his ideas and his alchemical formulas, going so far as to invoke a curse on Dee."

Sebastian's hands stroked my back. I shuddered back the anguish that welled up inside me at the memories, taking a small shred of comfort that the soulless, tortured Sebastian was one of the few people walking the earth who shared with me the ability to survive such profound torment. It was a bond of sorts, a wordless bond, but one I felt to my very bones as he offered me acceptance and understanding.

"He went to Prague to gain help from a sympathetic Emperor Rudolph in bringing Dee's downfall, but things soured, as they always did for him. When he was imprisoned in Prague by Emperor Rudolph, I was arrested as his assistant. My younger brother had been smuggled out of the country by my deceased mother's relatives, but I was beyond their reach. I was tried and sentenced as being in league with the devil. They burned me at the stake for the mere fact that Edward Kelley was my father."

Pain at the memory choked me. Sebastian said nothing, but continued to stroke my back. I burrowed deeper against him, allowing his comfort to slowly dissipate the agony within.

"Why were you brought back as a *tattu?*" he asked softly.

I let go of the breath I hadn't been aware I was holding. "My mother's mother was a powerful woman in her family. She had Egyptian blood and was viewed as being a noble in a society that did not commonly have such distinctions. She petitioned an archangel, pointing out that as I retained my soul, I could not have been involved in my father's sin of bartering with a demon lord for the curse on Dee. It took time, but eventually the petition worked its way to a sympathetic Power. Two lifetimes after my grandmother submitted the petition for intervention, I was declared innocent by the Power and granted another life to replace the one that had been wrongly taken from me."

"And when you were reborn, you were given another soul."

"Yes." I sighed. "That was a clerical oversight, actually. A new clerk only skimmed the resurrection order. He evidently saw the words 'demon lord' and 'curse,' and assumed I was being pardoned for a crime, and granted me another during rebirth."

"A small repayment for your suffering," he murmured, his mouth close to my ear. I squirmed a little. Baring my history to him hadn't been nearly as painful as I had imagined it would be, leaving me more than a little aware of just how tightly our bodies were entwined.

"I cannot pleasure you now, my Beloved," his voice rumbled in my ear, sending breathly little shivers of excitement down my arms. "I must destroy the threats to your safety first."

I pushed myself away from him, glaring

with every morsel of indigation I could rally. "Have you heard *nothing* I've said?"

"I have heard all you have spoken and read the words on your heart, as well." He caressed my lip with his finger. I jerked my head away.

"You stupid, arrogant, revenge-minded man!" I snarled, trying to escape his grip. "I will not go through this again. I will not suffer for yet another pigheaded male whose precious ego is more important than those he is bound to!"

"I do not do this for vengeance, Belle —"

"Like hell you don't!" Although my insides felt as fragile as cracked glass, I scrambled off him, furious that I was beginning to have feelings for someone who could be so indifferent to my concerns. I stormed to the door, fully intending to grab Damian and Sally and leave him forever.

Before I could so much as blink, Sebastian was in front of me, not only blocking the door, but holding me in a steely grip that was just this side of painful.

"You will listen to me, Beloved!"

"I've listened, and you're not saying anything different —"

He clamped me tight to his chest, holding me against him with arms that felt made of titanium or some other horribly unyielding metal. My face was squished into his shoulder, making it difficult to breathe.

"I am not doing this for revenge, Belle. You are my Beloved — I must protect you. If we do not wish to constantly look over our shoulders, waiting for Asmodeus to destroy one or both of us, then I must strike now, before he has had time to rally his forces."

"But —"

"No, it must be now. Salvaticus and Vexamen are times of unbalance in Abaddon — the demon lords are watching each other suspiciously to see who will emerge as premier prince. Their attention is divided, and it is one of the few times when they are vulnerable to attack. We have no choice. We must strike quickly."

What he said made sense to my brain, but my heart, oh, my poor heart flinched in horror at the thought of someone dear to me allowing revenge to rule him.

*It does not rule me, Beloved. You do.*

I gave a watery chuckle at that thought, unable to keep my body from melting into his. *You would do anything I told you to do, then?*

*Anything so long as it would not put you in danger, yes.*

I thought long and hard then. I listened to

the slow beating of Sebastian's heart, drinking in the sight and feel and scent of him, holding them close to my heart as I considered the idea that was slowly taking form in my mind.

"Can you destroy this demon easily?"

"Using the ring you have reformed, yes."

"Do you think it has told Asmodeus about me?"

"Probably, but I doubt if he has had time to act on the information yet." Sebastian was curious about where my questions were leading, but held that in check while I worked my way through my concerns, issues, and the burgeoning idea.

"If you destroy the demon, but not Asmodeus, what will happen?"

"Asmodeus will eventually track you down, and either trick you into his power, or use me to force you to surrender your extra soul."

I thought about that for a bit, and came to a decision. "Very well, I've thought about it, and I've decided that you can destroy the demon if you like."

Laughter was rich in his voice. "How very gracious of you."

I pushed back against now gentle arms, and gave him a glare. "However, I don't want you to make an attempt on Asmodeus until I talk to the Society."

The laughter in his face and eyes faded. "Belle, I have explained to you why it is important that I strike now —"

I bit his chin. "Yes, you have, but I think we have another option. However, I must first consult one of the directors at the Revenant Society to make sure what I have in mind can be done."

Softly, his mind touched mine, his curiosity so great it made me smile. Not one for mind games, I'd normally satisfy his desire to know what I was thinking, but this was a situation I wasn't even sure was possible. *I'll tell you about it the minute I know if it's feasible,* I told him.

A war broke out within him, a desire to show confidence in me fighting with the need to protect and safeguard. The fact that he struggled so strongly touched my heart.

"I think I could very easily fall in love with you," I told him, pressing a quick kiss to his delectable lips.

His eyes darkened. "Was that meant to be a kiss? Or did you mistake me for your grandmother?"

"Hey now!" I frowned, searching his eyes. "I'll have you know that none of my husbands, not one single one of them, ever complained about my kissing skills."

"They do not matter," he said, his voice a low growl that turned my bones to jelly. I sagged against him as his mouth descended upon mine. "*I* do. Either you kiss me as I deserve, or you will not kiss me at all."

I opened my mouth to tell him what he could do with such an arrogant demand, but fell victim to my own folly when his lips took charge. His kiss was hard, hot, and absolutely unyielding. His body moved against me, his hands touching and stroking whatever he could reach, his hips urging mine into a rhythm of desire. But oh Lord, it was his mouth I couldn't resist, his lips and tongue demanding a response that I couldn't deny. By the time he broke the kiss, I was breathless, gasping for air, my mind filled with the taste and feel of him.

He looked down at me with a smug satisfaction that was wholly male. I tried to rally a morsel of dignity, a tiny shred of indignation over such a chauvinistic attitude, but my mind refused to cooperate.

"You are not to leave the suite. I will return as soon as I have destroyed the demon."

He kissed me once more, sending the few wits I desperately tried to gather flying. It wasn't until he left, tossing commands to the revenants over his shoulder, that I could put myself together enough to protest his order.

"*Vous ressemblez à vous avez été* pulled backward through *le* hedge *du* prickly," Sally said, drifting over to where I clutched the door frame to the living area. "*Vive Monsieur le* Sexy Pants, eh?"

"And how," I answered, touching my lips. They were hot and tingling, the spicy-sweet taste of Sebastian still burning on them. It matched the burn he'd started deep in me, embers of an emotion too fragile to face yet. I shook my head, wondering how he had become so much a part of me so quickly.

Sally watched me for a moment before softly asking, "*Vous l'aimez?*"

I pushed myself away from the door and went to the phone, glancing at the open notebook Sebastian had left. The name and number of a London Guardian was written in a bold hand. I flipped through the book, feeling both pleased and guilty that Noelle's name didn't appear. How could I take such pleasure in a man when it gave pain to my friend?

"Take a number and join the queue," I said, praying Noelle would forgive me for pushing her to the middle of a list of things I needed to do before all hell broke out.

"What now?" Tim asked, wandering over as I punched in a phone number. "Are you ordering dinner? I admit I'm a bit on the hungry side, and William there keeps nagging about fading away to nothing if he doesn't get some sustenance."

"I'll order some dinner for everyone — vegetarian dinner — before I leave," I told him, glancing at the clock. It wasn't too late for the one director I knew to be in the office.

"Leave?" Tim frowned. "Sebastian said that no one was to leave the suite except the Guardian you were going to call. He didn't mention anything about you going off on your own."

"It doesn't matter," I said, waving a hand as I waited for the director to pick up the phone. "You'll all be safe enough once I'm gone. I'm just going to the Society and back. Hello, River? Ysabelle Raleigh here. I wonder if you have a few minutes you could spare me. Fabulous. I'll be there in about twenty minutes, all right?"

I hung up, intending to give a few commands of my own, but when I turned to face everyone, I was met with a wall of unhappy faces.

"Erm . . ." I said, a bit surprised by the solidarity of a group of people who had so little in common. Everyone, from Damian clutching William's head by his hair, to Sally, who was supposed to support me in all that I did, stood in a line with their arms crossed over their chests, identical frowns on their faces. "I take it that plan doesn't meet with your satisfaction."

"Sebastian said no one was to leave," Tim repeated, a particularly obstinate look on his face.

"Yes, but —"

"He said the demon would grab you if you left," Damian added.

I raised an eyebrow at him. "Since when do you care what Sebastian says?"

The boy gave one of his shrugs. "Nell says we should give him a chance to get over what was done to him, so maybe he's not as bad as Papa said he was. He likes you."

I was touched by the approval inherent in his statement. "Does that mean you like me, as well?" I couldn't help asking, half teasing him.

His dark blue eyes considered me for a minute. Then just as I knew they would, his shoulders twitched in a careless shrug. "You don't stink like other Beloveds. I like *that*."

Sally snorted as I was put so soundly into my place.

"We shall be grateful for small favors,

then," I told Damian, and considered the line of people bent on keeping me from my purpose. "I suppose a promise that I won't go anywhere but the Society headquarters and straight back wouldn't merit me parole?"

Six heads shook a negative answer (William appeared to be dozing despite being held up by his hair).

I sighed. "Very well, you can come with me then, although how we're all to fit into one taxi is beyond me."

There were a few halfhearted protests, but ten minutes later we emerged from the hotel onto the damp pavement outside the hotel, both William's head and Sally in their respective travel bags.

"Stop giving me that look," I told Tim in a quiet voice as the hotel doorman waved a taxi up to us. "I told you that I'm in no danger with all of you around. It's not as if the demon is going to spring out of nowhere and capture me."

Tim opened his mouth to reply, but I never heard the words he spoke. The demon that I'd seen earlier that day ripped open a hole in the fabric of being, wrapped both arms around me, and jerked me backward, away from reality as I knew it.

# Chapter Eight

The voices were the first thing I noticed. They were oddly familiar.

"Is everyone here? Did we all make it?"

"I'm here, although I'm fair starving to death. Someone lend me a hand. Or a foot. A thigh or two wouldn't go amiss, either."

"*Je suis ici,* as well. *Zut alors! Qu'est-ce le* hell?"

"Papa says they prefer Abaddon to hell," a childish voice said. I recognized it immediately as Damian.

"Do you think Ysabelle is all right? She is very still."

That had to be Tim. I was warmed by the concern in his voice, but a bit puzzled by my eyelids' apparent inability to move. They felt as if lead weights had been anchored to them.

"Is she dead?" William's voice was shamelessly hopeful and not in the least bit muffled, which meant Damian must have taken him out of the carrier bag. "Dibs on her if she is."

"It would take a lot more than a demon yanking me through the fabric of existence to kill me," I answered without thinking. A moment later I sat bolt upright, staring around wildly as my memory returned. "The demon!"

"*Il a disparu* bye-bye *avec* my boot on its derierre," Sally told me, hovering over me with a worried look in her eyes. "*Vous* okay?"

"Yes, I'm fine." I got to my feet, feeling a bit dizzy by the experience of having been pulled through to who knew where. "Erm . . . would someone like to tell me why you're all here? I don't seem to remember the demon grabbing everyone, and the last I saw of you lot, you were about to get into a taxi."

"*Je vous* grabbed." Sally patted me carefully, as if looking for broken bones or injuries. "All right, *vous n'êtes pas blessé.*"

"Thank you for that checkup, Dr. Sally."

She sniffed and tossed her hair. "*C'est* my *travail,* if *vous* recall."

"For which I'm very grateful," I said, giving her a little hug. "Now that explains how Sally got here, but what of the rest of you?"

Damian adopted an innocent look that

was wholly at odds with his character. "Sally had a hold of me when she grabbed you. I had William."

"When I saw them hauled away with you and the demon, we jumped in after you all." Tim beamed happily at me. It was on the tip of my tongue to tell him he had probably signed his death warrant, but I couldn't reward such an act of selflessness and bravery with a dire prediction.

"Where exactly are we?" I asked, looking around. We seemed to be in some sort of dimly lit cave alcove. Large outcroppings of rock obscured the view, but odd patterns of light danced high on the wall behind me. My stomach tightened as I moved to the entrance of the alcove, stepping clear of the rock.

Fire. There was fire everywhere. Not just little campfires, the sort I'd learned to act completely normal around . . . no, this cavern was filled with great pools of fire, burning from some unknown underground source. Snaking between the great, billowing flames, a stone walkway meandered to the far end of the cavern, where a plateau held what appeared to be an office, complete with desk, chairs, bookcases, and a couple of filing cabinets.

"Oh, God's mercy, we're in Abaddon," I

said as my lungs began to struggle for air.

"No, although I suppose it's easy to see why you could imagine that."

I whirled around at the mild voice that spoke behind me, my hand already at my throat. The sight of the flames, the smell of the smoke, threatened to overwhelm me. Desperately, I fought to keep under control the panic that welled within me. "Who are you?"

"I am Simon," the demon said. It appeared in human form, that of a young man with a weak chin and blond goatee. The demon waved its hand toward the narrow path. "I am the steward to Asmodeus. I have never met a *tattu* before — it is a great honor to have you here."

"Where is here if not Abaddon?" I asked.

"This is my lord Asmodeus's home. He prefers this design to the mundane houses, but technically, we are within the boundaries of London."

"This is all just an illusion, then?" Tim asked, looking around the huge, smoke-filled cavern.

The demon hesitated a moment. "In a manner of speaking, yes. This location is actually in a house, but it has been altered to an appearance more pleasing to my lord."

"Damian, come stand by me," I said

softly, holding out my hand for him.

Damian rolled his eyes, picked up William's head, and reluctantly joined me. I wrapped my arm around his shoulders, giving the demon a firm look to let it know I would defend the child at all costs.

"I wonder, what does demon taste like?" William's head asked no one in particular.

"Duck, I'm told," Simon answered, then gestured again toward the path. "If you please? Lord Asmodeus is most eager to meet you."

I glanced at the huge pits ablaze with the fires of hell, and shook my head. "Illusion or not, I'm staying right where I am."

Simon tipped its head to look at me. "Afraid of the fires, are you? That's not good. That's not good at all."

"How so?" I asked, one eye on the nearest conflagration. I felt sick to my stomach at its nearness, my psyche shrieking to get out of there by any means possible, but I couldn't leave Damian and my friends.

"I believe I'll let my lord answer that. If you please?"

I took a deep breath. "You can tell Asmodeus that I'm not going anywhere, and if he wants to talk to me, he can just get his pox-riddled behind over here to —"

A noise unlike anything I've ever heard in

this world or the next shook the cavern, echoing off the high stone walls, doubling and tripling on itself. The flame pits erupted in bonfires that nearly touched the ceiling, the fire and horrible scream almost enough to bring the entire structure down upon us. I pulled Damian behind me, trying to shield him as I backed up against the wall and prayed the glamour or whatever was being used to create this illusion was strong enough to protect the physical world from this nightmare.

Eventually, the noised died down, and the flames dropped to their normal level. My hands shook as I dusted off Damian, making sure he wasn't injured before turning to face the demonic steward.

Simon glanced nervously toward the distance corner of the cave. "I respectfully suggest you not anger my lord again. He does not take well to being told what to do."

"He can bite my shiny pink —"

Sally shut up with a look from me, but she muttered several rude threats in her odd mixture of English and mangled French. I examined my options quickly and decided that I really didn't have a choice.

"Fine. I will go speak to Asmodeus. But he must first release my friends." Sally, Tim, and Jack all protested, but I held up a hand to stop them, keeping my gaze firmly on Simon. "I will go just as soon as my friends are released, but not before."

I half expected another roar from the demon lord, but to my surprise, Simon smiled. "But, my good lady, your friends are not prisoners here. They may leave at any time."

"They may?" I blinked a couple of times, then glanced at the fire pits. There had to be a trick somewhere. "Very well. You will escort them out. Once they are safely outside this building, I will see Asmodeus."

The demon gave me a look that said it was humoring me, but put two fingers in its mouth and blew a sharp whistle. A small demon in running shorts and a dirty T-shirt appeared before it. "Wassup?"

"These people . . . er . . . revenents, Dark One, and spirit need escorting outside. See to it."

The little demon looked curiously at me, its eyes opening wide when it noticed my double souls. Its lips pursed together, but before my friends could protest again, it ripped open the fabric of being, shoving them through it with one last look at me.

"How do I know they're safe?" I asked, immediately seeing the flaw in my hastily thought-up plan.

Simon rolled its eyes, and gently shoved me toward the path. "Asmodeus has no interest in them. Mind the lava."

"Lava. Such a quaint touch," I murmured as I stepped carefully over a thin trickle of molten rock, careful to stay as far away from the raging pits of fire as was possible. I am not ashamed to admit that there were two times on the journey across the cavern floor where I came close to turning tail and bolting, but each time Simon seemed to sense my rising panic, and stopped long enough for me to regain composure.

"Here we are, then, all safe and sound. Well . . . for the moment." Simon's smile as we crested the plateau was feeble even by demonic standards, and did nothing to promote a feeling of security. "My most gracious lord, the *tattu* is here."

For the most part, my life has been sheltered. I've seen monarchs and politicians rise to power and fall away into obscurity. Radicals, geniuses, madmen . . . they've all crossed my path at some time or other. But with very few exceptions (Sally being one of them), they have all been mortal. The Society has been a recent phenomenon, forming a shy fifty years ago, and although my work there has afforded me a chance to mingle with other immortal beings, I seldom do. Asmodeus was the first demon lord I'd ever seen, and I had to admit that I was somewhat disappointed by the mundane appearance of the man who rose from behind a desk to greet me. He could be any fifty-something businessman crowded into the London tube, clutching a briefcase and a copy of a morning paper.

"If you like, I can adopt a more fearsome appearance," he told me, apparently reading my mind. "And no, I can't read your mind. That, to my great regret, has been a skill that has eluded me."

I blinked twice. "If you can't read minds, then how did you know what I was thinking?"

He reached out to touch my face. I took a step backward, out of his reach. Simon said something about attending to other business and slipped out a door built into the rock wall.

Asmodeus's hand fell. He propped one hip up on his desk, his arms crossed as he considered me. "I am quite adept at reading expressions, and your look of surprise at my mortal appearance presented no difficulty in interpreting. Do I frighten you?"

I swallowed hard, ignoring the urge to look behind me at the room filled with fire while wondering whether I could pull off a bald-faced lie. I've never been good at deceit, so I decided to go with honesty. "Very much so. What exactly do you believe you are going to do with me? I am a Beloved, bound to a Dark One."

"You are *tattu*," he said simply, falling silent for a moment.

I willed my body into quietude despite the horrible need to fidget . . . if not outright run away screaming at the top of my lungs.

"You have that rarest of things, a perfectly pure soul."

"I have two pure souls," I said, throwing caution to the wind.

"No, you have the soul you were originally born with and the second, which I assume was granted at a rebirth. The first is flawed; it is the second that I desire."

"You can't have it." I rallied enough inner strength to carry my trembling legs over to a chair, which I sat down upon in a sudden manner that belied my brave words. "It's mine. They both are, flawed or not. They're mine, and I have no intention of giving either up."

"Do you have any idea what a perfectly pure soul means to me?" he asked with deceptive mildness — deceptive but for the sudden light of unholy greed that shone in his eyes. Just meeting his gaze took a year or two off my life. I looked down at my hands, which were clutching each other. Chills ran down my back and legs, my stomach tightening into a leaden wad.

I shook my head.

"A soul affords me power. But a perfectly pure soul, one untainted by its bearer, can provide me with almost unlimited power. With a soul such as yours in my possession, my ascension to the throne of Abaddon is guaranteed."

My stomach roiled at the thought of my beautiful clean soul being soiled and ultimately destroyed in Asmodeus's attempt to become premier prince of hell.

"You can't have it," I said in a low voice, gripping the arms of the chair so hard my fingernails bent. "I will go back to the Akashic Plain before I allow you to destroy something so good."

He smiled, and for a second, I saw his true form. A red wave swept down over my vision, blinding me, stripping me of air and thought and, for a brief moment, the desire to live.

*I never thought of you as a quitter,* a soft voice said, imbuing me with feelings of being loved and cherished and valued above all things.

*Sebastian?*

*I am here, Beloved. I will be with you mo-
mentarily. Do not allow Asmodeus to frighten
you. I will not allow any harm to come to you.*

*Where have you been? Why haven't you
talked to me? You left and I couldn't mind-talk
with you.*

Regret mingled with sorrow leeched into
my brain. *I apologize. I was indisposed. But
now I am back, and together, we are more
powerful than you can imagine.* His mind
brushed mine with an emotion that I
couldn't mistake.

*Do you always fall in love with women so
quickly?* I asked, half joking.

*You are the only one, Belle.*

*Where are you?*

*Near. I will be with you in a few minutes.*

I lifted my chin, and kept my gaze steady
on Asmodeus. "I don't see that we have
anything further to discuss. I have no intention of relinquishing my soul to you, and
there is no way you can force me to do it."

He smiled again, but this time I was ready
for it.

*Good girl,* Sebastian said, his thoughts full
of approval. *You have been tempered. You
can withstand this.*

"I hate to disappoint such faith, my dear,
but time grows short." Asmodeus raised his
voice. "Simon, bring in Orinel."

The door opened just enough for Simon to poke his face through the crack. "My lord, there has been a . . . an unforseen event."

Asmodeus frowned. "Spare me your gibberish and summon Orinel and its prisoner to me."

If it were possible for a demon's face to grow pale, Simon's did. "Er . . . my lord . . ."

The door burst open at that moment, sending Simon flying into the room. He landed in a heap at my feet, but made no move to rise. I stood slowly as a man entered the room, moving as silently as panther. A blond panther.

"Asmodeus. I would be lying if I said it was a pleasure to meet you again," Sebastian said, holding out a hand for me. I stepped over Simon's inert form and took his hand, his fingers tightening around mine. "Although I admit to looking forward to this moment for a very long time."

The demon lord frowned a second time. "Where is Orinel?"

"The demon has been destroyed." Sebastian lifted his hand to show the ring of power on his thumb. "I believe I took it by surprise, since it spent a good five minutes before I dispatched it telling me of your plan to capture me and use me to force Belle into compliance."

At the sight of the ring, a red light shone in Asmodeus's eyes, but it quickly faded into one of speculation.

"That ring was destroyed."

"It was remade."

Asmodeus nodded. "The folly of alchemists and their precious carmot. Very well, we are at an impasse. You have my ring of power, and I have your Beloved. How do you suggest we proceed?"

Sebastian released my hand and pulled me close to his side. "Belle and I will leave with the ring in our possession. You will be allowed to continue as you are, until such time as you attempt to harm either of us. At that point, I will use the ring to destroy you just as I have done your minion."

*Is the ring powerful enough to destroy a demon lord?*

*In the right hands it is.*

Asmodeus looked thoughtful for a moment. "That is not acceptable. I, however, have a solution to the situation. In exchange for your Beloved's extra soul, a soul, I might point out, she has no need or use for, I will swear an oath to never harm you or your families."

Sebastian was shaking his head even

before the demon lord stopped talking.

I took a step away before Sebastian could refuse Asmodeus's ridiculous suggestion. Unless I did something, I knew the situation would deteriorate quickly.

"I just want to make sure I have this all straight in my mind," I said quickly. I backed up a couple of steps until my back was to the fiery hell pits. "You're not going to let us walk out of here unless I relinquish one of my souls, are you?"

Asmodeus pursed his lips. "No. Sebastian may hold the ring of power, and he may possess enough power to use it against me, but he would be destroyed in the attempt. You are his Beloved. He will not do anything to endanger you, including bringing his own life to an end."

I looked at Sebastian. The truth was in his eyes.

*Do not listen to his lies. I have power enough to destroy him.*

*I know you do,* I answered gently. But I also knew that Asmodeus spoke the truth . . . the attempt would end in Sebastian's destruction as well, and that I could not tolerate.

I looked at the cavern that yawned behind me, at the still-inert demon lying at the feet of the chair, at the man and the demon lord before me. A time had come that I suddenly felt as if I'd been waiting for all the years of my life. I prayed that what I was about to do would work. If it didn't . . . well, I'd been through that, as well.

"There is only one path open to me." My heart sang as I acknowledged the emotions that had been blossoming since I had first seen Sebastian. *I know you haven't asked me, and it's only been a short time that we've known each other, but somehow, I've fallen in love with you. I never thought I would willingly sacrifice myself for another, but you are more important than even my life.*

*Belle —* he started to say, but I held up a hand to stop him.

"A soul cannot be taken away by force," I said, my love for him all but bursting from me. "It must be freely given. Sebastian de Mercier, I do willingly cede unto you my soul. Bear it with all the love I have for you."

Sebastian knew at that moment what I was going to do. Asmodeus screamed as Sebastian leaped forward to me, but I stepped backward, off the stone plateau, down into the flames that called my name.

*I love you beyond life itself,* was my last thought to Sebastian before I was consumed by the fire.

# CHAPTER NINE

*Such a dramatic exit.*

  *Oh, be quiet.*

*If I'd known you were capable of such acting, I would have suggested that you simply brazen your way out of the situation.*

  *Such a funny man.*

*You had me believing you were sacrificing yourself.*

  *I wasn't sure it would work. I didn't have time to talk to the director about whether a soul transfer could be conducted via a sacrifice.*

  *Had I known of your plan, I wouldn't even have bothered to destroy Orinel. You could have acted him to a grave.*

I reached behind Sebastian and pinched his delectable rear. *One more smart comment like that, and I'll regret thinking I was dying for you.*

Immediately, my head and heart were flooded with a wave of love so profound, it made my breath catch in my throat. *Beloved, nothing will ever approach the unselfish acts you conducted on my behalf. I know what it cost you to believe you were sacrificing your life for me, and I will spend eternity humbled by your show of love.*

*That's a little more like it,* I said, allowing him to see the smile in my mind. I couldn't resist a possessive little touch to Sebastian's shirt as Sally opened the door to the suite. *They're here. Behave yourself.*

*I have promised to do so in front of the Betrayer. But once he has left, all bets, as they say, are off.*

The accompanying growl in my head left me breathless and wishing that Damian's parents would hurry up and take him off our hands so I could fling myself shamelessly on Sebastian and allow him to pleasure me in all the many ways he had been imagining since I had woken up in his arms.

*Those are only the tip of the iceberg,* he said with a silent laugh, stiffening slightly as an auburn-haired man entered the room.

"Hullo, Papa," Damian said, glancing at Adrian and a woman I assumed was his wife. "Hullo, Nell."

"Don't bother getting up on our behalf," Adrian told his son in a dry tone.

I looked him over, wondering what sort of life he had led to be named the Betrayer.

*You forbade me to dwell on it.*

"Sebastian," Adrian said, turning to face us, giving Sebastian a little nod.

"Betrayer," Sebastian said, making a stiff nod of his own. I elbowed him. "Er . . . Adrian."

I smiled at the love of my life, filled almost to bursting with the joy he brought me.

Adrian's dark blue eyes, so like his son's, passed over me with curiosity. "I do not know what miracle Ysabelle has wrought to turn you from predator to protector, but Nell and I are grateful nonetheless that you have kept Damian from harm."

Adrian held out his hand. Sebastian's jaw worked, but the rest of him was frozen into a big, unyielding block. I nudged him again.

*It wouldn't kill you to be polite, you know. He's offering you his hand, if not in friendship, then at least in peace.*

*He is the Betrayer —*

*Yes, I know, the one who handed you over to Asmodeus to be tortured, but you survived that just as I survived being burned at the stake. Twice. Tempered, remember? It's now time to move on, Sebastian. The present holds enough challenge — we can't live in the past.*

Sebastian's struggle was evident on his normally stoic face. I bit my lip to keep from

298

smiling as he wrestled with the memories of the hell he survived with an understanding of what I was asking of him.

"You can do it," Adrian said, dimples flashing to life for a moment. "It's painful at first, but it gets easier. Or at least my wife keeps telling me."

"Honest to God, these men. You'd think asking them to behave in a civilized manner meant the end of the world," Nell said with a roll of her eyes as she walked over to Damian and told him to gather his things.

The boy's nose wrinkled when she stopped next to him. "You still smell," he told her.

"And you're still obnoxious," she responded with a ruffle to his hair that spoke of affection despite her words. "Get your things and we'll stop by the museum so you can say hi to the mummies."

I raised an eyebrow at Sebastian. He was still imitating a statue, staring down Adrian, whose hand was still extended. "Stop acting so stubborn," I hissed, nudging him with my hip.

"I can stand here as long as you can," Adrian said, humor lighting his eyes. "You might as well give in."

Sebastian ground his teeth, his hands fisted tightly at his sides.

*You stubborn man. Don't you see that Adrian was forced to betray you by Asmodeus? If he didn't sacrifice you, who knows how many innocent people would have been killed? You wouldn't have wanted them to suffer in your stead, would you?*

It took a few seconds for him to sigh heavily into my mind. *No. But —*

I leaned into him. *The sooner you shake his hand, the sooner they'll leave and I can reward your generous nature.*

*You count too heavily on my ability to forgive, woman.*

*And you are adorable beyond words.*

"Pax, then," Sebastian said, grabbing Adrian's hand and giving it a hearty handshake. He all but ran to open the door for them, sliding me a look that expressed both his annoyance at having to forgive Adrian and his intention to claim his reward.

Adrian laughed, but said nothing as he collected his family and herded them toward the door.

"Can we stop at a supermarket before we go to the museum?" Damian asked, handing his stepmother a bulging carrier bag. "Be careful, he's sleeping."

"A supermarket? I suppose so," Nell said, looking curiously at the bag.

"Good. Belle said I can keep William,

although he's only to have vegetables and no meat at all."

"William?" Nell asked as she walked through the door. "Is William a hamster or something? I suppose we could handle a little pet, but nothing large . . ."

Sebastian closed the door just as she was peering into the bag. I held my breath for the count of five, expecting Nell to be pounding on the door asking what on earth we were doing giving the disembodied head of a revenant to her stepson, but for once, the Fates were with us.

"And now, my sweet Beloved, you will pay for forcing me to behave in a polite manner to the man who has so much of my blood on his hands."

Before I could protest — not that I intended to — Sebastian scooped me up and carried me into the bedroom in the best romantic hero tradition.

"You've been watching too many French movies," I told him with a kiss to the tip of his adorable nose. "No, Sebastian, seriously, we must talk."

"You may talk. I will feast."

"I can't possibly . . . wait." I pushed back on his chest until he put a few inches between us. "Are you hungry?"

His eyes went midnight gray. "I am hungry

for you, sweet Belle."

The flood of images into my head had my toes curling in delight. "Oh, that all sounds lovely — I particularly like that third idea you had; was that whipped cream and strawberries? — but what I meant was, are you *hungry* hungry? You know, for . . . er . . . lunch?" I tipped my head to the side and presented my neck.

Sebastian growled again, a sound that just about caused my blood to boil. His mouth was hot on my flesh, and I was tempted to throw morality and friendship to the wind and grab him, but fortunately, my errant companion chose that moment to check on me.

"*Les* zombies *sont partis aller* home, thank *Dieu*. How did — *sacre bleu* and all the saints! *Il* ravishing *vous?*"

"No, but —"

"Yes," Sebastian said, rolling off me and onto his feet. Sally's eyes widened as he stalked toward her, his hands on his shirt. With a short rending noise, he ripped the shirt off, two buttons flying right through her. "Yes, I'm ravishing her."

Sally looked in surprise at the buttons behind her, then back to the now bare-chested man approaching her. She backed up toward the door. *"Zût!"*

"Unless you wish to watch me make lengthy, passionate love to Belle, I would advise you to leave now," he told her, pausing to kick off his shoes.

Her eyes grew huge as he whipped off his belt.

I rolled over onto my side and admired the sight of the man I was bound to heart and soul . . . souls . . . as he did a striptease. It was funny how life worked out. I never in five hundred years would have imagined that I would fall in love with a vampire.

*Dark One,* a voice in my head corrected.

"Are you . . . you're not going to . . . Belle, he's not going to — holy *merde!*" Sally made an odd *eep*ing noise and disappeared through the door just as Sebastian's pants came off.

"You ought to be ashamed of yourself scaring her that way . . ." The words, which seemed to have no problem rolling off my tongue while I ogled Sebastian's backside, legs, and back, suddenly dried up when he turned around. "Holy *merde,* indeed."

Sebastian rolled his eyes as he strolled toward me. "I am just a man, Beloved. There is nothing here out of the ordinary. Well, perhaps *extra*-ordinary, but nothing to make that much of a shocked face over."

"My other husbands —" I started to say.

"We will not discuss your previous husbands," he interrupted, his movements like a big cat stalking its prey.

My gaze wandered across an incredibly broad chest, down abs that were impressive without being too sculpted, ultimately following a dark honey trail of hair that led to an impressive male endowment. "Fair enough. But —"

"No. You are mine now, Belle, and you will have no other man. What passed before we Joined does not matter to us."

"But —"

He pounced on me before I could finish the sentence, pulling off my shoes, pants, shirt, and underthings so quickly, I didn't have time to do more than blink before I was naked. He rolled me over until I was on my back underneath him, my breasts, my thighs, my hidden female parts all tightening at the sensation of his flesh against mine. Erotic images filled my mind, images of what he wanted us to do together, sending my temperature up several degrees. He kissed me then, a long, thorough kiss that lazily explored my mouth, demanding I respond without holding anything back.

"Yes, it does," I said a few minutes later when I managed to pull my mouth from his, desperately trying to hang on to the few fragmented wits I had left. "At least, one thing does — Noelle."

He froze at the mention of her name.

"I'm sorry, Sebastian." I put my hands on both sides of his face, willing him to understand my somewhat tangled emotions. "I love you. I love you more than I've ever loved another person, but she is my friend, and she has a bond to you —"

"You are my Beloved, not her."

"But she —"

His eyes lightened as he pushed back a bit to glare down at me. "You bring me happiness. You brought light and love into my life, ended my torment, and gave me the most precious gift anyone has ever been given. How can you believe you are not my Beloved?"

"Well . . ." I tried to come up with convincing proof, but he was right. The one thing I hadn't thought I'd been able to do for him had worked out.

*Perhaps it wasn't the traditional method of soul redemption, my love, but the result was just as successful. And I will be eternally grateful that I was blessed to find you.*

The words, and emotions behind them, were enough to make me blush, but one thing still bothered me, one problem that we had yet to overcome.

"I am willing to accept that we were meant to be together. But Noelle is a friend, and we've hurt her. I must do something about that, or it will taint our relationship."

He was silent for a moment, his beautiful face reflecting the thoughts he shared with me. "We've proven beyond any doubt that she is not my Beloved. Thus we will help her find the man for whom she was meant."

I nibbled my lip. "She's never been one for blind dates, but honestly, I don't see much of an alternative. I just hope she understands that we will be doing everything in our power to help her, though."

"We will make her understand," he promised, his mouth descending to mine, gently tugging my lip from where I was still nibbling on it. *Whatever it takes, we will do. I do not like these feelings of guilt within you. They distract you from the proper adoration of me.*

*Arrogant vampire,* I answered, gasping when he found a ticklish spot behind my ear. *You never answered me. Are you hungry? For . . . blood?*

I didn't want him to know, but I was a bit squeamish about the whole blood-drinking aspect to our relationship. I'd never been one of those women who thought vampires were sexy . . . the thought of someone feeding off me was almost repugnant.

*I will not feed, sweet Belle. You will provide life for me, but it will not be an act of feeding. You will give me life, and in return, I will worship you as a slave might.*

*I don't want a slave,* I said, my body burning as his mouth kissed a hot path down to my breastbone. *I want a man.*

*I am yours.* His cheeks, roughened slightly with golden stubble, brushed against my left breast. At the gentle abrasion it suddently became the most demanding part of my body.

"Oh," I gasped, waves of little shocks rolling down my body. Sebastian lifted his head long enough to send me a look so heated, it damn near set the bedding alight.

"I think we can do better than that," he growled, his mouth hovering over my suddenly insistent breast. Every muscle in my body was taut with anticipation, my breath so ragged it was a wonder I was getting any oxygen. When he took the tip of my breast in his mouth, I thought I would die. When he suckled that breast while gently tugging on my second nipple, I knew I was in heaven. And when he nuzzled the soft area on the underside of my breast, his teeth grazing the flesh for a second before piercing the skin, a white-hot pain dissolving into a feeling of profound pleasure that was multiplied by the joy he felt in taking life from me, I exploded into a nova of ecstacy.

*This is not feeding, my Beloved. This is a celebration of life — of our lives together, today, next month, and a millenia from now.* His voice was soft in my head, full of love and appreciation, and my heart swelled to know he was mine.

*Always,* he said, moving over me. I parted my legs, reveling in the purely physical pleasures to be found in the weight of him on me, of the sensation of my legs rubbing against him, of his chest hair teasing my already sensitive breasts. *You will always be mine.*

I bit his lip, sucking it into my mouth, and demanded that he do something about the tight ache he'd built up inside me. *I will hold you to that, Sebastian. Now stop tormenting me!*

His chuckle filled my mind when he entered me, the feeling of him gently pushing into my body a familiar pleasure, yet wholly different. I pulled my knees around his hips to accept more of him into me, digging my fingers into the muscles of his behind. His hips flexed as I twirled my tongue around his, drowning in the sensation of the taste, scent, and feel of him. He was everywhere, in my head, in my body, his mouth possessing mine until I broke free to breathe. His eyes were dark as night, but glowing with more love than I ever thought I'd see.

"I love you, my adorable zombie," he murmured against my neck.

"Revenant," I said on another gasp of pleasure as all my insides began to tighten even more. "I'm . . . a . . . rev . . . rev . . . oh, God's bones!"

My words trailed off into a high scream of absolute rapture as he surged hard into my body, his teeth deep in my flesh, the sensation of his approaching orgasm mingling with my own, as well as the sensation of him taking blood from me. My back arched as I clutched him, our bodies moving quickly in a rhythm that seemed to start in my heart.

*God's blood, I had no idea it was going to be like this. Why didn't I meet you a century ago?* I asked just before my being burst into a thousand little pieces of dazzling brilliance. Our souls, my own and the one I'd given him, touched, and for a moment, we were one glorious being as his orgasm claimed him, sweeping me along.

It seemed to take hours for me to finally come to my senses, but I'm sure it was just a matter of minutes. I was pleased to notice, as Sebastian rolled onto his back, taking me with him so I rested on his now damp chest, that he seemed to be having as much difficulty catching his breath as I did.

*Smug vixen,* he said, one hand caressing my behind in a gesture of love so sweet, it brought tears to my eyes. *What was that you were saying about your previous husbands?*

*What husbands?* I smiled into his head and let myself relax on the solid body beneath me, warm, contented, and for the first time in I don't remember how many centuries, truly happy.

# EPILOGUE

"Noelle —"

"No! I don't want your help! You and . . . and . . . blood boy there can just go about your merry little way. I can find my own man, thank you." Noelle stalked over to the window in the flat, the same window I'd been looking for such a short time ago. Her body language bespoke anger, leaving my heart aching to know I had caused so much unhappiness.

"I have promised Belle that I would help you, and I will, regardless of your pride," Sebastian said calmly. His hand slid around my waist. I leaned into him, the feeling of him next to me giving me strength. "I will personally see to it that every unredeemed Dark One in Europe is brought before you, so that you might find the one for whom you were meant."

I assumed Noelle would bristle up at that, but to my surprise, the look in her eyes when she turned toward us was more cautiously speculative than angry. "You think another Dark One is the answer?"

"I do." Sebastian nodded. "You are a Beloved — there is no denying that. Since there is also no denial that Belle is *my* Beloved, we can only assume that the one for whom you are intended is still out there, waiting to find you."

It took a moment for the meaning of what they were talking about to sink in. "Wait one minute!" I pulled out of his embrace to stand in front of him, my hands on my hips. "Let me see if I have this correct . . . she's a Beloved, originally yours until you met me."

Noelle straightened her shoulders and tried to look huffy, but sighed and slumped into a chair. "Oh, I give up. I'd like to be angry about this, I really would, but it's clear to me now what Sebastian meant all along. We just aren't compatible, and you two are."

"Well?" I asked Sebastian, nodding to Noelle to show her I'd heard her comment.

He looked momentarily disconcerted. "That is as good a summary as I believe can be made in a single sentence."

"In other words, you're saying Beloveds are not unique? That they can be passed along from Dark One to Dark One?" I poked him in the chest. He captured my hand, casting Noelle a long-suffering glance over my shoulder. It just made me want to poke him even harder.

A faint giggle escaped Noelle.

"It's not quite as stark as you stated, but in this instance, yes. Noelle was born a Beloved, but has yet to find the Dark One she was meant to redeem —"

I punched him on the arm. Hard. "You told me a Beloved was the one woman in the world who could save you. That is, one woman in the whole history of time who could bind herself body and soul to you, who would fulfill you, complete you and make you whole. And now you're saying that we're . . . *disposable?* I thought I was the only one for you!"

Noelle covered her mouth and pretended to cough, but I knew she was hiding her laughter. Sebastian made like he was going to pull me into another of his mind-meltingly wonderful embraces, but I held him off with an outraged glare.

"You are the only one for me, but since you bring it up, I would like to point out that you had five husbands before me. Five. Did you love them?"

"I . . . they . . . I was lonely. . . ." My teeth snapped shut over the protestations I wanted so badly to make, but damn it, Sebastian had a point, and he knew it.

"You see? You managed to have five husbands whom you loved, and yet you still love me to the exclusion of all else."

I grumbled to myself that I could change that if I really wanted.

"Add to which the fact that I don't love her," he said, pointing at Noelle. "I never have."

"You know how to make a girl feel so special," Noelle said, her lips twisting slightly.

Sebastian offered her an apologetic smile. "I meant no insult."

"Oh, none taken." She sighed again, then stood up and gave us a watered-down version of her usual cheery smile. "Men tell me all the time that they don't love me. It seems to be a frequent theme in my life. Very well, I give you two my blessing, not that you've asked for it in particular. I'm still a bit confused by this whole Beloved thing, but it's obvious to me how much in love you both are. I will hold you to your promise to find me a Dark One of my own, mind you, so don't think you're getting off easily."

"It will be our pleasure to help you," I said as Sebastian grabbed my wrist and started pulling me toward the door. "We won't rest until we've found the perfect man for you, one who is tender and witty and wholly deserving of your affection, not like this monstrous beast I seem to be stuck with."

Sebastian stopped in the doorway, raised one eyebrow, and growled deep in his throat.

My legs melted. *I just can't resist you when you do that,* I told him as he pulled me through the door into a blessedly empty hall.

*That is the plan, my sweet little zombie,* he said as I met him halfway in a kiss so hot, it came close to melting my shoes. *I'm so very glad it's working.*

Behind him, Sally appeared for a moment, smiled, then turned back into the flat. "Noelle! *Vous avez besoin de* a spirit guide *tres* groovy cool! Luckily, *je suis maintenant* available. Shall we talk about how *je peux aider* you be *tres jolie* Guardian?"

■ ■ ■ ■

# LUCY AND
# THE CRYPT CASANOVA
# BY MINDA WEBBER

■ ■ ■ ■

*To: Chris Keeslar,
a wonderful editor whose
humor adds greatly to the
story. Thanks for helping
me reach my potential.*

# ACKNOWLEDGMENTS

Thank you from the bottom of my heart to the top of it *Romantic Times BOOKreviews.* I was so pleased to win Best Historical Vampire Novel of 2005 for *The Remarkable Miss Frankenstein.* And to Carol Carrol for being a true family friend.

# Chapter One:
# Close Encounters
## of the Fourth Kind

"It was horrible, just horrible. You can't imagine the terror of it! Nobody should have to go through this, you know?" The black-haired girl cried out dramatically, and the lenses of the television cameras homed in on her big hazel eyes. She had an expressive elfin face; this was the main reason why she had been chosen to do the talk show instead of the four other abductees: her look of utter sincerity.

In the background, portions of the *Twilight Zone* talk show set stood out in stark relief. Strands of green ivy and lacelike cobwebs hung from the antique bookshelves. The shelves were full of marbleized skulls, gris-gris charms, and carved coffins hewn from a range of materials from wood to jade.

"Ya know, they had these really big black eyes staring at me. And they smelled, too!" the girl remarked adamantly.

Lucy Campbell, *Twilight Zone* host, nodded once. She was a West Texas girl who had sort of made it good. She was in the limelight — even if that limelight was rather peculiar, much like the guests on her show.

"What did they smell like?" she asked, wanting her guest, Carol Carroll, to reveal more of the strange encounter.

"Like really bad body odor, for sure," Carol replied. "And maybe some kind of dead fish thing."

Again Lucy nodded, commiserating with her guest. "And how long were you held captive?"

"Three days! Three horrible days filled with golden gooses and *fee, fi, fo, fumm*ing. And talk of blood!" Carol Carroll added, horror evident in her voice. "I was poked and prodded and fed golden eggs."

Lucy held back a grimace, thinking her guest sounded like she'd been held captive by a great big Easter bunny with a penchant for metallic spray paint, rather than an American Desert Ogre.

"Yes, it must have been quite an ordeal," she said neutrally, trying to keep an open mind. Personally she didn't know if she believed the girl, but there had been more than a few humans laying claim to having been abducted by American Desert Ogres in the last six years.

Searching Carol Caroll's hazel eyes for the truth, Lucy recalled her mom's sage advice: *Where there's smoke, there's fire.* So Lucy reasoned that where there were beanstalks, there might be ogres. In today's strange new world, anything was possible.

Thirteen years ago, monsters and all manner of supernatural creatures had come out of the closet — or rather, cellars and crypts. It had been the media event of the twenty-first century; probably of all centuries. At first there had been many skeptics, but one man changing into a werewolf and another guy drinking blood from a third guy's neck on *News 10* could quickly make believers out of even the most devout skeptics. Suddenly the unexpected and unbelievable were real. The American public and the world were expected to accept the impossible.

Almost overnight there were new legislation, new laws, and new attitudes on this startling and scary revelation. It had become a mad, mad, mad world; the whole world turned upside down. But American capitalists, always quick to profit, decided to make the best of the bloody business, and marketing departments everywhere began hawking Monster Madness, Monster Mania, and so forth. In short, monsters were marvelous.

Within three years, a bewildered and

bemused America had bought into the whole supernatural scene. And it was still going strong. People were corpse crazy, werewolf wild, ghost giddy — and witch and warlock woozy.

The most recent fad, which had already lasted more than ten years, was a fang frenzy. Life was a veritable Fangtasia, because everyone wanted in on the act — especially dentists, who were making a legitimate killing with the whole big teeth thing. You could get insincere fangs, sincere fangs, fake fangs, and fangs for the memories. Fangs that were eye-blindingly white, and fangs that were ebony black. And some people wore the two in combination, for a piano key effect. You could get newfangled fangs with intricate engravings, or bejeweled and bedecked biters. Small fangs and big fangs, monstrous fangs in snarling or howling mouths, all were displayed in every advertising campaign in America. Yes, wherever a person went, she was almost guaranteed to be flashed by fangs. Of course, fang flashing with intent was now a felony.

Along with the radically changing mix of human and non-human culture, other new opportunities had presented themselves, spawning a whole new category of television. There were supernatural talk shows like *Dr. Spook,* the premier spectral authority on adolescent ghosts, and *Haunted Home Improvement* hosted by T. Taylor Andrews. Comedy shows had sprung up for the walking dead, such as *Saturday Night Unlive,* and *The Tonight Show* hosted by Blade, a vampire with a razor-sharp wit. Not to be outdone, the shape-shifting community had developed the game show *Jeopardy 2,* where humans hid and ran from werewolves, werelions, and werebears (which were not cute and cuddly like teddy bears, if you were thinking they might be). In the last year, a program called *Supernatural Survivor* had garnered top ratings. The show was reality-based, and participants needed to survive nights in haunted houses, or in cemeteries while being chased by ghosts or ghouls.

New industries provided new job opportunities, which was great for people like Lucy. She had been in debt not only from finishing college, but also from paying her mother's medical bills. So, when opportunity knocked in the form of a talk show — even if it was really out there — Lucy had answered. She knew she might be sacrificing a bit of her journalistic integrity, but a job was a job; she'd decided to enter the *Twilight Zone.* And so Lucy had packed her bags and gone to New Orleans, which was now the major hub of supernatural activity. The city's new motto: "We'll raise your spirits."

But her talk show had turned out to deal with sensational and silly subjects of the supernatural realm. At first Lucy had hoped that she could guide the program into more serious topics, but since the *Twilight Zone* had been talk show sensationalism at its best before she replaced the last host, the producers demanded to continue in the same vein. No respectable or self-respecting monster would be caught on her show, dead or undead, so two years later found Lucy's professional reputation shredded by the sometimes-ludicrous stories she was forced to do in hopes of almighty ratings.

Like right now. Lucy silently sighed and turned her attention back to her guest.

"For sure, I'll never forget his big black eyes and that creepy goose he was holding. And that harp music."

"I've heard that ogres like harps," Lucy commented, a polite smile on her face. Harp music was synonymous with ogres. Lucy had done some research, and had learned that ogres were enthralled with the sound — or so every other abductee had said.

"I hate the harp, and that's all I heard night and day — that damn music! It was like being stuck in an elevator forever. Man, it was a bad scene."

When Lucy cocked a brow, the girl added, "You know, that horrible chamber music? I prefer Zydeco and hard rock, not some classical crap my ancestors listened to because they had nothing else."

"Of course," Lucy said.

"That harp music made me, like, bonky — along with all that yucky chanting."

"Chanting?" Lucy asked politely. The assistant producer of the show held up his fingers, indicating she had less than two minutes to close. Thank God.

"You know, the *fee,* the *fi,* and the blood-smelling stuff."

"Ah yes, the *fee,* the *fi* and the *fo*ing." Lucy nodded kindly. Was it really possible, or had Carol Carroll simply watched too many reruns of *The X-Files?*

"And did I tell you that overgrown ogre dropped beans on my head?" Carol Caroll asked, her eyes wide. "Beans! Over and over. That doesn't sound like much, but let beans get dropped on *your* head when you're trying to sleep!"

Lucy patted the girl's hand. "I imagine it's like Chinese water torture." But when the black-haired, tattoo-faced abductee looked blank, she added, "Never mind."

She wondered what the students of today were being taught: Spells in Sixty Minutes? Which witch is which? Where was all the classical Cold War history stuff? Lucy supposed that the Red Scare was now seen as the possibility of being sucked dry in the dark by a hungry vampire.

Giving a nod to her young guest, Lucy turned to smile into the camera. "Well, that's all for tonight. I want to thank our guest, Carol Carroll, for coming on and revealing her ordeal at the hands of her ogre abductors."

On cue, the audience applauded. The camera zoomed in, focusing entirely on Lucy Campbell, capturing her all-American good looks — blond, blue-eyed, and classically beautiful.

"Be sure to tune in to tomorrow's show: 'Voodoo priests who have fallen in love with their dolls,' " she continued, secretly cringing at the subject. How had she fallen so low? She wanted to do serious subjects, with prominent paranormal guests.

If only she could get real-life werewolves or vampires on the *Twilight Zone,* instead of wannabe bloodsuckers and men with hair-growth problems. Not to mention the less respectable witches and warlocks she'd booked, lesser shape-shifers, and the occasional troll or goblin. She had once almost gotten a demon to be a guest, but his price for appearing had been her soul. Lucy had quickly and quite firmly declined his offer and gotten herself out of the hot seat.

If only she could get a good guest, or break a good story. If only.

# Chapter Two:
## The Lucy Show

The elevator opened on the seventh floor, where the office of the owner of WPBS — the Paranormal Broadcasting Station — was located. Lucy walked across the plush gray carpet and announced herself to Mr. Moody's secretary. "The boss wanted to see me?" she asked the plump matron.

The secretary nodded, then added in a low, warning voice, "He's on the warpath."

Lucy thanked her; then, steeling herself for the meeting, she walked inside, wondering what burr had gotten stuck under the man's saddle now.

Glancing toward Moody's massive mahogany desk, she noted that the old crab was on the phone. Short, gruff, and about twenty pounds overweight, in broadcasting he was a force with which to be reckoned.

Mr. Moody hung up the phone and took in what Lucy was wearing, a cornflower-blue dress with a low-cut back and beaded bodice. "You must have a hot date planned tonight," he remarked.

Lucy shrugged. Her date was a first date, and she suspected it would be anything but hot. The man in question was handsome, but in a spoiled good looks kind of way. She wasn't sure why she'd agreed to the date.

She fought back annoyance at Moody's comment. What bad luck that he'd noticed. Usually she didn't date after her show, which was on weekdays and started at 9:00 p.m., an hour before primetime. Since the supernatural world had barged into the mortal world with much more bite than bark, most nations had revamped their workdays. The average shift now started at 11:00 a.m. and finished at 8:00 p.m., and many stores stayed open all night. This enabled paranormal clients and customers to shop 'til they dropped — unless they got home before sunrise.

"Is he a paranormal?" her boss asked curiously.

Lucy knew her personal life was just that, but what could she do? This was the boss, even if he was a nosy busybody who liked to point his pug nose into everything.

"No," she said.

Moody looked put out. "Damn! You need to make some better connections. You'd better start poking around in some coffins and *loup garou* dens."

Lucy frowned. She wasn't the type to sleep her way to the top, especially in coffins. Not after her past. Deciding not to reply, she sat down in a green plaid chair as Mr. Moody pointed his finger at her.

"I'm not happy with the cost of your show, Lucy Campbell. No, missy, I am not," he warned, his thick brows drawn together in a frown.

Lucy rolled her eyes. Her boss's name fit him like a perfectly tailored suit. He was cantankerous, contrary, cheap — and alternately creative and charming. One night he was as high as a kite, and other nights he was channeling Satan.

"So, I'm in the soup again, am I?" she said.

"I had to replace our specialty chair and the coffee table this week alone," he growled with firm displeasure. "And the show was a flop."

This was definitely one of his moody nights. Lucy grimaced as she recalled the Great Appalachian Troll. Over seven feet tall and massively built, the creature had flopped down hard on the specially made chair designed for guests who weighed more than three but less than five hundred pounds. There had been a loud creaking noise, and then suddenly both chair and troll had collapsed. Naturally the troll — never the calmest of species in the best of circumstances — had gotten angry and had smashed the matching coffee table as well, scattering cups and food everywhere. The guests had shouted and cheered, but Lucy had been left with coffee and egg on her face. And now this bill. Dang! Moody *would* bring up the troll episode.

"Who knew that Appalachian Trolls weighed over five hundred pounds?" she asked, her eyes wide with innocent indignation.

"Perhaps if you had researched a bit more about this particular guest?" Mr. Moody retorted.

"I did! But the troll must have been embarrassed about her weight and lied. She was a female troll, after all. And I apologized until I was blue in the face, but she was still surly. We also didn't have another chair sturdy enough to accommodate her, so she had to stand through the rest of the interview. I guess I have to admit the whole show went downhill from there."

Scowling, Mr. Moody made a face that made his thick brushy brows meet in the middle of his forehead, the look clearly saying the troll mess was all her fault. Dang, she had seen that look before. And so Lucy added, "I did stand up with her so she wouldn't feel out of place."

"You know she'll tell all her troll buddies about us. We'll probably never get another troll on our show again — at least, not on this side of the Appalachians!"

*That* would be a loss, Lucy thought snidely. No more egg on her face? But she said, "I'm sorry. Accidents do happen."

"You can say that again. You're accident-prone, Lucy. I tell you, accident-prone."

Lucy kept a straight face, neither accepting nor denying the statement. Just because she had been bitten by gremlins, slimed by ghosts, and cursed by warlocks, that didn't mean she was any unluckier than other people were. Other people just didn't spend their nights with the Amityville horror or wacked-out witches. Of course, there was one encounter in the past that made her feel unlucky. A vampire. One who . . .

She tore her thoughts away from that as Moody said, "I don't spend half as much money on my other shows as I do on yours. Why, *Creature Comforts* hardly costs a dime."

"Why should it?" Lucy snapped. "All your host has to do is walk around stylish homes of rich and famous monsters." Having seen mausoleums of some famous undead, Lucy personally thought it was a dream job — for a mortician.

Mr. Moody continued, ignoring her. "Besides the large antebellum ballroom, I hardly incur any expenses for *Monster Mash.*"

"What kind of expenses would you incur on a show where everyone is dancing? Maybe a few broken high heels? A lost sense of rhythm? All Ginger your ghost host has to do is announce the odd couples."

"They still don't cost much to produce," Moody grumbled.

Holding up a hand, Lucy defended herself staunchly — and with the few words that would most count. "I have the highest ratings of all the shows you produce."

Mr. Moody slammed down a bill from Billy's Barbecue on his desk. Giving her a black look, he asked, "Well, what the hell is this? Three hundred dollars for a single meal?"

"That was lunch, of course," Lucy explained patiently. The man could be an unreasonable monster at times, worse than a vampire trying to squeeze blood from turnips. But one had to be stupid to get in his way when he got on the warpath. "A five-hundred-pound Appalachian Troll has a mighty big appetite. Heck, when we were done, she ordered a whole goat to go."

Moody looked up at the ceiling as if the answer to his dilemma were written there. "Lucy, your show costs twice what my other shows cost. And may I remind you that I am paying you an exorbitant salary? Do I need to remind you that I gave you this job even though your only credits beforehand were merely some work in a small-town television station in Texas where you were the weather girl?"

Exorbitant salary, her aunt Fanny! Although Mr. Moody was paying her more per week than her job in Round Rock as a weather girl had, she would never be wearing Prada at this rate.

"I was a great weather girl," she argued. "That station loved me." Lucy had been slowly moving up in the ranks. "I also got to do the television news for two weeks when our anchorman got bitten by a ghoul. The ratings went up for those two weeks too."

"Only because you fell out of your chair twice. Hell, you weren't even drinking."

Lucy glared at him, mortified. "That could have happened to anybody. I was nervous, and miscalculated when I sat down."

Mr. Moody only shook his head. "That should have warned me."

"Besides, I was still upset about my mother's accident," Lucy continued. Ten months after she'd gotten the job, a grizzly werebear driver had hit her mother with his van. Fortunately her mother had lived to tell the tale, but unfortunately she didn't have any insurance. The medical costs were huge, and since the werebear had also been seriously hurt, her mother had been fined for harming an endangered species.

Staring hard at her, Moody conceded gruffly, "You were doing an okay job at that podunk station, but being a weather girl is not hosting your very own show. Think what you can accomplish here if you cut back expenses. You are doing important work, showcasing the supernatural!"

And she was killing all hope of any progress or of the more elite of the professional paranormal world to appear as her guests if the show didn't focus on more serious — or at least believable — issues. Well, as believable as any issue could be in a world where people could turn into bats or chomp your leg off if they got hungry on the night of a full moon and all the local takeout restaurants were closed.

"My fans love me," she said. For a long

time, she had wanted to be famous and respected like Oprah or Ellen. Now she was. And while those two women didn't have fans who wore black lipstick and stuck pins in dolls, fans were fans, and those fans provided almighty ratings. That was something.

It was funny. Lucy had always had something to prove to the world and to herself. Middle school had been a nightmare. She had been short, fat, and in eighth grade her skin had broken out. It was also in eighth grade that she'd learned what fear was — and that people were a lot like animals.

Chicks would peck and peck the runt of a litter, until they pecked it to death. The popular crowd had done the same to Lucy. She had been tormented and made fun of not once or twice, but daily for the whole of her eighth-grade year. Lunchtime had loomed, a hulking, menacing presence to be endured on a day-to-day basis, and Lucy had hid in the girls' restroom, hoping no one would find her. That had saved her from death by peckers.

In high school she had fortunately blossomed, losing her baby fat while her skin cleared up into a peaches-and-cream complexion. The ugly duckling became a pretty girl with an infectious laugh, and she had been head cheerleader, most popular girl, and most beautiful. But the earlier scars remained, and they influenced her life to this day. She had a driving ambition, a deep-seated need to be successful and famous; famous enough to show those hometown girls that she'd always been worth knowing and always would be — something they had been too superficial and self-involved to notice.

"Fans. Well," Mr. Moody said, hating to concede anything good about his most expensive employee. "You do seem to have a following. That's why you're still working, in spite of the exorbitant costs you incur."

"I'm always signing autographs," Lucy added, stretching the truth a bit. She had signed autographs now and again, but most people who came up to her told her how funny they found her show. If her show was a situation comedy she would have been a bit more flattered.

"Well, maybe you are. But if they knew the high costs that you run up . . ." Moody trailed off, mentally calculating the accidents, the destruction of property, the raise he was probably not going to give her this year . . .

"There was that Monty's python show. *That* was hard to swallow," he recalled grumpily. "I had to pay a fortune for that Harry Wizard fellow's warty, potbellied pig. He went potty! His grief counseling sessions — what hogwash!"

"I did try to keep that python from eating his pig."

"It was a disaster. In fact, I don't think I can ever look at bacon the same way," Mr. Moody went on, staring at Lucy. Shaking his head, he said, "Still, you do seem to have that loyal following. Despite the sliming and the leaf sprouting."

Lucy groaned silently. He wasn't going to bring *this* up now, was he? She recalled well enough the time when an enraged Druid warlock had put a curse on her, causing tiny leaves to sprout from her scalp. She had been doing the show for a little over six months, and had been wearing new high heels with wooden spikes — all the rage with the female vampire hunters on her show that day. Unfortunately, the spiked wooden heel had broken, and Lucy had fallen into the lap of the Druid warlock, Monsieur Chestnuts, causing her to squash monsieur's chestnuts along with his warlocky wand.

Mr. Moody rubbed his hands together gleefully, remarking, "The ratings shot up by six points. We should do that again."

"I . . . don't think so." Lucy declined with great conviction. It had taken her two days and numerous phone calls to find a hairdressing hedge trimmer who could deal with the leaves until she found a witch to lift the Druid's curse.

Glancing at her watch, she remarked, "Is that all? My date is waiting."

"All right, all right," Mr. Moody said. He watched her stand, his face craftily thoughtful. "But you do know Tuesday's show is dealing with witches and warlocks?"

"Yes," she replied. To be honest, she was a tiny bit uneasy. "The two covens have promised to behave themselves. We got their John Hancock on the agreement. No bespelling, no curses. None. Nada." And there'd be no wooden-spike-heel shoes for her, either.

Escaping Moody's office, she rode down in the elevator with her head leaned against the wall. She was tired and wondering how her date was going to go with Desmond. Maybe she would be pleasantly surprised and have a really good time — or at least an okay time. The way her dates had been going lately, she would settle for harmless.

And she didn't want to think about that vampire from her past. . . .

# CHAPTER THREE: CLOSE ENCOUNTERS OF THE CHEATING EX KIND

There was no way that Lucy could have known what little trick fate had in store for her that night.

*I should have just gone home after my meeting with Mr. Moody,* she thought in irritation. Why had she agreed to the stupid rendezvous with Desmond Tribideux? Maybe because she was lonely, and perhaps she really had wanted to see the art gallery's new exhibits. The show on The Art of Paranormal was supposedly excellent.

Lucy narrowed her eyes at her date, thinking that next time she was lonely she would stay at home with a good book and a glass of wine. Women, she mused thoughtfully, were such suckers. They had an intense need to connect, which meant they were constantly setting themselves up for disappointment, even when instincts warned them to beware. And Lucy had more reason than most to be unhappy with her lacking love life. She had been reminded of it this very evening. Once, she had been loved and cherished by the very best. How could anyone else ever compare?

Shaking her head slightly, she decided ruefully that some southern nights the only things worthwhile were old dogs, children, and dandelion wine.

"This painting reveals man's need to dominate and control his woman," Desmond remarked, winking at her.

Looking at the painting, which held shapes vaguely resembling human ones, also with a pair of large red eyes and a long black chain, Lucy smiled vaguely. "Really?" Actually, the painting's eyes seemed to follow her movements, making her uncomfortable.

Desmond seemed put out. "Come now, Lucy. I should think you would know a bit more about art than this," he remarked, his eyes dancing upon the cleavage revealed by her short blue beaded dress. The garment had been a definite mistake, Lucy thought regretfully. *I should have worn a turtleneck sweater — a baggy turtleneck sweater.* Except it was too hot in New Orleans for heavy-duty date camouflage like that.

"I'm not really into more abstract art," she protested politely. Desmond was ruining the art exhibition for her, just as he had ruined dinner with his prosing about the wine, his work, and his rudeness to the waiter. Not to mention the amount of touching he'd done all during dinner and their walk to the art gallery in the French Quarter.

Smiling suggestively, he motioned to another abstract painting. "I see my work is cut out for me. I'll be happy to tutor you in abstract art — and in anything else, for that matter. I'm quite an expert," he announced pompously, a leer on his face, "in pretty much everything."

*You're an expert sleazy troll,* she decided, brushing his hand off her bottom for the seventh time. Her date, this human octopus, had more moves than Chuck Norris. She was almost considering inviting him on her show as a guest freak. "Oh, I wouldn't impose. I've always thought ignorance is bliss."

But her stratagem didn't work. Ignoring her words, he began explaining the next painting, which was a series of bright blue circles with dark golden slashes and a faint distorted humanlike figure. "This painting represents woman's wish to be dominated by her passions and by her master. The woman's longings are evident in the work. She can hardly wait for the forceful thrust of his —"

Lucy interrupted. "I see." Her date had sex on the brain, there was no question. She needed to put the kibosh on that.

"The woman is in need — extreme need," Desmond continued. "Note the powerful brushstrokes around her thighs."

Lucy let his words flow around her and disappear. But he continued to talk, no doubt in love with the sound of his own voice.

Chalk up another dud evening and another date from hell. Again, she wondered why she even bothered. Four years of being constantly assaulted with unwanted sexual passes, listening to men moan about their work, their ex-wives or girlfriends was getting to be much too much. And the men believed that after two or three dates she would be happy to hop into a bed with them, because this was dating etiquette for the twenty-first century!

Although she wasn't a virgin, not at the age of twenty-eight, she certainly wasn't easy, being a two-fingered-hand kind of woman. Meaning she could count her lovers on one hand — holding up only two fingers.

No, she didn't want to sleep with someone on a schedule, nor did she want instant sexual gratification. She wanted to love, or at least to feel deeply about her sex partner. She didn't want to sleep with someone she couldn't trust or respect, and therein lay the problem.

Supposedly time healed all wounds. But not, of course, if they were made by a vampire. After four long, cold, bitter years, the ghost of a memory was still tormenting her. Five years before and to her eternal sorrow, Lucy had fallen deeply in love with an amoral immortal. She had been working on her last sixteen hours of graduate study in broadcast communication when she'd met Valmont Frances Pierre DuPonte. He had come to San Antonio, where Lucy was attending the University of Texas.

Val had been born in a time when women were put on a pedestal — before women had all jumped off like sky divers with no parachutes. He had been born when kings and queens ruled, and he had been a French count. When being a count counted for something.

Valmont now was a law enforcement officer, and he had come to San Antonio to teach the police force some newer methods in restraining and incapacitating dangerous preternatural predators. One night, the vampire had gone to the Riverwalk to drink in the view — and probably from a willing pretty neck or two in the shadowy alcoves of the riverbank — when he had met Lucy.

He had immediately knocked her off her feet — quite literally, since she had bumped into him and fallen into the river. But love was moving in the shadows that night, and romance had bloomed in the dark. Twenty minutes later they were having drinks in a pub that catered to vampires and other supernatural creatures, and Lucy had stared into the vampire's deep blue gaze and realized that this amazing male was going to be someone very special to her. She had wanted to waltz across Texas with him in her arms, never letting go. Fortunately, Val felt the same way, because he had begun courting her in an Old World fashion. Lucy had found it both delightful and unsurprising; he *was* over 360 years old.

She'd thought it would last. When his lectures at the police academy ended three months later, they had conducted a passionate long-distance love affair. For eight months Lucy had felt more alive than ever before, and all because of a man undead. She had begun planning weddings and her happily-ever-after — which was very possible with a vampire for a husband. Unfortunately, Lucy had decided to visit Val one weekday, and had flown in to surprise him in New Orleans only to discover that her true love was in reality a liar. She had found him with another female vampire, his fangs in her neck, the two-fanged four-flusher! Which proved another thing her mother always said: *"Once a bloodsucker, always a bloodsucker."*

She had called him every name in the book and then some. She had never really loved before Val, and at his loss, she was stripped to the bone, with nothing left for a long, long time. No, Lucy had never forgiven Val. Nor had she forgotten him.

"Lucy, pay attention! I feel as if I'm talking to the wall."

Drawing herself out of her bleak thoughts, Lucy focused back upon Desmond. He continued: "As I was saying, this painting here depicts fierce raging desires and man's responsibility to have sexual conquest wherever he can."

Why Desmond — who was an insurance administrator for necromancers and wizards — thought he knew beans about art was beyond Lucy's comprehension. Cocking a brow, she glanced at her date and then at the painting in question. At least she recognized the subjects. The painting was of a kitchen table with a giant swordfish lying across it, and a swath of white was a female form lying beside the swordfish. A bigger swath of a brown male stood next to the table, with an enormous purple penis.

"Can you feel the power radiating from it?" Desmond asked, staring at her, a look of what could only be called horniness on his handsome features.

"I can certainly feel something," Lucy muttered.

And it was true; suddenly the back of her neck was tingling. She felt like someone was staring hard at her, possibly someone she knew or had interviewed on her show. Everyone and their dog was here tonight at the gallery opening.

Turning around abruptly, she almost bumped into a drop-dead gorgeous female vampire dressed in a slinky red number. The vampiress had a cool narrow white face with fat red lips the color of ripe pomegranates, and was sporting a choker with a diamond the size of the Rock of Gibraltar.

"Pardon me for being so clumsy," Lucy apologized, then caught her breath as she glanced over to see the vampiress's escort. Speaking of dogs! Or rather, undead monsters, Lucy corrected in stunned recognition.

The moment seemed frozen in time, with

the past interceding into the present, every-thing blending together in shades of be-trayal, pain, and the ever-present hope of lost love becoming found again. Lucy felt a sense of dislocation, as if she were underwa-ter where everything was slow and wavy, for she stared at Valmont DuPonte, now the detective superintendent of the Supernatu-ral Task Force for New Orleans.

The vampiress smiled slightly, her smile widening as she took in Desmond. Lucy's date might be a tad conceited, a tad kinky, a tab obnoxious, but he was handsome. Lucy sighed.

Val, on the other hand, wasn't smiling — although he too looked wonderful in his black jacket and black jeans. He was still going for the austere look, Lucy mused, her long-suffering eyes drinking him in.

His dark black hair was pulled back in a ponytail that hung to slightly below his broad shoulders. His dark blue eyes were staring down at her from his wonderful height of six feet three — eyes that always had reminded her of the icy North Atlantic.

He looked great in those tight jeans. He had a good seat for riding, and rode hard and hot for somebody that wasn't a cowboy. Dang him! He just oozed sex appeal, and Lucy couldn't help thinking cattily that his date looked like she'd been around the block a few times — on her back.

"Lucy Campbell," Val remarked casually.

Lucy inclined her head, trying to regain her breath. Her body was heating up, her legs slightly shaky and her stomach doing somersaults. "Val."

What should she say next? She needed mundane words for this extraordinary situation. Finally she managed, "Long time no see." Four years, two months, and a week to be exact, with the exception of the times she had seen him featured on some news story about an exceptionally hard capture, like that charmingly lucky leprechaun who'd turned out to be a serial killer.

"Has it?" Val commented dryly.

Lucy fumed. Four years, two months, and one week might not seem like a long time to Mr. Immortal, but to her human mind it sure as heck was.

"*Cherie,* you must introduce me to your little friend," Val's Bourbon Street vamp said.

Lucy fumed harder. Little? She might only be five feet four, but it wasn't like she was one of the seven dwarves.

"Certainly, *ma jolie fille,*" Val remarked. He placed an arm around his date's svelte waist. "Beverly Perrogeut, this is Lucy

Campbell, an old . . ." Here, Val seemed to hesitate. "An old acquaintance of mine."

Even though he made her sound like an old shoe, Lucy held her smile firmly in place — likely resembling a deer frozen by headlights. Why couldn't she be nonchalant like Val was being? Well, she supposed she didn't have three-plus centuries of practice with meeting ex-lovers.

Her heart cried out with every cell of her body that had once known Val's body intimately. Once, he had cherished her like she was made of rare stone. They had been both lovers and friends. Now she was relegated to a position of "old acquaintance," which hurt.

Tearing her eyes away from Val's, she heard Desmond introduce himself to the vampiress. She in turn introduced Val.

"Have you been dating long?" Val asked, speaking to Desmond. He kept his expression deadpan, which was actually quite easy for a vampire like himself. Poor deluded male, he thought. Lucy was a hardheaded and hard-hearted female. She was also impossible and immature, with her idiotic twenty-first-century lack of understanding of what exactly honor meant to a man, and most especially to an Old World vampire.

"Tonight is our first date," Desmond

confided; then he leered at Lucy and pulled her closer. "But we are becoming acquainted very quickly."

*In your dreams, buster,* Lucy thought with irritation. Wanting to shove the jackass away, she instead resisted the impulse, hoping to spark a little jealousy in the old ex-boyfriend. Her mama had always said: *"A skinny worm might be worthless to a cat, but if you're trying to catch a bird, watch out."* And she recalled as well her grandma's sage advice for every situation: *"Remember the Alamo."*

Val kept his expression relaxed as he watched Lucy let Desmond hold her hand. The man was a randy goat with absolutely no *savoir faire* whatsoever. Even now, the idiot was trying to flirt with both women while also trying to stare down Lucy's dress — a dress that was too revealing for public viewing, low-cut and short, showing those muscular slim legs that had been made so remarkable by years of horseback riding. He fought back irritation.

Beverly flashed a very toothy smile at the human male, then looked the painting over. She loved competition, though she viewed no mortal as much of a serious challenge. She said, "I see this painting is done by Salvador. From his earliest period."

"I was just telling Lucy its very sexual implications. Such passion in the work. Look at the brushstrokes! Such primal desire. Such a forceful presence is the man. And the woman's face is remarkable — a true study in sex-slave ecstasy," Desmond explained with his slight hauteur.

*Such a big purple prick,* Lucy thought sardonically. Looking at the painting, her date and her ex-lover, she amended: pricks.

"Lucy didn't seem to properly appreciate the painting," Desmond remarked. "But with her beautiful face and body to match, I can tolerate that she's not knowledgeable about the art world. A man can't have everything, you know."

Wanting to slam his nose into the painting, Lucy instead remarked through clenched teeth, "Why, thank you, Desmond."

Val's mouth twitched, hiding a smile. He knew Lucy hated condescension. In spite of the pair holding hands at the moment, Desmond wouldn't be holding anything more tonight; Val was certain of that fact. Unable to resist stirring the pot a little, he asked, "What did you think of the painting, Lucy?"

She retorted flippantly, giving Desmond a long dark look and Val a hard glare. "It looks like a painting of a dead fish on a table to me, and a big prick." *Take that, you faithless fang-face,* she added hatefully. She knew her thoughts were rude, but she had had her fill of Desmond's condescension and Val's cool demeanor.

Val stopped the grin from coming to his face, wondering just which of them was the big prick Lucy had mentioned. Did she mean the painting? Or . . . She was glaring at both him and the human. He stirred the pot a little more by saying in a patronizing tone, "A prejudiced viewpoint never advanced the science of art."

Desmond, who was clearly embarrassed by her comment, nodded his head. "Lucy! You don't understand the painting or its theme of significant sexual bondage."

Val's date added her two cents, too, in a very superior manner. "It's a Salvador. Everyone just loves Salvador. Why, I have three of his prints. You must look beyond the obvious. But then, mortals are so often limited in their scope." Turning to Val, she shrugged sexy shoulders. "But what can you expect from the great unwashed."

"Excuse me?" Lucy asked, swelling with ire. "I may be a mortal, but I bathe daily and at least I don't go rolling in mudpiles at the cemetery like you dirt nappers. I don't make love in nasty old coffins, and I'm smart enough to know a dead fish is a dead fish. I like what I like, and I dislike pretentious people who run around spouting off popular mumbo jumbo about nothing."

Val watched with amusement. Lucy could do that better than anybody: go from irritated to full-out enraged in less than sixty seconds. He so enjoyed her pale blue eyes when they lit with that inner fire — whether passion or anger. And it appeared that four years had done little to dim her inner fire. It was such a waste, since she was untrustworthy and disloyal, a fickle female and a death-dealer to hearts, like that Buffy character or two.

"Stupid human. Just because you can't understand the otherworldly is no reason to disdain it," Beverly snapped, her cool demeanor vanished.

Lucy didn't care that she was creating a scene or enraging the full-blooded vampiress. She continued, "Otherwordly? This painting has nothing to do with the paranormal. It only makes me feel glad I didn't have swordfish for supper."

Desmond dropped her hand and took several steps away, frowning in disapproval.

Val's date sneered. "You know nothing about art or the paranormal! Who do you think you are, you insignificant piece of human offal, to ridicule my tastes? What utter rubbish. What conceit. I've lived centuries!"

Hiding the urge to laugh out loud when Beverly got on her high horse, Val decided to defuse the situation. He didn't want mortal and vampire to come to blows even if it would be amusing. "Settle down, *cherie*. Lucy does know a *little* about the supernatural. She's the host of the *Twilight Zone* talk show."

Lucy fell off her high horse, crashing to the figurative ground with a loud thump. Why did Val have to bring up what she did for a living? The vampiress's anger slipped away, and she actually giggled.

*"C'est vrai?"*

"*Mais oui* — it's true," Val replied.

The vampiress giggled again. "So that's why you look familiar. I've seen your show by accident once or twice. I couldn't believe it. I caught the tail end of the one about 'Men Who are Genies and the Women Who Rub Them.' I had tears in my eyes by the time that genie appeared in all his pinkish smoke. You were coughing, and your face had black tracks where your mascara had run. It was just so . . . camp."

Lucy's lips tightened. "I happened to have an allergic reaction to the smoke coming out of the genie's bottle, although I didn't know it at the time."

"Your face swelled up and you croaked like a frog!" the vampiress recalled, chortling gleefully.

"Too bad I didn't fall down and crack my head open. You could have really gotten a real thrill then. All that tasty blood," Lucy retorted.

"Fall down and crack your head?" Val asked. He couldn't resist. "But, didn't you do just that on the show where you had to chase those gremlins about?" Lucy glared at him, letting him know that he was definitely the big prick she'd been talking about earlier. Nobody wore a clearer "I'd like to kick you in the balls" expression.

Glaring at Val, Lucy recalled only too clearly how she'd had to go and get stitches after the gremlins fiasco. It had been her Easter show, and she had thought gremlins would be cuter than bunnies. Their cages had been decorated like Easter baskets, but the scheming little devils had made short work of those, chewing through the bars and snapping at her audience's pant legs. Recalling the whole sordid event, Lucy recognized that she probably hadn't thought the whole basket-cage thing through well enough.

"Yes. I ended up with six stitches," she admitted.

Suddenly realizing that the wily detective had made a deadly slip, she stopped glaring, a slight smile forming on her lips. "I didn't know you watched my show."

Val replied smoothly, inwardly kicking himself for admitting as much to the untrustworthy female. "Only when I'm in the mood for some good lighthearted comedy, Lucy." He would never admit that he watched her show whenever he got the chance, and that, when he didn't, he actually taped it.

"I live to entertain," Lucy replied. "By the way, I'm thinking of doing a show called 'Supernatural Cheaters.' You'd be perfect for it."

Val glared at her. "Not my style."

"If the show fits . . ."

"Fits? There is one thing certain in this life, *cherie* — the only way I'd do that sorry-ass show is over my dead body."

"Stake, anyone?" Lucy quipped.

Val's lips lifted in a sneer, and he went on the offensive. "I've often wondered. Did you catch all those little gremlins — especially the one that took a bite out of your finger?" he asked, his expression wicked.

Lucy shook her head, her face red with anger. "You know, some men don't have any moral compass," she said. Glaring first at

Val and then at Desmond, she retorted savagely, "Speaking of fingers," and then she shot Val one as she left. The two vampires and her date were given a view of her quickly retreating form.

She departed in graceful elegance, though inside her raged a storm of emotion. Unfortunately, while patting herself on the back for getting the last word and finger in on Val, she wasn't watching where she was going, and as she pushed her way through the crowd, she suddenly knocked into something.

Falling, Lucy at first thought that she had knocked over a life-sized statue of a gargoyle, tumbling them both to the floor. She hoped the statue didn't break. How could she ever cover the cost on her peanuts salary? But at the enraged shriek, much to her embarrassment, she realized the statue wasn't a statue but a real-life gargoyle in the flesh. How humiliating!

The gargoyle cursed her roundly, and in the background Lucy could hear Val's laughter stinging her very soul. It reminded her of another of her mother's quaint little sayings:

*"He who laughs last is usually the biggest ass."*

She couldn't agree more.

# Chapter Four:
# The
# Ex-Girlfriend's
# Grudge

The weekend for Lucy was long and boring after her disastrous date and run-in with Val and his nonhuman paramour. With fate conspiring against her, Lucy gave up men for Ben & Jerry. She ate two gallons of their delicious product not to mention two bags of dill potato chips and a whole pizza — and probably gained three pounds, she grumbled as she walked into her dressing room at WPBS on Monday morning. She had an hour to go before her show.

"Hey," Ricki called out, glancing up from the makeup case she was cleaning. Ricki was the *Twilight Zone* hairstylist and makeup artist. Her dedication to makeup was legendary around the studio, second only to the legend of her love life. Ricki had never met a man she didn't like. Of course, she only got involved with those males who were both intelligent and wealthy, so Lucy supposed she did okay.

"You look worried." Ricki's words were a question. "Is it the witchy-warlock show?"

No, it wasn't the show but her lack of a love life. Lucy shook her head, taking a seat in the makeup chair. Well, today's topic did make her a tad nervous. It was "Lei-line Warlock Magic vs. Wand-conjuring Witches," which made her role as host a bit tricky.

The two wizarding groups were very competitive, and each coven believed its magic was the best. Of course, the supernatural world was a very competitive one, filled as it was with predators, huge egos, and all manner of creatures.

Yes, she'd noticed, every supernatural group, pack, nest, or coven felt that it was head and shoulders above the others. Even though it was more than obvious that vampires stood five to six heads taller than goblins, talk to a goblin and that goblin would say it was tops, the highest creature on the old paranormal totem pole. Talk to a Lei-line warlock, and he would boast that his magic wand was bigger any day of the week — and especially at night.

Lucy had been surprised to find that the two magical covens were doing her show together, since animosity had always run rampant between the two groups, not to mention bitter spells and black clouds. Getting the two covens together was going to end in magic muttering, spellbinding mumbo jumbo — i.e., just the kind of stuff those television bigwig rating-cravers yearned for, like her boss Mr. Moody.

"You have purple bags under your eyes," Ricki remarked, dabbing white concealer beneath Lucy's eyes. "You need to get more sleep."

Right, Lucy thought. How could a person sleep when she was all tied up in knots like a really twisty pretzel? It had been three nights since she encountered Val at the gallery opening, and four years since she had slept with him. But her body felt as if it were only yesterday, and she was reliving with intensity the devastating passion the vampire had once brought to her life.

Yes, Val had once filled her life with such joy that every day was like Christmas, and their lovemaking had set off fireworks that eclipsed the Fourth of July. He had intrigued and enthralled her with his wit and wisdom. He had known more about history than any class she had ever taken, and knew more about detective work than *Columbo* and *CSI* put together.

Until Val, Lucy had always carefully guarded her heart; she had kept her feet on the ground. Letting herself go, she had ended up with her head in the clouds. And then, after loving Val, one dark rainy night, her world came crashing down. The bang had shattered Lucy's heart into so many pieces, she didn't think she could ever put it back together again.

That night, after finding Val, she had flown back to San Antonio, where it became crystal clear that she needed to go farther, home to the range. So, grabbing her keys and cash from the table in the hall, she'd driven straight through the black rainy night, even though she was haggard and hurting, trying hard not to fall asleep at the wheel. The old house where her mother lived was outside of Hawley, and a six-hour drive from River Walk City.

She had cried the whole way, raindrops on the windshield keeping pace with the tracks of her tears. Until that time, Lucy hadn't known a person had so much water in her body. Arriving home, she had been both waterlogged and dehydrated, and was longing for her mom's arms and the familiarity of home.

Half listening to Ricki's prattling now, as Ricki applied blush to her cheeks, Lucy knew that she had been in the forever-kind-of-love with Val. It hadn't mattered about their cultural differences, like she was alive and he was undead. She had ignored the fact that he drank blood and she drank Cokes, that he had nice straight fangs and she'd had braces. She had overlooked the fact that he was from Old World France and thrilled to the dark paths of the night with all its vibrating pulse, and she was the original sunshine girl from West Texas.

And she should have been prepared for the deceiving Damphyr's betrayal. She had been through the unfaithful bit before; her mother had been divorced twice, both times the result of her husband's unfaithfulness. Lucy's father was now married to a third wife, younger than Lucy by two years.

And yet, Val's infidelity and loss had left her disconsolate. She couldn't eat or sleep, feeling as if part of her was dying. Inside she had been so very cold and so very empty, except for the hurt that never quite dimmed.

Some redemption had come in the form of her mother's devastating car wreck, and in the frequent surgeries afterward. Lucy hadn't had time to cry over spilt milk — or blood as the case might be — and had no time to feel sorry for herself. Her mother came first, and Lucy had bravely and deter-minedly gotten over her debilitating depression and finally found work.

And if it wasn't the work she had once hoped for, at least her work paid fairly well and kept her dauntless curiosity and creativity well used. Her work on the talk show had helped her to cope with the loss of the one true love of her life, and her mother's recovery had helped her find her smile again.

To be honest, when Lucy had first received the offer to come to work here in New Orleans, she had secretly been hoping to run into Val again. A tiny part of her had hoped that just maybe he would beg her forgiveness, that he would tell her how much he had missed her in his life. In fact, when she'd first moved to New Orleans, Lucy had indulged in this little fantasy quite often. Sometimes she would imagine that she would laugh in Val's face for betraying her with that overstacked, overfanged, and underdressed vampiress. She would then order Val out of her house, his face shocked and sad, hers filled with the joy of gleeful revenge.

A few times her daydreams had gotten her and Val back together again. Well, to be honest, Lucy had mused on such a fate more than a few times, but her secret hopes and daydreams had been dashed. Even though she knew Val was aware of her presence in town, she had only seen him once — on a date at a jazz bar. He hadn't even noticed her; nor had he called since she'd arrived. Apparently, she was forgettable. And that was unforgivable, because Valmont DuPonte was anything but.

"Earth to Lucy," Ricki called. "Bags, Lucy girl, bags under the eyes! Not a good look unless you're a ghoul or a ghost. Now, why aren't you sleeping?"

Valmont DuPonte, Lucy thought angrily — the Don Juan of the dead. Once a vampire was in your blood, he was in your blood for good, like some damn parasite.

"I don't know," she lied at last.

Never again would she tell others about Val's betrayal and her broken heart. In Texas, everyone who had known Lucy knew about Val's infidelity and Lucy's love for the coffin-hopping, vampire-bopping creep. They could have written books. But no one in New Orleans even knew she had a history with this, the sexiest detective on the city's Paranormal Task Force. Which was perfect.

"I guess I've been working too hard. I've been too wound up after work to sleep."

"What you need is some good, hot, old-fashioned sex," Ricki advised.

"That's your suggestion for everything," Lucy replied, a smile on her face. Sex with Val had always almost burned up the sheets. Once he had filled her room with dark golden roses, calling her his Yellow Rose of Texas. It had been lovely.

"If it works, why knock it? Besides, whatever gets you through the night," the hairstylist commented, beginning to fluff Lucy's hair. "Hey, last night on the phone I forgot to ask about your date Friday. How'd it go?"

"He was a first-class troll."

Ricki stepped back, her mouth gaping open. "You're kidding, right? I thought you went out with Desmond Tribideaux. Instead you dated a troll? That's so gross. I wouldn't let one of those touch me with a ten-foot pole." Then, thinking about her remark, she added thoughtfully, "Although, I bet trolls might *have* ten-inch poles. Or larger. Hmm?"

Lucy arched her brows, giving Ricki a look of amused disgust. "Not a real-live troll. Just Desmond, who was being a first-class jerk with sex on the brain — sex in chains. Everything with him was sex and bondage, and he couldn't have cared less what I thought or what I want in life. Just what he wanted, and that was —"

"Some S & M big time, huh?" Ricki broke in.

"You got it," Lucy agreed, shaking her head. "He was almost worse than my last dinner date."

Ricki cocked her head and studied the effect of her work on Lucy's hair. "Yeah? The tax accountant?"

Lucy nodded. "I had one dinner date with the man and he was all over me. I tried to talk him out of walking me to my door, but he was adamant. Then, at the door, when he finally got it through that thick skull of his that I wasn't going to invite him in, he got all indignant and angry."

Ricki looked worried. "You didn't tell me about this."

"I was a little embarrassed at the time."

"What'd the guy do? He didn't give you any trouble that you couldn't handle, did he?" The concern in her voice was evident. Sex in today's modern world had been dangerous before paranormal predators were mixed into the lot; now sex was an impossible competition between human males and predatory paranormals. A female of any kind had to be extra, extra careful.

"Relax. When he started griping about how much money he spent on the date — over a hundred dollars, I guess — I just shut him up."

"How?" Ricki asked, intrigued. She'd relaxed now that she knew Lucy hadn't been assaulted by the tax accountant.

"I wrote out a check for fifty dollars and shoved it in his face, although I had another place in mind initially," Lucy replied, a grin on her face.

"You didn't?" Ricki started laughing. "Did he take it?"

"He did," Lucy answered, her eyes alight with humor. "And what's more, he cashed it."

"What a troll."

"My thoughts exactly," Lucy remarked as she and Ricki giggled. "Now, tell me why we females date males?"

Ricki wiped the laughing tears from her eyes, remarking quite earnestly, "Oh, that's easy. There's no one else to date."

# CHAPTER FIVE:
## LOOK WHO'S TALKING

Glancing down at her watch, Lucy noted that she had ten minutes to spare before her show began. Moving behind a curtain, she peered at the stage. Two cauldron-conjuring witches were standing by a large black pot with wisps of smoke curling from it, dropping in bits of what looked like dried bat wings.

*"Bon appétit,"* Lucy whispered, and her attention was drawn to two Lei-line warlocks who were standing nearby, their crystal-tipped wands in hand and somber expressions on their faces. Concealed behind the stage's pale black curtains, Lucy felt it was safe to inch closer, to try and hear what the warlocks were so urgently speaking about.

*"Mon Dieu!* Today you wouldn't believe what happened. Serena come by my house, you see, and upset she was. She had this scarf over her face, and when she pulled it off I got frightened, bad. She looks around

seventy. Her skin's all wrinkled, and her eyes are sunken in her head," the first warlock was whispering to the other.

"You mean that pretty little Serena Stevens of the Broomstick coven? Isn't she married to your cousin Arthur?"

The first warlock nodded.

The second warlock said, "Has someone put an aging spell on her? Serena's only, what — twenty-nine or so?"

"Thirty-three. But it's bad news, *mon ami*. Bad and scary. No way did I detect any spell or curse," the first warlock confessed. His expression was grim. "Just *Feu Follets* — evil spirits."

The second man frowned. His Cajun friend was the top warlock in the southern states. If a spell had been cast, he should be able to detect it.

Lucy listened in sly amazement. What a fascinating problem. She did so love riddles, although she also felt terribly sorry for the poor woman who'd turned old before her time. Imagine — one day whistling "Dixie," and the next day you're Whistler's grandmother!

"But that's impossible. People don't age overnight," the second warlock exclaimed. "Not without a spell, and a spell for aging would only last a week or two. And an evil spell like this would leave a black magic stink."

Clasping his arm tightly, the first warlock hissed, "*C'est assez* — that's enough! They might hear, those attention-starved cauldron crones. Wouldn't they just love it — *mais oui* — to stick their warty old noses in our business? I can see the headlines: Cauldron-conjurers out-magic Lei-line warlock's family. No way would we be able to keep our wands up in public. *Mon Dieu,* the humiliation!"

The second man nodded thoughtfully. "You're right. Those cauldron crones are always big on publicity, what with their shiny black cauldrons and their eyes of newt. Just because their witch heritage relates them to MacBeth, Sleeping Beauty, and the Witches of Eastwick — that's no reason to go and act so magically superior."

"*Pas de be'tises.* No joke. Remember how they go on and on about the Salem witch trials, yes? So some were hanged, so what? They never hush their mouth about it. You'd think their witch ancestors were the only ones to suffer persecution. Burned at the stake, my ancestors were — which beats hanging any day of the week!"

Hmm, Lucy thought shrewdly. A case like this could bring a lot of attention to whoever solved it. This was a serious crime, with serious repercussions. Some nasty old monster couldn't just go around aging others with a snap of his fingers; there weren't enough old folks homes around! And what would it do to Social Security, which was on its last legs anyway?

Her grandmother had always said that a person's character determined her fate, and Lucy knew she was a character, so she would be safe. Besides, public safety would be served along with her own self-interest if she could help solve the crime. People would begin to see her show in a more serious light, and even the elite of the supernatural world would have to take notice, to pay her a little respect.

She grinned in anticipation. Finally, she had something she could sink her teeth into — and she wasn't even a vampire!

Glancing over at the two warlocks, she waited for more revelations, which she was glad were quick to come.

"Her aging is downright eerie, *mon ami.* Arthur is worry-sick, and Serena is complaining of hard hearing and wanting to eat supper at four in the afternoon. I tried every spell I knew to de-age her. *Mais non,* I couldn't. What's been done? Me, I don't know. But it's not black magic like I know.

374

I'm at my warlock's end."

But Lucy wasn't. She firmly planted the names of Serena and Arthur Stevens in her mind. If she played her cards right, mortals and paranormals alike would soon see her as something more than a pretty face. Tomorrow she would go and visit the poor woman, then have a meeting with the oldest practicioner of black magic in New Orleans: Marvin Laveau, great-grandson to Marie Laveau, the voodoo queen to end all voodoo queens.

The two warlocks took a seat, and Lucy quickly patted her hair. The assistant producer of the show called out, "Four minutes till airtime."

Walking out from behind the curtains, Lucy took her place in the leather chair situated between the black leather sofas where the two warlocks and three witches were now seated. The segregated groups were shooting daggerlike looks between them, their hostility clear.

Lucy smiled at both groups and sat, hoping that open magical warfare wasn't about to erupt. There was not only her safety, but Moody's complaints about the repair bills to consider.

"Three minutes till airtime, Lucy," the assistant producer called out.

Turning her attention back to her guests, Lucy glanced down at her notes. "Now, I know we will all have a good time on the show today, and we will behave ourselves as befits adult warlocks and witches," she reminded them. "No casting spells or curses. No bewitching. And remember we have an audience, so no cursing. After all, we are prime time."

The two warlocks looked slightly affronted. "We know how to not cause trouble. After all, we're descended from noble stock — Merlin of Camelot!"

"Sorry," Lucy apologized.

"We come from noble stock also," one of the older witches retorted.

Before more could be said, Lucy cut everyone off. "I'm glad. That means this show will be quite a success with the dignity and aristocratic bearing you all will want to display on it."

Both sides seemed appeased, and they tried to outdo each other in their noble silence.

Lucy breathed a sigh of thankful relief. Today's show was going to be fine. There would be no problems, no chairs breaking, no egg on her face, no ghost sliming goo all over her Diordi pantsuit, nobody's pot of gold stolen, and no leprechaun curses flowing over her head. And most important of all, no reason for her boss to fire her tonight.

And things went fine for a bit. The show was dandy until one of the cauldron witches remarked that sometimes a wand was only a wand, and then only as good as the hand that held it, but that a cauldron was a cauldron.

The warlocks both shouted, "*Mon Dieu!* Isn't that just like the pot to call the kettle black?"

And the show went rapidly downhill from there, black magic, white magic and every other color flashing as well. Spells and stinky odors filled the air, and Lucy was hard-pressed to tell which witch had done what.

After thirty minutes of that, Lucy found a frog in her hair as the warlocks sent the things raining down on the cauldron-conjuring witches. The witches, not to be outdone, decided to conjure up cats, all manner of shapes and sizes, like a berserk *Cat in the Hat* book, felines appearing everywhere.

Lucy sighed in resignation. Yes, it was raining cats and frogs. Mr. Moody was going to be hopping mad about tonight's janitor bill. It seemed everybody wanted to rain on her parade.

Still, she had a lead to a better story.

# Chapter Six:
# Marvin's Voodoo
# Room

The sun, a bright orange ball, was sinking slowly into the horizon as Lucy parked her car on Potion Ninety-nine Street, an ancient road settled directly in the center of the voodoo triangle, where most of the *traiteurs,* priests, and priestesses lived along with several witch covens. It was the day after the shower of frogs and cats, courtesy of those overly sensitive witches and warlocks.

Getting out of her car two houses down from Marvin Laveau's house, Lucy breathed deep, noting the air was heavy with the smell of wisteria and honeysuckle, along with the crisp odor of burnt milk — the scent of magic. Locking her car, she went back over her conservation with Serena Stevens.

Two hours earlier, she had convinced Serena to speak with her. It hadn't been easy. Serena hadn't wanted to see anybody, much less talk to anyone about her ordeal. But

Serena had eventually shown Lucy a photograph taken four months earlier.

Lucy had been shocked, trying valiantly to hide her amazed revulsion. Serena had been a beautiful thirty-three-year-old witch, the picture of health and vitality. Now she was an old woman with liver spots everywhere, and all the wrinkle cream in the world couldn't help her now. Serena had aged forty years overnight. Or, to be more precise, Serena had aged after a kiss at the hands of a supernatural predator, a heinous creature who was apparently on the loose in the Big Easy, a monster who had to be stopped.

Serena had told Lucy that she and her warlock husband had been having some problems in their marriage, and that she had been going out bar-hopping with her friends for several weeks now. On her first girls night out, Serena had met a very handsome man with deep violet eyes and dark black hair he wore in a waist-length braid. He called himself DeLeon, and had a scar on his cheek that began under his left eye. Instead of taking away from his massive sex appeal, the mark only seemed to add to it.

At first Serena had thought the gorgeous male was a vampire, and since vampires and witches generally got along like a pot on boil, she had flirted mercilessly with him at the Overbite Bar. But the next night she'd had too much to drink, and she'd gone into the alleyway to share a passionate kiss with him.

The kiss had quickly swirled out of control. Serena had tried to break away, but DeLeon had held her fast. He had ripped off her panties and begun assaulting her, and she'd felt her heart beating so hard that she'd thought it was going to burst out of her chest. Her skin had started to burn, and the very essence of herself had started to fade into nothingness.

Fortunately, some college students had wandered into the alleyway to release some of the beer they'd downed, and the timely interruption had saved Serena's life. Unfortunately, the three drunks hadn't arrived in time to save her youth.

Lucy sighed. Pushing open Laveau's wrought-iron fence, she saw a few raindrops splatter on the crumbling sidewalk in front of her. She quickly stepped over a crack in the sidewalk where a large root had pushed its way through the cement. She didn't know what the new monster was that had attacked Serena, but she intended to find out. If Marvin didn't know what kind of monster could steal people's youth, then no one did.

Marvin Laveau had actually just been on her show about "Voodoo priests who fall in love with their dolls." The man might be crazy in love with his life-size doll, and he might be just plain crazy, but he was one of the world's oldest voodoo masters. He knew more in his little fingers about bad scary things than most people could dream up in their nightmares.

Walking up the steps to the large veranda, Lucy used the pentagram knocker. The door was answered on the second knock, and Lucy was led inside a large room and told to wait.

The room's windows had dangling glass beads and bones hanging in the place of curtains. Old books and sheafs of papers were nestled among the floor-length shelves, and the jars that covered every surface were filled with wiggly inhabitants or dried herbs. One jar appeared to be staring at her.

Lucy looked closer, and she gasped. Eyeballs filled the jar. Reading the label, she hit her forehead with her hand. "Of course! Eyes of newt." Picking it up, she studied it closer. "So *that's* what it looks like."

"*Mais oui,*" Marvin Laveau said as he entered.

Lucy turned, pasting a smile on her face.

"Thanks for seeing me on such short notice," she said.

Marvin was over eighty, with hair long silvered with age and eyes a startling emerald green. His skin was the color of burnt molasses, and his long life was reflected in the many lines of his austere face.

"*Ma petite,* you said it was important." Then, seating himself in a chair behind his rather impressive oak desk, he motioned for her to sit as well.

Lucy nodded her thanks, and reclined in a chair covered with a lace cloth directly in front of his desk.

"Ouch." Jumping back up, she reached under the heavy lace and pulled out a rubber chicken. She stared mutely at the rubber hen, a dumbstruck expression on her face. Then: "I thought you used real chickens in your ceremonies. Although . . . I do see how plastic ones would be better. No blood and no stink," she guessed.

Marvin's laughter filled the room, and he leaned back in his chair. The sound boomed everywhere.

Lucy frowned, putting the plastic chicken on his desk. Once again, she felt the butt of a joke.

"It's *ma 'tite fille* — my little girl. My granddaughter. It is her idea of a joke."

"I see," Lucy replied. She grinned. "I bet she's a handful."

*"Oui."* Still chuckling, Marvin added, "Ah, youth. It so often wasted on the young."

Which was a perfect opening, Lucy thought, and she began her tale about the young witch who was now old. She explained concisely and precisely the events that had led up to and followed Serena's rapid aging. Marvin listened quietly, his dark eyes going from warm laughter to grim concern. *"Bon Dieu avoir pitie!"* he said at last. The confusion must have shown on Lucy's face, because his next words translated, "Good God have mercy."

Lucy nodded. "You said a mouthful. Can you help me?"

"You want to know who or what could do this to someone?"

Lucy nodded again. "Do you know?"

Marvin frowned, then got to his feet and walked over to a bookshelf. Pulling down a weathered-looking book with yellowed pages, he flipped through. As he found what he was looking for, his frown deepened, carving deep black scowl lines in his forehead. He nodded to himself. *"Mais oui.* It is just as I thought."

"What?" Lucy asked in breathless anticipation.

"This is pure evil. *Ancient* evil," he said, his voice harsh with concern. "The monster you seek is called an incubus. A Ka incubus to be precise, one that feeds off a person's youth like vampires feed off blood."

"An incubus?" Lucy felt goose bumps up and down her arms, as if the universe was warning her away. "I've heard of incubi that feed off lust. But I thought they were extinct."

"*Non.* Not extinct, but very rare. And these are even more so. Few know about the Ka incubi. I had thought they were in the Big Sleep between worlds and shadows. But it appears that one is here in the Big Easy." Marvin shook his head. "*Ma amie,* this is very bad. Very bad magic."

Suddenly time seemed to slow, if only for a moment, and Lucy knew that she had crossed a line. She was nearing the dark side, hunting for this predator who stole a person's life-force. She could end up dead, or she could end up sixty-four, with lined skin and nobody to love her — and all in the next few days. Still, she wouldn't let the opportunity pass. Her mama didn't raise no fools.

Watching Lucy's reaction, Marvin nodded somberly, his green eyes fraught with some emotion Lucy didn't understand. An image of Serena thrust itself into her mind: Serena's misery, her lack of hope, the dying emotion and life in her eyes. "Can Serena ever get her youth back?" she found herself asking.

"*Oui.* If someone can capture the incubus fairly soon and submerge him in salt water for a day and night, then part of the life-force he has stolen will be given back to those whom he has robbed."

"How do you capture something like that?" Lucy asked.

Marvin stared at her. Then he explained how to capture an incubus with an ancient spell. It included chanting, some green powder, and unfortunately a dead chicken. Lucy had him write it down.

Before she left, Marvin warned her to be careful, and then he made her a protection *gris-gris.* It included some herbs, a small stone, and a few bones. The last ingredient, much to Lucy's disgust, was a small chicken foot.

Chickens, chickens, chickens. She hadn't liked the things since she was a girl, and had had to gather eggs in the henhouse on the small ranch her family owned in West Texas. She still had the tiny scars on her arms from chicken-pecking during her egg-gathering experiences. An irate chicken was damn mean — like an eighth-grade girl — and it pecked anyone who was stupid enough to go after its eggs. As Lucy got older, she'd given a wide berth to rampaging chickens, even going so far as to swear off fried chicken, her grandma's specialty. Now it seemed she was back in fowl territory.

Thanking Marvin sincerely for his help, she walked outside and fingered the *grisgris*. Her thoughts were whirling around and around like a potter's wheel. She didn't really believe in lucky charms, but one couldn't hurt. Although, now she was stuck wearing a chicken's foot around her neck. At least it didn't peck and didn't stink. Her life, she mused wryly, was a feathery flap of a farce.

# CHAPTER SEVEN:
## HANK WILLIAMS HAD
## IT RIGHT

Fingering the *gris-gris* that Marvin had given her earlier in the day, Lucy walked up the steps to the entrance of the Overbite Bar, DeLeon's supposed hangout. Marvin's and Serena's warnings echoed in her ear, ghostly whispers of dread. Still, Lucy knew that some stories had to be told. It didn't matter that danger lay hidden deep in the shadows, concealed behind smoke and mirrors; all that mattered was the story, and that she would be the one to expose the Ka incubus on her talk show. However, caution would be her word of the day. She didn't intend to go from being a talk show diva to queen of a nursing home all in one night.

At the door, two large signs read: VAMPIRES DO IT WITH A PRICK and WEREWOLVES DO IT WITH THEIR CLAWS ON. Lucy frowned. That was too much for her. Still, paying her cover charge, she walked inside.

The Overbite Bar was a place where wannabes, a few real vampires, werewolves, and other supernatural creatures sometimes stopped by for a drink or a quick bite. The club was fairly crowded tonight, and it looked like everyone and their dog was here. Around Lucy, vampire wannabes were dressed in black capes and black pants, their dark shirts open to the waist, exposing their jugulars. Others were dressed in red.

For some strange reason, humans had gotten it into their heads that vampires only liked black and red. Vampires *did* love the color red, but mostly flowing out of bodies — to drink and not to wear.

And vampires apparently loved flowers. The male vampires here wore flowers in their buttonholes, and the vampiresses wore them in their hair or on their clothing, and it was clear each vampire was specific about which flower he preferred. Val must have preferred golden roses.

Choosing a table in the middle of the bar, Lucy glanced up at the open balcony above, noting where the true vampires were sitting. The tables they sat at had an array of night-blooming flora in vases. The vampires were dressed in an array of bright colors, skintight dresses or pants. Lucy caught a glimpse of disgust cross their faces every time the humans below vied for their attention in their Bela Lugosi costumes and faux vampire creations.

A waitress dressed in a skimpy black dress with almost no back leaned down and asked, "What's your poison?"

"Lone Star longneck," Lucy responded, scanning the crowd.

"Hey, aren't you that host for the *Twilight Zone?*" Lucy nodded, glad to be recognized, and the waitress continued enthusiastically, "I just loved that one show with all those Draculas in drag."

Lucy smiled. "It's one of my favorites, too. Kind of like a Victoria's Secret catalog meets *Fangoria.*"

"I know! I'm just dying to know where that green-haired drag queen got that cute little leafy number."

Lucy laughed. The leafy number had just the right amount of strategically placed foliage, giving the drag queen a kind of Tarzan-meets-Dracula chic. "He told me he bought his outfit at the Yolanda G. store," she confided.

"Thanks!" The waitress looked thrilled, flashing a toothy smile — complete with fake fangs, of course. "Well, let me get your beer."

Two drinks later, Lucy still hadn't spotted

her quarry, and had turned down four offers to dance and one to buy her a drink. She was getting antsy from sitting still for so long. Shaking her head, she sighed. She'd had no idea surveillance work was such a dull detail. No wonder cops sat around on stakeouts eating donuts and drinking tons of black coffee, with scowls on their faces; they were probably bored silly.

Glancing down at her watch, she noted it was approaching one in the morning. She was tired and she had been here for over three hours, hoping to use herself as bait, yet so far she had received no useful bites. She hadn't even spotted anyone that resembled the description of DeLeon, and certainly not anyone with violet eyes, a color no other supernatural predator she'd seen could claim.

"Well, well. Look who's here."

Turning slightly, Lucy found herself face-to-face with Detective Valmont DuPonte, and she choked on her drink. As usual, his presence was electric. Her pale blue eyes watering, she wondered what the coffin-hopping, fang-banging worm was doing here.

As her eyes quit watering, she took another long look at her ex-lover. He might be a cheating worm, but Val was an attractive worm, and he wore authority well. This vampire, who had made his own rules for centuries, was like a giant straddling the world.

He was staring at her neck. She shivered, remembering that necking with a vampire took on a whole new meaning — and that meaning was a far cry from the necking with a redneck in a pickup truck that all good — or not-so-good — Texas girls had done in high school.

Her heart began pounding, and she felt an adrenaline rush much like the ones she got when she ran. Runs always made her slightly dizzy and sick at her stomach. That, she supposed, was why she rarely ran or jogged.

"Fancy meeting you here, Lucy. Slumming and dressed like an Elvira reject?" Val pulled out a chair across from her and sat down.

Lucy narrowed her eyes. Her dress might be a tad on the Goth side, but it was none of her ex's business.

"Hardly slumming," she replied, willing her brisk heartbeat to slow down, willing the butterflies in her stomach to settle and stop trying to crawl up into her throat. "I don't remember asking you to sit down."

"Now, *ma petite,* your bad manners are

showing." Val stared at her fringed sleeves with tiny feathers attached and grimaced. "Definitely the Elvira look. Or maybe Morticia Addams."

Glancing away from Lucy, Val took in some of the other mortals. They seemed dressed more for a Halloween costume ball than a nightclub. His blue eyes lit with scorn. Humans were always trying to imitate what they admired, and most of them were hoping to live forever. They never learned that it wasn't the number of breaths a person took, but the quality of those breaths. A person could live to be a thousand, but that wasn't the key. If he wasn't happy with himself as a mortal, he would probably despise himself as an immortal.

Lucy heard the scorn in Val's voice. She knew he despised Goth clubs and all humans who longed to be something they weren't. It wasn't that Val was a snob; it was just that he believed those who longed to be vampires and leave behind their humanity had little idea what being a vampire really meant. He had explained it all to her: Vampirism wasn't about sex, blood, and violence all the time, or about unending power and very long lives. Rather, being a vampire was a culture within itself, with very strict rules and responsibilities.

Even though she understood his point, she didn't like his disdain. Especially not directed at her. "What cactus bit you in the butt?"

"*Cherie,* how you've changed since . . ." He hesitated, the implication clear.

"You mean, since that night we broke up?" Lucy finished crossly. Oh, how that night lived in infamy in her mind.

"Since you ran away like a *pichouette* — like a little girl. You acted like a spoiled brat, breaking up with me without hearing my explanations." Val hadn't meant to get into their separation, to show that he held any feelings for her whatsoever, but seeing her up close and personal had really tested his resolve. Lucy was still as beautiful and spirited as when he'd first met her. He recalled the strawberry birthmark on her right hip that turned scarlet red when she climaxed. He longed to forget her totally, but he also longed to hold her in his arms.

He leaned back in his chair. Her scent was still managing to arouse him to a painful degree, his preternatural senses running amok with his hormones. He shouldn't feel anything for this woman who could turn away from his love, who could not trust him never to betray her. Her lack of trust had wounded him deeply, especially after he had given her his whole heart. "You wouldn't even take my phone calls," he reminded her coldly.

"You quit calling after six weeks. Such devotion," Lucy asserted. "Romeo would have called Juliet for at least six months before he gave up on her . . . if they had phones back then," she finished lamely. Just because she had screamed at Val to never call her again was no reason that he had to obey. He should have just climbed up her balcony.

"You told me you loved me, Val. Man oh man, was Hank Williams right!" Lucy said disgustedly.

"Hank Williams?" Val cocked a brow, trying to follow Lucy's slippery thoughts. Sometimes it was like trying to walk on a tightrope covered in grease being cut at one end.

"Your cheating heart will tell on you! You betrayed me with a vampiress. *A vampiress!* You swore to me that you didn't mind me being human, and yet you made love to another of your species while you were supposedly in love with me! Well, let me tell you something, you crypt Casanova — what goes around comes around!" she snarled, her pale blue eyes darkening. "You didn't find me with *my* teeth in someone else's neck that night! You're as bad as my father and stepfather." So far, her father had been married three times, and her stepfather had left her mother for a twenty-two-year-old with two big boobs and one tiny little brain.

The muscles in his jaw tightening, Val growled, *"E' spes'ces de te'te dure."*

"Oh, speak English!" Lucy grumped.

"You hardheaded thing. I did not betray you. Not once. Not ever!"

Val's voice rose on his last two words, and the sharpness of it grated on Lucy's nerves. How dare he criticize her when he was the lecherous leech who couldn't keep his fangs in his mouth? "Liar, liar, pants on fire," she spat out. Then, realizing what she had said, she prayed for the floor to swallow her whole. "Well, that was certainly mature," she said after a moment. And although her face was red, at least she had beat him to any comment.

Relaxing slightly, Val crossed his arms over his chest. "I rest my case. You are as stubborn as a mule and you still haven't grown up."

"Why, you randy horse's ass. Just because I'm not over two hundred years old doesn't make me immature."

"Your age has nothing to do with it, *cherie,* just your attitude. Deep inside you're still that little girl whose father left her mother for another woman," Val remarked. Watching her angry face tense with the mention of her past, he went on. "You never really gave me a chance. I tried hard to prove to you that I was trustworthy, *cherie.* I let you see more of me than I have ever shown anyone besides my immediate family. But when push came to shove, you shoved me away."

"Jeez, Val. Since when did you get the psychology degree?" Lucy sneered. He had no right to condemn her when he had betrayed her trust. "My mom was right. Dogs are loyal. Men aren't."

Val glared at her. "You're not the only one who got hurt. You should have just taken a stake and stuck it in my heart. Because that's what it felt like when you threw away our life."

Lucy held up her thumb, making it go around in a tiny circle. "See this? It's the world's smallest record playing 'My Heart Bleeds for You.' "

Val sighed. "Were you always this cruel, or had I forgotten?" He should be over her. There had been other females of all colors, species, and sizes. And yet . . . none of them compared to Lucy, even on her bad days.

"I'm not some dumb blonde, Val. I know

what I saw! You had your fangs in her neck and you were both naked underneath those robes!"

At that moment, Lucy hated Val with an intensity that shocked her, and wanted him with a desperation born of lost closeness. Part of her was crying out to run her fingers over that wonderfully sleek body. It had been so long since she had felt the incredible mind-altering passion he stirred within her. She found herself wondering how a heart could be filled with such hurt, and yet want so much to brave that hurt again.

Val stood up to leave, graceful as always.

"Wait!" The word tore from her throat in its urgency, but Lucy couldn't and wouldn't beg to have him back. Campbell women were made of sterner stuff than that.

Still, before she knew what she was doing, she'd already asked, "What *happened,* Val?"

He shook his head. "Once I would have explained my actions. Once I tried to explain my actions. But you didn't want to listen."

"I . . ." Lucy choked on the words. Suddenly she was dying to know why her love had cheated on her, wanted to forget her pride and her past. "Why were you with that vamp that night?"

Val studied Lucy's high breasts, and the

way her skirt skimmed over her hips, hugging their slender shape. But then he decided, "Once those words would have meant the world to me. Once. You know something, *cherie,* you're a martyr to your past."

And before Lucy could say another word, Val was gone; the dead man was walking, leaving her a dead woman inside once again. He was right; she knew that her past had shaped her into the woman she was today. Her decisions, values, hopes, fears — it all came from what had happened to her as a child, both the big traumatic heartbreaks and the small inconsequential things that filled the everyday life. After hearing Val tonight, Lucy wondered if her eyes had been so clouded with what had been that she'd refused to see what could have been.

Two tears coursed down her cheeks, and Lucy had a feeling that she had might have made a mistake four years ago. In a life fraught with errors and her accident-prone character, losing Val might just have been the biggest mistake of her whole life.

No. Who was she kidding? Losing Val *had* been the biggest mistake of her life. Getting up from her table, she resolved to leave. She was too depressed for any more stakeout duty. And as she walked out the door of the bar, Lucy sighed mournfully.

"If only." They were two small words, which meant everything if a lonely person could go back.

*If only.*

# CHAPTER EIGHT:
# I USED TO LOVE
# LUCY

Everyone, human or supernatural, carried his past with him, like so much unwanted baggage. If a person was smart and self-aware, he lightened his load. But Lucy hadn't lightened her load at all, Val realized despondently as he hurried out of the Overbite Bar.

Shaking his head, he walked to his car. He had loved Lucy once, deeply and passionately, in spite of the fact that she had turned his undead life upside down with her accident-prone and chaotic lifestyle. Lucy was intelligent, passionate, and most of all she made him laugh. She had a bulldog determination in whatever she undertook, and an air of innocence about her that he had always found refreshing. He had loved to listen to her West Texas accent she couldn't quite get rid of, especially with words like "oil," "wash," and "nine." The way she slurred them out, she sounded like she was from another planet.

The first time Val met her had been at the Riverwalk in San Antonio. When she had fallen into the river, he had fallen hard. Later that night, they had danced to a golden oldie by Tony Orlando called "Tie a Yellow Ribbon Round the Old Oak Tree," and Chicago's "Color My World." Those two songs became their songs.

Three weeks later they'd made love for the first time. The Eagles' "Take it to the Limit" had been playing, and their two pulses had beat in rhythm to the music and their dance of love as old as time. Val had taken them both to the limit, over and over, as the dark shades of evening faded to the grays and purples of darkest night. Lucy had been everything he ever imagined in a lover. Of course, she had also been fairly inexperienced.

Yes, Lucy had become his daydreams, and she had filled his nighttime with true happiness, a *bon viveur* he had not felt in over two hundred years.

On the downside, Lucy had always been argumentative, stubborn as a mule for someone not of the shape-shifter weremule set, suspicious, and immature. Her pride was almost as strong as his own. And the most daunting thing about her was that she hadn't outgrown her past. She probably never would.

The ringing of his cell phone captured his attention as he put his car into gear. Glancing down at the display, he noted it was his partner in the paranormal task forces. "What's up, Chris?"

Chris's husky voice drew him back from his dark thoughts about lost love. Christine was a vampiress, and had been his partner for over four years. She had once been a lover. In fact, her relationship with Val was what had sparked her interest in law enforcement. Christine had gotten her degree and become a police officer for the night shift back when women were still scarce in the force.

"What's happened?" he asked her.

"We got a dead one. Strange, Val. It's really strange," Chris said.

"Where at?" Val felt his face muscles tightening. If Christine said it was strange, that was a bad sign. As partners, they had seen some really gruesome murders, from deranged ghouls to rogue werewolves.

"Down at the French Quarter on Voodoo Lane, a block from Addams's Familiars."

Addams's Familiars was a favorite of the wizard and witch world, as well as with gargoyles who liked having something fuzzy to play with while in flesh form. Cats, frogs, bats, hamsters — any number of familiars were available at the store, in all shapes, sizes, and colors.

"You there now?" Val asked.

"*Oui.* Just got here and saw the body," Christine replied, her voice filled with tension.

"I'll be there in five," Val responded. He flipped off the phone. If Chris was this upset, something big, bad, and ugly had gone down tonight. Val knew, because he knew his partner. Even though they hadn't been lovers in over eighty years, he still cared about her and always would. She hadn't ever been the love of his life, but she always stood firm as a friend that he could count on. He owed Christine a lot, in spite of the fact that she was the vampiress Lucy had seen with him that ill-fated night four years ago.

Hurrying to the scene of the crime, he could see the yellow and black police tape billowing softly in the light wind. Val's nostrils dilated at the smell of garbage tinged with the hot sultry air of the Louisiana night. Beneath the putrid scent of rotting trash was a different smell of decay.

His partner was standing by the victim's body. Christine's skin was the color of creamed coffee, her lean, muscular body a stark contrast to the victim. The dead woman was older, her body curled into the fetal position, and she had heavily wrinkled skin on her face with eyes clouded white from age. The corpse had little muscle mass left in her legs and arms, and her skirt was hiked above bony hips. Underwear hung around her right ankle.

It was the expression on her face, mouth frozen in a scream of horror, which caused a wave of sympathy to sweep Val. Nobody should die in a dirty alley like this, left to rot like so much trash. And soon the victim would be just a number in the morgue. Val wondered what her last thoughts had been. The woman had been terribly afraid; he could still smell the emotion in the air.

Clenching his jaw, he surveyed the area and approached the victim. The scene showed signs of rough sex: bruises on the skin and ripped underclothes.

Kneeling, he studied the victim as dozens of scents filtered through his nose. Something supernatural had used this woman and destroyed her; Val could smell it in the scents of night, in a faint damp smell of the grave. He didn't believe a vampire had done this, but something with a similar smell — something probably a close relative to the

Nosferatu species.

"*A la fin!* Welcome to the end," Val hissed, his dark blue eyes fierce. And, shaking his head, he turned away from the frozen scream and wide milky eyes of the corpse. "Who found the body?" he asked.

"Some kids. They were drinking pretty heavily and wandered outside to be sick."

Val nodded. "Coroner?"

Christine glanced down at her watch. "ETA is sometime in the next ten minutes." She turned back to the victim's corpse, sadly shaking her head. "She looks like she's been raped. Who would want to rape an old woman? And why is this old woman wearing red bikini briefs with lace hearts? And look at the old gal's shoes! Four-inch spiked heels? How can someone this frail even walk in them?"

Val shook his head. "The sex started out consensual, I think. And she smells like she's been dead maybe three hours. Not more than four."

Sniffing the air carefully, Christine concurred, her chocolate-brown eyes filled with worry. Lifting the victim's purse, she grabbed the wallet inside.

"What on earth could have done this?" she asked, glancing through the wallet.

"You mean what in *hell,*" Val said savagely.

Even after all the years he had lived, death was never a pretty sight. He knew it was never a welcome one for mortals.

"You think we're looking for some sort of demon work?" Christine asked.

Val shook his head.

"A *traiteur* voodoo?" Christine suggested, holding up the victim's driver's license. "Says here that her name is Caral Jones. She was only twenty-four. Damn, it looks like she got a reverse face-lift."

"Or something worse, much worse," Val agreed. He hated to see this waste. Life was precious, both human and paranormal. This young woman had once laughed, had probably strolled along the French Quarter in the morning, sitting at a café with a cup of chicory coffee and a plate of warm beignets. This woman had once loved and been held tenderly by someone who cherished her. Her hopes and potential were now gone forever, all taken by an act of cruel intention and insidious hunger. To stop things like this was why he'd joined the police.

"How was this done? If this is her license . . . how could she age to death this quickly?"

"With a lot of help from something other-worldly," Val replied. "Something real other-worldly. Something I thought was still sleep-ing, which was sleeping for over six centuries."

"What are you talking about? What did this? If it was black magic, then it's stronger than any I've ever seen."

Val lowered his head as he studied the body, replying tersely, "This isn't simple black magic, Chris. This was something feeding."

His partner looked incredulous. "Feeding? What feeds on youth?"

"An incubus. A Ka incubus to be exact."

"But I . . ." Chris hesitated, her confusion evident. "Incubi feed on lust, I thought. And there aren't many of them left."

Glancing back at his partner, Val nodded. "You're half right. Incubi who feed on lust are called Eros incubi. They're very old, and since they can't create more of themselves, they're a dying race. Maybe there are eleven left from the Old World. Those, supposedly, in Europe."

"Then what's a Ka? I've never heard of them."

Val sighed, adding in a grim tone, "Not many know of their existence. They feed off youth, like the Eros feed off lust. There's only supposed to be three or four Kas left, and they have been sleeping the Big Sleep. Nobody knows where. It was rumored they were around the Ural Mountains. It appears

the rumors are wrong," Val finished sardonically. He glanced down at the aged remains
in front of him.

"Let me do some checking, and I'll get
back with you on this," he said after a moment. If what he was thinking was true, then
the Big Easy was in for a world of hurt.
Incubi in general felt the world was their
oyster. Kas liked to eat oysters raw. They
were generally very intelligent, lusty, attractive, and cruel. And hungry. They were
always very, very hungry.

Christine started to argue, but Val shook
his head and started toward his car. "Look,
I've got some research to do, and some calls
to make to the League in Europe."

"The League of Vampires?" Christine
asked, surprised. Val hated to ask for help,
and especially from the League. They always
required a favor for anything they did.
Sometimes those favors had a decidedly
nasty edge.

"Chris, use your paranormal contacts to
check out the supernatural community, and
see if there have been any more bodies that
have aged at a rapid rate. I know there are
no cases like this anywhere in New Orleans
or even Louisiana, or we would have been
contacted. But try out the Federal website
for similar crimes and see if anything else is

stirring."

Christine nodded and Val left, his thoughts in turmoil. If a Ka incubus was feeding in New Orleans, what a plentiful supply of food the monster had. Partygoers of every age, size, shape, and beauty, everyone was drinking and enjoying the good life, not realizing that paradise always, always, had a dark side, a cruel, ugly side.

Val cursed. The Big Easy was appropriately named.

# Chapter Nine:
# Lucy in the Sky
## with Diamonds

After a sleepless night, regrets filling her for both listening to Val and not listening to Val, Lucy had gotten out of bed on the wrong side. Nothing had gone right lately. She hadn't found DeLeon at the Overbite Bar, and Val's comments had been earth-shattering. For four years she had refused to listen to him, and now she was dying to hear his explanation. And if that didn't beat all, she didn't know what did.

Eating a late lunch in front of her television, she found a newscast that caught her attention like the snap of a line when a big old catfish took the bait. The newscaster was talking about the recent violence in New Orleans, the newest death. And Lucy was struck by the description of an old woman who had been found raped and murdered. Her name was Caral Jones. The unusual spelling had stuck out like a sore thumb.

As luck would have it, Lucy had interviewed a Caral Jones eight months ago for one of her shows. Caral had been twenty-four.

In trying to get answers from the New Orleans Paranormal Task Force, Lucy was unsuccessful. She encountered a big blue wall, as if she had run smack-dab into a Blueberry Ogre. No one was answering any questions, which only encouraged Lucy's suspicions. As her mother always said: *"You can douse a skunk with perfume, but it still stinks."*

Yes, the New Orleans PTF stunk to high heaven. Caral Jones's murder had been done by a preternatural creature unlike any New Orleans had ever seen or smelled before. The perp was a Ka incubus, and the powers that be were keeping mum.

Calling Caral's number, Lucy quickly learned that the girl had died last night, a victim of a foul attack. The chances of two women with the same unusual spelling of the name Caral both dying on the same night were just too much, and so, in typical fashion, Lucy came up with a plan. She had been tempted to tell Ricki, to get her help, but decided at the last moment that tracking down a Ka incubus was too dangerous to include close friends or even enemies.

Putting her plan into action, she dressed in beige khakis with a white lab coat thrown over her blue T-shirt. Her hair was in a tight bun, and she put on a pair of tortoiseshell spectacles, hoping to disguise her looks. She might not be as famous as Sandra Bullock, but she did have some following in New Orleans.

On the pocket of the lab coat she wore, Lucy pinned the name tag for a Dr. Craig. Her badge at a quick glance looked like any other badge worn by members of the New Orleans morgue staff; however, if she was unlucky and someone inspected the badge closer she would be caught for sure.

She was unlucky. Within ten minutes, Lucy had been caught by a junior G-man wannabe, the assistant to the assistant coroner. She had been thrown unceremoniously out of the morgue, and escorted outside by a security guard with a stern lecture on illegally gaining entrance.

Back at her van, Lucy eyed the hospital building, a huge Gothic-like structure built of cement, limestone, and steel. A small light above the imposing entrance revealed two thick glass doors, a yawning opening like a huge glass mouth.

Lucy stared hard at the entrance, her thoughts tumbling everywhere. At this rate, she thought derisively, she would never get close to Caral Jones. But the old woman's body in the morgue must be the same Caral Jones that Lucy had interviewed, and a person didn't have to be Sherlock Holmes to figure out that the Ka was on the attack.

Putting on her thinking cap, Lucy reviewed her options. She had to get into the morgue to view the evidence. Just because she had been bodily escorted out, that did not deter her. Campbell women weren't squeamish or quitters. They were, however, adept at adaptation.

Watching an ambulance pull in, Lucy noticed the attendees wheeling a covered body on a stretcher into the morgue.

"A covered sheet . . . a body. Oh yeah!" she said, her pale blue eyes lighting with inspiration. Jumping into her van, she took off like a bat out of hell.

Thirty minutes later, Lucy had secured a gurney and sheets from St. Elligus Hospital, a parish hospital that was so busy a person could steal a dead body away with no one the wiser. This bizarre event had happened a time or two in the past, as Lucy knew from interviews on her show.

Unloading the gurney from the back of her van, Lucy cursed as she dropped one of the wheels on her toes. "Hell's bells," she said as she hopped around on one foot. "That really hurts." Who knew that a gurney was so heavy? Paramedics should get hazard pay.

Reaching inside her van, she grabbed a king-sized bottle of ketchup and began squeezing it into the sheets. After she finished, she rubbed it onto her pants, T-shirt, and arms, then smeared some into her hair. At last, closing the van doors, she began her secret trek to the morgue by route of a line of trees around the building. She wanted absolute silence, but finally decided that an occasional curse and the sound of twigs snapping under the gurney wheels would be acceptable.

"Damn it all," she said. A gurney had wheels and rolled, so therefore it should be reasonably easy to push across slightly uneven, unpaved ground. Who would have known it would take a bodybuilder to accomplish it? At this rate, she was going to miss her show, which just wasn't acceptable — not to her, and, more especially, not to her boss, Mr. Moody. She sped up, in spite of the protest from her aching muscles.

She had to duck far back into the tree's shadows with the gurney once, as an ambulance came to a screeching halt in front of the morgue. Waiting for the attendants to leave, Lucy began to get impatient, feeling terribly creepy standing smothered in ketchup in the shadows, cavernous darkness at her back.

Suddenly, her scalp started itching and she felt the hairs on the back of her neck stand up, just like in a horror movie. Someone or some*thing* was watching her; she just knew it. It was probably plotting how best to eat her alive, or to drink her blood, to drain her dry. And she'd already applied the condiment.

A ghostly whisper of sound had her cringing, and Lucy felt the cold at her back. Beyond that were the black recesses and dark depths of the unknown. Her breathing quickened and she took deep breaths, the metallic taste of fear filling her mouth. She didn't want to be a blurb on the nightly news, "Talk show host found eaten like a hamburger." She didn't want to be any species' food for thought.

Reaching inside her pocket, she found her can of mace. She wanted to turn around and look, but fear held her immobile until the crackling of tree branches behind her preceded the word "Who?" That startled her into reacting.

With lightning reflexes born of fear, Lucy whirled, expecting to see some demon from hell, or some ghoul or ghoulish freak who liked to hang out near morgues. Instead, her eyes, now more accustomed to the darkness, met two other eyes staring at her from the top of an oak.

"Hooo," the sound came again.

Shoving a hand to her mouth, Lucy barely stifled her relieved giggles. Her menacing presence was an owl! Shaking her head, she stepped back and checked again on the ambulance. Its attendants were just now getting inside.

As she stood there, Lucy felt a sting on her ankle, followed closely by another. "Ouch!" She hopped on one foot, swiping at her pantleg, finally managing to raise it. Finding an ant, she moved away from the anthill she had disturbed with her gurney.

"What rotten luck! I'm somebody's food after all. Probably a fire ant too," Lucy grumped. She hated the tiny little menaces. Their bites were painful and left big red lumps. "What *else* can go wrong tonight?" she asked.

At last the ambulance sped away, and Lucy cautiously tugged and pushed the gurney over the uneven ground until she reached the back parking lot. Glancing right and left, like a sprinter in training, Lucy ducked low and prepared. Then she shoved the gurney hard in front of her, running, the gurney's wheels spinning crazily. Huffing and puffing, she started to feel dizzy. Still, she reached her goal.

Her victorious "Yes!" punctuated the night. With true grit, she had made it to the side of the building that was heaviest in shadows. "John Wayne, you'd be proud of me," she muttered as she stared at the entrance. "Now to wait for another ambulance."

She didn't have long. Within minutes, another ambulance had pulled up to the morgue, quickly and efficiently unloading its cargo and going inside, the glass entrance doors sliding open with a *ping.*

Lucy pushed her gurney hard, rushing for the doors. Glancing quickly inside, she noted that the security guard had again followed the ambulance attendants down the long hallway to find out all the gory details. Lucy had noted the guard's ghoulish curiosity earlier, after the first paramedics brought someone in. Campbell women had a keen eye for detail. After all, God was in the details — that and in cooking ingredients.

Shoving her gurney through the doors, Lucy pushed it quickly down to the opposite end of the hallway, where she settled the heavy metal stretcher. Lifting the messy sheet, she scrambled onto the gurney and threw the sheet over her body and face. All she had to do now was pretend to be dead, and they would wheel her into the main part of the morgue, right next to the autopsy room. Hopefully the ketchuped sheets would look like a bloody mess, and no one would be tempted to look underneath. Even if they did, she felt sure she could hold her breath for a few minutes. How hard could playing dead be?

More sounds came from the back of the morgue. Lucy listened intently, taking tiny breaths, hoping no one could see any infinitesimal movements of the sheet over her mouth. She hoped she didn't hyperventilate. How inconsiderate of the paramedics and guard to keep yapping when she might do just that.

Finally she heard the other gurney being wheeled out, its wheels making a *cha-chink* sound on the worn linoleum tile, and the guard and the paramedics talking about the car wreck that had just claimed two lives. Suddenly Lucy heard them call a greeting.

"You here for the Jones autopsy, Detective DuPonte?" a male voice asked.

Lucy stifled a groan. Of all the morgues in all the world, why did the grand detective of the undead have to show up at hers? She supposed it was because Val had a nose for sniffing out conspiracies. Although her conspiracy wasn't important in the great scheme of things, it was still a conspiracy, which to Val would be like waving a red flag in front of a bull. Or red gunk in front of a vampire.

Remaining very still, Lucy held her breath as she heard him acknowledge the question. He then began walking toward the autopsy room, passing Lucy by.

Suddenly the footsteps stopped, only a few steps past the hallway where Lucy lay in wait. Lucy froze every muscle in her body, her heart pounding. Could this fiendish Don Juan of the undead hear her heart beating like a demented drum in her suddenly very tight chest?

Four steps later she had her answer, as she felt the sheet being whisked off her. She didn't open her eyes, wondering briefly if she could just continue to play possum. She supposed things had taken a wrong turn at the condiment tray. Maybe she should have thought it through better.

# CHAPTER TEN:
# WASH THAT MAN
# RIGHT OUT OF HER
# HAIR

---

*"Merde."* Val laughed as he yanked back the sheet. "What do we have here — Sleeping Beauty?"

Lucy kept her eyes firmly shut, wishing she and her gurney could disappear into thin air. Where was a witch's broomstick when she needed one?

"Well, well, *cherie.* First I catch you dressing like Elvira, now I find you playing dead in the morgue. Are you trying out to be undead, or just bored?" Val stared, wondering what Lucy was playing at. What was she doing in the morgue with ketchup smeared all over her?

He goosed her. "Rise and shine. And by the way, you overdid the Heinz."

Lucy opened her eyes, the color of her face a match for the condiment in her hair, and Val stared down at her as if she had stepped on his grave. Lines of concern twisted the corners of his mouth. As if she didn't know the gravity of her situation!

Standing directly behind Val was the security guard, whose eyes and mouth were wide open.

Blinking, Lucy sighed. The jig was up, and humiliation was once again her middle name. "How did you know that there really wasn't a dead person under here?" she asked.

Val leaned over and sniffed disdainfully. "How else?"

Foiled, and caught red-handed. And -bodied. And -haired. What wretched luck.

Getting to her feet, she pushed away from Val. "Your nose should be in the Guinness Book of World Records. Are you sure you aren't part werewolf?" she snapped.

She could see a slight grin tug at the corners of his mouth — a mouth she wanted to kiss. Hell's bells! Why couldn't she just forget him? She needed to wash him right out of her hair, along with about thirty gallons of ketchup.

The security guard was scowling at her as if she had stolen the Hope Diamond, and he finally put in his two bits. "You're the lady that pretended to be a doctor earlier." Glancing at Val, he added suspiciously, "Detective DuPonte, I've already had to throw her out of here once. You ought to arrest her for breaking and entering."

"Tattletale," Lucy groused. "And I didn't break and enter. The doors were open, and you weren't at your post."

Hands on his hips, the guard scowled. Pointing a finger at her, he glanced over at Val. "Then arrest her for impersonating a dead body."

Val chuckled. "That's not illegal. Especially here in the Big Easy."

The guard started to protest, and Lucy grinned. A wave of relief washed over her. She wasn't going to be hauled off to jail after all.

Val put up a hand as he noticed Lucy's smile. Whatever chaos she was up to, he was going to nip it in the bud. He said, "However, entering the morgue under false pretenses can get a person into big trouble."

This time, Lucy scowled and the guard grinned. "Good. I've got a pair of handcuffs if you need them," he suggested helpfully.

Val shook his head, his deadpan expression revealing nothing. "Thanks, Max, but I'll take it from here." And with a motion of his hand, he dismissed the guard.

Lucy could hear the grumbling as Max stalked off down the darkened hallway. Glancing at Val's rather grim expression, and seeing the slight glare in his vampiric gaze, Lucy decided that fleeing the scene of this tiny little crime was probably her wisest course of action. She took three steps backward.

Val shook his head, his blue eyes dark with emotion. "*Viens ici!* Come here."

Lucy obeyed, took two steps forward, albeit warily.

"What are you doing here, *cherie?*"

"Would you believe my laundry?" Lucy replied. She hoped that humor would somehow defuse the situation.

"This isn't funny, Lucy. I can take you into the station for this. I probably should." She was up to her pretty little eyeballs in something, and he was going to get to the bottom of whatever crazy scheme she was hatching.

Setting her jaw, Lucy spoke with a confidence she was far from feeling. She held out her hands, her expression defiant. "Do your worst. Haul me in. Beat me with your nightstick." Campbell women didn't back away from danger, even two hundred pounds of mad, sexy vampire. Campbell women embraced danger, they ran toward it. Of course, Campbell women often had short life spans.

"I don't carry a nightstick, and you know it. *Merde!* I ought to take you over my knee and spank you, is what I ought to do."

"You wouldn't dare. I watch Court TV. I watch *Law & Order.*" But she wasn't so sure. Val looked angry enough to dare anything. "You touch me and I'll scream police brutality. *Big-time* police brutality. I'll tell all New Orleans that you're a monster. A betraying brute who threatens helpless women with handcuffs and worse."

"*Mais oui* — yes, you would, wouldn't you? Do you see any handcuffs, Lucy?" he asked tiredly. His next glare was an exact replica of his last. Jeez, the vampire had no range of expression.

Lucy dropped her arms as he shook his head, and he said tersely, "You always were hysterical, and willing to embellish the truth. I remember when I flew to talk to you in San Antonio, and you stood on that balcony screaming at me. You shouted that I should be hauled off by Robespierre, and cursed me for peasant abuse — all when I haven't had peasants on my land in two hundred years. I remember you throwing a vase of flowers at my head and screaming obscenities," Val continued, visions of spanking that pert bottom flashing through his head. Baring that bottom, and then the rest would be . . . something he did his damnedest to forget.

"You deserved worse, you blood-sucking betrayer!" Lucy waved her finger at him, remembering more of her mama's sage advice: *When verbally attacked by an irate male, deflect, deceive, and demand.*

"You mistrustful malicious mortal," Val replied. His eyes glowed with the fires of injustice. Lucy made him angrier than any other female in his entire existence, and that was saying quite a lot. "Shut up, Lucy. You don't know what you're talking about."

Lucy glared at him, her hands on her hips. Anger flooded her system like the sugar from four too many Fig Newtons. "Don't you tell me to shut up, you two-timing satyr! Don't talk down to me. Don't act like I'm some blond bimbo you can crush under your feet like some rider-stomping bull longhorn. I expect your respect," Lucy shouted. "No, I *demand* your respect! And I want none of your irritable male syndrome!"

Val narrowed his eyes. "Irritable male syndrome?" What the hell was that? Well, he'd show her an irritated male, all right. "*Merde.* You're an expert in deflection and diversion for one so young," he admitted. He still needed to find out exactly what Lucy knew, and listening to his nether region crying out for a hot time in the old town tonight would get him nowhere.

No, he certainly shouldn't be finding her attractive — not in one of her temper tantrums, standing there covered in ketchup. But he was either sick or he had gone too long without mind-blowing sex. Lucy was the only mind-blowing sex he had experienced in over three hundred years, and she was driving him crazy.

"I never said you were a bimbo, Luce," he said with a sigh. "Stop the stalling techniques. What the hell are you doing here?"

"Research," she answered.

"For what?" Val had a sudden glimmer of suspicion that Lucy knew something about the incubus. Earlier today they had discovered the existence of another victim. Fortunately, the woman was still alive, and Christine was interviewing her at this very moment. Hopefully, when Val met back up with his partner at police headquarters, they would both have considerably more information to share about the youth-stealing monster.

"Research . . . for a show," Lucy lied, trying desperately to come up with some reasonable explanation to be here in the morgue. But it was hard with Val standing there so tall, dark, and handsome, with his unphony French accent. Campbell women could come up with a great white lie or two

— or even three, if absolutely necessary — in any situation or circumstance, except where handsome hunks of the walking dead were concerned. Just because Val looked like some pirate out of a romantic fantasy, what with his sexy smile and that dimple in his chin, that was no reason for her to lose her old Campbell common sense.

"What show?" he pressed.

"I just knew you were going to ask that."

"Imagine," Val remarked wryly, his suspicions growing stronger.

Lucy glanced away from those beautiful blue eyes, thinking that Val should be declared a criminal, even if he was the city's ace detective. How beautiful he was. How tempting. She wanted him and didn't want to want him. She loved him and despised him. How typically Pisces.

Val thought Lucy looked tired and messy. But then, that was her — his ex-love who created mayhem and havoc wherever she went. Damn, how he wanted to lay her down on that ketchup-smeared gurney and sink into her hot, wet depths. It had been so long. But his body wouldn't have its way. He was stronger and harder than that.

"What show?" he repeated.

"A show about corpses," Lucy said.

"Corpses? What kind of corpses?" Right.

What cock-and-bull stories she could come up with! He would give her an A for effort. He always had.

"Dead ones," Lucy explained, then turned to leave. "What else?"

Grabbing her arm, Val stopped her, his fingers and brain registering the warmth of her body and the smell that was all her — a bit wild, a bit earthy, and a bit like gardenias, although it was perverted by the pungent scent of ketchup. "*What* corpse show, Lucy?" And why on earth did he care? He should just let her go.

"None of your business," she snapped. That fired his ire.

"I'm making it my business."

"Oh, go find a stake and put it where the sun doesn't shine." Lucy yanked her arm out of his hand. Her skin burned where he had touched her. Her heart had sped up. She wanted to lean into him and kiss his soft, angry lips . . .

But she didn't.

"*Tu es trop grand pour tes cullottes.*" He didn't have time to verbally fence with Lucy; he had an autopsy to attend. Yet here he was, savoring her temper and her words. He was a fool. A great big vampire fool.

She looked annoyed. "Quit spouting French at me and talk English."

"You're too big for your britches," he explained. Did she know or not know about the Ka? Val stared hard at her, shaking his head. At last he warned, "Stay out of the morgue. Stay out of police business, or I'll have you arrested. Keep that enormous and poky nose of yours occupied by staying home. I mean it, Lucy," he finished.

Jerking her arm free, she turned abruptly and walked off, seething. She was uncomfortable and sticky. Her foot still hurt where she had dropped the gurney on it, and she was beginning to get a backache. All she wanted was a hot bath, and then to be held and comforted. She certainly didn't want to be dictated to by some two-timing tick of an ex-boyfriend, especially one who had absolutely no right to dictate to her. "Oh, screw you and the horse you rode in on," she muttered, forgetting about vampires' supernatural hearing.

He called out after her, "Me? In your dreams, Luce. In your dreams! Though you can ask the horse yourself."

Damn, he was quick. Lucy felt herself blush, and not at his insult. No wonder he was the whiz kid of the New Orleans PTF. She was on TV, and a damned fine actress; she knew how to hide her feelings. So how

430

did the clever bastard know that he still held a starring role in her X-rated dreams?

# Chapter Eleven:
## Mama, Don't Let
## Your Babies Grow
## up to Love Vampires

The next night, the phone was ringing when Lucy unlocked the door to her apartment. Dropping her purse and kicking off her shoes, she answered.

"Hello?"

Her mom's West Texas accent filled the line. "Lucy, sugar, I just loved your show tonight. That wererat impersonator — he did such a good impression of Jimmy Cagney! And you were just wonderful."

"Thanks, Mom," Lucy said, sitting down wearily. She was tired, and still had to go out and make her rounds of the Overbite Bar. Not to mention that tonight was Friday the thirteenth. Friday the thirteenth might not be Mardi Gras, but ever since monsters had come out of the proverbial closet, this particular date was a big deal in New Orleans.

Yes, parties were thrown everywhere to celebrate the unlucky day. She knew the Big

432

Monster Ball was being held at the House of Usher, just a couple of blocks west of the Overbite. Lucy had promised her boss that she would put in an appearance, as he still wanted her to mix and mingle with some of the more elite ranks of supernatural celebrities.

"I'm just so proud of you. Your show is better even than that *Tonight Show*," her mom remarked. "And Blade has those flashy big teeth, and all that black leather. He looks like some kind of vampire James Dean!"

In spite of her weariness, Lucy smiled. No way her show could compare to the vampire's. His cutting style, his awesome guests . . . Blade always had the most interesting preternatural predators. But then, this was what mothers were for, to value their kids above all others.

"That vampire is just too pretty for a man if you ask me. I wouldn't believe a word he says, since a girl can't trust a man who is prettier than she is. Pretty soon they start staying out late and showing up with lipstick on their collars, and it isn't even your shade."

"I know, I know," Lucy agreed. Val *was* prettier than she, and even though he hadn't had any lipstick on his collar that ill-fated night — he wasn't even wearing a collar — she had still caught him cheating, the promiscuous parasite. Hadn't she? His protestations flashed again through her mind.

"Do you have a date tonight?" her mom asked, drawing her thoughts away from the stark recollection of a nearly naked Val with that bloodsucking bathrobed bimbo.

Lucy pulled out a slinky green number that just screamed for sin and laid it on the bed. She planned to wear her matching bite-me heels, just in case she ran into Val. "Not tonight," she admitted.

"Are you dating anyone special, hon?" her mother pressed.

Hmm, Lucy thought, what an easy question to answer. How sad. "No, Mama, I'm not."

"What about that nice man on your show tonight? He was tall, dark, and handsome."

Lucy sighed in exasperation. "And hairy, Mom. He was a *wererat*. I date enough human rats as it is without dating the supernatural ones," she added truthfully, moving to run some bathwater. "He also had beady little black eyes."

"Oh, Lucy. What am I going to do with you? I want grandkids to spoil, and at this rate I'll be ninety before that happens."

Lucy shook her head. Her mom must have been talking to her sister, whose two married daughters had five kids between them. "Maybe someday, Mom. But right now I'm focusing on my career."

"That shouldn't stop you from dating!"

"All the good guys are gone — married or dead or something," Lucy snapped, tiring of being hounded. But her mother seemed unfazed.

"Don't give me that old song and dance. I know you. You've never gotten over that Cajun detective, have you? I know you don't talk about him anymore, but I remember how devastated you were when you caught him cheating on you. If the man hadn't been dead already, I'd have made sure he was! After what he did to you, my little girl — that supernatural skunk should have been hanged. I should have kicked his arrogant ass from here to Mexico."

"Mom, this isn't up for discussion. I'm over him," Lucy lied. Her mom sounded unconvinced.

"Lucy, hon, you need to get back in the saddle. Just because you've had a major spill doesn't mean you can't ever ride again."

But Lucy didn't think that was true. After riding Val and Val riding her six ways to Sunday, galloping off into the sunset for a happily-ever-after with some other man just didn't seem possible. Because — and this was a big because — when you've had the best, you couldn't try the rest.

"Look, Mom," she said, "I have to go out again on some business, and I need to get ready. I love you, and I'll call you on Sunday."

Lucy got off the phone and into her bathwater, but as she lay back, she thought about Val. Meeting and loving him had been like a wild hot wind had swept them up and tossed them into the eye of a tornado. And in the end he had been nothing but a heartache, a big old larger-than-life heartache that had taken her for one hell of a spin. "Fangs for the memories, Val," she grumbled.

Frowning slightly, Lucy soaped her arms. She'd suddenly remembered how Val was angry with her. Why? He was the lying, lecherous leech who had been unfaithful! She had been pure as the driven snow. But there was not the slightest doubt in her mind that Val was really ticked. Did that mean he felt slighted? *Had* he been slighted? She'd been thinking it earlier, and doubt reared its ugly head once more. Could she have been wrong in what she saw? Could he possibly have had a reasonable explanation for sipping on someone else?

Lucy sat up slowly, tiny droplets of water sliding down her back, making her shiver. Had she done the right thing in not listening to Val's explanation? Had she been hardheaded and stupid? Of course she couldn't have. When was she so stubborn?

Disgusted with herself, she stood up and grabbed a towel. Glancing into the mirror, she saw confusion staring back at her. Maybe she *had* been wrong.

No, she told herself. Maybe mountain oysters were really chicken livers, and cows jumped over the moon.

# CHAPTER TWELVE:
## OLD UNFAITHFUL?

As Lucy walked up the cobbled sidewalk to the House of Usher, she listened to the music that spilled out through the bars surrounding the old antebellum home. The structure had been renovated and turned into a club three years earlier, and it was now the hangout for the elite of the supernatural world — and it required a membership for all but special occasions like Friday the thirteenth or Halloween.

The music, rich and vibrant, was almost a living thing as it poured into the night from nearby bars. The air was fraught with sounds of zyedeco, jazz, and blues. Lucy loved that about New Orleans: the killer music and the mouthwatering food. Texas might be a state of mind, but New Orleans was a feast for the senses.

The inside of the club was cool and dark, and it smelled of incense and a hint of orange blossoms. A huge mahogany bar with brass rails stretched all along the ballroom floor. The floor was tiled in black and white marble, and couples were dancing and swaying upon it to a soft tune.

The club was packed to the rafters, and that made her search more difficult. Lucy sighed. "Everybody and their dog and cat is here," she complained. But she hadn't really expected anything else.

She spent the next half hour wandering through the house, studying the faces and looking for a creature with violet-colored eyes and a scar on one cheek. And perhaps she was also hoping for a detective with eyes the color of an arctic sea.

She also did as her boss had bade her do, mingling and mixing whenever she could with the elite of the paranormal world. After about twenty minutes, Lucy found herself chatting with one of the blues' undisputed kings. His name was Holiday, and he had a way with the sax that should be declared illegal. He was also a werewolf, the head of the Pirate Alley Clan. Maybe, just maybe, if she played her cards right, she could get him to do her show.

Unfortunately, Holiday had had too much to drink and was being a little too frisky for her comfort. As his hands latched on to her buttocks for the fourth time, Lucy tried to brush them away . . . only to feel a strong wrist and hand touch hers. Glancing back, she found herself staring into Val's face.

"Val!" she said, her heart pounding.

He gave her a look of angry disgust, then went about sending Holiday off with a flea in his ear about treating a lady with respect. Just seeing Lucy with the lecherous wolf made Val feel as if someone had poisoned his Bloody Mary.

Turning back to Lucy, he gave her a dark look. "What's gotten into you, *cherie?* Why were you letting that fur ball feel you up in public?"

"Letting him? A lot you know! I was removing his hands from my butt, you ass."

But he just gave her his inscrutable look — a look that had used to infuriate Lucy when they were going out. He'd made it whenever she tried to make an important point that he felt was silly.

"I could have handled him," she growled.

Val nodded. "It sure looked that way. And he could handle you. Another few seconds and he'd have had your dress up to your waist." Val's blue eyes blazed. Seeing Holiday's hands all over the behind of the woman he'd once loved was bringing things to the front of his mind — feelings that were better left buried.

Glaring, Lucy pointed a finger at him, retorting, "I'm a big girl, Val. I can handle myself."

He saw the pulse beating rapidly in her throat. Once he had kissed that throat, bitten it. Her blood had been spicy rich, and he had never tasted anything so good. The thought made him angry. He was no fledgling vampire to be led by his emotions, by lust, but that was exactly what was happening.

"What were you doing with Holiday, anyway? Just because he can play a sax like an angel doesn't mean he is one. That wolf's a real dog when it comes to women. Strange, *cherie,* you used to have better taste." *And you used to taste so good.*

Lucy snorted. "I suppose you mean you?"

Val said nothing, just gave her a knowing smile.

The smile clearly made Lucy angry. "I know what Holiday is, and I wasn't flirting with him. I was just doing my job. My boss wants me to mingle tonight, to scare up some guests for the show."

This time, Val snorted. "Scare up is right — or dig them kicking and screaming up out of the grave."

"And just what does that mean?"

Val shook his head. "Well, you must admit

441

your work's not *60 Minutes.*"

"It may not be now, but that doesn't mean it couldn't be if I got more serious-minded guests!" How dare he insult her show? Even if he was right — which he was — who did he think he was, judging her show like some Ebert and Roeper?

"No one of any importance in the supernatural community would be caught dead on your show — or undead," Val remarked.

His words hurt, because Lucy knew they were the truth. She'd said the same thing herself. And he not only knew it was the truth, but knew that she knew it was the truth. She knew her show could be better, and having him say so really cut into her confidence. She glanced away, managing to hold her tears at bay. She didn't want Val to see her cry again. He had seen enough of her pain.

Seeing Lucy's reaction, Val knew that his careless words had cut her deeper than he'd intended. He'd been through some bad, some truly sad times because of this woman, the heartache of losing her never completely dissipating. Still, Lucy had once been the light of his life. So why was he hurting her?

Touching her arm, he apologized. "That wasn't very nice," he admitted. "I've got my mind on a lot of things going down tonight.

Friday the thirteenth is not a fun, crazy time for us cops. We're the ones who have to stop all the craziness."

Lucy nodded stiffly. She was glad for his apology, glad for the words, but his comments still stung. If only they weren't true. "You sound almost human," she murmured, not meaning anything negative.

"Can't have that, can we?" He grinned, much like his old self. She had a flash of memory, a flash of all the old reasons for loving him. "If I do anything human again, you be sure and let me know," he added.

Lucy smiled. "I guess you're working, then?" she asked.

"Unofficially," Val replied. "Now look, *cherie,* it's getting late. You should go home. It's not a good night to be out and about. Too many *feu follets.*"

Rolling her eyes, she shook her head both in confusion and frustration, and Val couldn't help but think that she would be perfect prey for an incubus. Their paranormal senses let them detect those wounded in spirit, whether it be loneliness, desperation, heartache, or disillusionment with life. Lucy needed to go home now and stay behind locked doors.

"Evil spirits. Monsters on the prowl," he explained.

"Of course. New Orleans is a monster haven — or monster heaven, take your pick. But I've lived here two years and nothing bad has happened to me."

Watching Val, Lucy wondered if she should say something about DeLeon. If she did, would he reveal anything about the youth-sponging monster? In a perfect world, she and Val would be partners. But then, in a perfect world they wouldn't have broken up.

Feeling it was appropriate, she went for broke. "But, then, nothing like an incubus has been in town before, has it?" She waited for any sign of reaction.

It wasn't long in coming. Val cursed a Cajun blue streak, then drew her back into a shadowed alcove. *"Mon Dieu! Cést une erreur."*

Lucy gave him another irritated look. "English, please."

"You're mistaken."

She snorted. "No, I'm not. I know, Val. I know about the Ka."

He went even whiter than his usual vampire complexion. "How the hell did you find out? Who told you?" His suspicions had been right all along; this menacing mess of a miss had stuck her pretty little nose into something that wouldn't necessarily get it bitten off, but more likely aged by four or five decades. *Mais oui,* that pretty little nose just might get her a pretty little headstone in the not-too-distant future — or at the very least end up permanently wrinkled like a Sharpei.

"I can't reveal a source," Lucy protested.

Val shook his head, glaring at her. "Serena Stevens! I should have known. My partner told me Serena acted funny when asked if she'd told anyone else about her attack." He wished he had a switch to take to the broomstick witch for having talked to Lucy.

"This isn't *The X-Files,* and you aren't Fox Mulder," he told her. "Stay the hell away from this, Lucy. It's police business, and none of yours."

"Why haven't you told the public about it?" Lucy demanded, her mouth turning down at the corners. "Don't you think everyone deserves to know that a new monster is in town? That a kiss can kill you. That, if you get lucky, you'll only get a quick trip to Florida and retirement."

"We don't want John Q Public up in arms," Val said. "We need to avoid mob mentality, humans with garlic and stakes attacking every vampire in sight. So . . . if a leak comes about the incubus, I'll know just where to look," he warned her.

Lucy started to argue, but Val was familiar with her tactics. He stalled her by adding, "We're calling a press conference in two days to inform the public." He didn't like informing the public, because that meant the incubus would know his cover was blown, perhaps making him harder to track. In the worst case, the incubus would move to a different territory, making him impossible to catch. He'd have to work fast to catch the beast.

Lucy closed her mouth, appeased. The public was going to be warned. But that also meant a slew of bounty hunters would be on the prowl for the Ka, which decreased her chances of finding the youth-stealing critter first. She didn't like that possibility.

"Just go home and stay out of this," Val advised her sternly. He was hoping that for once Lucy would use what little common sense God had given her and back off. "No story is worth your life."

"I know what I'm doing, Val," she replied. "I'm not a beef-witted simpleton."

The look he gave her said different. "Lucy, with your record you will either have the Big Easy in a big uproar, or end up with varicose veins and and a berth in a coffin. You *don't* know what you're doing."

"I do so," she snapped. "I'm a qualified

professional."

"You were a weather girl. Now you do a talk show that's the joke of the paranormal world. Chet Huntley, Connie Chung, or Barbara Walters you are not. So stay the hell out of this!"

Every word stomped harder on her pride. "I might not be fricking Connie Chung, but I'm trying! And just why the hell do you care?" she hissed.

Val leaned against a column, staring hard at this hardheaded, distrustful, misguided mortal. She had a suspicious nature, which he abhorred, and she was so unruly that she created anarchy wherever she went. "You know what, *cherie?* I wish the hell I knew why I bother. I wish the hell I knew why I care."

Lucy's temper, which had been a roaring blaze, did a slow burn and then fizzled out as the import of his words struck. Val still cared! But just how much? Reaching out her hand, she gently touched his arm. "You do bother. You do care. Warning me? That tells me something."

His deep blue eyes were smoldering, but he shook his head. *"Trop retard."* Lucy opened her hands, palm up — she didn't understand — so he went on: "It's too late, Lucy. Too late. You didn't trust me. You didn't love me enough."

"But I did, Val. Surely you can't believe I didn't love you. Why, I loved you like nobody I've ever loved in my entire life. You were my moon and my stars."

"Whether you did or didn't, it's a little late now. That's all spilt blood, not to be cried over. It's in the past."

Lucy leaned into his chest, staring up into his eyes with earnest intent. She could sense something new, something she'd never seen. Something she'd never allowed herself to see?

"Forget the past," she said. "I'm listening now. I really want to know what happened that night. I really *need* to know."

Touching a finger to her chin, he bent his head toward hers. "I don't want to talk about it. I can't forget that you honored me so little. Trusted me so little."

She circled his shoulders with her arms, and reaching up and drawing his head down for a kiss. The kiss was scorching hot, burning with need and fever. Lucy's insides heated up, too. She had so missed Val's lips on hers. His soft, hot mouth, and the way he made her feel inside — all melting and sugary. This was heaven: being in his arms again, his lips on hers after four long hot summers and frozen winters. There was nothing but this moment in time. She wished it would last.

Val wanted to lose himself in these sweet hot passions that were unique to Lucy alone. But he couldn't. He didn't trust her anymore, not with his heart or his desires.

Lucy was jerked back quite unwillingly into the present by the sound of Val's name being called.

"Ah, Val, I've been looking for you everywhere, and here you are. You said you'd be bored at the Monster's Ball, but you don't look bored to me."

Both Lucy and Val drew apart. Val looked a little uncomfortable, and Lucy was dumbstruck. It was her: the slutty, villainous vampiress who had vamped Val! Lucy hated her, despised her, wanted to kick her bloodsucking butt from there to Fort Worth.

The woman seemed amused. "Val — aren't you going to introduce me to the lady you've been kissing?"

Val looked put out, but reluctantly complied. He said, "Christine Armstrong, this is Lucy Campbell."

Lucy glanced from Val back to the vamp. She was dressed in a tight golden dress that revealed most of her chest and her upper arms. The female vampire was muscular, but in a feminine and curvy way. The name

Armstrong seemed to fit. This viperous vampiress could probably bench-press Lucy at least twice over.

Still, Campbell women being Campbell women, Lucy wanted to deck her — or at least pull her hair out or something equally humanly fiendish. This was the home-wrecker! And she was still around Val, while Lucy was long gone?

Her gaze hot and furious, it raked over the vampiress and then back to Val. "Damn you to hell, Valmont DuPonte," Lucy said. "I almost bought your act. I thought maybe, just maybe, I had been wrong about what I saw that night!"

Lucy clenched her fists, her breathing tight, trying desperately to control the tears that were in her eyes and in the back of her throat. Once again, Val had branded her heart without even showing up for the roundup. More of her mother's sage advice suddenly rang in her ears: *If a rattlesnake bites you once, you're damned unlucky. If you get bit twice, your mama raised a fool.*

"What a laugh!" she continued. "You made a fool of me then, and I'm a great big fool now. Foolish, the Queen of Fools. I hope you're satisfied, Mr. Two-timing Tick! I was ready to throw myself at your feet and listen to your explanations. If I had been wrong, I would have begged your forgiveness for being too suspicious. For not trusting you more. But you're still with this woman! How dare you? So I'm human, and evidently my poor mortal blood isn't good enough for you. So you cheat on me with this fang-faced viper? Well, Val, here's a big surprise: I'm proud of my human blood and my talk show. I wouldn't invite you on if you were the last bloodsucker on earth. So take that, you big leech!" And with those words, Lucy turned and ran off into the crowd, her eyes full of tears of hurt and humiliation.

Val and Christine watched her go, bumping into every person on the dance floor as she passed.

"She still loves you, *mon ami,*" Christine remarked thoughtfully. With a girlfriend like Lucy, Val would be up to his neck in trouble trying to keep up with her. Which was perhaps just what her morose partner needed — a lover who would shake him up like a blenderful of margarita, and keep him laughing as the nights turned to years turned to decades.

Val snorted. "And that makes everything all right? She didn't trust me enough to listen to what I had to say. No, it's all blood under the bridge now."

"She would have listened tonight. She still will if you go after her," Chris advised, recalling the look of terrible pain in Lucy's eyes.

Val shook his head. "You can't have love without trust," he said tersely.

"Val, your love life since Lucy has been dead as a doornail. For eighteen months you tore everybody's head off like a rogue werewolf. Talk to the lady. Work it out."

Val growled. "Go stick your nose someplace it's wanted, and leave my love life alone," he said, and then he stalked off.

"*What* love life?" Christine called after him, shaking her head. The male species really was quite stupid at times, and quite stubborn. It was a good thing that females knew just how to handle them. Laughing, Chris dubbed herself the matchmaker from hell.

And she was about to do a little business.

# CHAPTER THIRTEEN: LIAR, LIAR, PANTS ON FIRE

Lucy hurried outside the club and began walking back to her car four blocks away. Tears were running down her cheeks, along with a thin trail of mascara.

"Damn, I must look like a raccoon," she muttered to herself. She wasn't going to be doing any more hunting tonight for De-Leon. Val's latest deception had devastated her, made her fit only for the dogs.

Her high heels made a *clip-clop* noise on the sidewalk through the mist swirling at her feet. Behind her, she could hear someone's fast approach. She felt a twinge of unease at the hurried purpose of those steps, but, taking a quick peek behind her, she stopped suddenly, anger overriding her sense of caution.

"What the hell are you doing following me?" she snapped. At the moment, she didn't care if the female vampire wanted to have her for lunch; Lucy felt sure that at the very least she could tear out all the vam-piress's lovely black hair at the roots. "Come to gloat?"

The woman stopped in front of her, shak-ing her head. "That was pretty stupid back there," she suggested.

"Thanks. I really appreciate you coming after me for an extra insult or two. What is this, some new vampire fad?" Lucy stuck a finger in the air, then pointed it. "Well, I can come up with a few insults of my own. You're a coffin-jumping, neck-licking, freaky-fanged vamp!"

Christine laughed softly. Then, seeing Lucy's hands clench into fists, she wiped the smile off her face. If she went and punched out Val's one true love, her partner might get a bit testy. "You've got it all wrong, Lucy," she said.

The mortal rolled her eyes. "Sure," she said sarcastically. "It's in a frog's nature to hop."

Christine blinked. "What's a frog got to do with Val?"

"It's the nature of the reptile — or the beast or vampire or whatever," Lucy ranted. "A cheater cheats."

Christine hissed at Lucy, angry. "Val would *never* betray anyone — especially not you. You've got it all wrong. Val and I aren't lovers. We haven't been for over eighty years. I'm just his partner in the PTF. I have been for the last four years."

"Oh, right. I'm too dumb to notice his fangs in your neck that night, and you both practically buck-naked! He was going at your jugular like a wino with a bottle of Thunderbird."

Christine shook her head. "It wasn't what it seemed. And we both had bathrobes on."

Lucy raised her eyes to the heavens. "Bathrobes! Well, I saw what I saw — and you're obviously with him tonight."

Christine shook her head. Humans could be so very . . . human at times. "I'm his *partner.* That's why we arrived together at the House of Usher. Duty and all that."

"Go on." Lucy felt a strange feeling come over her. Like she was being . . . stubborn. Stupid. Again.

"The night you dropped in to surprise Val, well, we had been involved in a werewolf pack rumble. Val took a silver bullet meant for the chief of the Lafitte clan. He had lost a lot of blood, and was replenishing it off me when you arrived. We were dressed in robes because we'd both had blood all over us, and had showered just a few minutes before." Seeing the doubt and disbelief in Lucy's eyes, Christine added, "I took a shower in the *guest* bathroom."

"You expect me to believe this?" Lucy asked, her thoughts whirling like a rider on El Diablo, the meanest bull in Texas. What if these things the vampiress said were true? What if Val was truly innocent? What if Lucy had been a world-class idiot, what with her lack of trust and refusal to listen?

"Why didn't he tell me?" she asked.

"He tried more than once. You didn't listen," Christine snapped. "You ripped out his heart better than any slayer ever could."

Lucy gulped, her stomach queasy. "I didn't mean to. I thought he was cheating on me," she said. She might have made a big mistake five years ago. She might have made the biggest mistake of her life, and then, like the world-class idiot she was, gone and done it all over again. "Why didn't *you* tell me?"

"I didn't think anyone who could treat him like that deserved him. He loved and cherished you, and you crushed him."

Lucy hung her head in shame. She couldn't bear to see the accusation in the other female's eyes. And . . . "Why tell me now?"

"I thought about calling you when you first moved here to the Big Easy, but after watching your show a couple of times, I decided you weren't the brightest bulb on the tree. But maybe I'm wrong. Or maybe it doesn't matter. Either way, Val never got over you, and he deserves to be happy."

Lucy's eyes glistened with tears. Her heart held a glimmer of hope. "You don't think he's over me?"

"No, I don't."

"Then why isn't *he* here?"

Christine shrugged her elegant shoulders. "Because he's a male vampire, and they do the dead-man-walking-away trick better than any other species. Because you broke his heart and didn't believe in him. Honor for a seventeenth-century vampire is everything."

"I have my pride, too —" Lucy began, but Christine cut her off.

"Pride is a cold bedfellow. And besides, Val is worth more. You know that."

Lucy thought over what Val's partner said, and Christine was right. Pride was pride, but good love was better every night of the week. Yet, was everything ruined? She had not believed in her true love's fidelity. She had martyred herself for her past, for her mother's past, letting the burdens she carried convince her to distrust everyone else, and to hurt them before they had a chance to hurt her.

"I've done Val a terrible wrong. How could I?" she whispered.

"Yes, you did a bad, cruel thing, and Val didn't deserve it. He's a wonderful, loyal, loving, and passionate vampire — a credit to our species."

Christine stared at her, and looking into those warm brown eyes Lucy tried to see within the vampiress's heart. "Do you still love Val?" she asked.

Christine heard the concern in the mortal's voice. "I love Val as a partner and friend. Yes, we were lovers, but only for a short while. Less than six years. Besides, I'm with someone, and I have been for the past twelve years. And I'm not giving that up."

"I don't know how to thank you," Lucy said with a sincere smile. Tears glistened in her pretty blue eyes.

"Easy," Christine replied. "By sucking it up. Go apologize to Val. Make him listen. It won't be easy."

But suddenly, before any more could be said, Christine tilted her head to one side. Lucy started to ask her what was wrong, but the vampiress silenced her with a slash of her hand, her mouth becoming a tight, hard line.

Handing Lucy a cell phone, she commanded, "Call Val. Tell him where we are. I think our monster has just struck. . . . Hit one on the phone," she explained when Lucy paused. Then, when Lucy did as instructed, Christine took off running. Kicking off her high heels, she headed toward a back alley across the street.

After calling and alerting Val, Lucy took off after the vampiress. She was both curious and concerned, so Val's curses to stay put served no purpose but to ring idly in her ears.

The alley was dark and curving. Lucy could hear Christine's feet against the wet asphalt, slapping fast and furious as the vampiress ran.

By the time Lucy reached the end of the alley, she heard the sounds of a fight. The alley had an overflowing Dumpster and open stacks of boxes and smaller tin garbage cans, many filled with rotting fruit. A large single lightbulb hung above a doorway, illuminating the struggle taking place between Christine and another paranormal creature. On the ground beside the Dumpster lay a young woman.

Lucy ran to what was clearly DeLeon's latest victim and checked her pulse. From the light above, Lucy could see that the woman's mouth was bruised, tiny wrinkles radiating out from her mouth and eyes. The woman's skirt was hiked up, but her panties were still on. Had she been raped? At least she was still alive, even if she was unconscious.

The sound of someone being thrown into a trash can caught Lucy's attention. Glancing up, she saw Christine lying in a heap by the can and a tall figure with dark hair hanging in a thick fat braid to his waist. He was crouching down, ready to launch himself at Christine, who was shaking her head as if dazed.

Without really thinking, Lucy picked up a wine bottle and threw it at the creature's head, screaming, "Remember the Alamo!" It hit with a *crack*.

Surprised more than hurt, the creature turned to look at Lucy. In the dim light, she gasped and froze like a deer caught in the headlights. The monster had violet eyes — strange, empty dead eyes — along with really ugly reddish fangs. It was the Ka incubus in the flesh — and unfortunately, up close and personal!

What irony. She had been looking for the menacing monster for over a week, and here he was. She had found him all right, and he was just a tad irritated at her. Maybe she shouldn't have thrown that bottle of cheap wine at him. Maybe she shouldn't have drawn his attention to her. After all, she wasn't Superwoman or a super vampire. Maybe she hadn't thought her distract-him-any-way-you-can plan through completely.

What to do with him? Lucy was nearly in hysterics as the incubus leapt toward her. But again, her subconscious came to her aid, and she grabbed up a trash can lid and held it like a shield.

The incubus continued attacking, so Lucy hit him in the face with the trash can lid. She could feel it dent, and his weight threw off her balance. She stumbled into a trash box with the rotting, slimy fruit, and landing in the mushy and smelly things had her gagging and cussing while the incubus rolled away and came to his feet.

"You youth-stealing swine! You red-fanged freak! Why don't you pick on somebody your own size? Cowardly creep! You sidewinder incubus, you!" Lucy shouted, trying to keep the monster's attention on her instead of Christine. She struggled to her feet, slipping inside the large box as she danced around on rotting grapes, peaches, and bananas. Suddenly she felt like she was in a B-grade horror movie — but in Tuscany, complete with wine-making. "You life-snatching sneak of a skunk!"

DeLeon growled at her insults, reddish fangs gleaming a bright crimson and growing another inch. He blinked, wondering why this mortal female wasn't cowering in fear or crying for mercy. She was different than most humans . . . but still wasn't enough of a curiosity to keep him from killing her.

Lucy gasped. "Oh, yuck!" DeLeon really had a dental problem, what with those foul-looking fangs of his. No way did she want those things anywhere near her. She shuddered in revulsion.

Smelling her fear, DeLeon laughed and slowly stalked her. Lucy's plan was working. He had clearly momentarily forgotten in his anger that another supernatural creature was behind him lurking in the dark, waiting for the perfect time to strike.

"Hell's bells," Lucy muttered, maneuvering out of the trash box, large globs of smashed grapes and bananas on her clothes, peaches in her hair. As she stepped accidentally into another small box, it lodged on her right foot. Unsuccessfully she tried to kick it off, then gave up and began backing away.

"Hold on to your cowboy hats, you've found what you were seeking, Lucy, and this is going to be a bumpy night," she muttered to herself, not really thinking about what she was saying. How could she? This monster took a person's life without remorse. He aged women so he could be forever young, and didn't care about the wrecked lives he left behind.

"You're nothing more than a necrophiliac," she accused him. "And having sex with women until you age them to death? You ought to be ashamed! You amoral immortal! You ought to be rotting in hell, you chicken-shitted, troll-dunged youth-sponger! What makes you think you can age a woman, having her act like and buy purses like her mother forty years too soon?"

DeLeon halted in his stalking. He gave his prey another close inspection, reassessing his earlier opinion. The mortal was a muddled moron, an escaped lunatic! Had she truly come looking for him?

Lucy smiled. Though feeling grim, she was also pleased. Her plan had worked. An age-old Campbell family strategy was confusion to the enemy. And behind him, in the corner of her eye, she could see that Christine had gotten to her feet.

"I'll make you pay for those words, foolhardy human," DeLeon snarled. He lunged at her, but behind his back Christine went on the attack. The vampiress's lunge caught him in the lower back. Unfortunately, while the tackle sent him to the ground, it also knocked Lucy back into the trash pile.

"Hell's bells!" she exclaimed. "I'm in the fruit again."

The sounds of shouts and running feet and the flicker of flashlights lit the alleyway behind them. Behind that noise came the insistent call of police sirens, still distant but closing in. Hearing this, DeLeon threw Christine off his body, slamming her into the wall, then he took off running, jumping the nearby chain-link fence as easily as if it were a puddle. A moment later he had disappeared into the hot, dark Louisiana night.

Catching her breath, Christine spoke up. She said brusquely, "Tell Val what happened. I'm going after him." And before Lucy could argue that the incubus was too much for a lone vamp to handle, the vampiress was gone.

Pulling herself out of the garbage, Lucy stood. The pounding footsteps and bright lights neared. Instinctively, she knew that it was Val running to her rescue.

She almost groaned. In spite of her recent fall, the box was still stuck to her foot. A banana peel rested on her right shoulder, along with smashed grapes all over her clothes and knees. Large gobs of fruit were dripping down the side of her cheek from her hair. She had always been told she had a peaches-and-cream complexion, but this was ridiculous.

Taking a clomping step forward, she wiped slimy juice out of her eyes. She was an unappetizing mess of fruit cocktail, looked as bad as she possibly could look . . . and yet she had never been gladder to see Val in her entire life.

# CHAPTER FOURTEEN: THE GRAPES OF TRASH

Val ran down the alleyway, his flashlight bobbing, his movements fast, and he hoped his expression was a grim reminder to not mess with anything that went bump and bit really hard in the night. Lucy and Christine were in danger! His heart was pumping double-time in his chest as he burst onto the scene.

He saw Lucy standing slightly bent over, as if from a blow to the stomach. Her heart was beating a fast two-step; Val could hear it from where he stood. Once again, she was in the thick of things — covered in grape goop, a banana peel on her shoulder, and somewhere she had picked up a box she was now wearing on her foot. She looked like someone with a bit of a fetish for fruit, but otherwise seemed unhurt.

To the right of her, a young woman lay moaning softly. Good, Val thought, the victim was alive, and so was the lack-witted Lucy.

"Where's Christine?" he asked.

Lucy stared at him, then replied, "She chased DeLeon." She took a step closer, the cardboard box clumping along with her.

Lucy wanted to throw herself into Val's arms, but his grim expression stopped her. Besides, she looked like a vegetarian nightmare. Despite the fact that this strong, handsome knight had come running to rescue the fair maiden, this was certainly no Hallmark moment. An insidious killer was on the loose, Val's partner was chasing him, she owed Val a big apology for her years of mistrust, and she looked like some sort of rotting fruitcake.

"How do you know it was DeLeon?" Val asked brusquely, moving to check on the other girl. Two more policemen had just arrived on the scene.

"Violet eyes, a scar . . . and the guy really needs some major dental work. His teeth are this really awful red, and they aren't as sharp as yours. They're kind of thick, and longer." She hoped she hadn't hurt Val's feelings by the bigger-teeth bit. Men were so sensitive over the subject of size — or at least her mother had always said so.

Val nodded, then motioned the patrolmen

over, commanding the two officers, "See to the lady and watch out for Lucy here. Don't let her get into any more trouble than she's already in." He gave her fruit-smeared body the once-over.

"Wait, Val. Where are you going?" Lucy asked, her tone high and scratchy, revealing just how frightened she was. She wanted to cringe, thinking that she sounded like a scared mouse, some silly female waiting to be rescued. But then, she *was* a silly female waiting to be rescued. Lucy knew she might be able to handle some paranormal creatures, but a monster like a Ka incubus was big time.

Val looked grim as he replied, "After Christine. DeLeon's too much to handle alone. She could be killed."

"No need, partner," came a voice. Christine materialized out of the shadows at the back of the alley and added, "And I'm alive because Lucy here helped out. She drew DeLeon's attention away when I was down. He would have gotten me." Walking up to Lucy, the vampiress gave her a hug, in spite of the garbage hanging off Lucy's clothing and in her hair. "Thanks, Lucy, you saved my *'tite* ole vampire butt."

Lucy hugged Christine back, surprising herself. This was the female vamp she had hated for over four years, the coffin-wrecking *femme fatale!* But she had been wrong about Christine. She had been wrong about a lot of things. Guilt was gnawing at her insides like a hungry mouse. She owed Val, huge.

"How's the victim?" Christine asked.

Val looked away from his partner and the princess of pandemonium over to the ground where one of the policemen had lifted the young woman into a sitting position. "She's okay. She may have lost a few years, but at least she's not dead."

"I don't think she was raped," Lucy remarked hopefully.

Val sniffed the air carefully, filtering through the smells of rotting garbage, urine, and dank decay. "No. She wasn't," he agreed.

"Good," Lucy stared at the victim, but she was secretly wishing Val would take her in his arms. She was wishing this was four-plus years ago, and that she hadn't been a major-league fool.

Christine moved closer, saying, "He got away, Val. He's fast. Really fast and strong. I followed him down the last few blocks of Pirate Alley, but lost him in the warehouse district."

Val nodded. "I'm glad you weren't hurt,

and that you knew better than to try and apprehend the suspect by yourself. One vampire isn't quite strong enough for a Ka incubus!" he said accusingly.

"I had help," Christine protested. "I had Lucy."

"Ah. Lucy." Pointing a finger, Val turned his attention from his foolish partner to the source of his real anger. His voice taut with suppressed rage, he hissed, "She's a civilian. A chaos-causing, accident-prone civilian. *Merde,* Chris — look at her!"

The vampires turned in unison, staring at Lucy. She had been listening to their conversation in ire, tugging the box off her foot and almost toppling over. To think she had thought Val was a knight in shining armor. Hardly!

"Well, thanks a bunch, Val!" she snapped. "I might look like a tossed fruit salad, but I can take care of myself." And with that, she threw the offending box over her shoulder. Her eyes opened wide when she heard a yelp.

Glancing quickly back, she winced. She had hit one of the policemen on the head. "Sorry about that," she mumbled, busying herself picking her purse up off the ground. Reaching inside, she withdrew a gun and thrust it up in the air.

The second policeman went for his pistol. Val quickly stopped him, blocking his view of Lucy. "Just what the hell is that thing supposed to be?" he asked. "It looks like a water pistol."

"It is," Lucy replied, stung by the disdain she could hear in his voice. Four minutes before, he had desperately wanted to save her. Now he seemed to want to strangle her — a meddling, muddling mortal.

"You're running around the Big Easy with a water gun, and that's supposed to protect you?" he asked. "How easy do you think it would be for a criminal — or a paranormal, especially — to spot a water pistol?" He bit out the words. This daft woman was impossible! And why did he care? Just sign him up for the Dumbest Dick of the Year Award.

"I'm not stupid! Just because you think so doesn't mean I am. How stupid would I have to be to carry around a water pistol with just plain water in it? Pretty stupid, huh? Well, don't hold your breath." Lucy snorted, shoving the pistol back in her purse. "Oh, that's right. You don't *have* to hold your breath, do you, you big dead dufus!"

"Dead dufus?" Christine repeated, trying to keep a straight face. What a comedy of errors. Val was livid — and that really meant something for the normally stone-faced detective.

Turning to Christine, Lucy explained. "He's a dufus, all right, if he thinks I would try to scare a real live monster with a water gun. This contains *holy* water." And before Val could comment, she added, "I also have regular mace and laced mace."

"Laced mace?" Val couldn't help but ask. He felt as if he were watching a train wreck.

"Yes." Lucy reached inside her purse and pulled out a mace bottle. "This one has silver nitrate for shape-shifters and gargoyles."

"I see," Val said. And he did. Her down-home weapons would be deadly if used correctly. But with Lucy . . . "That's why they're still in your purse?" he asked.

"I don't understand," Lucy said, but Val cut her off.

"*Mais, non.* Of course you don't. *Cherie,* nobody ever was protected by a weapon still in their purse."

Lucy looked at him as if he was crazy. "I know that."

"You do? Then why are they still in your purse?" he persisted, certain she must see reason before he turned five hundred years old. Not that five hundred was too far off.

"Because it all happened so fast," Lucy

answered reluctantly. Suddenly she saw where his questions were leading, and it wasn't down a primrose path or anything so sweet-smelling. Dang, the man was sneaky, and he could go right for the jugular when he wanted. And yep, he definitely thought she was a fruitcake.

"Right. That's why preternatural predators are called predators — because they're lethal and fast. Very fast, Luce. Too fast for humans, smart or otherwise."

Scowling at him, Lucy shoved her mace back in her purse and began to walk away. Her walk was lopsided, since she had lost a shoe somewhere. Her clothes were sticking to her, and she heard herself squelching as she went, peach goo dripping into her eyes.

Humiliating! She could feel Val's eyes upon her, just as she heard the sound of the ambulance siren head down the alleyway.

But then a voice called out, "Wait up, Lucy! I'll drive you home."

It was a command, and Val turned and gave instructions to the other police officers to secure the scene, then asked Christine to accompany the victim to the hospital.

Lucy halted, listening to his instructions, and to his domineering tone of voice, and suddenly she shivered. She remembered all too well that voice whispering instructions in her ear as they had wild vampire sex. Instructions about where to touch him, where to bite him, and just where he was going to touch her.

Oh, how she wanted that back. She wanted *him* back, even if he was a tad authoritative. Even if he drove her crazy sometimes with his protective instincts and the draining way he sucked on her neck. She sighed. Her neck was very sensitive, and nobody knew how to suck one better than a vampire. They were experts at necking. In fact, they had probably invented neck-sucking, horny, toothy race that they were.

Val caught up just as Christine called out, "Hey, Lucy, that battle cry of yours — remember the Alamo? I like it."

Lucy turned around and nodded slightly, her eyes a bit glazed. "Thanks. It's my grandma's saying. Her only saying, really. She says it when she stubs her toe, when she's hoeing the garden, or before we eat."

"You need a battle cry to eat dinner?" Christine asked in confusion.

Val didn't let her answer. Grabbing Lucy's arm, he began escorting her to his car. He answered himself over his shoulder. "Not really. Lucy's grandmother is just mad as a hatter."

Lucy punched him on the shoulder. Christine stood still, grinning.

"She is not, Val. She's just . . . a little eccentric," Lucy said.

Val sighed. "*Cherie,* the woman wears a lamp shade on her head to commune with Albert Einstein." And then the darkness swallowed them up.

Christine chuckled softly to herself. Val had his hands full with this one. Lucy Campbell would lead him a merry chase, and such a mess couldn't have happened to a better vampire. She wondered what Mr. Einstein would say about it all.

# CHAPTER FIFTEEN:
# CLOSE ENCOUNTERS
## OF THE SEXTH KIND

Lucy lived two miles from the House of Usher, so the ride home was fast and filled with lectures about not sticking her nose into police business. She could have been hurt. She could have been killed. She could have chipped a nail. She could have aged thirty years — or, on the other hand, she could have skipped thirty years of income taxes. Still, police concerns and finding De-Leon weren't foremost on her mind right now.

She let Val's stern lectures wash over her, and she thought about how best to take the bull by the horns. She had to frame her apology for mistrusting him in a manner that he would find irresistable. He *had* to forgive her and take her back into his life; she missed him too much for him to do anything else. But wearing smashed grapes and bananas on her clothes and peaches in her hair wasn't conducive to groveling —

not unless she was apologizing to a fruit fly.

Outside her apartment, being the protective old-fashioned gentleman and eagle-eyed cop that he was, Val escorted her to her door like she knew he would. She asked him to come inside for a moment. She noted that he accepted with reluctance, almost as if he expected some form of ambush. Clever vampire.

She stalled him from asking any questions by saying she needed a quick shower. Then, ten minutes later she was out of the shower and dressed in a robe. Val eyed her with both trepidation and a hint of simple male appreciation.

"Okay, Lucy, what did you want to talk to me about?" he asked.

"Us."

"There is no us," Val reminded her firmly — although he had gotten misty just a moment before while holding her hand. She had given him both the best years of his life and the worst.

"There used to be an us," she suggested, "which was a good us, a great us. Now there isn't an us, but that doesn't mean there can't be an us again. And a great us, not just a good us, because without us, I do okay and sometimes not even okay."

Val's eyebrows wrinkled and he stared

hard at her.

"That didn't come out quite like I imagined," Lucy said. Romantic it certainly wasn't. "I meant to say, I'd like us to have a second chance."

"I thought you hated my two-timing guts," Val replied somewhat coldly. Not that his voice didn't always sound a bit cold, him being undead as he was. "At least I remember you shouting that all over San Antonio."

"I didn't mean it! You had broken my heart — or at least I thought you had broken my heart until I learned tonight that I'd broken my own without your help. I'd suspected I'd been a big ol' fool. Now I know for sure." Lucy began to wring her hands, knowing that she was messing up her apology big time, but she couldn't seem to help herself. It was as if some babbling idiot had taken over her body, possessing her and causing her to blurt out inane things when this conversation might just be the most important one of her life.

Crossing his arms over his chest, Val asked quietly, "What are you trying to say?"

"I'm sorry. I was wrong about you," Lucy finally managed to get out. "I am so sorry."

"Chris told you the truth about that night?"

Lucy nodded.

"You believe her when you wouldn't even listen to me." Val bit out his words.

"When I first saw you two together, I was too hurt to listen to anything. My worst fears had come to life. I just wanted to lie down and die," Lucy explained, her eyes pleading with Val.

"What kind of love can there be without trust? With a woman not willing to listen?"

He stood so remote from her, as if he were on some distant cliff a thousand miles away. She had to bridge that distance. She fell to her knees, taking his hand in hers and bathing it with her kisses and tears. "I'm sorry, Val. I was stupid and I let my past dictate to me."

Angered, Val jerked her to her feet. "Don't debase yourself. Don't . . ." His words trailed off as Lucy pulled his head down and kissed him with all the hunger she had shelved and saved for so long. His lips were better than anything she had ever tasted. His body was firm and hard with muscle. His erection jutted against her thigh, causing the heat already growing between her legs to intensify. She wanted him hot and hard and now.

She rubbed her body against him, hearing him moan. "I need you, Val. I need you," she whispered as she kissed his neck. Then she bit down, knowing that he loved such foreplay. But then, what vampire didn't?

He groaned. Lucy was so soft and warm, and his longing increased. He needed and wanted to hold her tight, to forget their past and to hell with the future. The traitor in his jeans was clamoring for Lucy's attention.

His hunger ignited, Val began caressing her breast, finally moving to take it in his mouth. He shoved her robe back off her shoulders. She tasted like the same wild spice she always had, and he wanted to lick and suck on her all night long. She made him so hot that he thought he would explode before he even got his jeans off.

As if she could read his mind, Lucy unzipped his pants, dragged them down his hips. He helped her, shoving them off his legs as she grabbed hold of his sex.

"I love your body," she murmured. "So big and hard. I love it when it comes into me over and over, the tightness and the heat."

The words shredded his control, and Val forgot that Lucy didn't trust him and had shattered his heart. He forgot everything but his need for her, because his body was screaming at him to possess her thoroughly and all night long. " 'Tite ange — my little angel."

Picking her up in his strong arms, he sped through the living room into the large bedroom at the end of the hall. Placing her on the bed, he followed her down, his lips sucking on her rose-tipped nipples as his hand delved between her legs. She was hot and wet with wanting him.

He growled possessively as he moved over her and thrust home into her hot, liquid depths. She climaxed immediately, and it took great restraint for him to not follow her. He gasped, "My *jolie fille,* your skin is so soft and sweet, like golden honey." He could not find words for his joy.

Lucy felt tears slipping down her cheeks as Val thrust into her body over and over, his mouth feasting on her breasts and neck. This was heaven to her — heaven lay in his arms. This was her man, and his loving was like hellza-poppin. She would never be the same. It was strange what a little moonlight, danger, and an apology could do.

"I love you, Val — oh, how I love you." Lucy moaned as she kissed his neck, rubbing her hands across his buttocks, feeling their strength as he pumped into her.

*"Mon coeur."*

"My heart," Lucy repeated back to him.

481

His eyes were tender as she spoke, her body taut with the upcoming release, her hips pumping in wild rhythm with his own. Her senses were so alive; and she was cresting high on the wave of a whirlpool.

The tension in Val built and built, cresting until his blood burned like a raging wildfire. Then, with a loud shout, he climaxed.

As he rolled over onto his side, Lucy stared at him and knew that if she lived to be a hundred years old, she would never find a more perfect example of the male animal, unless it was a werewolf. Val was magnificent in his nakedness, what with his marbled pallor and beautiful symmetry.

Sitting up, Val reached for his jeans.

"Where are you going?"

He glanced back her, his expression resolute. "I've got a murder to solve and an incubus on the loose."

Her eyes filled with confusion. "I know that. But our lovemaking was so wonderful, and you used to . . ." She hesitated as he turned away and zipped his jeans. "You used to love to cuddle afterward."

Val hesitated a moment, then spoke as if he were fighting some internal conflict. "This . . . shouldn't have happened."

Lucy was confused. They had made love, and it had been even better than before.

Surely everything was all right. She believed in Val now. She would never distrust him again, and she had wholeheartedly apologized. "Why shouldn't this have happened?" she asked carefully, terribly afraid that his answer was going to crush her heart.

"Because we aren't a couple anymore, and we aren't going to be a couple."

"But why not? I apologized to you. I meant it. I love you. You must love me. At least, you made love to me like you do."

"I may still love you, Lucy. But love isn't enough." He pulled on his shirt and headed toward the living room.

Heedless of her nakedness, Lucy followed him like a rat terrier nipping at his heels. Val felt her presence behind him, smelled her sweet earthy smell, the aftermath of love. Yet he didn't look back, because if he did, he just might weaken and take her back to bed.

"Love's not enough?" Lucy shouted. "What is that? The slogan for Stupid-asses of America? If love isn't enough for a relationship, then what the heck is?"

"Trust." Val jerked on his jacket, feeling cruel. He could hear the tears in Lucy's voice, but he just didn't want to go through all this again.

"I *do* trust," Lucy wailed. "I really do."

*"Tu menti."*

Lucy snarled. "Oh, for crying out loud, speak English if we're going to fight."

Val turned to look at her, at war with himself. He forced himself to verbalize his fears. "You lie. About trusting me or anyone."

"What? Do your vampire powers now give you the ability to read minds?" Lucy snapped. "I didn't lie, and I mean it. Not about lying, about meaning that I didn't lie. I trust you. I really do. You should trust me to trust you, because I do."

Val's eyes almost crossed from her convoluted speech. She was driving him so crazy, he didn't know his right foot from his left — as evidenced by him putting on his boots incorrectly.

"You say you do right now," he said, "but wait until something happens that makes you lose that trust. Then where will we be, when you no longer are trusting because I did something that made you think I couldn't be trusted, but didn't really?"

This time it was Lucy staring at Val with a dazed expression in her eyes. He knew it well. He had worn that look often, whenever Lucy went on a rant.

Hitting his forehead with the palm of his hand, he remarked remorsefully, "*Merde,*

I'm beginning to sound like you! That's all I need."

Lucy took that cue. "What you need is *me.* Do you know that when you used to kiss me I could hear violins playing? Now someone's pulling the wrong strings. What you have is a hole in your head. How dare you lecture me about trust? You can trust me to know that I made the biggest mistake of my life when I let you go. You can trust me enough to believe in me. I *will* trust you, Val. Forever. I give you my word that I won't ever doubt you again. And Campbell women don't lie about something so important."

*"C'est assez,"* Val muttered, his hand slashing down. "That's enough. This does neither of us any good." And with that, he opened the door.

"Don't go like this, Val," Lucy pleaded. She hated begging; Campbell women didn't. But then, Campbell women weren't usually stupid enough to get rid of the best thing that ever happened to them. "Forgive me."

Val glanced back once, then walked out the door. "I do forgive you, Lucy. But I can't forget. You tore my heart to shreds when you left me. I don't want to go through that again, not even for you."

The closing of the door was symbolic.

Lucy felt as if it had slammed shut on all of her hopes and dreams of a happily-ever-after with Val, and only after five minutes of stunned bewilderment and a boatload of tears did she think of a few things she should have said.

Opening the door, she shouted, "Don't let the door hit you in the butt."

Her neighbor stuck his head out of his apartment and glared at her. Lucy glared back, unremorseful. She'd had to respond to Val's rejection somehow. Better late than never.

# CHAPTER SIXTEEN:
## IF LUCY FELL

Three days had gone by, and three nights, and the badass brownshoe of Bourbon Street still hadn't called her. No, Val hadn't contacted her at all after they'd made love, and while Lucy wanted to get in his face and yell at him, honesty made her curb her temper. After all, she'd been the one at fault. She should have trusted him. She should have listened to him at the very least, in spite of her very incriminating eyewitness evidence of his cheating.

Lucy morosely poured herself a glass of bourbon in a shot glass. Her show was finished for the night, and she was depressed — so depressed that she was sitting in the coffee room at the WPBS television station feeling sorry for herself. Logically Lucy knew that Val had said their making love was a mistake, but Lucy had hoped that after Val reflected he would realize he was wrong. She hadn't expected hearts and flowers, but she had hoped for a call to see how she was doing. Surely he missed her just a little bit.

So, she had been wrong once. So what? Lots of people in life made mistakes. Val should forgive her mistake, because make no mistake, Lucy would never make that mistake again. Not even if she saw him in bed with three vampiresses. She would now believe anything he said, even if he told her they were all just trying out a new mattress. Never again would she accuse the vampire she loved of being unfaithful or untrustworthy, if only the stiff-necked neck-sucking stiff would believe her. She had to get another chance!

He had called her *"mon coeur"* when he was making love to her. But if she was his heart and he was hers, how could they not be together? His comment "Love is not enough" was pure blasphemy. Love was always enough, presuming one partner wasn't being pigheaded. Lucy had to make Val see that the past was the past, and that the future could still be theirs.

Ricki the makeup artist came in, interrupting Lucy's pity party and switching channels on the television set. Glancing up, Lucy caught sight of Val on the screen. "Turn it up," she urged, surprised to see a reporter interviewing him.

Apparently, last night the New Orleans Paranormal Task Force had released information about the incubus. Tonight Val was telling what was being done to track down the monster. Lucy listened intently to Val's interview, frowning when he began to criticize the incubus, calling the creature's methods messy and unrefined, and hinting that the only way the incubus could "get it up" was to rape, terrorize, and age women. A little death really meant a lot of death with him. Val's condemnations were so harsh that any vampire would find them offensive, since vampires, even the subspecies, were concerned with prestige and power. And Ka incubi were even worse.

Val hadn't pulled any punches in his criticism of the incubus, which Lucy knew was totally out of character. He could be silent as a corpse when he chose to be.

Ricki shook her head. "What your detective just did is like sticking a hot iron up the ol' wazoo of that DeLeon."

"He's not *my* detective," Lucy answered, wishing that he were. Besides, Lucy recognized what Val was doing. He was making DeLeon madder than a snake in hopes that the youth-sucking creature would make a mistake.

"But you wish he was," Ricki remarked, knowing her too well. She tapped her long red nails on the tabletop.

Lucy grumbled. "I never should have told you about us." Yesterday, Ricki had caught her crying into her café au lait, and had poked and prodded her until Lucy had caved in and spilled the beans about everything.

"But you did tell me," Ricki crowed. "*Finally!* And a good thing, too. Broken hearts are too bad to be kept to one's little old self. We all need a shoulder to cry on. Although preferably a big strong male one."

Lucy shook her head. "Been there, done that. Crying, I mean. I about flooded West Texas with my tears last time," Lucy admitted. A gleam came into her eye. "This time, I think I'll try something different."

Noticing the sudden twinkle, Ricki laughed. "Hmm . . . whatever you are going to do to that handsome Cajun detective, count me in."

Lucy nodded. "All right. Let's go," she said, and she picked up her purse.

"Where to?"

"I'm going to do a little old fashioned wooing," Lucy replied mysteriously. "At Val's house."

"Oooh! Sounds romantic! This could be

fun!"

Two hours later, Ricki took back her words. "This isn't fun at all. I can't believe I'm doing this," she complained.

"Oh, hush," Lucy said, dusting off her Levis. "I said I was sorry you tore your pants. But you should have climbed up that tree and over the fence like I did, not climb the fence with those iron spikes on the top."

"Well, why does your detective have to lock his fence? Hell, why is his property even fenced? He lives twenty minutes from town. Who'd come all the way out here to rob him? Besides, he's a vampire! A crook would have to be crazy to jack a vampire. And how the hell should I know how to climb over fences? I'm a hair and makeup artist, not a two-story man. And what's with that 'Remember the Alamo' stuff?"

"Texas tradition."

Ricki shook her head in exasperation. "Thank God I'm from California. In fact, I don't even like the country. I don't like the bayous or the swamp."

Lucy had to smile. "This isn't exactly the swamp."

Ricki sniffed and pointed out the large cypress and oak trees lining the front of Val's house, which was settled back deep in shadow, only slightly lit by the half-moon. The trees were covered in gray-black pieces of moss, which swung like long feathered boas in the night wind. "That's moss, isn't it, and I can smell the bayou. It stinks."

"You're smelling humidity and lots of vegetation. There's some magnolia with night-blooming jasmine thrown in," Lucy volunteered. The scent was strong but earthy, combined as it was with the rich scent of decay. To her right, a huge magnolia tree stood, branches dark like shadows, silvery-looking flowers peeking from the darkness. The magnolia blossoms themselves, a rich pungent smell of sweetness, reminded her of warm southern nights and Southern Comfort in a glass. The South in a nutshell.

"So good to know that I'm keeping company with a botanist," Ricki said, stomping toward the largest oak tree near the veranda. Her flashlight bobbed up and down, the beam cutting through the shadows. "Let's just get this whole thing over with."

Lucy hurried to catch up with her friend, tugging her bag of ribbons with her. Reaching the oak, she pulled out the long yellow one.

Ricki had set her flashlight to the left of the massive oak, lighting the tree so that they could do their work. Within minutes, they had a long chain of yellow ribbon winding around the trees.

"Well," Ricki admitted, getting into the spirit of things, "this is kind of romantic, and maybe just a little bit of fun. Imagine his face when he sees his trees covered in yellow ribbon. Just like that song!"

"Yeah, I hope it works," Lucy agreed. "I really miss him. I really *need* him." She sighed. "I may not deserve him, but I want him back. Because life without Val is an empty bowl — without cherries, without pits . . . Empty."

Ricki threaded the ribbon higher up the tree, but just then it began to rain. Large fat drops. "I spoke too soon," she said. "This is not romantic. This is not fun. I want to go home."

"Come on, Ricki," Lucy coaxed. "We've only got two more trees to do. What's a little water between friends?" She smiled, hurrying over to the next oak, and the salty smell of the rain filled her nostrils.

Ricki didn't answer. Before she could, something loomed up in the darkness behind her. Lucy screamed out a warning, swinging her flashlight around, highlighting the scene of horror. Ricki glanced back in time to see the Ka incubus start toward her, hands outstretched, long, sharp clawlike fingernails gleaming in the moonlight.

"Run, Ricki, run!"

But Lucy's warning came too late. Before Ricki could move, Lucy saw her grabbed by the monstrous DeLeon. A slash of lightning leaped across the sky.

Her heart crashed against her ribs in anticipation and sheer terror. A brave person would go help her friend. Strange, Lucy thought, she'd rather be a coward and run screaming into the night. But as she took a step backward, longing to run and needing to scream, her throat was too dry and she realized she wasn't thinking clearly. Where was the cavalry when a person needed them?

Ricki screamed for Lucy to help as the incubus bent his head toward her, and he caught her scream in his foul mouth. Soon Ricki was giving awful little noises. Those shrieks were what finally mobilized Lucy. She might be stupid at times. She might be accident-prone. She might not be the most trusting of girlfriends, but she would not be a coward and let her California friend end in retirement in the swamps of Louisana. No, she would go down fighting.

"I love you, Val — and remember the Alamo!" she yelled. And with that she charged, a yellow ribbon trailing behind her.

She tripped, which probably saved her life. Instead of charging directly into DeLeon's back, she ended up clipping him in the knees, knocking the incubus, Ricki, and herself to the ground. There they proceeded to roll around in the mud, name-calling, hissing, fangs flashing and so on, until De-Leon finally gained purchase on the slippery ground. Grabbing Lucy by her neck, he quickly flipped her over on her back and threw himself on top of her.

Ricki was frozen in terror, whimpering on the ground. Lucy discerned the words "gray hair" and "plastic surgery."

Staring up into the incubus's empty eyes, Lucy felt her future doing a flashdance before her eyes. She was going to be wearing support hose and dentures — if she was lucky. If not, tonight was her last night on earth, and Val hadn't come back to her. Dang him! She briefly wanted to take a stake and stick him where the sun didn't shine.

Yes, it was his stubbornness that had led to her coming here to surprise him. Well, she hoped he would cry over her grave, the stubborn dirt ball. If he had called her, she wouldn't be stuck mud-wrestling with this incubus. No, she would never forgive the fickle Frenchman for putting her in this life-threatening danger. Not unless he saved her with some sort of miracle.

Unbeknownst to Lucy, Val's house was being watched. It was all part of the plan to capture DeLeon, the plan where Val had given the interview on television, insulting the incubus in hopes that he could make DeLeon strike back at him. Now, as Lucy was contemplating all the mean things she was going to yell at him, Val and Christine were sneaking up around the back of his home. Val had gotten a call earlier that someone had climbed over his fence.

What greeted his eyes when he and Christine rounded the corner made him curse in French. Lucy and her dimwit friend! They were tangled up with the incubus, covered in mud from head to foot. Still, it made things easier, now that his prey was pre-occupied.

Taking aim, Val shot the incubus with a stun gun designed especially for supernatural creatures of DeLeon's kind. In the background he could hear police sirens shrieking, closing in fast.

The dart punched into DeLeon's cheek. The incubus howled in anger, then a second later fell over sideways as the potent garlic and silver nitrate drug took effect.

Ricki was babbling hysterically. "I'm never listening to another idea of yours again — not as long as I live, Lucy Campbell."

"You'll probably live longer," Lucy agreed, her face as pale as that of a vampiress, her teeth chattering in shock. She shoved De-Leon's leg off, finally managing to stand on her own two shaky feet. "You saved me," she said to Val.

She was a muddy mess, with grass sticking to her in clumps, and a yellow ribbon dangling from her wrist. But Val suddenly thought she had never looked lovelier. He wanted to kiss her and strangle her all at the same time. He opted for something safer. "So sue me," he said.

Lucy's mouth popped open, and Christine knelt down by Ricki. The vampiress folded the distraught young woman into her arms.

"What the hell where you doing out at my place this time of night?" Val asked. His anger began to grow as he thought about the situation. Lucy, in her cavalier, chaos-ridden characteristic way, had managed to get herself almost killed by involving herself. "How did you know about the operation?" he asked.

"What are you talking about?" She was filthy and she had scraped her elbows.

Longingly Lucy looked at Val, willing him with her eyes to hold her in his arms and take away the weight of the world. The big ol' undead dufus wasn't cooperating. Didn't he know that she was one step away from hysteria?

"Why are you here at my house? Why did you climb over my fence in the middle of the night?"

"I climbed over the tree. *Ricki* climbed over the fence," Lucy corrected automatically. Why wasn't he walking toward her? "Why are you scowling at me? I . . . I could have been killed proving my love for you," she defended. That would be against everything you read in books. However, see if she ever decorated his stupid trees again!

Val was not convinced. "What? Love? Why are you here?" he demanded, his voice rising to an almost shout. Definitely unvampirelike, Lucy thought.

"I put ribbons on your trees." She pointed to the massive oak by the front door.

Val glanced at the tree, then turned back to her, his expression unreadable.

"Yellow ribbons," Lucy added, her heart in her eyes and her throat. She prayed he would understand. She had risked death and sacrificed her pride to show him that she loved him. "I'll always want you. I'll

498

always love you," she said.

Val began cursing in French. He pointed a finger at the oak tree and said, "If that isn't the stupidest stunt you've pulled off yet."

Glancing at him in stunned disbelief, Lucy opened her mouth to tell him to just shut up when she suddenly felt dizzy and light-headed. She would think that she was going to faint, but Campbell women never fainted, not even in the days when it had been considered ladylike.

The last sound Lucy heard was Val's *"Merde."*

"Oh, speak English," she mumbled. Then the ground rose to meet her.

## CHAPTER SEVENTEEN:
## I LOVE LUCY!

Lucy was sunk in depression. After Val's less than gallant rescue from the incubus, she had gone home and waited for a phone call. Two nights later she was still waiting, fool that she was.

Last night the capture of the incubus had been featured on all the major news stations, with Val and Christine prominent in the media frenzy. Lucy had watched with eyes filled with hope. Her hope was starting to dim as the nights passed by into misty mornings with no word from Val. It appeared that even if he still loved her, he meant what he had said about love not being enough.

"Earth to Lucy," Ricki said, prodding Lucy's shoulder. "Your hair is done and it's time to get your butt moving and go do your show."

Lucy turned misery-filled eyes to Ricki. "Val hasn't called, and I don't give a fig about tonight's show," she groused.

Ricki patted her shoulder in sympathy. "The night's still early, and how can you not be excited about tonight's show? I've never seen a naked mummy before."

Lucy almost cringed. Tonight's show was "Mummies Who Want to Join Nudist Colonies."

"Do you think they have to wear sunscreen?" Ricki asked. "I wonder what sort of SPF ratings they need."

Lucy gave up and got to her feet, letting Ricki lead her to yet another really stupid show.

"I wonder if they're going to lose any body parts when they unwrap?" Ricki continued cheerfully.

As they got to the set, Lucy could hear the producer call out "One minute till airtime!" Sitting down in her chair, she was surprised that Ricki joined her, sitting in one of the guest chairs to her right.

"What are you doing?" Lucy asked. "And where are the mummies?"

"Change of plans," Ricki answered.

Before Lucy could ask more, the show began, and Val and Christine walked out onto the set and seated themselves on the guest sofa. Blinking her eyes, Lucy wondered if she was having a brain freeze.

"Where are the mummies?" she asked in a weak voice, totally dumbfounded.

Val hid a grin. Lucy had that look down pat. He loved it. Just as he loved her.

"Egypt?" Christine replied with a shrug.

Clearing her throat, Ricki opened the show. Giving a bright smile, she said, "There's been a change of plans for tonight. Detective Valmont DuPonte and Detective Christine Armstrong are here to tell us about the capture of the infamous Ka incubus! And they had a little help from yours truly, and from our very own Lucy Campbell."

The audience cheered, while Lucy sat in shock. Val was really here on her show, and he was smiling at her like she was the finest thing he had ever tasted. Forget the past and forget professionalism, she wanted to know what was going on with him. "You're on my show. You said you'd never do my show," she mumbled.

"Ah, *cherie,* how could I not be where you are? You're my heart — *mon coeur.*"

His answer made her forget the audience, and made her forget her duties as host. "You forgive me?"

"I do. Appearing on your show is my way of saying I want you. *My* yellow ribbons," he said. After nearly losing Lucy to the incubus,

502

Val had realized in his heart that his life would be so much less without her. He wanted to share his life with Lucy. He wanted to teach her about honor and trust. She would keep him laughing and happy. And he wanted that partnership to start as soon as possible.

Staring at him, Lucy felt her heart melting. "I thought you said love wasn't enough," she remarked.

"I was wrong." Val shook his head, his heart in his eyes. "I was a big undead dufus. I can't live without you. My crypt just isn't the same with you gone." And with that he went to Lucy, crouching down in front of her. "Isn't it obvious? I love you with all my soul and all my heart."

The audience oohed and aahed, and when Christine nudged him Val added, "By the way, that was a very nice touch with the yellow ribbons."

"You hated them," Lucy reminded him. But the quiet desperation had fled her eyes, leaving her the soft and luminous look of a woman in love.

"No. I loved the ribbons. I hated the fact that you put yourself in danger," he remarked. Drawing her to her feet, he held her in his arms. Lucy felt warmer than she ever had. Happier.

"Oh, Val. I love you too." Her words were barely audible, and Val stole her breath with a passion-filled kiss.

The audience hooted and hollered, and Christine smiled merrily.

Ricki's grin grew from ear to ear. "For those of you who missed the opening," she joked, "I want to thank you for tuning in to the 'I Love Lucy' show." When Val and Lucy's heated kiss continued, Ricki did as well. "As you can see, these two lovebats are going to fly happily-ever-after off the set and into the night."

Christine laughed, watching fondly the fiery kiss between the couple. "I think this show will be a hard act to follow," she said.

Ricki agreed.

When the kiss finished, Lucy's sigh was pure bliss. She had gotten her second chance at happiness, and Mr. Moody was surely in ratings heaven. "Oh, Val — I love you. I've missed you so. And again, I'm so sorry."

Ricki piped up, saying to Christine, "I bet she'll just be living for sunsets."

Leaning over, Val whispered to her provocatively, "We never did get to have make-up sex."

Lucy got a gleam in her eye, and she grabbed his hand. "Let's go. Sunrise is in nine short hours."

Val threw back his head and laughed, and the two ran from the set to the sound of thunderous applause.